D0669204

016

# IN
# THE
# BLUE
# HOUR

PALM BEACH COUNTY
LIBRARY SYSTEM
3650 Summit Boulevard
West Palm Beach, FL  33406-4198

# OTHER BOOKS BY ELIZABETH HALL

*MIRAMONT'S GHOST*

# IN THE BLUE HOUR

## ELIZABETH HALL

LAKE UNION
PUBLISHING

This is a work of fiction. Names, characters, organizations, places, events, and incidents are either products of the author's imagination or are used fictitiously.

Text copyright © 2016 Elizabeth Hall
All rights reserved.

No part of this book may be reproduced, or stored in a retrieval system, or transmitted in any form or by any means, electronic, mechanical, photocopying, recording, or otherwise, without express written permission of the publisher.

Published by Lake Union Publishing, Seattle

www.apub.com

Amazon, the Amazon logo, and Lake Union Publishing are trademarks of Amazon.com, Inc., or its affiliates.

ISBN-13: 9781503939394
ISBN-10: 1503939391

Cover design by Shasti O'Leary-Soudant

Printed in the United States of America

*For Bill and Mary*

# PROLOGUE

The night waited. She could hear the flakes of snow as they pillowed on the ground, heard the hoot of an owl, hidden in the brush of the pines. And somewhere, deep beneath the surface of that heavy silence, she could hear the beating of her own heart. It was keeping time, marking the minutes, the seconds, which had slowed to a frozen crawl. From a distance came the sound of the car, making its way up the hillside of the mountain pass. The muffled sound of tires, crunching through patches of snow, interspersed with the slapping sound made by contact with wet pavement. Getting closer.

From the air above, the car looked like a soft gray pearl, rolling along the side of the mountain. Elise watched, as if she were already a part of the heavens, a part of the moon and stars, as her silver vehicle rounded the curves of La Veta Pass in the moonlight. She could see patches of snow sticking to the ground. The trees were coated with thick white icing. Fat flakes continued to fall, a thick blanket, tucking in the world like a mother would her child.

The sky was a deep gray-black, the color of midnight on a moonlit night. Clouds scuttled across the landscape, and for moments at a time, the moon would disappear altogether. Fingers of fog reached out from the canyons, snaking their way across the road, obscuring the sight of the silver car as it traveled. Then the fog would shift, the moon would find its way out again, and the soft light cast a sea of jewels on the snow, lighting the ice on the highway like diamonds. Pale light glittered on the roof of the car as it negotiated the turns of the frosty pass.

From her dreamlike vantage point, somewhere in the sky above, Elise watched, mesmerized, as the car failed to make the next curve in the road. The tires slid, unable to find traction on a patch of ice. The car glided sideways, sliding to the edge of the road, and in one smooth motion, skated off the side of the mountain. For one brief, eternal moment, it hung suspended in the night sky, like a silver bird that had forgotten how to flap its wings.

Then the car dipped and curved slowly to the canyon below. Clouds moved to block her view, but Elise could hear the sound of the vehicle crashing against rocks and trees, metal screeching and crunching in the freezing night. She heard the branches of trees snapping and breaking, the pounding of rock and earth disturbed by the heavy impact. The car settled somewhere near the river, snaking its way through the trees at the bottom of the canyon. She heard the sound of the engine, ticking like a heartbeat. She heard the hiss of steam from the smashed radiator. The river murmured, its song soft and muffled by snow and ice. She heard the flap of a bird's wings, swooping up out of the canyon, and watched as the black bird flew off into the night.

Elise, watching from above, felt no pain.

# CHAPTER ONE

Elise rattled the key in the lock and pushed open the door to Michael's studio. She stepped inside and pressed her breath out in one long, slow stream. Despite having been locked up for seven months, the air was still sweet, pungent with the aromas of cedar and sage and pine and earth. Smells that were woven, inextricably, with him.

The studio was just as he had left it. Wood shavings littered the concrete floor. The long workbench, covering the entire north wall, was lined with his carving tools: handsaws, chisels, brushes, tiny slivers of metal that looked like the probes of a dentist. In one corner was a collection of dead wood—cedar, piñon, bristlecone pine—pieces he picked up in the woods every time he went out. Elise trailed her fingers over their rough edges, and for a moment, she couldn't breathe. It was as if they were waiting—waiting for Michael's hands to caress the knots and twists and turns, waiting for Michael to uncover the treasure that lay within. Waiting, like mistresses, for their lover to return. Waiting, just as she had been doing, all these months.

Elise turned. The table in the middle of the room held the piece he'd been working on the day he died. It was a raven, more than two feet tall, standing proud and perfect, its head turned slightly, staring over one shoulder. Elise touched the folded wings, brushed her hands over the shovel-shaped tail feathers. The delicate lines of each feather had been painstakingly revealed by Michael's chisels. He had stained the wood a deep coffee color, fixed obsidian stones for the eyes. The eyes were perfect; they followed Elise as she circled the bird, when she stepped back, when she wandered around the room, as if they were wary of this blonde-haired intruder.

Other pieces lay scattered about. On one table, the head and shoulders of a red-tailed hawk emerged from a heavy knot of cedar. The natural color of the wood was perfect. Elise knew at a glance that Michael would not have stained this piece. She drew her hand along the table and found a branch of weathered gray pine, the tiny markings of a chickadee rising from the depths.

The realization hit her: she was not crying. Her eyes were dry. All this time, all these months, she had avoided coming out here, avoided looking at his work, avoided the shop where he had spent so much of his time. She had been certain it would break her—that she would dissolve into a puddle of sobs on the floor, unable to ever get up again. Instead she felt serene, calm and liquid in all her movements, like a well-trained dancer. All the love that Michael poured into his carvings, his birds, was still floating in the air, riding on the dust motes, surrounding her with his essence. It was peaceful here. Peaceful in a way that their too-quiet home was not.

Windows wrapped three walls of the work space, and Elise turned and stared outside. The light was fading. Sunset, with its rose and apricot and russet, was burning away, light bleeding from the sky. Elise stood still, close to the raven, watching as the colors outside slowly faded. All those months she had avoided coming out here, and now she did not want to leave. She could smell Michael in the air; she could feel the calm aura that always surrounded him when he worked. She turned and took one more look around the shop.

Her eyes came to rest on the obsidian eyes of the raven. "Oh, Michael," she whispered to the dark glass. She stared at the bird, caught in one of those moments, still so frequent, when she could almost believe that Michael was still alive, that she would turn a corner and he would be there, waiting. Caught in that narrow space of unbelief, when it was still possible that nothing had changed.

Elise sighed and walked to the door, stepped outside, and pulled it closed behind her. She turned the key in the lock. It was the only thing she ever locked, up here in these mountains. The only place that she felt a need to protect. Their home was so isolated, so far from any town, and in all the years they had lived here, they'd had only a handful of visitors. They used to joke that if they ever sold the place, they would not be able to find the keys for the front door. So isolated that it was rendered safe.

Now, though, with Michael gone, the isolation felt different. Instead of secure and protected, Elise felt alone, vulnerable. Cut off from the world. She turned and headed up the path toward the cabin.

The sky had deepened into the deep ice-blue of dusk. The blue hour, her grandmother had called it. That time when the veil between the world of the living and the world of the dead was the thinnest, that time when it might be possible to catch the finest thread of connection with the departed. Elise stood still for a moment, her eyes searching the black of the forest around her.

She remembered standing outside with her grandmother, when she was no more than seven years old, in the deep-blue dusk. A heavy silence, like thick fog, had descended on the two of them in that time right after her mother had died. Both of them stood still and hushed in the gloaming—memories of Elise's mother touching their faces and arms, making the hair on their necks stand up.

Elise shuddered. It had frightened her back then, the idea of communicating with the dead. She knew all about zombies and ghosts and *la llorona*, the woman who waited by the water, ready to snatch a child who stayed out too late or played too close to the river. It made her shiver, standing in the blue light with her grandmother beside her, waiting for the ghost of her departed mother to break into the silence.

It had never occurred to her then, as a child, but now she looked back on those evenings and wondered why it was that Beulah wanted so much to communicate with Rose. She had never had much to say to Elise's mother, her own daughter, when Rose was alive. So why was it that she spent so many evenings, just at dusk, either standing outside in the garden or sitting close to the window in the living room, staring as the sky deepened into night?

Elise started up the path to the cabin. Her boots scrunched on the gravel. A soft breeze whispered over the tops of the trees and sighed as it dropped from the canyons in the mountains above her. She pulled her sweater tighter against her thin frame.

The hair on the back of her neck went up, a feeling as if she were being watched. From the depths of the porch up ahead, the tinkling of chimes filled the air. Elise stopped and turned slowly. Her eyes scanned the black silhouettes of the trees surrounding her. They had lost all their depth, nothing but flat black shadows, framed against the darkening blue. She looked back at the studio. Through the window, the black eye of the raven glittered at her.

For a moment, the sounds around her seemed magnified. The dead leaves of the cottonwoods rustled in the breeze, clicking against one another, like castanets. Water trickled in the stream, just beginning to feel the icy embrace of the coming winter. Down the hillside, she heard a lone coyote howling into the dusk, followed a few seconds later by the barking of the dog that lived in the house down the hill.

Elise turned in a circle, her eyes sweeping the dark woods around her. "Michael?" She whispered his name, just a soft breath of sound, a barely audible brush of air.

So many times in the past few months, she had started down the path to the shop, wanting to tell Michael some news. So many times, she would stop short after a few steps, remembering. So many times, she had turned her head and thought she had seen him, standing out at the woodpile, or coming up the steps of the porch. As if the memories of all the times he had done just that were imprinted on the present moment, faded shadows of his energy. Sometimes she turned her head and there was movement, some nameless something, just at the edge of her vision. But as soon as she turned toward that brush of motion, it was gone, teasing her with its illusiveness. She couldn't trust her own senses.

Elise forced herself to exhale slowly, made her feet move in a deliberate, measured walk to the porch. The porch railing, the dark wood of the cabin behind her, the roof over her head—all wrapped her in a sense of safety, and she stood at the railing and breathed easier, scanning the woods one more time.

The wind had stopped. The air was still now, thick with quiet. She stared into the dark for a moment longer, shaking her head at her own foolishness. Then she turned and went inside. The screen door slammed behind her, the chimes tinkling with the vibration.

"Ken? It's Elise . . . Elise Brooks." Elise stood in the kitchen, the phone in her hand, staring out the window into the dark. She ran her fingers absentmindedly up and down the surface of the kitchen table. For months, she had dreaded this call.

"Elise! It's so good to hear your voice. How're you holding up?"

Elise bit her lower lip. She'd never trusted Ken Black. She was almost certain he didn't give a damn about how she was holding up. Ken owned an art gallery in Santa Fe, a high-toned, upscale place that reeked of money and pretension and speciousness. Elise had never been comfortable in the gallery, or with Ken and his thin, bottle-blonde, perfectly polished wife. But Ken had been selling Michael's work for years, and Michael had long ago learned the value of holding both your tongue and your judgment when it came to the people who were selling Native art to rich tourists.

"I'm managing," Elise muttered through her teeth.

"Good, good. Glad to hear it."

There was a pause, as if Ken were ticking off the appropriate number of seconds until he asked his next question. "Elise . . . have you had a chance to check the studio?" She almost smirked. Right down to business, Mr. Black. Right back to what interested him most: money, and the possibility of more money.

Elise swallowed. "Yeah. Yes, I have."

"So? Anything we can put in the gallery? I sold Michael's last piece two weeks ago. His work is getting really hot, you know. Prices are going up since . . ."

Elise cut in before he could finish that dreadful sentence. "No, Ken. There's nothing. He had a few pieces started . . . nothing that's anywhere close to gallery ready." Elise fought the waver in her voice. She'd never been much good at lying. The eyes of the raven floated back to her. That piece was ready, but Elise knew deep inside that she could not part with it, no matter how much she might need the money. That raven felt like the thread that still held Michael close to her, the piece he had touched before leaving for the last time.

"Hmm. I could have sworn Michael told me he had something that was almost ready." There was a long pause, as if he expected her answer to change if he just waited long enough. He coughed. "And you, Elise? Are you making ends meet? I know how hard it must be, now that . . . well . . ."

Elise felt her jaw clench. It was none of his damn business if she was making ends meet. And no matter how bad her life might be, she would never confide in Ken Black. "I'm managing."

"That's good. Well. Thanks for checking the studio. The collectors have been hounding me, you know. But . . . if there's nothing else, then there's nothing else."

Elise felt her heart skip. "Sorry."

"Keep in touch, Elise. If there's anything I can do . . ." Ken's voice trailed off. Elise could almost hear the cogs in his head clicking away, calculating which of Michael's works he could reacquire and sell for more money. "And Elise, if something should turn up, be sure and let me know, okay?"

"Yeah. Okay." Elise clicked the "End" button on the phone and laid it on the kitchen counter. Her shoulders drooped with relief, and she walked to the window and stood, staring out at the night. The house behind her was completely dark, totally quiet. Since Michael's death seven months ago, she rarely turned on a light, never turned on the television or radio. She felt closer to him, somehow, in the dark. In the quiet.

Elise wrapped her sweater tightly across her chest and crossed her arms in front of her. A thin sliver of new moon hung in the western sky, Venus nearby, like lovers out for an evening stroll. They turned the sky a lighter shade of black, cast a soft glow on her face, reflected in the window. Just enough light to catch the golden flecks of her long hair. Just enough light to catch the tear on her cheek, like one tiny, perfect moonstone.

# CHAPTER TWO

"Get your skinny white butt in the car." Monica stood in the kitchen, hands on her hips. Fighting stance. Her black eyes flashed.

Elise caught the look and dropped her gaze back to her coffee cup. She ran her finger around the rim. "Mo, I . . ." She stopped herself before she could finish the sentence. She had known Monica since first grade, and she certainly knew her well enough to know what that gleam in her eye meant. Disagreeing with Monica took far more energy than Elise could muster.

Monica Madrid was tough as nails, no matter that she stood only five foot one, a hundred pounds after Thanksgiving dinner. Maybe it was her small size that had turned her into such a fighter; maybe it was growing up with three brothers. A mixture of her Taos Pueblo mother and her Apache father, Monica had shoulder-length black hair and the blackest eyes Elise had ever seen. There was depth to those eyes, a darkness that never let on what might be lurking beneath, like looking into well water. They flashed now, waiting for Elise to say something—anything would do. Monica was in fighting mode, and crossing her would be almost impossible. Elise had been only six years old the first time she witnessed this side of Monica's character, but it had left an impression she would not forget.

Elise and her mother had just moved back to Amalia, the small town in New Mexico where her mother had grown up, and where her grandmother Beulah still lived in a four-room adobe house. Elise's whole world had turned upside down. First her father, killed in an accident. She was only five at the time. With his death she had lost the feeling of laughter and warmth and safety that came from having him around, of having a family that was whole and happy. And before she could even begin to absorb that loss, her mother had loaded the car and headed back to New Mexico.

Now her mother was quiet. She never laughed; she never smiled; she seemed not to notice that she had a daughter at all. The drive across country, leaving Tennessee, had been as silent as a prayer: no radio, no singing, no joking around the way they had always done when her dad was in the car with them. She could remember the way he used to sing to them, a boisterous version of "Hey, Good Lookin'" that would send both her and her mother into fits of laughter. Now there was only the sound of the tires whining on the pavement, the sound of the gas being pumped into the tank every time they stopped, the clicking sound of her oxford shoes on the cold linoleum of the gas-station bathrooms.

They had left behind everything Elise had ever known. And this new town, sitting at the base of the Sangre de Cristo Mountains in northern New Mexico, was completely different from the hills of Tennessee. The air was dry and brittle: Elise had a nosebleed every day for a month. She stared out at sagebrush and chico and Indian ricegrass, and she picked the spines of prickly pear cactus out of her sneakers every time she ventured more than ten feet from the house. The landscape was parched and dusty, a mirror of what her life had become after the lush abundance of Tennessee and a family intact.

The adobe house that Grandmother Beulah lived in was small and cramped. Elise and her mother now shared a tiny bedroom. The room was painted bright blue, and the linoleum on the floor curved downward at the walls, where the heavy adobe bricks had settled over the years. The room was pretty enough, with two iron beds and chenille bedspreads. But being in there with her silent mother was worse than going to church. She felt stifled, unable to breathe. The sadness was thick enough to choke on.

Grandmother Beulah was just as quiet as her daughter. She and Rose had never been close, and Beulah seemed surprised to find her back—tall, quiet Elise in tow—settling into the adobe house not out of desire to be close to her mother, but simply because Rose had no place else to go.

All the words had gone out of Elise's life. At dinnertime, instead of conversation, there was a bare minimum of spoken language: "Pass the salt." "Tortillas?" "I'll wash up." Elise heard only the sounds of knives and forks on the pottery plates, the sounds of chewing and swallowing. She often sat at the dinner table, pushing her food around her plate, wishing that someone would speak. She wished she could hear her father's voice, telling a story about his day. She wished she could look up into his twinkling blue eyes, wished she could see him wink at her. She wished she could hear him laugh, and watch her mother's face light up and laugh with him.

School was no better. Two months into first grade and Elise still felt like a flamingo, transplanted to the desert. She was too tall, even at six. Fair skinned, fair haired, blue eyed. She spoke no Spanish, which came flowing like mountain water out of the mouths of all the other first-graders. She wore dresses, plaid with Peter Pan collars, and white ankle socks edged in lace. Everyone else wore jeans. But the J. C. Penney in this small town didn't bother to carry anything resembling long, and Elise was stuck, her dresses just deepening the divide between her and the others.

At recess, Elise walked around the perimeter of the playground, kicking her black-and-white loafers against the red gravel. She toyed with the buttons on her sweater, a coarse gray wool that Beulah had knitted, insistent that warm and practical was much more important than soft and pretty.

Monica was on the jungle gym, her knees locked over the top bar, hanging upside down. Her hair hung down, like blue-black raven feathers. She kept it chin length, unlike the other girls, who all had long braids. Even at six, Monica was too much of a tomboy to worry about her hair. She never wore a dress; Elise had seen her only in jeans and snap-up cowboy shirts, hand-me-downs from her three older brothers.

Lloyd Bunker, the undisputed class bully, sauntered over, his two buddies, Charlie and Glenn, right behind him. He was tall, like Elise, but stocky. His face and arms were covered with freckles. His dark-red hair stood up in spikes that refused to bend to his mother's comb and water, and she had long ago given up trying to tame his hair or his manners.

"Well, well, well." His voice and his posture were all stage manners, designed to show Charlie and Glenn and anyone else who was watching that he was the boss. "Look at the monkey Injun, hanging in the trees."

Monica pulled herself into an upright position and jumped to the ground. She spread her feet slightly. Her hands clenched and unclenched by her sides. Her black eyes flashed. She was at least a head shorter than Lloyd and many pounds lighter, but she did not seem to notice.

"What did you say?" Her voice was barely audible.

"I said . . ." Lloyd drew out his words, enjoying the power, enjoying the attention that was gathering around them. "Look at the monkey Injun."

He turned slightly, grinned at Charlie standing behind him on the right. "I wonder what's worse? Being a monkey? Or being Injun?" He raised a finger to his chin and tipped his head as if he were lost in deep thought. "Or . . . is it the same?"

Charlie and Glenn laughed.

Lloyd turned back to Monica, his eyes growing flat and hard. "Even a dirty Mexican is better. Can't think of anything worse than Injun. Maybe I should call John Wayne, tell him we got an Injun that needs killing."

Monica jumped, her body lifting and slamming into Lloyd. He fell backward to the gravel, and Monica sat on his chest, pummeling his face with her fists. The children gathered around them, yelling.

Mrs. Valdez hurried over, shouting, "Stop it! Stop it this instant!" She broke through the ring of children and pulled Monica, kicking and punching, from the pile. Lloyd sat up, blood covering his mouth and nose and dripping onto his shirt. Charlie and Glenn were quiet.

"I'll get you, you son of a bitch!" Monica yelled.

"Monica! That's enough." Mrs. Valdez shook her. She moved to help Lloyd to his feet, but he scrambled up without her help. "All right, young lady, let's go. Lloyd, come on. You need the nurse."

Lloyd followed at one side, and Mrs. Valdez held Monica stiffly on her other side, yanking hard on the girl's arm as they moved toward the office. "Such language," she gasped, her fingers pinching Monica's upper arm. The bell rang, and everyone lined up, watching, solemn faced, as Lloyd and Monica were marched toward the door.

"Mrs. Valdez?" Elise could not believe she was speaking, but there it was—her voice calling after their teacher before they could get inside. Mrs. Valdez turned to look at the line of children by the door. Elise stepped forward.

"Mrs. Valdez?" Elise glanced first at Monica, then at Lloyd, who was still bleeding.

"Yes? What is it?"

Elise took a big breath. "He . . . Lloyd . . . was calling her names. That's why she hit him."

Monica's eyes went wide. She would never have spoken up for herself. She had already learned that the truth rarely helped, and that the word of an Indian was not worth a piece of gravel. There was never any benefit to be had from trying to explain.

"Oh?" Mrs. Valdez glanced back at Lloyd, who stared at Elise, his eyes spitting fire. "What kind of names?"

"He called her a . . ." Elise paused and looked at Lloyd again. Lloyd glared back at her, his jaw clenched. She looked back at the teacher. "He called her a dirty Injun."

Mrs. Valdez pursed her lips. She turned to Monica. "Monica, is this so?"

Monica pressed her lips together and refused to answer.

"Lloyd?"

Lloyd glared at Elise.

"Did anyone else hear this?" Mrs. Valdez scanned the line of first-graders. A few looked down at the ground. Feet scuffed in the gravel. Lloyd's power was already well established, even this early in the school year.

"Mrs. Valdez?" It was Esperanza Mondragon. She was a little slip of a girl, almost as quiet as Elise, but tiny and thin and rarely one to speak. "I heard him say it, too."

Other children began to nod, braver now.

"All right, young man. March. You'll both get the paddle." The teacher turned and pressed her hand into Lloyd's shoulder blade, squeezing hard.

After school that afternoon, Elise walked slowly down the red dirt road toward her grandmother's house. She was weighed down with loneliness, with the sadness of losing her father, with the impossibility of learning to live in this new, dry place. She didn't fit in at school, but at least in class there was talk and laughter and sound. She could barely put one foot in front of the other, barely force herself to walk back to her grandmother's silent house and those two silent women.

Monica ran up beside her. "Why'd you do that?" she demanded. "I don't need a white girl to rescue me."

Elise stopped and stared at the small, dark girl. She shrugged.

"Now he's gonna be after you, you know." Monica said.

Elise turned and looked down the road. "But he's so mean to everybody. It's not fair . . . that you would get in trouble when he started it."

Monica laughed. "Fair? That's a good one."

Both girls turned and walked down the road.

"Well, don't worry," Monica continued. "If he comes after you, I'll get him."

Elise glanced sideways. Monica was a head shorter than Elise. She was thin, like Elise. But on Monica it was more like wire, stretched tight and strong. Elise's brand of thin looked like twigs that could snap at the slightest pressure.

Monica started running, calling, "And I'll tell my brothers to watch out for you, too." She stopped, a hundred yards down the road, and turned toward Elise. She grinned, tipped her nose in the air toward Elise, and turned and ran off.

"I'm not taking no for an answer." Monica's voice was fierce.

Elise looked up from her coffee cup. "Mo, I just . . . I just don't feel like going out, you know? Being around people."

"I don't care whether you feel like it or not."

Elise exhaled.

"Look, Lise." Monica moved closer to the kitchen table, her voice and eyes softer. "I know you're sad. I miss him, too." There was a catch in Monica's voice. Michael was her cousin. They'd all grown up together.

She took a deep breath. "But you haven't been out of here in months. You can be sad in Taos just as well as you can be sad here."

Elise sighed. Arguing would be pointless once Monica had her mind made up. "All right. All right, I'll go. But I reserve the right to make you miserable all day."

"Fine." Monica set her mouth in a prim line. "Go ahead and try if you want to. But as you already know, I am completely immune to the manipulations of white women." She smiled at her friend. "So . . . you gonna walk to the car? Or do I have to throw you in?"

# CHAPTER THREE

They sailed down the highway toward Taos. It was a perfect fall day. The sky was sharp and clear, like blue crystal. The aspen on the mountainsides flamed orange and gold, the leaves flittering in the breeze. Purple asters bloomed in the fields, a bright contrast to the yellow flowers of the rabbitbrush. The smell of desert sage filled the car. Elise felt her spirits lift. She loved this drive, loved this land, now that she had spent more than forty years of her life here.

Monica's Honda hit eighty, and she turned up the music, belting out the words of Santana as she shimmied in her seat. She knew every word to every song on the *Supernatural* album, and Elise had to smile. Monica rushed toward life. She grabbed what she wanted. So totally opposite of the way Elise approached everything.

Elise turned back to the highway just in time to see them barreling up on an old white pickup. Elise slammed her foot on the passenger-side floor.

Monica breezed around the truck, speed never faltering. "Damn fool's doing the speed limit." She blew a bubble and popped it back into her mouth with a crack. "And by the way, Lise, the brake is on this side of the car." She looked at Elise's foot, still stretched out to the floor as if she could actually slow the car down.

Elise smiled. Then it hit her like a brick, her momentary reprieve shattered. She pictured Michael inside that silver car, sailing off the snow-slick highway on the pass, flying into the air. Her smile evaporated.

Monica glanced over at her friend. She reached forward and turned the music down.

"I should have stopped him, Mo."

"What? What are you talking about?"

Elise shuddered, as if the cold of that snowy night in March had found its way into the car. She stared out her side window. "Michael. I should have stopped him, and I didn't."

"Elise, I always knew you were crazy, but this is over the top. How could you possibly have stopped him?"

The seconds ticked by. The words were buried deep, and it hurt to bring them to the surface. Her throat burned. "I dreamed it. The accident."

Monica let up slightly on the gas, every fiber of her being taut with attention.

Elise sighed. "Maybe a month before it happened. I had this dream. My car, driving down the highway in the dark. I could see the head-lights, lighting up the road just in front of it. It was snowing. There were patches of snow and ice on the highway. And then it just went off a curve, up near the top of the pass. Nothing sudden, no swerving to avoid a deer. Just hit a patch of ice and went right over the side, sailing out over the canyon below."

"You could see Michael in it?"

"No. No, that's the thing. It was my car I saw sailing off the moun-tain. But I couldn't see anyone in it." Elise glanced at her friend again. "It jolted me awake. Like I just knew that if I had stayed in the dream any longer, I would never wake up. My heart was pounding. All that time, those weeks after I had the dream, I thought it was me—that I was the one who was going to die." Elise turned her head to look out the window. "I never told Michael anything about it."

Monica was silent, soaking up the words of the story.

Elise swallowed. "And then, maybe a week after I had the dream, I went for a walk in the middle of the day. I was rounding this corner, up by Elk Meadow, and I saw an owl, sitting in a ponderosa pine. Right in the middle of the day. He just sat there on that branch, staring at me. Watching as I walked toward his perch. Even turning his head to watch me when I went past him up the road."

Monica shuddered. Her whole family had an absolute dread of owls. Monica had almost hit one in her car one morning, the same day her father died of a massive heart attack. To the Madrid family, owls were the forerunners of death.

"It scared the hell out of me, Mo. All those things we've heard about owls. Connection with the world of the spirits. Death. I was shaking for a while after that. Convinced that I was going to die."

Elise looked down at her lap and laced her fingers together. "I never told Michael any of it. I thought all the signs pointed to *me* being the one to die. I did not want him to worry."

Monica exhaled slowly and trained her eyes on the highway stretching out before them.

"I was completely wrong. The dream, the owl . . . I read it all wrong. Completely screwed up." Elise lifted her head and stared at the passing chico brush, the blurs of purple piñon asters and yellow rabbitbrush in the fall landscape. A tear started its slow slide down her cheek.

"That day, the day it happened, I wasn't even thinking about the dream. I was working on a weaving, frustrated because I couldn't get the colors right. Nothing seemed to be working. I was just tearing out three hours' worth of work. And Michael came in from his shop, in a hurry, because he'd spent too long working out there. He grabbed my keys off the hook by the stairs. Stood in the doorway and told me his truck wouldn't start, that he was late for his meeting. He said he was going to take my car."

"I barely even glanced at him, Mo. I was so caught up in what I was doing. I think I mumbled something about how it would cost him, but sure, go ahead."

A thick silence descended in the air around them. A slender trail of moisture snaked down Elise's face. "The dream never crossed my mind. I made my dinner later, and read for a while. Went to bed about ten. And then, around one in the morning, I bolted awake. And I knew."

Elise turned to face her friend, and Monica met her eyes for one brief instant. "I knew I'd gotten it all wrong—what the dream meant. I knew that *he* was going to die—was probably already dead at that very moment." Elise swallowed. "I was sitting on the porch when the state patrol showed up."

Elise brushed the tears from her face. Seven months had passed since Michael's death, and this was the first time she had told anyone about the dream. The guilt had completely encased her, like a suit of armor.

"Lise, dreams are one of the hardest things to figure out. Even Uncle Wes says so. You can't beat yourself up like this." Uncle Wes was Monica's great-uncle; he practiced traditional ways on the Taos Pueblo.

Elise shrugged. "But why didn't I tell him, Mo? I always told him everything. You know how he was about dreams . . . about visions. He might have figured it out. Or at least he might have been more careful. Maybe he wouldn't have tried to drive the pass that night." Elise sucked in a deep breath. "I never even said good-bye."

Monica stayed silent. In Monica's world, and the world of her family, dreams were important. Owls were important. Messages came in many forms; knowledge came from many sources.

Michael, like everyone else in the family, had been very comfortable with dreams and visions and had always paid great attention to them. He was completely at ease with the idea of spirits. The entire family was that way. They left food outside in small bowls for the spirits to eat. They offered tobacco to the spirits of plants and animals. They prayed and sang and beat drums for the spirits. They participated in the feast day ceremonies at the Taos Pueblo and at the Jicarilla Apache Reservation, where Michael was born.

Michael listened to nature: the trees, the birds, the stones. He believed there were many ways to gather information, and listening to the spirits in the life around him was one of the most important. He told her that the white man was stuck on scientific proof, on logical sequence, but Indians, almost all indigenous cultures, knew there were infinite possibilities for acquiring knowledge.

Elise had watched Michael and Monica and the family for years now, fascinated by their connection to the world of spirits. But she herself had never felt that connection in the same way. She had tried, had spent chunks of time outside in the quiet, trying to hear what the spirits had to say. But somehow, it eluded her, that wisdom. That voice. Those spirits. She was never quite sure if she was hearing spirits or if it was just the chatter in her own mind.

Now she couldn't stop blaming herself. "If I had told him about it . . . maybe he'd still be alive."

"And maybe it wouldn't have mattered. Uncle Wes says when it's your turn, it's your turn."

The two women were silent, staring at the road ahead.

When she spoke again, Elise's voice was low, almost a whisper. "Sometimes . . . at dusk . . . I feel like he's out there somewhere. Watching. Waiting." Elise looked down at her hands, lying helpless in her lap. "Like he wants to say something. I'll turn my head, and it's like . . ." She turned toward Monica, almost ashamed of her words. "Like there's a movement in the trees that I can't quite pin down . . . can't quite catch. It's always just at the edge of what I can see."

Monica glanced over, and Elise turned to watch the sage out the side window.

"I wake up sometimes in the middle of the night . . . listening. Wondering if I really heard something, or did I just dream it?" Elise continued to stare out the window. "Sometimes I think I hear the car pulling up in the driveway. Michael's footsteps on the stairs."

She turned to face Monica. "At first, I would get up and go look. Check the stairs, check the kitchen . . . go to the front door and look outside." Elise looked down at her hands again. "There's nothing, of course. Nothing I can see."

She waited a long moment before continuing. "I don't turn on the television or the radio. I don't turn on the lights. I keep the house completely dark, completely silent. Just in case . . ." Elise heaved a huge sigh. It was such a relief, to have unburdened herself of her guilty secret. "Just in case he's trying to tell me something.

"It seems that's all I ever do, now. Wait. Listen."

Monica took a deep breath. She kept her eyes straight ahead, on the curve of the road in front of her. She waited a beat, allowing the heaviness of the revelation to pass. "Well, that's your problem, then. Maybe you should get off your bony white ass and make him a sandwich."

# CHAPTER FOUR

Fall in Taos was magical. Brown adobe houses, nestled into the mountains and canyons and next to the arroyos, flushed with the golden light of autumn. The cottonwoods glowed yellow, blazing against the crisp blue of the sky. Wild plum trees, thick with fruit, bent under the weight of their bounty. Birds careened through the sky and the branches, raucous and giddy with the feast.

They parked in the lot by Our Lady of Guadalupe and cut through the Bent Street Plaza, headed for Kit Carson Park. Music danced in the air. The scent of roasting green chiles, as much a part of a New Mexico fall as the cottonwoods, wafted on the breeze. Elise inhaled, drinking in the colors, the aromas, the sounds. As much as she had fought coming, the trip was lifting her spirits. Her shoulders were straight, her chin was up, as if a puppeteer had pulled the strings and straightened her.

They entered the art fair at the park and stopped in front of a booth with crates of homemade soaps. Each of them picked up a round ball of softness and inhaled: lemon, gardenia, lavender.

"Here, woman, you need this." Monica held a ball of lilac soap to her friend's nose. "You're starting to stink like an old bear, the way you hibernate up in that cabin."

"Very funny." Elise held the pale-purple ball to her nose and closed her eyes. She recoiled instantly. "Not lilac. Lilac makes me think of death."

Monica studied her friend for a moment. "Okay, not lilac." Monica picked up three soaps and whipped out a twenty-dollar bill. "How about these instead?"

"Come on, Mo. I don't smell *that* bad."

"You only say that because you're used to the smell. You should get a whiff of you from where I stand."

Elise smiled and stuck out her tongue.

They wandered through the booths, taking in the familiar collection of jewelry, leather purses, woven shawls. Pockets of people wandered the isles, trampling the last of the summer grass. A crow cawed from one of the cottonwoods, and Elise shaded her eyes to look for it.

"Oh, good. Just what I was looking for," Monica said. Her eyes were glued to a booth across the way. "Want a lemonade, you no-good stinking whore?"

"Watch it, Madrid. You might get hurt, talking like that."

Monica smiled. That comment sounded more like Elise, the pre-trauma Elise who used to banter back and forth all the time.

"Every bone in my body is quivering in fear. I might even need to sit down for a moment." Monica raised the back of her hand to her forehead and feigned a swoon. Then she smiled and pushed through the crowd toward the fresh-squeezed-lemonade stand.

Elise caught a glimpse of a dark-haired man up ahead, his hair pulled back in a long ponytail. Her heart stutter-stepped. He had hair just like Michael's: long, thick, and black. The man was one of the musicians, and he was playing a wooden flute. His side was to Elise. Andean music filled the air, flute and guitar and the heartbeat rhythm of a drum. Elise felt the familiar weight of grief settle on her shoulders. A few minutes ago, her spirits had lifted with the sounds and smells and activity of the art fair. That musician, with his long black hair, took her right back to thoughts of Michael. She sighed heavily and turned away, trying to lose herself in the booth on her right, full of stone and crystal jewelry.

The woman behind the table caught Elise's eye. She wore the gypsy style of clothing so common in Taos: long flowing skirt in burnt orange, a handwoven shawl of red and yellow and orange and pink wrapped around her shoulders. Strands of thick salt-and-pepper hair escaped from the bun at the nape of her neck.

Elise dropped her gaze to the earrings on the table. Citrine, carnelian, and garnet caught the sunlight. She ran her fingertip over a carnelian earring.

"He's still with you, you know," the woman whispered.

Elise looked up. The woman had large, dark eyes. Her skin was smooth, her eyes and face calm and serene, as if she had seen it all and nothing had the power to ruffle her any longer.

"Excuse me?"

"Your husband. He hasn't really left you."

Elise stared. Her heart skipped a beat.

The woman looked away for a moment, her eyes scanning the crowd. "That man?" She tilted her head toward the musician playing the flute, the one with the long black ponytail. "Playing the flute? He looks like your husband, no?"

Elise stopped breathing.

"He was"—she closed her eyes, swayed slightly back and forth— "quiet, gentle." Her eyes remained closed. She brought her hands up, moving as if she were working with tools. "He worked with his hands, yes?" Her eyes shot open and bored into Elise.

Elise swallowed. Her finger still rested on the carnelian earring, and she lifted it quickly, as if the stone held some kind of electrical current that was allowing this woman to see into her life.

The woman closed her eyes again. ". . . I see a car. Sailing off the road, into the air." She stood, her eyes still closed. One hand fluttered to her heart, and she swallowed. "An accident?"

Elise was lost in the woman's words, in the dark depths of her eyes. She could no longer hear the music, the milling of people behind her. She had lost her sense of everything except those eyes, those words that poured out, thick and slow, like molasses.

"He has something he wants to tell you," the woman whispered, her body swaying toward Elise, her eyes suddenly enormous.

"Here, grump." Monica appeared beside Elise, holding a red paper cup, the Coca-Cola label blazing on the side. The smell of fresh-squeezed lemonade perfumed the air.

Elise did not take the cup; her gaze never left the woman standing behind the table. She barely registered Monica at her side or the bright-red cup held at the edge of her peripheral vision.

The woman flicked a card from her sleeve and held it toward Elise. "Come see me."

Elise took the card in her hand, her eyes brushing over it, seeing none of the writing, only the pale-purple color of the paper. She could barely breathe. She turned away slowly, intentionally, as if she had to break a series of threads that held her bound to the woman, like a bug caught in a spiderweb.

"What was that about?" Monica whispered as they walked away.

"I don't know," Elise breathed. She stopped and scanned the lavender card in her hand. "Says here she reads tarot cards."

"Jeez. It's getting to where everyone in Taos County thinks they're psychic. What a load of shit." Monica sucked hard on her straw.

"Mo?" Elise looked into Monica's eyes. "She knew about Michael."

Monica pursed her lips in protest. "What do you mean, she knew about Michael?"

"Honestly. She knew about the accident. She said . . . he's still with me."

"He's still with you? That's what she said?"

Elise nodded.

"Yeah, well, that seems pretty general to me. She could say that to anyone who walked up to her, and it would be true in some weird way. A father. An uncle. Everyone on earth knows at least one man who's passed. 'He's still with you!' Wow. I'm impressed. *Amazing* insight." Monica's eyes spit disgust.

"She knew he was an artist." Elise stopped suddenly, and a woman behind her bumped into her, sending a wave of lemonade over the front of her cup.

"Let me see that." Monica slipped the card from Elise's grip.

Monica scanned the card. "Celestina Redbird. Another damn wannabe. All these white people taking Native names." Monica's eyes flashed. "Everyone wants to be Native. Wants a Native name. Wants to do ceremony. Wants their own personal medicine man. They just don't want to hire us, or wait on us in restaurants, or have us living in their neighborhood, or . . ."

Elise stopped walking, remembering the day that Michael had come home from a solo trip to Santa Fe. He had taken several pieces down to the gallery. Elise was tied to a deadline on a weaving and had not gone with him. Michael had driven down early in the morning, delivered his work, and started the drive home. He'd stopped at a restaurant next to the Rio Grande, a place with outdoor tables that both he and Elise loved. But this time he sat for twenty minutes, watching as the waitress took orders from several tables that had come in after he had.

On her next sashay past his table, eyes averted as if he wasn't there, he'd stopped her. "Miss? Could I get a bowl of red chili?"

She stopped and looked him in the eye, took in the long black hair, tied into a ponytail with a piece of red leather. She took in his jeans and scuffed boots and worn denim shirt. "Humph." She snorted. "You gonna pay for it?"

It had stopped Michael cold. He'd been in that restaurant countless times, though never alone, as he was at that moment. The woman had no idea who he was. She had no idea that he was an up-and-coming artist in the Santa Fe market, that he'd been sober for over twenty years, that he owned his home in the mountains, completely free of debt. All she saw was the dark skin, dark eyes, long black hair. All she had seen was Indian. And she had lots of ideas about what Indian meant.

Elise remembered Michael coming home that night, fueled by anger and by something even worse. Judged by a woman who knew nothing about him. Inadequate. Unacceptable. Too much risk for her establishment to handle. And all because of the way he looked.

Elise glanced back at Celestina once again. "How do you know she's white?"

"By the smell. You white people smell funny."

Elise watched as Celestina waited on two teenage girls looking at crystals. She exhaled. "Well, whatever she is, she knew an awful lot about Michael." Her eyes came back to Monica's.

Monica handed Elise the card and turned back for another look at Celestina. "She knew? Or did she guess? Because you have never been any good at hiding anything. Your face always gives you away."

"Maybe." Elise fingered the card.

"She just wants your money."

"What are you talking about? I didn't pay her anything."

Monica stopped walking, and raised her eyebrows at Elise. "Not yet."

Elise smiled. "Oh, I see. Now *you're* reading the future?"

Monica shrugged. "Bunch of New Age crap. Hook you in with a few very general observations that could be true for anyone in the world, and the next thing you know, you're walking in her door, laying down the dinero."

"New Age isn't really that new, you know. Reading cards has been going on since at least ancient Egypt," Elise protested. She wasn't quite sure why she was defending the woman. She stopped walking and looked at Monica. "So you're saying the only way to know something is rational . . . scientific?"

"Of course not. That's the Western way of thinking."

"So what's the difference? Between reading cards and . . . I don't know . . . a dream . . . a vision."

"They are different, Lise." Monica stopped again, planted her feet in warrior stance. "If there's something you need to know—it comes to you. Directly to you. In a dream, or a vision, or in the sweat lodge. That's why we go on vision quests. Sure, there's a medicine man down the hill, praying for you and ready to help if you get in trouble. But you go on the hill by yourself." Monica glanced back at Celestina's booth. Celestina met her eyes. "And whatever you need to know comes to *you*, not filtered through some psycho wannabe."

Monica turned and glowered at Elise again. "You don't need psychics or card readers or crystal balls. You don't need anyone else to tell you. That's the difference."

Elise exhaled; her shoulders drooped. "Maybe not. But I didn't do such a great job at figuring out that last dream." Her eyes scanned the crowd; she fought to keep her emotions in check. "And by the time I did, it was too late."

Monica's face softened. She put a hand on Elise's forearm. "Maybe you weren't supposed to figure it out. Maybe it was only . . . I don't know . . . a way to show you something. Maybe just to show you that you know more than you think you do. Maybe it doesn't mean what you think it means."

Elise shrugged. "Maybe." She turned her gaze to the trees in the park.

They both stood still, sunlight playing in their hair. Monica looked up and nudged Elise's side with her arm.

"Wanna go pee on Kit Carson's grave?"

# CHAPTER FIVE

*"Elise?"*

Her eyes shot open, and she inhaled sharply, holding her breath. Elise lay in the dark, her ears straining for sound. For several nights now, she had awakened thinking that she heard him, calling her name. She lay completely still, listening intently.

She let her left hand drop to Michael's side of the bed. The sheets on that side were cool to the touch, and that absence of warmth hit her once again. Every time she woke, the knowledge was a fresh assault on her senses. It was still a shock, the memory flooding back every time like it was brand-new information. *Michael is dead. He is not coming back.* She would never again hear his footsteps coming up the stairs or feel his weight as he lowered himself into their bed after a long night of working in the studio. She would never again hear him whisper her name, checking to see if she was awake, so he could tell her what he was thinking.

Elise sat up and looked at the clock. It was three in the morning, but she knew there was no point in trying to go back to sleep. Once she had jolted awake, slammed into remembering the new circumstances of her life, there was no going back to any semblance of rest. She pulled on her sweater and slippers and started down the stairs.

At the bottom, she stopped and looked out the window of the front door, gazing out at Michael's studio. White light glowed on a window in the studio, and for one brief second, she thought that Michael was out there working late. He had always been a night owl, sometimes staying in the studio until early in the morning hours. Elise stood, watching the light, moving her body slightly to get a better angle. It took her a moment to figure out that it was only the reflection of the moon on the glass, and she exhaled.

Padding into the kitchen, she started the motions of making coffee, exhaustion numbing her. She spooned coffee beans into the grinder and pushed the button. The noise was overwhelming in the quiet, and it stole up on her, that voice, whispering her name once again. *"Elise?"*

She took her finger off the grinder and listened, chills running up her spine. Elise turned and walked back to the window, staring out at the studio. There was nothing. No movement. No light. No sound.

The dog at the house half a mile away began to bark—the frantic, steady bark that normally meant a bear on the prowl. Elise listened. It was late in the season for the bears to still be out. She shivered again, as if the cold finger of the past were rubbing against her, tracing the line of her back. Just a whisper, the faintest breath of touch. And yet there it was, the sense that she was not alone.

Her whole world had tipped upside down, yet again, like that first year in Amalia, that year in first grade. Her father was dead, his absence a huge hole in her heart, her home completely changed from the one she had always known. She couldn't relate to any of the fourteen children in her class. She lived with a grandmother she'd never met before, who rarely talked and never, under any circumstances, showed any emotion.

Elise remembered coming home from school, just a few weeks into this strange new world of the Southwest. She was excited, eager to tell her mother about the song she was learning in Spanish. It was a version of "Old MacDonald," and Elise had been singing it to herself all the way home. *Allá en el rancho bonito, donde tengo un patito. Cuando me miran venir. El patito dice "quack quack." Hay que bonito patito.*

She had bounded into their little blue bedroom only to find her mother sitting in a chair, staring out the window. Since their return to New Mexico, Rose was only a stone carving of a woman; nothing about her seemed lifelike. She was nothing like the mother who had filled Elise's life when they lived in Tennessee. Elise had stopped cold, a shiver running down her arms. She did not tell her mother about school; she did not sing the song she had practiced.

Instead, she turned quietly and went back outside, and climbed up into the crotch of an old cottonwood tree. She pulled her knees up to her chest, wrapped her arms around them, and wished that she were back in Tennessee, wished that life were the way it used to be. Wished that she could curl up with her little dog. Wished that they were all out in her father's bright-blue fishing boat.

She could remember sitting in the middle, in the bottom of that boat, half-heartedly attempting to fish, since it seemed to be something her father liked so much. She could remember him, twisting the worm on the hook. She hated it when the guts squished out, and her father laughed. So did her mother, sitting at the back of the boat, holding an umbrella up over her head to shade her pale skin from the sun. Elise remembered turning toward the sound of her mother's laughter, floating and bouncing over the lake water. She remembered the way her mother threw her head back, her teeth gleaming, her neck long and milky. Back then, Rose had been a flesh-and-blood mother, a mother who laughed and played and sang as she went about her work.

Now they were both here in Amalia, laughter a long-forgotten memory. The land was dry and brittle and consisted of several shades of brown and gray, similar to living with the woman they both called Beulah. She was never Mom or Grandma. There was a formality between Rose and her mother, as if they'd both been starched into stiff, silent versions of themselves. Elise sensed something humming under that stiffness, something unspoken and uncomfortable, but she had no idea what it might be. She only knew that the house was too quiet, that her mother was lost in some silent world that she could not escape, and that her grandmother was unable, or perhaps unwilling, to bridge the divide to reach either of the two younger females.

Winter came, and snow and cold settled around the house, a mirror of the cold quiet that lay within. Rose began to cough, and there were several times when Elise came home from school to find her lying in bed, curled on her side, facing the wall in the room they shared.

One afternoon in late February, bright with blue skies and a brief warm spell, Beulah had met Elise walking home from school. "Come with me," she commanded. Elise joined her in walking down the dirt road. Beulah never asked about school, never asked how Elise was doing, and this day was no different, despite their time alone together. They walked in silence to an old adobe house at the end of a dirt road, nestled in several giant old cottonwoods. Elise could hear the muffled sound of a stream close by, water trickling under the ice. The house was dirt brown, but the door and windowsills were painted bright-turquoise blue. A fence of log poles, only a few inches thick, planted vertically, surrounded a side yard. The whole area seemed much more lush with vegetation than Beulah's home did. There were currant bushes by the fence, piñon and cedar surrounding the house. She and Beulah stepped up onto the portal, a wooden porch supported by heavy, peeled logs. The screen door flew open, and Monica and an older boy came running out of the house, the screen door banging behind them.

"Hey," Monica called as she ran, obviously too busy avoiding her brother to give Elise more than a passing shout.

Elise turned from watching the two of them sprinting down the road and found herself looking into the eyes of one of the most beautiful women she'd ever seen. Monica's mother, Lorena, stood in the doorway. She was small, a compact but beautifully curved frame, and her eyes were as dark and gentle as a pool of snowmelt on the forest leaves.

"You must be Elise." She smiled. "Monica has told us all about you."

Elise blushed, a smile flashing in her eyes. She and Beulah passed inside the door of the house. The front room was warm and smelled of piñon, though only red coals remained in the fireplace in the corner. There were several chairs and a sofa, and all of them were covered with striped wool blankets. A rug, woven of the same shades of brown and gray, with turquoise-and-deep-crimson stripes, covered the floor.

Beulah and Elise followed Lorena into the kitchen and sat down on wooden chairs painted a bright canary yellow. Elise twisted in her chair to examine the woodwork, the sunny yellow color, the intricate pattern of leaves that was painted on the slats of the back of her chair. This was more color than she had seen in months, a warmth in both the yellow color and the air that made her feel better.

"My husband made these chairs," Lorena said. "He's good with a paintbrush, don't you think?"

Elise nodded, unable to find her voice in the presence of this woman.

"Coffee?" Lorena held up a gray enamel coffeepot that had obviously been in use for quite a while.

"Yes, thank you," Beulah muttered.

"Elise? Coffee?"

Elise was stunned. She had never been offered coffee before. She shot a quick glance at Beulah. Beulah nodded her head, just one small dip, and Elise smiled. "Yes, please."

Lorena brought her a green milk-glass mug, filled with a mixture that was heavy on the cream and sugar. Elise could still remember the wonder of that cup of coffee. She wrapped her hands around the cup, the way she had seen her mother do, and she leaned over it to breathe in the aroma, dark and rich and earthy. She felt suddenly grown-up. She straightened her body in the wooden chair and watched this amazing woman who sat across from her.

"Her mother," Beulah began, flicking her eyes toward Elise, "has a pretty bad cough. I can hear her lungs gurgling sometimes. Lots of phlegm."

Lorena's eyes grew sad and somber. She nodded thoughtfully. "Yes. Grief settles in the lungs."

"The doctors say . . ." Beulah stopped, a catch in her voice. The sound caused Elise to look up at her grandmother. Beulah turned away, cleared her throat, and started again. "The doctors say that it will just have to run its course—they've done everything they can."

Lorena glanced at Elise and then back to Beulah. She reached across the table and laid her small, dark hand over Beulah's speckled old fist. Elise was stunned. She had never seen anyone touch her grandmother before. Beulah didn't flinch, didn't draw back. Her white, wrinkled skin was covered by Lorena's long, tapering brown fingers. "She has lost her will to keep going," Lorena whispered.

Beulah nodded and turned her head away again. Elise thought she saw the glistening of a tear on her grandmother's cheek. She could hear her grandmother swallow. A small knot of fear formed in Elise's stomach. Beulah never showed emotion, and Elise became hyperalert to the atmosphere in the room.

Lorena studied Elise across the table. Then she stood and walked to an old red cabinet, the paint chipping and peeling away to reveal the gray-brown wood beneath. "I can give you something to make her more comfortable," she said, reaching inside and pulling out two small brown bottles, small enough to fit in a fist. "This will ease her cough, help her to rest." She stood next to Beulah and placed her hand on the old woman's shoulder. "I don't have any tinctures for a troubled spirit. Best thing I know is to get her outside, if you can. She needs nature to heal her."

Beulah shook her head. "I've tried. She says all she wants to do is rest."

Lorena pursed her lips and nodded. "Then bring the outdoors in. Boughs of cedar, some pinecones, dried grasses. Maybe some dried flowers. Whatever you can find. Put them all around her bed, all around her room. And right next to her head, something with a wonderful aroma. Cedar, maybe. Or pine."

Beulah nodded.

Suddenly the back door slammed open, and Monica came bounding into the room, her face glowing from running, her eyes lit with the triumph of eluding her brother.

Elise waited for Lorena to say something, to tell her to slow down, or close the door, or not to run in the house. That's what Beulah would do. That's what Rose would have done, back when she still noticed such things. Lorena only smiled at her daughter and stood to close the door.

"Want to see our baby lamb?" Monica asked Elise.

Elise remembered walking home beside her grandmother later that afternoon, unable to stop herself from an occasional skip step. What a wonder it had been, to see the place where Monica lived, to meet her beautiful mother, to drink her first cup of coffee, to watch the week-old lamb standing snuggled up against her mother. She had completely forgotten the shiver of dread that had crawled on her skin just a few hours earlier.

That was the beginning. Soon, she was spending almost every afternoon at Monica's house, including Saturdays. She loved it there. Monica and her brothers were as wild and reckless as young colts, constantly running and teasing and bantering with one another. They rode horses, and fished, and hiked in the hills. They played cowboys and Indians, but in their games, the Indians always won. At night, the family sat around the adobe fireplace in the front room, eating piñon nuts and listening to Monica's father tell stories of the Jicarilla Apache people he'd grown up with.

Elise fell completely in love with Monica's mother. Lorena's large dark eyes noticed everything; her copper-colored skin glowed. She wore her long black hair loose or in one long braid, except for the times when they visited her home at the Taos Pueblo. Elise loved to watch as Lorena twisted her hair into a knot at the nape of her neck and tied it with a piece of red calico. She told Elise that only young girls wore their hair loose on Pueblo lands, that once a girl had become a woman, she had to keep her hair tied. In the evenings, they snuggled under handwoven blankets to stay warm, draping them over legs or shoulders. It was from those early days of fingering the wool that Lorena had spun and dyed and woven herself, surrounded by the warmth and companionship of the Madrid family, that Elise first developed the desire to weave.

Lorena knew every plant and how to use it, from the ricegrass and chico and rabbitbrush on the flatlands to the mugwort and amaranth in the mountains. She showed Elise how to wrap pieces of sage and cedar into sticks for smudging; she made teas; she made tinctures that looked a horrid yellow color and stank like skunk. But everyone came to her, asking her advice for some problem, whether it was related to health or to life in general. She told Elise that when she was out wandering, looking for a cure for some problem, she could just stand and listen, and the plants would tell her what she needed to know. "The plants are my friends. When you find the right plant for the problem, it says, 'Pick me, pick me.' It almost glows, because it is excited to be used."

Lorena could do anything, it seemed. Elise loved to watch as Lorena worked at her pottery wheel, throwing pots of black micaceous clay. When several pots were sitting on boards, dry from the high mountain sun, she would build a fire in a pit in the backyard and bury the pots in sawdust. She only used cottonwood for the fire, which smoldered and smelled and made everyone cough with smoke as thick as sheep's wool. "Like someone is pissing on the fire," was how Monica's oldest brother put it. It never burned hot and clean like the piñon they used to heat the house, but it was perfect for the slow, smoky burn necessary to fire the pots.

The Madrid home was overflowing with activity and laughter and jokes and stories and cooking. Even so, Lorena always had a moment to touch Elise, even if was just to stroke her pale hair or rub between her shoulder blades. Elise loved it there, so completely different from the cold silence and unspoken tension that filled the rooms of Beulah's house.

And when Rose slipped away late in the spring, off to the land of the spirits to join her husband, it was Lorena who stood behind Elise at the grave, her hand resting on Elise's shoulder. It was Lorena who took Elise on long walks through the fields and the woods, who told her to listen for the spirit of her parents in everything around her. "You can always ask them for help," she told Elise. "They will watch over you. Take care of you."

But Elise had never talked to the spirits of her mother or her father, had never asked them for anything. She could barely remember her father; her mother had become unavailable and silent long before she actually passed. Elise had learned not to rely on parents. Even if she could have spoken to them, she had no idea what she would say.

Michael, though, was another story. She had known Michael since that summer between first and second grade, right after her mother died. He and his brother, Andres, came to Amalia every summer and spent several weeks with Monica's family. The children were cousins; their fathers were brothers who had grown up on the Jicarilla Apache reservation. Every summer since first grade, Elise had been included in their adventures. She and Michael had almost grown up together, and she never thought about him in any way other than as a cousin, at least not until the summer after sixth grade.

It was a beautiful day in early July. Heat waves were washing over the valley below, but up here, high in the Sangre de Cristo Mountains, the air was still early-morning cool. Elise was in the back garden, helping Beulah pull weeds from the tomatoes. She heard the horses' hooves pounding the ground, felt the vibration through the soles of her bare feet, and looked up to see two horses coming toward the fence. Monica was behind her older brother, Narciso, on a brown-and-white paint. Michael rode on a spotted gray, a gelding that hadn't quite forgotten that he was once a stallion. When they stopped at the fence, the gray pranced sideways. Michael sat tall on the horse, his back straight. He rode bareback. He was fourteen, and had been quieter, moodier, this summer than Elise had remembered in the past summers. She stood up, and brushed dirt from her hands.

"We're going to the lake. Mama wants trout for dinner. You wanna come?" Monica called down.

Elise looked at Beulah, sitting on her haunches in the red dirt of the garden. Beulah's long gray hair was tied in a knot at the back of her neck; a battered straw hat shaded her eyes and face. She met Elise's eyes and nodded. "But I only want rainbows," she sputtered. "Don't you bring me those little teeny brookies. You catch brookies, you just throw 'em right back."

Elise smiled, just slightly, and ran inside to grab her shoes. She pulled them on as she ran across the yard, hop-skipping as she did so. She stopped when she reached the two ponies, unsure what to do next. Michael bent, held out his hand, and she swung up behind him.

That was it. She knew it, knew it like she knew the smell of cedar and sage and the sound of the ravens when they flew over the house. He became part of her landscape, settled down into her heart, into her bloodstream, into her bones. There could never be anyone else.

And it stayed there, locked in her heart, coursing through her blood, even when Michael turned into a monster. The following winter, his brother, Andres, was killed. Seventeen years old, not driving, but just as drunk as the other four kids in the car. Michael changed completely. When he came back to Amalia the following summer, he was sullen and dark, angry and hateful, like an afternoon thunderstorm raging in the mountains. He guzzled beer on their fishing trips. His eyes were constantly rimmed red. He sometimes forgot to shower, stayed in the same dirty jeans and denim shirt for two or three days. Elise didn't like him then. But she knew, inside, what he was really like—what he could be when he wasn't drowning in pain.

She understood pain. She understood loss. She'd certainly seen enough of it in her young life. She watched him, waiting. Hoping. Whispering prayers to some unknown spirit that Michael would recover.

In August, he left. But instead of heading back to Dulce, to the reservation and his grief-stricken mother, he fled to Los Angeles. They heard, through the Native grapevine, that he was heavy into drugs, too doped up to have any idea what was going on.

She didn't see him again for seven years. She was twenty and had just finished burying Beulah, her last blood relative, her last tie to family. She was in the backyard at Beulah's adobe house, cleaning out the raised beds of the garden. She and Monica had left Amalia after high school. They'd moved to Albuquerque, enrolled at the University of New Mexico. Monica quit after one semester, saying that city life was not for her. Elise managed to stay on, alone, until spring break. She went home to her grandmother's, home to Monica and her brothers and her mom and dad, and couldn't tear herself away to go back. Now she was waiting tables at the local café, living by herself in Beulah's old adobe.

She sat on a railroad tie, her eyes locked on the dead yellow vines from last year's tomatoes. A shadow fell across the garden. She turned, and there he was, sitting tall on that gray gelding he'd ridden so long ago. The horse had lost most of its prance and stood still, his eyes locked on Elise.

"Hey," Michael called.

Elise raised her hand to shade her eyes. "Hey." He looked different. His hair was long, almost to his waist, tied in a ponytail. He was taller, broad shouldered, his jaw that of a man.

"Sorry to hear about Beulah."

Elise swallowed. She nodded.

He made no move to get down off the horse, just leaned forward, resting his arms on the horse's neck. His eyes traveled from the mountain peaks in the east, to the scraggly mass of dried-out garden, to the adobe house. He didn't look at Elise.

It was Elise who broke the long silence. "When'd you get back?"

"Been back in Dulce about a month. My mom wanted to see the family, so we drove over yesterday."

Elise nodded, bent her head to the dried stalks in front of her. "How is your mom?"

Michael smiled. "Glad I'm sober." He turned his eyes to Elise then, and she could see the teasing, gentle light that used to be there.

"Wanna go for a ride?"

Elise looked up at him, her hand over her brow. She nodded. And this time when he reached down to pull her up, she knew he was back for good.

They wandered that day. No galloping, no hurry, just that old gray picking its way through the cactus and sage and rocks. Michael talked about LA, about how he'd lost himself in the city, in the strangers and the drugs and the anonymity.

They stopped at the top of Red Hill, and Michael dropped the reins and let the horse graze. He and Elise rambled, gazing at the valley below them.

"One morning, I woke up, hungover as usual, and stinking to high heaven. I had passed out in an alley. And here's this old guy, shaking me." Michael smiled and shook his head. "His face was all dark and crinkled, eyes black and laughing like I'd done something funny. Long gray hair tied back with leather."

"He was running a sweat lodge over at a treatment center on Ninth. Lakota man. A traditional. Anyway, he got me up, took me back to the center. I had a cup of coffee. And a few hours later, I was sitting in that sweat lodge with him." Michael stared off into the New Mexico landscape. "Something about the dark, you know? So pitch-black you can't even see your hand in front of your face. And the stones, the grandfathers, glowing red in the center pit. Steam that burns your skin and sears your lungs. It all came out then. Everything I'd been holding in since Andres was killed." Michael kicked the dirt with the toe of his boot.

"That old guy kept singing, pounding the drum. Pouring water. We were in there for hours. I must have sweated out at least a month's worth of alcohol." He glanced sideways at Elise. "And maybe seven years' worth of tears."

"When I came out that day . . . well, that was it. I haven't had a drink since." Michael turned and stared down at the valley below them.

"I started helping him. I chopped wood. I tended the fire. I helped cut willows when we built a bigger lodge. He taught me the songs . . ." Michael put his hands in his pockets and drew a deep breath. "In Lakota, of course. Different from Jicarilla, but still. It was the old ways, the old wisdom. Exactly what I needed."

Elise spent the next twenty-five years watching him practice the old ways. She had witnessed firsthand how much Michael needed those traditional ways of being. How close he became to the earth, and the trees, and the stones. How he listened to the birds and the wind and the elk in the meadow. How he could pick up a piece of deadwood, and turn it slowly in his hands, and begin to see the winged creature that lay trapped inside. As if he understood that his work in this lifetime was to give them wings to fly, to release them from bondage.

Birdsong started from the cedar tree, and Elise found herself standing at the front door, staring out as the night slipped away, memories thick and heavy around her. She scanned the trees, looking for the flutters of bird wings.

*Oh, Michael,* she thought. *I don't know how to do this. I don't know how to go forward. I don't even know the first step. How the hell am I supposed to go on without you?* Those thoughts had come so often these past months.

Elise turned away from the door, turned away from the ghosts of memory that hung thick around her. The pale light of early dawn spilled onto the floor and up the stairs. The lavender color stood out and caught her eye, like a bright jungle bird. The card must have fallen off the table, and Elise bent to pick it up. "Celestina Redbird. Psychic. Tarot reader. 147 Paseo de Pueblo Norte. Taos, New Mexico." Elise turned the card in her fingers and stared as the blue light of dawn filled the house.

Outside, a gentle breeze caressed the pine trees, whispered across the floorboards of the porch, brushed like a feather over the chimes hanging from the rafters. The notes floated, bells from another world, whispering her name.

# CHAPTER SIX

The shop was in an old adobe building, surrounded by a rickety picket fence, set back from the street several feet more than the shops around it. A huge cottonwood stood sentinel at the gate, dropping slender golden leaves onto the stone walkway. The dried ghosts of summer flowers filled every inch of ground near the path. Lavender, daisies, flax, poppies—all stood at brittle attention. The gate was painted bright orchid, as were the windowsills, the porch, and the wooden door that stood wide open. The porch almost glowed with lavender-colored light. A breeze rustled the leaves and set the many sets of chimes on the porch to singing.

Elise stepped through the front door. There was no one in the room, and she turned slowly, taking it all in. To her left was a glass counter, filled with stones and jewelry and a stunning blue crystal ball. Crystal prisms danced in the window, ballet dancers doing pirouettes on their long strings, sprinkling multicolored gems of light on the floor and walls and ceiling. Elise turned. To her right were shelves of candles and incense. She could smell nag champa, caught a whiff of gardenia from the white candles burning in the corner. Behind the candles, the back corner of the room held purple shelves, filled with the books of the New Age trade.

Elise moved to the shelves and ran her fingers along the edge, staring at the titles: *Encyclopedia of Angels*, *Astrology of the Moon*, *Book of Witchery—Spells and Charms*. She picked up a book, *Guide for the Practitioner of the Magical Arts*, and flipped through the pages. Connecting with the phases of the moon, learning to tune in to the plants, observing the cycles of the seasons—Elise was surprised that some of the headings were so similar to the things she had experienced with Monica and Michael and Lorena. Not at all what she had expected when she pulled that book off the shelf.

"I knew you would come."

Elise spun around, caught off guard, and absentmindedly placed the book on the shelf.

Celestina stood framed in the doorway to the kitchen. A beaded curtain clicked and danced around her. She stepped into the front room, her green skirt swaying, her silver earrings flickering. The woman was draped in a shawl of bright-green-and-purple flowers; her hair was pulled back in a bun, strands of silver escaping like slender beams of moonlight. Elise stared at her dark eyes, at her smooth skin and high cheekbones, and wondered just how old this woman was. She had to be something past sixty.

Celestina's eyes were dark, but completely closed off, like trying to see through a brick wall. They gave no sign of the woman within, as if she deliberately veiled the contents of her own mind and heart. As if she had put up a gate that would not allow anyone else access to her inner being.

"You've driven quite a distance," she said.

Elise swallowed and nodded. "Yeah."

Celestina took a step and leaned against the glass counter at the front of the store. She watched Elise and chose her words carefully. "And now you are having doubts about all this." Celestina raised her arm to indicate the crystals and books and incense that surrounded them. "But there is nothing to be afraid of. What harm could come from listening? No one can force you to accept anything you don't want to. I only offer what I see and hear. You decide if there is any part of it that feels true *for you*." The woman stopped, her brow furrowed as she gazed at Elise. "Everyone needs help now and then. A little guidance from spirit."

Elise thought about her dream all those months ago, how she thought she knew what it all meant. The cost from that mistake had been enormous. At this moment, she didn't trust herself to know right from left. She remembered waking early this morning, feeling as if someone were calling her name, remembered turning from the doorway and finding that lavender card lying in the middle of the floor as if it had been dropped there on purpose. She did need help.

Celestina held out her hand and lifted a curtain to another small room behind the bookshelves. "Yes?"

For a moment, Elise stood frozen. Then she forced herself to exhale. "Yes," she whispered, and followed Celestina through the curtain.

The space was tiny, no more than eight feet square, and dark. There was no window in this room. Along the back wall were shelves and alcoves built into the thick adobe walls of the building. They were filled with statues of the saints: Niño de Atocha, Our Lady of Guadalupe, Saint Jude. Candles flickered, shadows danced on their carved wooden faces. On one shelf was a crystal vase full of red roses. Red petals lay scattered below, at the feet of Our Lady. The scent filled the room, a mixture of the sweetness of rose and the faint hint of decay. A bottle of rum stood next to Niño de Atocha, a shot glass half-full in front of his feet. On a silver tray lay a partially burned cigar.

"He likes good rum and Cuban cigars," Celestina explained. "And I like to keep him happy." She kissed her fingertips and touched them lightly on his feet.

In the middle of the room was a small oak table, two wooden chairs with woven seats resting on either side. The table was covered by a fringed shawl and held an unlit candle, a brass bell, and an incense burner.

"Sit," Celestina whispered, indicating one of the chairs.

Elise slipped into the chair. Celestina sat down across from her and lit a stick of incense. The scent of nag champa wafted into the space, quickly overpowering the rose and rum and cigar smells that lurked beneath. She lit another match and touched it to the candlewick. Their faces took on a soft golden glow.

Celestina's movements were measured and tranquil; they exhibited none of the agitation and anxiety that racked Elise. The older woman pulled cards from some hidden fold of her skirt, held them between her hands, like a prayer, and closed her eyes. Her body swayed slightly; there was a vibration, a low hum, from somewhere deep inside her. Every movement was slow and calm and liquid, like honey pouring from a spoon. She opened her eyes and laid the cards on the table. "I will call my spirit helpers now," she whispered. After staring at Elise for a long moment, she picked up the brass bell and gave it one clear chime. The sound bounced around the small room.

Elise straightened in her chair; a shiver climbed her spine and raised the hair on her arms.

Celestina straightened her back, shuffled her body slightly to fit the chair, and closed her eyes again. She took a deep breath and laid her fingertips on the deck of cards, as if they held some invisible cord that allowed her to see into other worlds. Her eyes remained closed; her body swayed back and forth. "He did not suffer," she whispered.

Elise stopped breathing. The question of how much Michael had felt that night, how much pain he had endured, had been a constant hum in her mind, compounding her guilt for not telling him about her dream, for not stopping him from going.

Celestina's voice dropped to a whisper. "I can see the moonlight on the car. It is dropping . . . sailing into the canyon below. But he is not in it. There is a bird flying from the car . . . soaring into the air. He is free now, flying with the birds that he loved so much."

A sound escaped from Elise, something between a moan and a sob. Regardless of whether it was true or not, the image of Michael, free as a bird and leaving before the pain could hit, brought her comfort. Emotion rushed at her like an oncoming train, and she dropped her eyes to the candle flame, the image warped and distorted by her tears and the way her body had started to shake.

Celestina began to sway again. "Mmm," she muttered. Her eyes and the corners of her mouth drooped. "I see you have many relations in the spirit world," she whispered. "Too many, for one so young."

Elise swallowed; her eyes burned. She fought to stop the trembling that was now racking her body.

Celestina stopped and raised her hand to her chest. Her face contorted, as if she were in pain. "Pain in the chest . . ." Celestina coughed, as if the vision was settling in her own lungs. "Coughing. I smell roses. Someone very close to you."

Her eyes flickered open.

Elise swallowed the lump in her throat, and nodded. "My mother. Her name was Rose. She died of pneumonia." Elise shuddered. She was now completely entranced with this woman, completely lost in her words and the emotions that fluttered across her face. Elise felt a shiver on her neck, and a fresh wave of goose bumps snaked down her arms.

Celestina closed her eyes again. She swayed forward and back, her hands rising into the air between them. "I see . . . strings . . . balls of yarn. You work with wool?" Her eyes popped open, searching Elise's face for the truth of what she had seen. Elise nodded.

"But you have not been able to work since the night he died. Your creative voice is blocked. Silent."

Elise dropped her eyes to her lap. Weaving had always brought her such comfort, such a sense of calm and peace. She loved the feel of the wool in her hands, the rhythm and trance of work. But since the night

Michael had sailed off over La Veta Pass, to the land of the spirits, she had been unable to lose herself in the gentle motion of placing the weft, of beating the yarn into place, of the color and pattern and texture of the wool. She had missed it, almost as intensely as she had missed Michael. It was as if she was a double amputee, losing everything that she had ever relied on to keep her functioning in the world.

Celestina sat completely still. She was silent for a long, tense moment. Elise sat up straighter, on edge about what the woman might say next but completely mesmerized by all that she had already seen.

"It isn't just the weaving, is it?" Celestina's eyes searched those of Elise. "Nothing in your life is working. You can't eat. Can't sleep. You don't know which way to turn. You don't know what to think, what to do." She waited, searching Elise's face with an intensity that burned the skin. "Almost as if you are . . . paralyzed."

Elise dropped her eyes to her lap, unable to meet Celestina's gaze. Her exhalation confirmed the truth of those words.

Celestina was silent, swaying back and forth. "Up until now, others have made decisions for you. You have never had to make it on your own before." The woman stopped talking, gazing at the flame of the candle between them. "Your husband cast a very long shadow, no? And you were swallowed by it—lost in the edges of his life. You have not found your *own* way in this world. Your own voice."

Elise straightened her back, her mind immediately resisting. She started to speak, to say, "That's not true," but Celestina held up a hand to stop her.

"You live in the mountains, yes?" Celestina did not wait for a reply, did not search for confirmation. It was as if she could see it all before her on the table, and she shook her head back and forth at the sight. "But you are too much alone, with only the dead for company. You cannot continue to stay up there, alone all the time." Celestina's eyes snapped up, and they met Elise in a hard, penetrating look. "Too much isolation can be . . . treacherous."

Elise forced herself to swallow. The words hung in the air between them, and Elise felt the impact vibrating through her. She had always loved the solitude. But what she was going through now, without Michael, was much worse than solitude.

Celestina continued to stare at Elise, but her eyes glazed over and lost focus. "Spirit says to spread the cards." She cupped one palm over the deck of playing cards on the table and slowly fanned them out, face side down, an arc of pattern before her. She let her hand hover over them. Without looking, her finger dropped and hit one card. She slid it out from underneath the others and flipped it over on the table: nine of clubs.

Celestina gazed at the card and then raised her eyes to Elise. "You are lost. There is darkness around you, wind and rain and night. You are lost in the storm, unable to see the way forward. And you are too terrified to move—afraid you will make a mistake and fall off a cliff."

Elise shuddered. The woman's choice of words was uncanny, the images so similar to her dream all those months ago.

"But you must move. Standing still is even more dangerous than moving in the wrong direction. Movement is crucial. When nothing is working, when everything in your life feels wrong, then you must make changes. This is the message of the card. Even if you can't see very far ahead, it is time to take a step."

Celestina pulled back, and without looking down, she flipped another card. The five of hearts lay on the table before her. "You are going on a journey?"

Elise shook her head.

"Yes," Celestina corrected. "You *are* going on a journey." She closed her eyes, her head tipped to one side. "A journey through the darkness. Toward the rising sun. To the east."

The older woman stared at Elise, their eyes locked on one another. Again, without dropping her gaze to the cards, she held her hand slightly above them, swaying back and forth, like an ocean wave at low tide, in a soft, steady rhythm. She flipped another card and dropped her gaze to the jack of spades.

"A man in your life. A man with dark eyes."

Elise's whole body thrummed with electricity. "Is it my husband?" She could almost hear the beating of her own heart, waiting for Celestina's answer, waiting to hear what Michael had to say. She was certain the message was from him, had known there was a good reason for her drive down here today.

Celestina continued to stare at the card, lost in concentration. Finally, the woman looked up and shook her head. "I do not know. The only thing that is clear is that it is a man, with dark eyes." She reached across the table and placed her hand on Elise's forearm. "But remember. This is the one-eyed jack. He can help you. But he can also take you off track. Even if this *is* your husband. Even the people who love us do not always know what is best. You must be very careful. Because this man"—she dropped her gaze to the card in front of her—"speaks with both sides of his tongue. A trickster."

The room became very quiet. Celestina sat, eyes closed, and started to speak. "Your name is Elise?"

Elise gasped. "Yes."

"Someone is calling your name. Someone from another world."

The words stopped Elise cold. She could not breathe, remembering the way she had awakened just this morning, hearing someone calling her name. Every fiber of her being pulled tight, frozen, waiting to hear. She knew Michael was trying to tell her something. She *knew*.

Celestina shook her head and looked at Elise. "That's all I can hear. Someone calling your name." She dropped her eyes to the cards on the table in front of her. "Spirit says to pull one more card," she whispered. "But you must choose it."

Elise bent forward and let her hand linger in the air a few inches above the cards. She stared at Celestina, not the cards, and let her finger drop. Her finger rested on the corner of one card, almost completely covered, and Elise slid it out from under the others. She flipped it over on the table between them.

Celestina gasped. The ace of spades lay on the table between them. She stared at it for what seemed like far too long.

Elise felt her heart speed up, felt the blood pounding in her neck. "What . . . what is it?" she whispered.

Celestina exhaled slowly, and her eyes drifted up to Elise's face. She swallowed, her words barely audible. "It is the death card."

Elise pulled back in her chair. "The death card?" She dropped her eyes to the card on the table, as if she herself could read what was written there. "My death?"

Celestina raised her shoulders and tipped her head. "The death card can mean many things. It could be your death. It could be the energetic residue of your husband's death. Or someone else in your family. You certainly have had more than your share of death around you. I could see it, permeating your aura when you walked in today. Death has created all these dark swirls, mixed into the colors of your being."

Celestina paused and studied the card again. "It could be symbolic—like the death of your old way of life. Like a snake, shedding its skin. It does not have to mean your physical death. The cards . . . just like dreams . . . can mean many things."

Elise nodded, her mind reeling. It was too much to absorb, and suddenly, now that it was too late, she realized she didn't want to know what the future held. She didn't want to know what was coming, in the same way that she resented the burden of the dream all those months ago, and the sick realization that no matter what warning she might have been given, some things could not be stopped. Elise wished she had not come; she wished she was back in her cabin on the mountain, alone with the quiet and no death card staring up at her. Tears snaked their way down her cheeks; she shook as if she were cold. "But it could?"

The woman pursed her lips and nodded, slowly.

Elise exhaled and asked the only question that came into her mind. It made sense, in some ways—the dream of her car flying off the mountain, the death card lying on the table in front of her. "And my husband? The message from my husband? Is this what he's trying to tell me? That I am going to die?"

Celestina closed her eyes again and sat slumped in her chair, her head tipped to one side. She appeared to be listening intently. "Hmm." She pursed her lips and began shaking her head back and forth. "There is a message . . . but I cannot hear it clearly. Someone is blocking the energy. Someone who was close to you. B . . . Bella?" Celestina's face scrunched with the effort, and her eyes shot open. "I can't quite get the name. But she is standing right behind you."

Elise jumped. She could almost feel Beulah's touch on her shoulder.

"And she's furious that you are here. Pretty angry with me, too, I'd say. Doesn't believe in all this . . . gibberish." Celestina's head straightened, a smirk crossed her face. "Tough old bird, that one." She took a deep breath. "I'm sorry. She's completely blocking the energy now. Nothing can come through with her standing right there."

They both sat silently. Elise watched as the heat from the candle flame climbed into the air, warping and twisting. She smelled the roses, the rum, the heavy scent of incense burning on the table between them. She was acutely aware of the silence, of Celestina's breathing, of the eyes of the saints evaluating her from their shelf on the wall. All around her, she felt the presence of death. Dead saints. Dead spirits. Dead rose petals. Death breathing down her neck and running a skinny finger up her arms.

Celestina forced a long, slow breath and gathered the cards together in a neat pile. She slipped them back into her pocket, as if she could take back the impact of the reading, of the negativity of her words. She blew out the candle on the table and reached forward to put her hand over Elise's forearm. "You will find your way. You will find the answers. I know what you are going through. I know what it is like, to find yourself alone. To not know the way forward. To be caught in the storm and the fog."

Elise met Celestina's gaze. Her fear had not dissolved, but something in Celestina's dark eyes pulled her in and softened the impact of the revelations of a few moments earlier. Elise felt connected to her, as if some invisible thread now wrapped them to each other.

"We came here over thirty years ago, my husband and I. Three little children. He put all our money into this torn-up old house in Arroyo Seco. The place was a disaster—no running water, no electricity. The roof leaked like a sieve. But he wanted to be here, with the other artists. Thought he could make his name, make his fortune as a painter. Tore us all away from Brooklyn. Brooklyn, of all places. My mother. My brother. Real pizza." Celestina smiled at the thought.

"And then he died. Up on the roof, during a storm, trying to cover one of the thousand holes. Slipped and fell two stories." Celestina stopped for a moment, her eyes lost in some distant time. "Died instantly. Left me with three children, the oldest only eight. No money. And a home I could never sell. We'd been here less than a year. I knew almost no one."

Celestina sighed, and her eyes found those of Elise. "I thought I would never stop crying. Prayed and cried, cried and prayed. I must have shed a million tears. And then one day, I was searching my dresser, looking for a necklace that my mother had given me. I was planning to pawn it, just to get a little money for food. I looked everywhere, but I could not find that necklace, even though I was sure I had worn it since we moved here. What I did find, in all that frantic searching, were these." Celestina pulled the deck of cards from her skirt and gazed at them.

"My mother gave them to me when I was fifteen. I didn't want them, and she knew it. Back then, all I wanted was to get away from her, to get away from cards and readings and all that crazy spirit stuff. I hated it, growing up with all that. I wanted to get away from spirits and messages and the never-ending line of people with questions about the future, questions about the departed. But she put them in my hands and told me to save them—that there would come a day when I would need those cards to survive.

"I was so determined that my life would be different from hers. But when she told me that, it scared me. I had seen what my mother could do with cards. I had seen what she could do, communicating with spirits. I had seen how many times she was right about something or someone."

Elise sat completely still.

"My father left us when I was five. Just my mom and me and my brother. She had to have a way to support us, and she did what she had always known. She started reading cards. Put up a sign in our apartment window. Sometimes, on Friday nights, she would hold a séance down in the basement. She practiced Santeria, just like her mother before her." Celestina smiled. "It runs in the family, you see.

"I hated it. Hated it. Hated how the other kids in the neighborhood always made fun of us. Hated that she had to be so *different* from everyone else. As if I was part of a family of witches. All I wanted was to put it all behind me, to run away and never look back. But I knew better than to get rid of those cards, after she gave them to me. I knew my mother had seen something or she wouldn't have done it. And as much as I hated it, I had to acknowledge her power. I threw the cards in a suitcase and tried to forget their existence.

"For a long time, I did forget. I forgot that I had them. And it wasn't until after my husband was dead, and I was completely lost about what to do, looking for a gold necklace to pawn. That's when they appeared in my life again. Instead of the necklace, I pulled these cards from a pocket in my suitcase. It made perfect sense, suddenly. My mother had managed to support us, all those years. With her cards, her readings, her communications with the spirits. We always had food on the table. As soon as I touched those cards, I knew. She had seen what was coming in my life. She had known there would come a time when I would have to support myself and my children. She had known that these cards would save me. And she was right. I did it. I raised my three children, even managed to fix up that wreck of a house he stuck us with."

Celestina smiled. "Some things do not make sense at first. But you will find your way, my dear. You will. Sometimes a card . . . like the death card, is only meant to help guide you. To keep you on your guard, watching . . . aware of everything around you. Someone . . . something . . . will show up in your life to help you. Stay alert."

The bell over the door in the front room jangled, and both women jumped, startled at the sudden sound. They heard the conversation of a man and a woman, a woman's voice calling, "Celestina? Are you here?"

"I'll be there in a moment," Celestina called out. She leaned forward and placed her hand over Elise's own. "Take whatever time you need back here. I do not have any appointments for a while." She looked at Elise, her face troubled. Then she stood and swept through the curtain, the beads dancing and clicking as they settled back into place.

Elise could hear Celestina's voice, different from the voice she had used in the back, in the dark, in the reading. Her voice now was cheerful and full, singing out in a higher key as she greeted her friends in the front.

Elise forced her breath out slowly and turned her head to look at the statues of the saints, candles flickering and bending in front of them. This was not at all what she had expected. She had come here wanting the message from Michael. Wanting, desperately, to talk to him. Wanting to know how she was going to live the rest of her life without Michael by her side. She did not want to know about a future that included a journey or a man with dark eyes or yet another death.

Elise took a Kleenex from the box on the shelf beside her and blew her nose. It was too late now. Celestina's words had entered her consciousness. Like the dream of her car, sailing out over the canyon, the words had already settled into the crevasses in her mind. A brainworm, like the way the words of a certain song will sometimes enter the mind and repeat endlessly. Celestina's words had entered her awareness, and she knew they would not leave. She forced herself to take a deep breath. Then she stood, her legs shaky and uncertain, and walked through the curtain.

Celestina turned to look at her. "Elise, I want you to meet my friend Sonia. She's a weaver, too."

Elise moved toward the woman standing near Celestina. She was beautiful, with long, thick black hair and dark eyes. She was dressed in a simple white blouse and jeans. Silver earrings danced at her ears. Around her neck was a lovely handwoven scarf, in autumn shades of orange and red and gold and purple. The two women shook hands, and Elise was instantly captivated.

"Very happy to meet you." Sonia smiled.

"Did you make that?" Elise asked, indicating the bright scarf.

Sonia looked down and picked up an end of the scarf in her hand. "Yes. Years ago, actually. When I first bought my big loom."

Elise smiled. "It's lovely."

"Thank you." Sonia smiled. "Elise, this is my friend Tom Dugan."

Elise turned to the man standing next to Sonia. He was around six feet tall, with curly brown hair, a few fine streaks of gray at the temples. He had brown eyes, but they were warped and distanced by the thick glasses on the bridge of his nose. He seemed uncertain, shy and awkward like a teenager.

He tipped his head, pushed his glasses up on his nose, and examined Elise. "Have we met before?"

Elise studied him carefully. There was something about him that was familiar. It happened often, really, after all these years in the Taos area, and all those years of selling their art at art fairs and openings at the gallery. She had found that people often remembered meeting the artist, even if she and Michael did not recall meeting them. Elise shook her head slowly. "I don't think so."

He lifted his eyebrows and shrugged. "Well, nice meeting you."

Elise turned toward Celestina, who had moved behind the counter. "How much do I owe you?"

Celestina's eyes were soft and liquid. "You don't owe me a thing. Spirit told me to help you—when I saw you at the park that day." Celestina's eyes twinkled with laughter, and the corners of her lips rose. She leaned forward and whispered quietly, "Tell your friend I don't want your dinero."

# CHAPTER SEVEN

The sun was sinking, lighting the entire Sangre de Cristo range with the bloodred alpenglow that had inspired their name—Blood of Christ. Elise drove home in a daze, emotionally drained, her mind endlessly looping through Celestina's words, reliving the flick of each card she had flipped onto the little table. She could still feel the hush that had come into the room when she flipped the ace of spades, could still hear that sharp little gasp that had escaped from Celestina's mouth.

Once again, Elise had forgotten to eat. She'd driven right past her favorite restaurant in Taos, had turned her head to look in the window at Lopez Market in Amalia just a few minutes ago, without registering that it was her last chance to buy food. A trancelike state had enveloped her in the back of Celestina's shop and had continued for the entire fifty miles of the drive home. It required all her concentration to maneuver the truck, to stay on the road, to make sure she didn't slip as she climbed the ravine-ridden gravel road up to the cabin. By the time she turned into the driveway, exhaustion, hunger, and the effects of dehydration were playing havoc with her mind and body.

Monica's white Toyota work truck sat slightly askew, as if she'd pulled in fast and the truck had fishtailed as she parked. Monica sat on the front porch, tipped back in a chair, her feet on the railing. She watched as Elise got out of the car and forced her exhausted legs up the gravel path to the house.

"I must have started a trend," Monica deadpanned. "This makes, what? The second time you've left the house in the last six months?"

Elise tried to force a smile. "Sorry, Mom. Next time, I'll ask permission."

Monica held up a bottle of wine. "Medicine for your misery. Got any food to go with this?"

Elise stopped and mentally scanned the contents of her kitchen. "I think there's a box of Cheerios in the cupboard. Probably stale."

Monica nodded, her lips pursed. "Mmm. That's what I thought. I can't believe you can survive on cereal and popcorn. Good thing my mom made a pot of green chili. Homemade tortillas, too."

"That's the best news I've heard all day." Elise pushed the door open and was immediately met with the smell of chili on the stove. She dropped her purse on the table by the door, next to the lavender card that had inspired this whole adventure, and turned to Monica, who was now hunting up a corkscrew in the kitchen. "You didn't have time to change?" Elise asked, taking in the drywall dust and paint smeared down the front of Monica's clothes.

Monica and her brother ran a remodeling business and enjoyed a fair amount of success. Completely comfortable with tools of all kinds, Monica often had a tool belt around her waist and some implement of construction in her hand. From changing the oil in her car to fixing the old truck they used on the farm, Monica could do just about anything. With help from her brother, they had built a home for Monica next to her mother's house, even managing the wiring and plumbing. She had an absolute flair for tile work, which made her much in demand around Taos. Elise had never known anyone so thoroughly strong and independent, and often covered with grease, or drywall dust, or paint, or some artistic combination of construction residue.

Monica looked down at the mess that covered her coveralls. "Hell, no. I had to pry you out of this place a few days ago, and this morning you went sailing right past me without so much as a one-finger wave. I knew you were up to no good."

Elise dished up bowls of chili and collapsed into a kitchen chair. She took the glass of wine that Monica offered and sniffed: Canoncito Red from the winery south of Taos. Her favorite. "I wasn't up to anything," she said, savoring her first sip. She dreaded Monica's reaction to her trip but squared herself to telling the truth. "I went to see that card reader."

Monica brought the covered pottery dish of tortillas to the table and sank into the chair with a loud sigh. "I knew it. I knew you wouldn't be able to resist. Oh, the allure of easy answers." She shook her head and dug into her chili, not coming up for air until she'd managed several bites. "So. Have you gone completely insane?"

"Not completely." Elise dropped her eyes to her bowl, too tired to really savor Lorena's cooking. "Not yet, anyway."

"What did the Indian wannabe have to say?"

"Not an Indian wannabe. She's from Brooklyn. Your psychic powers are a little rusty, Mo." Elise chewed a bite of tortilla and stared into the dusk outside the kitchen window. "She was pretty amazing, actually. She could see Michael's accident—sailing out over the canyon. Said he's flying with the birds he loved so much." Elise dropped her eyes to her bowl and took a minute before she continued. "She knew that I'm a weaver."

"Lucky guess," Monica growled. "This is Taos County. Everyone and their aunt Edna is a weaver."

"You're not." Elise raised her eyebrows. "And she picked up on my mom. The pain in her lungs. Figured out her name." Elise stared out the window again.

They were both silent for a moment. Crickets filled the night with song.

"She tell you anything about Michael?"

Elise focused on her food again and shook her head.

Monica pushed her bowl away and lifted the glass of wine to her lips. The deep-crimson color was almost black in the dim light, as if she were drinking the night. "Did she tell you anything you don't already know? Anything that was remotely useful? Because coming up with your mother's name and how she died is not really helpful at this point in time, is it?"

Elise dropped her gaze to her half-eaten bowl of chili. She was almost too tired to finish eating, and she certainly didn't have the energy to rehash the quiet tension in that dark alcove in Taos. "She flipped a few cards. For my future."

Monica's brows went up.

Elise shrugged. "I guess it was about what you would expect. Big changes ahead. Man coming into my life who will help me. Going on a journey. Standard card-reading stuff, I guess." There was one part of the reading Elise knew she couldn't talk about with Monica. Not now. Not tonight. At the moment, it was more than she herself could process.

"Good Lord. A man coming into your life?" Monica pursed her lips. "Now there's a prediction that wouldn't work for just anyone who walked in the door."

"You are such a cynic."

"One of us has to be. And a journey, huh?" Monica threw her head back and laughed. "That's rich. A journey. Physical? Spiritual? Will you be taking peyote with the hippies on Blueberry Hill?"

"You can be quite a smart-ass, you know."

"Elise, you've known me for over forty years. You ought to be used to it by now." Monica twirled the glass in her hand. "Don't you think these 'predictions' are a little generic?"

Elise shrugged and ran her finger around the rim of her wineglass. "Maybe. But she got everything else right. About my past. About my family. About what my life is like right now. How could she know all that?"

"Well, for one thing, because you can't hide anything you feel. You wear your heart on your sleeve, and in your face, in your body. For instance, right now, you're all slumped over like you've been kicked. You need to take a few lessons from the People. We know how to play it straight."

"Are you saying she couldn't read your cards?" Elise pulled herself up from her slump. "I could be very interested in that kind of psychic experiment."

Monica put her glass down and stared at Elise. "That's it. Now I know you've gone off the deep end."

Elise turned to stare out the window. The trees were flat black; the sky had faded to a deep shade of blue. A few stars blinked over the valley, above the thin gold line that rimmed the western horizon. When she spoke, her voice sounded far away, lost in a tunnel a million miles from the kitchen, where they sat. "I think Michael is trying to tell me something. Something important."

Monica turned to look at Elise.

"I keep hearing him, calling my name. Just soft enough that maybe I imagined it. But just loud enough, often enough, that it could really be happening. I heard it this morning. I thought maybe that card reader could help."

Elise tipped her glass of wine, watched as the liquid swirled in the glass. "Mo? Have you ever actually seen a spirit? A ghost?"

Monica got very quiet. Her life was rich with the idea of spirits. Her mother, Lorena, always put out a spirit bowl on feast days—a bowl of food, just a bite of everything the family was eating, placed outside to feed the spirits. The family had always been part of the celebrations at the Pueblo: the Green Corn Dance, the Deer Dance, numerous celebrations and ceremonies that took place every year. Monica's uncle Wes was considered quite a medicine man. Living with spirits was something they'd been doing for generations.

Monica leaned forward in her chair and put her arms on the table. "Remember when my grandpa Lopez died?" Monica smiled at the memory. "We were at the cemetery, after all the singing and drumming and eagle feathers were all over with, and the wind came up—sharp and fast. All the women who were wearing dresses had to fight to keep their skirts from flying up. Legs and panties flashing all over the place."

Elise smiled. She did remember it, all the tittering and laughing, and everyone saying that it was just like Old Man Lopez, one last chance to lift the ladies' skirts.

Monica turned to Elise. "And then, just as quickly as it came up, the wind was gone. We started walking toward the car, and my mom heard it first. She stopped and looked up at the sky, and there was an eagle, pretty high up, circling the cemetery. We could hear it calling. And as we stood there watching, this feather floated down from the sky. Slow motion, back and forth, back and forth. It landed in a clump of wild rosebushes, and my mom went after it, never mind the thorns and her good dress. She keeps that feather on her dresser. Calls it a gift from her father."

They both sat quietly, soaking in the memory of the funeral that day, more than fifteen years ago. The silence stretched out, comfortable and quiet. Monica's smile dropped, and her voice, when she finally spoke, was quieter than Elise had ever heard her. "I never told anyone this," she whispered.

Elise looked up at her. The one thing Monica never had any trouble with was saying what was on her mind, exactly the opposite of Elise, as if she and Elise were the yin and yang of expressing their thoughts.

"After my dad died. Maybe two or three weeks after. I'd been at the house with Mom. We ate dinner together, watched a little TV. She went to bed, and I fell asleep on the couch. And in the middle of the night, I got up to go to the bathroom, and there was my dad, sitting in his leather recliner. He nodded at me, and I said, 'Hey, Dad,' and headed down the hall. It was a sight I'd seen so often in my lifetime that I never really thought about it. I was in the bathroom before I remembered, 'Wait a minute. Dad's dead.' When I came back out, there was nothing there." She glanced at Elise. "For a minute I just shook my head, trying to wake myself up. And then I moved over to his chair and put my hand on the cushion. It was indented, and still warm. Just like it would be if someone had actually been sitting there."

Elise absorbed the quiet words, remembering Monica's dad, sitting in that chair, eating piñon nuts and telling stories. His eyes were always laughing, like he knew the inside joke about life and was pretty tickled by it.

"Have you seen Michael?"

Elise pinched her lips together and shook her head. "No. But I keep seeing this movement—some flash of something—out of the corner of my eye. It's like I can feel him out there." She tipped her head toward the window. "Like he is watching me. But I never quite catch it."

Monica was quiet for a few moments. "Lise? Did you ever think it might not be Michael?"

Elise turned quickly. "What do you mean?"

Monica met her gaze in the dark. "You have a lot of people in the spirit world. Maybe it isn't Michael. Maybe it's Beulah or your mom. Maybe even your dad. Or maybe someone completely unrelated."

Elise sighed. "I guess I just figured it would be him. Since it was only a few months ago that he passed . . . since we were together for so long."

Darkness had fallen all around them. Outside, the sky had turned dark, and neither of them had moved to turn on a light. They sat quietly, both of them staring out at the night.

"Elise? Maybe you should come down and stay with me, or with Mom. Get away for a while. It's so . . . isolated up here."

The words struck Elise, like the twang of a tuning fork, reminding her of what Celestina had said just a few hours earlier. *You cannot continue to stay alone up there. Isolation can be treacherous.* Elise forced her breath out, a long, slow stream to help her regain her equilibrium. Sometimes that was exactly what she wanted—to get away from here. To be somewhere that didn't include being alone every moment. To be somewhere that didn't have Michael stitched into every surface, every tree, every board of this house. But how could she go? Not now. Not yet. Not with this overwhelming feeling that Michael was trying to tell her something. That he was out there, somewhere, just beyond what she could see, waiting.

Monica let out a long sigh. "Or maybe you need to go see a medicine man. Sometimes they can see things that we can't. Why don't you talk to Uncle Wes? Whenever I don't know the answer, I go to Mom or Uncle Wes."

Elise glanced up. "When have you ever not known the answer?"

Monica tipped her head. "Theoretically speaking, that would be who I would ask."

Monica lifted her foot and nudged the bottom of Elise's shoe. "Lighten up, would you? I won't hold this against you. You can't help it if you sometimes do weird things. Psycho card readers and such. It's bound to happen. You are white." Monica raised her eyebrows and smiled.

Elise couldn't help herself. She laughed.

After Monica drove off, Elise collapsed into the leather chair in the living room and slipped off her boots. She raised her feet to the ottoman and lay back in the chair, light-headed from the events of the day. How was it that a few words from a perfect stranger could send her mind into this unsettling new awareness? Because it was true, what Celestina had said. Nothing in her life was working right now. The words of the reading swirled around her, like inky black smoke. *Too much alone. Too isolated. Your husband led the way; now you don't know which way to turn.*

Elise loved this place, this house, these mountains. They were a part of her, no different from her hair or the color of her eyes. But she was too much alone now. She talked to Monica on the phone every other day, and Monica came up once a week or so. The tiny hamlet of Amalia was a good half-hour drive, and Elise went down for supplies every other week. But that was it, for the most part. Her nearest neighbor was half a mile away.

For more than twenty years, she had loved being here. It was her refuge, a place of quiet and safety and beauty. She remembered how excited Michael had been when he found this property. Fifteen miles from the town of Amalia, up a twisty red gravel road, often rutted and strewn with rocks. But the property was on the stream and had great views of the valley below. The land here was fairly level, and the trees were thick and old and contained a little of everything: piñon, juniper, cottonwood, spruce, even a copse of aspens. It was rare to find a piece of property with so much variety in one spot.

"You'll never guess what I found." He'd been almost beside himself with excitement, his body fairly vibrating with joy. They'd been married almost a year, living in the house in Amalia left empty by Beulah's death. He took her up to the property, let her walk every inch of it with him as he laid out his vision for the cabin, and a studio, and maybe someday a garage. He helped her imagine the porch, looking out at the valley below. He stopped her in midstride, in the middle of a grassy area, and said, "Right there. That's the fireplace. Can't you see it, Elise? River rock? Maybe a few pieces of copper thrown in to make it interesting."

She remembered laughing, feeling caught up in his excitement. It was a dream, the idea of building a cabin in the mountains, their own place, their own design, using their own hands. A new beginning, a fresh start, away from Beulah's house with all the uncomfortable memories of silence and death.

She had always wanted to live in the mountains, to smell the pine trees and hear the stream. The views of the sunsets over the valley were incredible. Living in the mountains with the man she had loved almost her whole life, hiking the hills looking for inspiration for their work. It appealed to her in so many ways.

At first it had been an adjustment, living up here without Monica and Lorena in easy walking distance. She hadn't realized just how often they had stopped in at one another's homes—sometimes several times a day—and she missed that proximity to the two women who had meant so much in her life. And after they had been up here less than a year, Elise had given up her job waiting tables at the Main Street Café in Amalia, the only job she'd ever had. The drive up and down that rutted road was just too much for the sometimes-meager income, and Michael had encouraged her to quit and concentrate on her weaving.

Never had she imagined that she might end up here, in this cabin, alone. Winter was approaching, and she would have to deal with finding firewood. Michael had always taken care of it—just as he kept the fire going, adding wood in the middle of the night when he came in from the studio, keeping the house warm for Elise. It was Michael who had maintained all their solar panels, Michael who had been the primary breadwinner. Yes, Elise sold a few weavings here and there, but she'd never had to worry about making ends meet with her own work. Since Ken Black had discovered Michael's carvings, Elise had not had to worry about her own sales, or more appropriately, the lack of sales.

She dreaded the coming winter, living alone up here, without him. Being this far from town, up that washboard road, made her think twice about going to the café for a cup of coffee, or popping in to see Lorena or Monica if she was feeling a little low. It was simply more hassle than she could manage.

Elise let her eyes travel around the living room of the home they had built together. Along the north wall was the rock fireplace, just as he had imagined it all those years ago. He had placed a few pieces of rough copper at random places, and the blue-green color of the jagged rock sometimes caught the light and turned the fireplace into a work of art. Opposite the fire, against a large window, stood the worn gold-colored couch they had inherited from his uncle. The chair she sat in was one that Michael had picked up on one of his trips to Santa Fe.

She looked around the room. Was there anything in here that she had picked out? That she had wanted and decided to buy? She'd made the curtains in the kitchen—yellow calico with tiny blue flowers. She had made the quilt on their bed. A couple of her weavings hung on the walls, mostly experiments with color and technique—nothing that she would consider a fine piece of work that she loved.

The room was filled with things they had picked up on their walks: antlers, the skulls of small critters, feathers, the jawbone of a coyote, teeth still intact. Artwork filled every available wall space: photographs and paintings that Michael had traded for, back when they had very little money and were making most of their sales through art fairs. But as her eyes scanned the room, taking in the books and paintings and photographs and odd fragments of nature that had found their way inside, Elise wasn't certain what was *she* and what was Michael. She had never really believed there was a difference—that their tastes, their desires, were intertwined, interchangeable, almost indistinguishable. Monica had once described the two of them as bookends—one dark, one light—but mirror images of the other.

And now, without her mirror image in the room, she wasn't sure about anything. What did *she* like? What did *she* want? Who was she, without Michael to reflect her back to herself? Elise had no idea.

# CHAPTER EIGHT

It was Friday. Elise hated Fridays, or to be more precise, she hated Fridays *now*, since Michael had died. Most of the time, she barely knew what day it was, but Friday always marched into her consciousness like New Year's Eve: all noise and fireworks and anticipation. There was a sense of expectation, a sense of completion, a sense that there should be some sort of celebration despite the fact that she did not live the normal nine-to-five existence of most Americans.

Friday had always been the day when she and Michael kicked back and relaxed. Despite working at home, despite the fact that work, for both of them, was creating art, Friday had always been the day when they wrapped up a few loose ends and quit early. They would drive into Taos, have dinner at the Apple Tree or Doc Martin's. Sometimes they would stay the night at the Taos Inn so they could listen to music until late in the night, dancing until they leaned on each other in exhaustion.

Earlier in their marriage, back when they were still doing the art-fair circuit, Friday was often the day to set up for the coming weekend, or sometimes it was the first day of the show. The day always held a great sense of expectation, the adrenaline rush of possibility and expansion that made it more glamorous and glittering than any other day of the week.

The pieces of one particular Friday came back to her now. She and Michael were sitting at a table on the patio at the Apple Tree restaurant in Taos, directly beneath the actual apple tree. The perfume of the apple blossoms over their heads sweetened everything they tasted. They were sharing almond-crusted brie and remarking that the restaurant was a microcosm of the world. They could hear Portuguese being spoken at one nearby booth, Spanish at another, and at the table behind them, two couples were exclaiming over the food in French. She and Michael were eavesdropping, trying to see how many of the words they recognized.

Ken Black, the owner of the art gallery in Santa Fe, and his wife, Elaine, she of the perfectly coiffed bottle-blonde hair, came through the door from the restaurant, following the maître d' to a table on the patio. Ken was scanning the restaurant to see if he knew anyone, and his eyes locked on Michael's. "Here we go," Michael whispered to Elise and raised his eyebrows.

Michael stood and shook Ken's hand and invited the couple to join him and Elise. Elise knew he would, knew that he felt obligated to invite them, but her stomach flipped over at the thought of sharing her Friday evening, and a perfectly wonderful dinner, with oily Ken and his Barbie-doll wife.

Elise had tried, over the years, to find something she and Elaine could talk about, but so far she'd been unsuccessful. Elaine was big-city; she had long red fingernails and wore a mountain of makeup. As far as Elise had been able to discern, her only reading material was *Cosmo*. Elise read constantly, lived outside a town of fewer than five hundred people, and never wore makeup or dyed her hair. They had nothing in common. The two women greeted each other, Elaine with the kiss-kiss that never quite landed on Elise's cheeks. They quickly turned most of the conversation over to the men.

"So, Ken, what brings you up to the high country?" Michael asked in between bites of mango chicken enchiladas, his favorite dish on the menu.

"An artist, of course." Ken laughed. "In the canyon, headed toward Angel Fire. A weaver, actually." He nodded at Elise.

Michael glanced at Elise. "And? What did you find?"

Ken chewed his steak thoughtfully and rested his hand on the table, fork pointed toward Elise. "Technique is excellent. Good color choices." His eyes dropped to his plate. "But there's something missing." Ken nodded toward Michael and continued his assault on his steak. "I see the same thing so often. Someone who has learned their craft, who has really perfected the techniques of weaving or carving or painting, or whatever it is. But there's no spirit in the work. No heart. No voice that speaks to me."

Elise rested her fork on her plate and watched him.

"And then there are the artists who have *not* perfected the technical aspects of the craft, whose work can only be described as primitive. But the spirit of the piece just jumps up and grabs you by the throat. That is true art—a connection to the muse, to the creative spirit, that just comes right through the work." Ken tapped his closed first on his heart. "The heart of the work." He turned and looked at Michael. "Something that you do very well, Michael."

Ken had never said that Elise's work lacked heart. He had never actually said anything about her work. But he didn't have to. His message—that she was not good enough, that her work was not good enough—had come through loud and clear from the very first day they met Ken Black.

She and Michael were working the art-fair circuit, as they had for several years. They'd set up a ten-foot-square canvas tent and filled it with their work: Elise's tapestries along the sides, Michael's birds perched on tables in the middle. This particular Friday, they were set up on the plaza in Santa Fe and had just finished putting out the art earlier that morning. Elise had wandered off to find coffee for the two of them. She returned to find Michael engaged in conversation with a man who was dressed in black—black shirt, black pants, black sport jacket and boots. The black of his clothing set off his Navajo belt buckle and bolo tie. Elise slipped into the back of the tent and listened as Ken Black expounded on all the Native artists he had discovered over the years, as if he were responsible for the beautiful art they produced. She listened as Ken told Michael that he would like to represent Michael in his gallery and that he would take every piece Michael had on hand. Ken was certain they would be able to push prices higher over the next few months.

Just like that—just that fast—their whole lives had changed. Ken never mentioned her weavings that day—only Michael's birds. Michael had introduced her as his wife, "Elise Brooks, the weaver," holding out his hand to indicate her weavings around them. But Ken barely glanced at her work.

Elise was happy for Michael. He began to get attention for his work. An article in the *Santa Fe New Mexican*, a whole spread in *Southwest Art*, numerous articles in *New Mexico* magazine and the *Albuquerque Journal*. Ken sold every piece Michael brought in, and prices rose steadily. For the first time in their lives, there was enough money. Michael bought her a new car but kept his old beat-up truck for hauling deadwood for his work.

When the applications for art fairs started coming in for the following year, Elise had thrown them in the trash. She didn't want the hassle of setting up the tent, of sitting in the rain or sun or snow or wind for three days if Michael wasn't a part of it. Michael had told her she could do it if she wanted to, that he would help her set up and tear down. And she did that, for one fair in Taos. But she had never really liked it, sitting out there in the open, watching as people walked by and made judgments about her and her work. Without Michael, it was not the same, and she quit doing the art-fair circuit.

She sold her pieces at a couple of small galleries in Taos, but never more than a few a year. She wove when she could, took her weavings to the shops in town, but her role seemed to change, from struggling young weaver to the wife of Michael Madrid, the Jicarilla Apache artist who carved incredible birds.

Elise loved Navajo patterns, had always loved the exquisite beauty of the colors and the stories and history that went with them. Several years before, she had spent two weeks living on the reservation, studying with a renowned Navajo weaver. The patterns spoke to her: old-style Crystal, Teec Nos Pos, Ganado, Two Grey Hills. She loved the stories that went with them; she loved the way her teacher had talked about yarn and color, and the way they touched each other to create a new story.

But there was nothing of *her* that came through those weavings. Navajo patterns. Navajo colors. Nothing of the vision and voice that made up Elise Brooks, that made her want to sit at the loom and pull yarn through the warp. Because deep down, Elise had no idea who she was. She did not feel a connection to the ancestors the way Michael did. She didn't have a connection to the land that went back hundreds of years, the way Monica did.

That feeling of disconnection, of not belonging, went back as long as she could remember. And now, without Michael, it was even worse. She was lost in the darkness, just as Celestina had said.

Elise had tried, in these months since Michael died, to sit down at her loom and weave, to find that gentle rhythm that took her into the zone of creation. But after only a few lines of weft, she gave up in frustration. The muse had deserted her, just as Michael had, as if they had driven off the side of the mountain together, leaving her completely barren of ideas and inspiration and companionship. Completely cut off from the one person and the one activity that had always brought her comfort and wholeness.

She knelt in front of the woodstove. The chill of this October morning had forced her to try and light the first fire of the season. It sputtered and smoked, and she drew her head back, coughing and waving the smoke away. She wondered when the chimney had been cleaned last—yet another in the long list of chores that Michael had taken care of, another in the long list of items that she was now going to have to figure out on her own.

"If you were going to go and die on me, couldn't we have planned this a little better?" she growled to the smoking stove. What she had once loved—the seclusion of the mountains, the rusticity of not having a central heating system, the way they had relied so much on each other—was now choking her, making her gasp for air. She had no idea how she was going to live up here, alone. She had no idea how she was going to earn a living. She had no idea how she was going to get through another Friday, another weekend, without him.

Elise bent forward and laid her head on her knees. She forced a long, slow breath, filled with frustration and anger and an aching, wrenching pain. When the phone rang, the sudden noise made her jump. For a moment, she thought about not answering, about giving in to this depression and just lying on the floor all day. But the sound was overly loud in the still morning air, and she forced herself up to find the phone. "Hello."

"Elise? Elise, is that you, dear?" The woman's voice was distant and unclear, as if she were speaking from the far end of a tunnel. For one weird, crazy moment, Elise thought the voice was that of her own mother, dead more than forty years. She shook her head, trying to clear it. Her mind had been much too focused on the dead these past months.

She cleared her throat. "Who is this?" The chimes on the porch began to dance and jingle, and the sound pulled at her. She glanced outside, wondering if wind was about to mar the perfect fall day.

"It's Celestina Redbird. From the shop in Taos? I hope you don't mind. I did a little detective work to find your phone number. Good thing I have access to so much information." Celestina laughed.

Elise said nothing, but she wondered what that meant exactly—some kind of psychic white pages? She heard the chimes again, and her eyes scanned the tops of the trees for movement, looking for evidence of the wind. They did not sway and dance; nothing moved, and she stood with the phone pressed to her ear and inched closer to the window in the front door.

"Not to worry. I just asked a few friends if they knew a weaver in Amalia whose husband died recently. Nothing terribly exciting or psychic."

"Ah." Elise nodded.

"I wanted to invite you to our little get-together tonight. A potluck. The widows' and orphans' club. Not a club, really. It's just a few of us who get together and have dinner. Socialize with our own kind."

The words sent Elise's heart into jumps and flutters, like the sharp maneuvers of a hummingbird. Widow. Orphan. What loathsome words they were. She'd never thought of herself that way before. Was that really who she was? A widow? An orphan?

Elise stood still, hearing sounds on the front porch.

"Elise? Are you still there?"

"Yeah. Yes, I'm here." Elise heard the chimes on the front porch again, and she moved to the door. She looked out the window and scanned the porch. No one was out there. No wind moved the treetops.

"It's a little tricky to find the house. Have you got a pen?"

Elise scrambled for paper and wrote down the instructions. She hung up the phone and laid it on the table by the stairs, silently cursing herself for agreeing to go. As much as she hated spending Fridays alone, she didn't really want to spend tonight with perfect strangers, either. Turning around, she caught the flutter of movement in her peripheral vision. She moved slowly to the window in the door once again. This time, though, she kept her head slightly sideways, an attempt to sneak up on whatever it was that had been eluding her.

A raven sat on the railing of the porch, one foot lifted to scratch his head. His eyes scanned Elise, and he put his foot down and tipped his head to one side, examining her with one glassy black eye. The raven made a soft clucking sound, like a chicken on its roost. Their eyes locked on one another for a moment. Then he stepped off the railing and soared away.

# CHAPTER NINE

The sun was sinking. Elise had slowed the car to a crawl, searching for the driveway Celestina had described. She'd made all the hairpin turns through the sleepy village of Arroyo Seco, passed the Taos Pueblo reservation lands on the right, and had started the climb into the foothills of Taos Canyon when she found her turn. The mailbox by the road was painted a bright turquoise; on either side of the driveway stood three log poles in descending heights. They had once been painted bright turquoise, lavender, and bloodred, but time and sun and weather had dulled the colors and chipped away at the paint. Even so, they were still distinctive enough that she knew this was the place. She turned into the driveway, dark and narrow from the tall trees on either side.

The smell of pine rushed in through the crack in her window, and she was struck by the still-bright symphony of colors in the fall trees. A clump of aspen sang out in yellows and oranges; the cottonwoods blared like trumpets over the road with bright-gold, narrow leaves. Bushes of oak and sumac pounded red and rust in the fading light. She was surprised by how rich and verdant the land was—so different from the dry flatland she had left behind just moments ago. There had to be a stream somewhere close by.

The driveway circled in front of an adobe house—a patchwork of what must have been a traditional, old one-story home on the right and a soaring two-story addition of wood beams and expansive windows on the left. The house was pumpkin-colored adobe, with windows and doors that glowed with golden light, like the face of a jack-o'-lantern.

The place was serene and quiet and oddly comforting. Elise felt none of the fear or anxiety that she had felt pulling up to Celestina's shop less than a week ago. She was completely calm, and everything around her slowed to a midnight hush.

She turned off the engine and sat for a moment, staring out at the fading light. Bats swooped from the trees; she could hear the hoot of an owl nearby. Elise left the shelter of the truck, every sound magnified: the clicking noises of the engine, the clang of the metal as she closed the door, the scrunch of her boots on the gravel, the breeze rustling the leaves of the aspen trees.

She felt as if she were walking down a tunnel; everything to the side and overhead had faded into obscurity, and she could see only the faded turquoise door ahead of her. The moments took on a slow-motion quality—every second of time, every sound, every sensation around her exaggerated. She remembered a similar feeling, years ago, when she was just learning to drive and her car tires had lost contact with the pavement and had started to spin on the snow-covered blacktop—the sense that her life was out of her control, that there was nothing she could do to stop it, the feeling that all meaning was distilled into just this moment. She had that same sense of time suspended.

She heard the whoosh of wings and turned to her left. A raven flew over her head, and she could see that it was missing a feather, on the left wing. It settled into the branch of a ponderosa pine, and Elise shook a shiver off her shoulders.

Sonia stepped out on the porch, in blue jeans and white blouse and bare feet. Her long black hair was wet. She smiled. "You made it. This place isn't easy to find."

Elise smiled. Sonia had to be close to sixty, but she was beautiful in an easy, timeless way that gave no indication of her age. Elise took her hand and they kissed cheeks, as if they'd known each other a long time.

"I'm so glad you are here. Come in, come in." Sonia led the way into a hallway, lost in evening shadow. Elise hung her jean jacket on a hook by the door. To the right side was the original adobe house, low and squat with thick walls, similar to Beulah's old house. To the left was the newer addition.

She followed Sonia down two stone steps into the center of the room. A rock fireplace dominated one wall; the rest of the room curved around it with twelve-foot-high windows. Elise was entranced by that curve of windows. It made the room seem as if it were part of the outdoors, as if the trees and grass and bushes outside were somehow part of the furnishings. She could see the lights of Taos sparkling in the near distance.

Sonia moved next to her and sighed. "I love it here. Love the trees. Love the view. Love the deer that stop by for a snack." She pursed her lips toward the four does and three fawns that were grazing outside.

They stood, soaking in the beauty of the surroundings.

"You lost your husband recently?" Sonia murmured.

Elise nodded. "Last March."

Sonia sighed heavily. She kept her eyes focused on the view as she spoke. "I think that first year is the worst." The sounds of the birds singing their end-of-day songs came through an open window. "My Victor has been gone for six years already. I can't say that it is *easier*, but it is different now. At least now it doesn't feel like an open wound all the time. At first, just about anything—a smell, a song, finding his reading glasses—sent me right under. Just like you've had all your skin ripped off, and everything that brushes up against it is excruciatingly painful."

Elise shivered and ran her hands up and down her arms. She would never have thought to describe it like that, but the image was startlingly accurate.

"I met him when I was fourteen. And fell instantly in love, if you can believe that. I never had to face being an adult without him." Sonia stared out at the garden.

"Same with Michael," Elise whispered. "I've known him since I was little." She hadn't expected to talk about him, to talk about being a widow with someone who was a perfect stranger.

"That doesn't happen very often," Sonia whispered. "Not anymore."

Sonia's eyes stayed glued to the scene outside. "My Victor had a heart attack. All very sudden. One minute, he's outside working in the garden"—she pursed her lips to indicate the area just in front of the window—"and the next . . . my whole life has changed. I heard something . . . like a word or a cry . . . and by the time I got outside, he was gone. That fast."

Sonia did not turn to look at Elise. Outside, light was fading, slowly turning the sky a deep teal-blue. "In one moment, my whole life flipped. It felt a little like being out in the middle of the ocean, at night. No boat, no life vest. Nothing but darkness. Disoriented, like I didn't even know which way was up. It was all I could do to keep my head above water, and not go under. I had to remind myself to breathe. Took enormous effort. I was tired all the time, and yet I could never manage to sleep for more than an hour or so without jolting awake. And always, those first few seconds, when the memory comes crashing back. He's dead."

Elise pressed her lips together, fighting to keep herself from crying. How could this woman, this complete stranger, understand so perfectly what Elise had been going through these past few months? She swallowed and murmured, "That's exactly the way I feel."

Sonia met her eyes and smiled. "So there we are, barely surviving. And then add to that the way our society handles grief—or doesn't handle it, is more appropriate. People didn't want to be around me—almost like I had a disease or something. Afraid they're going to catch it. On those rare occasions when I could force myself out of the house, it was almost excruciating. They don't know what to say, or how to act. They don't know whether to talk about him or not. Many of them just avoided me altogether. Double whammy.

"I met Celestina during that first year, when things were so bad. And we'd get together every month, just to talk and cry and not feel like we had the plague. Celestina had already been a widow for quite a long time. But she had not forgotten how it feels." Sonia turned to look at Celestina, sitting across the room. Her eyes flickered back to Elise. "And that's why we asked you to come, Elise. Getting together with someone who understands what you're going through—well, I don't know how I would have made it otherwise."

Elise felt her shoulders relax. She was glad she'd come, glad she'd forced herself to get out of the house and drive for an hour. And glad to meet this woman, to hear those words. To know that she was not alone, and probably not losing her marbles, the way she often felt.

"Come and meet everyone," Sonia murmured, taking Elise by the elbow.

Elise followed her to a long, rustic table, surrounded by carved wooden chairs in the Spanish colonial style. Celestina stood and kissed Elise on the cheek. She took both of Elise's hands and looked in her eyes. "I'm so glad you came."

Sonia introduced a woman named Cynthia, who stood and took Elise's hand tentatively. She seemed fragile, in both looks and mannerisms. Her eyes flitted; her hands barely touched Elise's. She had silver hair and blue eyes, and she dripped with wealth, from the cut of her hair to the manicured nails to the rings and bracelets and diamond-encrusted watch that circled her wrist. Elise found herself suddenly conscious of the fact that her shoes were scuffed and she hadn't been for a haircut since before Michael died.

Sonia smiled. "Cynthia has found a new love. In addition to reading cards, Celestina loves to play matchmaker."

Cynthia swallowed, and her shoulders stiffened. "That didn't work out, actually."

Sonia laid a hand on Cynthia's arm. "I'm sorry to hear that. You certainly don't need any more pain in your life."

Cynthia raised her eyes to Sonia. "It was too soon. I'm not ready yet."

Sonia let her hand rest on Cynthia's arm for another moment and then pulled her attention back to her guests.

Sonia held her arm out. "This is Pablo. His partner died almost a year ago."

Pablo was shorter than Elise, thin and dark with huge dark eyes. He took Elise's hands in his. "Very happy to meet you, Elise, although I wish for all our sakes that it had been for some other reason."

Elise nodded.

"Don't forget me." The voice came from the shadows, and Tom Dugan rose from his chair. "We met at Celestina's shop." He moved forward and held out his hand. "Tom Dugan. Nice to see you again."

Celestina put her hand on Tom's arm. "Tom is not one of us." She laughed.

Sonia threw her head back and also laughed, a laugh that came from deep inside, a laugh that crinkled her eyes and made Elise smile at the sound. "Got that right," she blurted.

Celestina looked at Elise and raised her eyebrows. "He is not a widower. But he helps us"—Celestina's arm swept out to include everyone at the table—"with little projects that we all need to have done. He was here this afternoon, chopping wood for Sonia, and she invited him to stay for dinner."

"Ah," Elise responded. "Nice to see you again, Tom." The words left her mouth, polite in the way Beulah would have approved, but she did not feel the corresponding emotion. There was something about Tom Dugan that made her uneasy. She didn't like feeling his eyes appraising her through the thick lenses of his glasses. She felt a little like an insect under a microscope.

Elise turned away from him to look at Sonia.

Sonia turned and held her arm out to the table by the window, laden with dishes of green chili and enchiladas, kale salad, chips and guacamole. "Well, let's eat. Shall we?"

There wasn't much in the way of light—none of the lamps had been turned on. The last remnants of the sunset had long since fled. A fire burned in the fireplace, and framing it on both sides were two leather sofas and a heavy wood coffee table. Candles burned in the center and on the dining table they had just vacated, but other than those, the room was dark.

"Shall I turn on some lamps?" Sonia asked.

"No, my friend. Let's stay in the dark." Celestina leaned forward and set her glass of wine on the low glass coffee table. "It reminds me of when I was little and my mother would hold séances in the basement. Spirits like the dark."

Elise sat with her legs curled up under her on one of the sofas, glass of wine in hand. She had been more comfortable with this group of strangers than she would have thought possible. That thread that bound them all together, that understanding of grief and loss, was strong. But Celestina's words caught her in their net, and she sat up straighter, staring at the older woman. "Séance?"

"Every Friday evening, people would line up outside our house in Brooklyn. Sometimes there were so many. Right at seven sharp, my mother would open the door. She would wander up and down, looking into the eyes of everyone who waited in line. And then she would pick maybe ten or so to follow her down the stairs. It might be the first people who lined up, and it might not. But no one ever complained, even if they had been waiting awhile. They knew—we all knew—that my mother had her reasons for those she picked. She just seemed to know who really needed a message. Or maybe which ones had messages waiting to be delivered."

Celestina sat slightly tipped to one side of her chair and stared at the fire. "It scared me so much, when I was little. We would follow her down the stairs, my brother and I, and sit at the table with her and the neighbors. Scary, scary. And totally fascinating." Celestina turned to Elise. "I could not believe the things that came through on those nights."

From the chair directly across from her, Tom let out a long sigh.

Celestina sighed. "Tom does not believe. He is blind to the spiritual world."

Elise glanced at him, and he looked at Celestina, his face a perfect canvas of exasperation.

"But that is because he has not been trained to see." Celestina tipped her head, gazing at him, her mouth raised in a smile that intimated she understood the secrets Tom did not. She turned to the others around her. "Becoming attuned to the spirits requires a . . . slightly different way of looking at things. Like an artist. Some people can take a pencil and draw the lines and the shading and all the intricacies of a vase or a landscape. They have trained their eyes to see those lines. Learning to hear spirits is much the same. It's there, all the time. But some people"—she turned her gaze back to Tom—"have not yet learned how to hear them."

Tom crossed his arms and leaned back in his chair. He let out another heavy sigh. "Bunch of hooey," he grumped.

"Is that a scientific term, Tom?" Celestina looked at him, a long, hard look. "We try to forgive him for his ignorance. Someday, maybe, he will learn." Celestina turned toward Elise. "My mother, on the other hand, grew up listening to spirits. She was quite a medium. Nothing frightened her." Celestina's voice dropped to a whisper. "Not the case with me. I'm still a little afraid of a séance, of the spirits that come through." She shivered dramatically. "Gives me the willies. You can never really be sure who might turn up. There are always a few vaga-bonds out there in the ethers that we don't really want to have at our table."

Elise glanced around, into the dark corners of the room.

"I cannot do what my mother used to do. I don't want to. But sometimes, after dinner, when we're just sitting here, and it gets quiet and dark, sometimes . . . I hear something. Something from the other side. Most of us, not all"—she nodded her head toward Tom—"have someone important in the spirit world, and occasionally, I can pick up something they are trying to say."

Elise looked around at the group, scattered on sofas and chairs, sip-ping wine and staring at the fire. No one seemed particularly alarmed by the information. Everyone sat in a circle, surrounding the candlelit coffee table. Cynthia, Elise thought, looked the least like the rest of the group—her obvious wealth drawing an absolute line of divide between her and the other widows. She wondered how they had ever managed to come together, wondered if Cynthia, like herself, was another lost soul who had wandered into Celestina's shop, looking for answers in the cards.

"Elise, have you have had a visit from your husband yet?" Sonia leaned forward and placed her wineglass on the table. Her eyes were bright and serious.

"Excuse me?"

Sonia nodded. "His ghost. Every one of us in this room . . ." Her eyes traveled around the circle and stopped at Tom. "Well, almost every one of us has had some kind of . . . encounter."

Elise straightened her legs. "Oh?"

"A few months after Victor died, I got the flu. I hadn't been eating right—I couldn't sleep. All the usual symptoms of grief. But then I got so sick. Feverish. I lay on that couch for two days. Couldn't even bring myself to go upstairs to the bedroom. Several times, I woke up and I could feel Victor, sitting in his chair by the fire, watching me. It wasn't scary. I wasn't worried. Just kind of like he was keeping an eye on me. In my fever, I guess I forgot that he was dead. It just seemed . . . normal that Victor would be there."

Celestina leaned forward. "I was at the shop. It was really quiet: wintertime—very few customers. I was in the kitchen, making tea, and I felt this cold rush of air next to my arm. And I looked up, thinking someone had come in the front door. There was Victor, standing in the front room of the shop. He looked me right in the eye. And then he was gone.

"I knew right away that I had to come up here, to Sonia's," Celestina continued. "I closed the shop and drove up. Found her on the couch, burning up with fever. She was so out of it, she'd been forgetting to take aspirin. I made sure she did. I made her some chicken soup and started pushing liquids. Stayed up here all night. Me and Victor, sitting in these two chairs, watching until her fever broke."

Elise eyed the two chairs next to the fire. Celestina now sat in one, Cynthia in the other. Chill bumps crawled on her arms.

Sonia turned to Elise. "I don't know how it works—on the other side. But I do know that every single time I needed help, I got it. Ask him. Ask your husband to help you. Anytime you need it, for anything."

Elise let out a long exhale. She wasn't sure whether to speak; she looked around at the faces of the group, pale gold in the flickering candlelight. "Have any of you . . . did you ever feel like your husband"—her eyes flicked to Pablo—"your partner . . . was trying to tell you something?"

Pablo straightened his chin and bit his lip. "This is a really weird story. I'm an artist . . . watercolors. Only after Robert died, I was having trouble working. Just couldn't seem to find the energy. Couldn't focus. Money was really tight. I would lie in bed at night and get these panic attacks. I couldn't catch my breath. It felt like the room was crushing me. I was so afraid I was going to lose everything. We have . . . I have a nice place near the plaza. And one afternoon, I was walking in the plaza, just kind of spacing out. Not thinking. Not really looking where I was going. And all of a sudden, I turn and there's Robert, sitting at one of the little benches in the middle of Bent Street Plaza. And he looks at me, and says, 'Pablo, go home.'

"I kept telling myself that it wasn't real, that I had imagined it. That it was exhaustion messing with my mind. But I started walking back toward the house. I turned and looked over my shoulder, to see if he was still there. He wasn't. No one was there. It didn't make any sense at all, but I went home anyway. And the minute I walked in the door, the telephone rang. It was this man in LA who had bought a few of my paintings several years back. And he said he was in town for the day, and he really wanted to visit my studio.

"I didn't have any new work—not new in the past few months. But I did have several pieces that I'd done before Robert died. And this guy came over, and he bought three of my paintings. When he left that day, I was several thousand dollars ahead." Pablo let out a long sigh. "But I would have missed him completely if it hadn't been for Robert telling me to go home." Pablo turned and looked at Elise. "I imagine you'll hear from your husband at some point. I think we all have, eventually."

They all sat quietly, absorbing the story, breathing in the dark and the quiet and the awareness of all the dead spirits around them.

"Elise?" Celestina sat forward, her head tipped to one side, her eyes staring but unfocused. "Elise. Someone is calling your name."

Elise felt her breath catch. Her whole body froze. Everyone in the room went completely still. All eyes turned to Celestina.

Her head still tipped to the side, she whispered, "Smoke gets in your eyes. Ah!" Celestina straightened her head and fanned the air in front of her face, as if actual smoke were right in front of her. "I smell smoke. Like a cigar, or maybe a cheroot, something like that. A message—in the smoke."

Celestina sat up straight, her eyes wide and dark and focused on Elise. "He's here," she murmured, her brows shifting upward. "The one who will help you."

Elise froze. And then she remembered the raven—the one she had seen on the porch earlier today. The one she had seen flying overhead when she got out of the truck a few hours ago. She scanned the darkened trees outside the window, just behind the other sofa, searching for sign of that raven. There was a flutter of movement in one of the trees; Elise could see the reddish light of two eyes, staring at her from the dark. He was out there, in the trees.

A crashing noise broke the intense silence, and everyone jumped.

Sonia stood from her seat on one of the couches. "Don't panic! My dog is getting old. Sometimes she wanders into a corner and can't find her way out. She probably knocked something over. I'll go look."

Elise glanced outside again and back to Celestina, sitting in the chair by the fire. Their eyes locked.

"Found it!" Sonia called. She came back into the big room, holding a walking stick out before her like a talisman. "He got trapped in that corner by the front door. Knocked over my husband's favorite walking stick."

She stood next to the coffee table; the others were silent. "I'm so sorry, Celestina. I hope it didn't scare anyone."

Pablo stood up and stretched his arms. He turned his head to indicate Celestina. "Walking stick. Do you suppose that's our cue? Time to go?"

Celestina laughed.

The energy in the room changed. Everyone rose and moved away, taking dishes to the kitchen, gathering up the remnants of the potluck, all the noises wrapped in the quiet murmurs of conversation. Instantly the room and its inhabitants had returned to the normal, everyday world of the living, all thought of ghosts and spirits pushed to the background.

Except for Elise. She shook her head, willing her heart to beat normally. She turned to look out the window again, scanning the trees once more. She could see no sign of the raven. For a moment, she thought perhaps she had only imagined it, that the whole spirit-communication idea was making her see things.

Her gaze shifted back inside. Tom was sitting directly across from her, looking at her as if she were a botanical specimen he'd never before encountered. The candlelight jumped and bounced off his glasses.

Their eyes locked, for one small moment. Then Elise turned away, a shiver creeping down her spine.

# CHAPTER TEN

Tom Dugan was lost, in far more ways than one. He leaned his arms against the steering wheel of the truck and thought, for perhaps the hundredth time this week, *What am I doing?* Immediately, he corrected himself. He couldn't say for sure that it was a *hundred* times; he hadn't actually counted. As a man who had spent his entire adult life with mathematical equations and meticulous observation, it was important to be precise. But that question had dogged him for several months now, had repeated and repeated in his awareness. *What am I doing?*

Here he sat, in a beat-up old Ford pickup, the contraption that had once belonged to Celestina's dead husband, completely turned around and unable to use either his cell phone or Google maps. The truck had been built long before GPS was available. And beyond the physical realities of this particular situation was the question of *What am I doing?* as applied to his life in general. He had a master's degree in electrical engineering, thirty years of work experience designing software and circuit boards for all types of solar equipment. He'd run his own successful business back in Tucson, but had left it all, less than a year ago, to do what, exactly? He was an intelligent man, even if it was a self-assessment, which is generally unreliable in any scientific way, but still.

For almost a year now, he'd been living in a little casita on Celestina's property, living rent-free in exchange for menial labor. Tom Dugan, the brilliant mathematician and scientist, hauling wood and fixing faucets for Celestina and all her crazy woo-woo friends.

He had pulled into Taos one winter night almost nine months ago. The check-engine light had just come on in the Jeep, and just as soon as he noticed it, smoke had started curling up from the radiator. He pulled over at the first available spot and turned off the engine.

It was after six on a Thursday evening in the winter, and most of the storefronts around him were dark. He had no idea where he might be able to find a mechanic or an auto-parts store, although at this hour, it was unlikely he would find either. He could have taken out his cell phone, searched Google for a motel or a nearby restaurant, which was exactly what the normal Tom Dugan would have done. But that night, for whatever reason, he did not reach for technology.

There was one store that still had lights on, and he was parked directly in front of it. He headed inside, not knowing what kind of store it was, not paying attention to anything other than the fact that the lights were on and he was stuck.

An older woman with dark eyes sat behind the counter. She had cards spread across the glass top in what looked to Tom like some very strange version of solitaire. Celestina raised her eyes to his and murmured, "I've been waiting for you to get here."

Those words stopped him, and he pushed his glasses up on his nose. He had never been to Taos before, didn't know a single, solitary soul. Tom looked at the door behind him, as if maybe another person had come in with him and that was whom she was actually addressing. "Excuse me?"

"You can quit running now."

"Uh." Tom turned sideways, staring back at his Jeep sitting at the curb. "I'm not running. I'm having car trouble."

Celestina stared at him. "Yes. I know."

For a moment, Tom contemplated going right back out the door. Then he took a breath and continued. "I was wondering if you know of an auto-parts store, or a mechanic, that might be open?"

Her eyes took it all in; she stared at Tom and his smudged glasses and his unironed shirt. She looked out at the Jeep, parked outside her gate. "Your car is not the only thing that needs help," she said, gathering the cards in her hands and tapping them into a neat pile. "The car is simply a reflection of the problems in your life."

*Oh, shit,* Tom thought. *I've wandered into the web of a total lunatic.* He started backing toward the door. "Thanks for your help. I'll see if I can find . . ."

Celestina shrugged. "If you wish. But it isn't going to get any better until you face it."

"Face what?" Tom found himself responding.

"Oh, I think you know. Too many lies in your life, yes? Lies, lies, lies."

Tom stood still, his mouth slightly open. "I'm not sure I know what you're talking about."

"Oh, but I think you do." Celestina stared at him. "I can help you, if you allow it." She began to flip cards onto the glass countertop again, slowly, rhythmically. He heard the slap-slap-slap as the cards hit the glass.

Despite his misgivings, he continued to stand there; he even took one step closer to that countertop and those cards. One step closer to the strange woman with the dark eyes who was reeling him in like he was a fish on a hook.

She flipped a card, stared at it as if it were his curriculum vitae and she was examining his background. "I have a casita in the back of my house. Just one room and a bath." She looked up at him again. "You can stay there. For tonight. Until you get . . . things . . . figured out."

So he had stayed. And apparently, he still didn't quite have things figured out. Nine months later he was still there, living in that casita, rent-free, in exchange for whatever job Celestina thought needed doing. Sometimes it was for her, sometimes for one of her friends. But Celestina did all the directing. And truthfully, he was enjoying the parade of lunatics that marched through Celestina's shop, with their absolutely stupefying belief in the woman's psychic abilities. It was entertaining, a bit like watching professional wrestling on television, except that those on television *knew* they were engaged in a spectacle of entertainment. The people who streamed in and out of Celestina's shop did not appear to be as highly evolved.

He supposed, too, that his continued acceptance of this so-called life of unemployment and menial labor had something to do with Celestina and the way she coddled him. She acted like a mother hen, clucking and cooing and trying to protect him from the dangers of the big bad world and all the mercenary women it contained. Her most frequent question seemed to be, "Have you eaten yet?" And then she'd force him to sit down and suffer through a bowl of homemade soup or chili or a plate of enchiladas. It felt good, to be clucked over like that. He loved the way she fussed over him and fed him and tried to fix all those cracks that had appeared in his psyche since that mess in Tucson.

He told himself, repeatedly, that he had never really loved Alana, his recently exed-wife. They had nothing in common, except that he made money and she spent it. But he did love the *idea* of Alana. The idea of going home to another human being, the idea of occasional words, sometimes whole sentences, that passed between them. The idea of sleeping next to her warm and fragrant body, and particularly the idea of how friendly she could be whenever she wanted something expensive. That BMW, for instance, had definitely been a worthwhile expenditure. Alana could be strikingly attractive with the light of dollar signs in her eyes.

Tom had been a registered loner his entire life and had been both shocked and awed when they got together. He could not believe his luck—could not believe anyone who looked like *that* would actually be interested in *him*. As it turned out, *he* was not really what she was interested in.

The worst thing, by far, from the whole episode was that he had walked away with a complete lack of confidence in his own powers of observation. He truly was the last to know. He had spent his whole life as a scientist, carefully trained in the powers of examination, making detailed notes and painstaking scrutiny of conditions. How could he continue to call himself a scientist when he had completely missed all those clues about what the two of them were doing? How could he have lived with her, slept next to her, and not seen the obvious?

Circuit boards and programming languages were so much easier than the murky field of human behavior. He didn't understand it and never had—had always preferred the company of equations and concepts and coding to that of human beings, which had left him flustered and frustrated as he tried to interpret even the most simplistic signals of emotion.

Before he left Tucson, before he ditched his former life and ran away, he'd been making friends with Jack Daniel's. He continued that relationship when he got to Taos but did his best to sneak the bottles off the property without Celestina seeing them. It didn't matter how careful he was; she knew. He didn't have any idea how she did it, but once again he found her sitting at the counter in the shop, laying out tarot cards on the glass next to the cash register, waiting for closing time in the quiet dark. Almost as if she had to check to see if there was anything she needed to know before she closed up and headed home. Tom had been in the back, fixing a broken shelf in the kitchen, and came out front to find her flipping cards. Without even looking up, she said, "The answers are not in that bottle, Tom. If you keep drinking with Jack, you're going to drown in your own misery." She had raised her head then, flashing those dark eyes like six-shooters.

It had given him chills, that. How could she have known? He never drank to absolute stupor. He showered the smell off every morning. He was careful to dispose of his bottles at another location. He never went anywhere or called anyone once he started drinking in the evening. But instead of giving her the satisfaction of knowing that she had hit the nail on the head, he had simply looked at her and murmured, "Good night, Celestina."

"You have better things to do with your time, Tom. And you will need all your faculties for the road ahead."

He turned and met her eyes for a moment, wondering what it was that she had seen. He shook himself and turned away. There was no way Celestina could actually *see* things in those cards; he knew that absolutely, unqualifiably. But that evening, he went home and made a frozen pizza and poured two fingers of JD into the glass, no ice. Her words came back as he was standing at the sink, about to take his first sip. He did not for one minute believe in all this psychic business. But Celestina scared him, just a little. He'd heard too many of her stories, had seen too many customers who came back again and again because she was right so often. And that tiny sliver of doubt, the same doubt in his own powers of observation that had haunted him since the fiasco with Alana, now came back to whisper in his ear. What if Celestina *had* seen something? What if there was some future headed right toward him that would require a clear head?

The rational, scientific part of his brain kept repeating, *Nonsense.* But he had missed all the signs with his ex-wife and his business partner, so maybe the rational, scientific part of his brain wasn't working as well as it should. And that was enough to stoke the fire of fear, to make him think that maybe he should actually listen to this crazy lady with the tarot cards.

He turned and poured the contents of the glass down the sink and followed that with the remains in the bottle. That was six months ago, and since then, he really had been trying to pay attention. To make careful observations of all the relevant conditions. To try and keep a running tally of the number of people who *believed* in what Celestina had to say and kept coming back for more.

But if Celestina had given him really useful directions to Elise's cabin, he'd have been there by now. Tom exhaled and backed the truck around yet one more dead end. He'd been up in these mountains for more than an hour now and was no closer to locating Elise or her house.

Tom put his hands on the top of the steering wheel and leaned forward, putting his chin on top. "Damn it, Celestina. What the hell do I do now?" he muttered. From somewhere just outside the truck, he heard a *quork, quork* sound, overly loud in the quiet of the fall day. A raven flew right in front of the truck and settled on the branch of a cottonwood tree. Tom looked at it. Their eyes met, and the raven dipped his head twice. Then it left the branch, turning in a graceful arc, and flew down the gravel road. Tom put the truck in gear and followed, not because he thought the raven was talking to him, or leading him, but because—what the hell? He couldn't think of anything better to do.

The afternoon sun lit the hillside with gold. Elise stopped and gave herself a chance to breathe normally. She'd been walking, hiking almost straight up, as fast as she could. Sometimes, when the pain and grief burned in her veins and smashed her lungs, she felt desperate to walk—to pound the pain through the soles of her feet, to lose herself in the mountains around their cabin. As if she could make the physical pain sharp enough, solid enough, to drown out the endless loop of desperation and loneliness and self-doubt that played through her mind.

She stood still, waiting for her breath to return to normal. She heard the aspen leaves ticking together, their golds and oranges bright against the deep greens of the ponderosas and piñons and cedars. Leaves dropped from the tree, winding downward, lodging in the branches of the pines below them like Christmas ornaments. The sky was brilliant, like blue glass, and for a moment, at least, the beauty soothed her. She could smell the sweet spiciness of the cottonwood leaves, the heavy musk of the pines.

She started walking again, slower this time, not quite as desperate with pain as when she had started out from the house an hour ago. She topped a small hill and dipped down into a meadow, thick with golden grasses, bending and stretching in the breeze. The cool fall weather had soaked the last of the green from the grass. Everything in the meadow was golden, as if a painter had coated the scene with liquid amber. Elise stopped again, her heart pounding. There was something about this meadow, this honey-colored light, that felt familiar. She turned slowly, taking it all in—the gray-brown bark of the cottonwoods along the edges, the way the wind whispered through the leaves. Had she dreamed this?

She sat down on a rock and gazed at the meadow. Listened, the way she had seen Michael do a hundred times. The way she had seen Lorena do when she was out gathering her plants. She *had* dreamed it, she felt certain. Just last night, but every scrap of the dream torn away with the light of dawn. Now it came back in pieces, like fragments of a broken pot, and she had to try to figure out how the pieces went together again.

A field, much like this one. The grasses dry, brittle and rustling, gilded in amber. A man, standing in the middle. He was grinning, and his smile was bright in his sun-darkened skin. His arms were brown, the biceps bulging. His blue eyes danced with laughter; his black hair was thick and wavy. He bent down in the grass and held out his arms to her.

The shirt he wore was denim, the sleeves cut out to reveal those strong brown biceps. In one pocket on his chest she could see the bulge of a pack of cigarettes. His voice drifted to her from far away. "Coming, Elise?" She ran through the dry grass, just a little girl, exerting enormous effort to lift her legs high enough to stay above the bristly stalks. He lifted her in his arms and swung her in a circle, and she laughed, giddy with dizziness. She couldn't have been more than two or three years old.

Elise stared into the empty field before her now, listening to the wind dancing through the grass. She had never had a scrap of memory of her father to hold on to. But she knew, standing in this field of golden grass, that it was her father. She let herself get lost in the sensation when he had lifted her and swung her in the air—a feeling that she was safe and warm and completely protected. Like she was home. The same way she had felt the first time Michael wrapped his arms around her.

She walked a few feet and sat down on a fallen aspen log. The bark was smooth and white, and she ran her hands over it, her eyes searching the field, trying to pull back that feeling—trying to sink back into the warmth and comfort of that dream, into the arms of the father she'd never really known.

She had so few memories of him. She was barely five when he died. She had no idea how soon afterward, but she knew that her mother had loaded the old Chrysler and driven the two of them back to New Mexico, to the home Rose had grown up in. Elise had a vague recollection of sitting in the backseat, surrounded by piles of clothing and blankets that her mother wanted to keep. She remembered leaning her head back against the cushions, watching as the world sped by outside her window. She remembered the back of her mother's head, just ahead of her in the driver's seat, an occasional sound like hiccups or crying that came from up front.

"Mama? Are you all right?"

She heard more sniffling. "Fine. Just a little tired, that's all." Rose had reached for the dial on the radio, and Hank Williams's voice filled the car with the heart-twisting words of "I'm So Lonesome, I Could Cry."

There had been no questions, no talk about Elise's father, about their lives before coming to New Mexico, as if when Rose headed west she had left it all behind, locked up forever in the silent vault of her heart. And after she died, less than two years later, Elise lost all connection to her past, to whatever had happened to her before living in that quiet four-room house with her grandmother. Beulah was old-school: she didn't talk much herself, and she lived by the adage that children should be seen and not heard.

Growing up in that silent house, Elise had often pictured herself as a foundling—a mysterious girl who appeared without benefit of parents or memories or roots. She felt her father only as an absence, like the space left behind when a tooth has fallen out. No pain, just a hole, an emptiness where something should have been. She noticed it only at certain times: leaving school at three thirty and seeing Esperanza Mondragon run out to her daddy, who waited outside his truck in the street. Or when she was a teenager and the girls at school would complain about how their fathers didn't approve of a certain boy.

There was no one who waited for Elise outside the school building. No one who forbade her to date a certain boy. There was only the quiet of dinners with Beulah, the empty chairs at the supper table, the scrape and click of their silverware on the plates, the heaviness of a million unspoken thoughts. Absence. Loneliness. Separateness. Those were feelings that had marked Elise's life; those were the feelings she knew well, as if they were part of her skin. Until Michael.

And now, here she was, over fifty years old, and back in it again. Alone. Separate. Different.

A shadow flew across her vision, and Elise looked up. A raven settled itself into an old, dead aspen nearby. A widow maker, dry and match tender, ready to fall at the slightest wind. Elise held her hand over her eyes and stared up at the bird. She forced herself to sit still, to watch and listen, as Lorena had told her. She wondered vaguely if this was the same raven that had sat on her porch a few days ago, the same raven that had shown up at Sonia's house in Arroyo Seco, and then shook her head at her own foolishness. Why would one raven be following her around?

The bird preened itself, cleaning its feathers. Elise had always loved the ravens, loved the *quork* sound they made when they flew over, loved their keen intelligence. They had been her favorite bird for a very long time now. This one eyed Elise and began to cluck, like a hen with its chicks. Elise smiled. That was a sound she had never heard from the bird before: tender, loving, almost maternal.

She remembered the stories Michael had told her about when he first started carving birds. He'd been back from LA six months, working odd jobs, trying to find a life for himself back in New Mexico but not having any idea what that might be. One of the elders from the Jicarilla reservation had put him on the hill—sent him up into the mountains on a vision quest. For four days and three nights, Michael had stayed in one small spot, an area marked off by prayer flags, only ten feet square. No food, only one blanket for the cool mountain nights.

Michael told her later that nothing happened until the fourth morning. He'd been preparing himself to go back, to tell the old grandfather that he hadn't had a vision. Michael was disappointed. Though he knew that it happened, that there were numerous young men who had gone on the hill and not seen anything, still—he had hoped. He had prayed. He had offered tobacco, sung the songs.

He was sitting cross-legged on the ground that last morning, staring out at the valley below him. A granite boulder, marking the northeast corner of his spot, shifted slightly at the corner of Michael's gaze. He didn't move his head to look at it directly; instead, he gazed from his peripheral vision as that stone changed completely. It moved, altered, grew feathers, and lifted into the sky, screaming the call of the eagle. Michael shaded his eyes to watch the bird it had become. The stump of an old ponderosa pine several yards distant was next. Michael watched as it morphed in his vision, stretched itself and took flight, the red tail of a hawk blazing against the blue sky. Birds began to take shape all around him. Stumps, rocks, branches turned into ravens and flickers and chickadees.

Michael picked up a piece of firewood, a twisted gray branch of piñon. He cupped his hands around it, watched as it transformed before his eyes. He was suddenly holding a dove. And that's when he knew—knew how he would make a living, knew what he was going to do with his life. He took down his prayer flags, walked the half mile down to the camp of the Jicarilla elder. He started carving the same day. Spirit birds, he called them. Spirits of the ancestors. The spirit of his brother, Andres, dead several years.

Carving, shaping deadwood into birds, had transformed Michael. He grew calmer, more self-assured. He listened, intently, to the wisdom of the trees, the rocks, the animals and birds that crossed his path. Especially the birds. "Messengers," he told Elise. "When they cross your path, pay attention."

She looked up at the raven, sitting near her in the tree. "I'm listening," she whispered. "What do I need to see?"

The raven swooped off the branch and flew just over her head, so low that she raised her arms and ducked. She stood up and started walking in the direction it flew, back down the road toward the cabin.

Even before she reached the cabin, she could hear the sound of a vehicle coming up the road, pulling into her own driveway. She hurried through the trees and stopped short. A beat-up old Ford truck was parked in front. It wasn't a truck she recognized, and it was loaded with firewood. Probably someone lost, trying to deliver to one of her neighbors.

On her porch, a man stood, crouched by one window, his hands around his eyes, trying to peek inside. Elise watched as the raven flew to a nearby tree.

Tom Dugan turned and looked at her, pushed his glasses up on his nose, and said, "There you are. I wasn't sure I had the right house, and no one answered my knock. You are harder than hell to find."

"What are you doing here?" Elise stood with her arms crossed over her chest, slightly chilled by the breeze in the air.

"Celestina seems to think you need firewood. And from the looks of that pile"—Tom walked down from the porch and pointed at the few pieces of wood that were left in her woodpile—"she was right about that." He pulled the truck up next to the former woodpile and killed the engine.

Tom stepped out and pulled on leather work gloves. "For a psychic genius, so-called, she sure is terrible at giving directions. That crystal-ball thing isn't exactly crystal clear. I've been driving around for an hour now, trying to find this place."

He opened the tailgate on the truck and stepped up. "Shall I stack it here?"

Elise turned to look at the few pieces of wood still left in the wood-pile. There wasn't enough wood there for more than a few days of cold temperatures. Monica and her brother Narciso had promised they'd bring her a load, but they were busy with the remodeling business and hadn't quite gotten around to it. "Right there is fine," Elise replied.

"So Celestina loans me this truck—her husband's, of course. Older than dirt, and no GPS. And she tips her head"—Tom demonstrated by tipping his head to one side—"and gets all goofy eyed, the way she does, and says, 'Take the road up the mountain, outside of Amalia. Turn left at the third tree.' Like there's *one* road up the mountain outside of Amalia. Like there's not a whole *forest* of trees." He raised his arms to indicate the thick woods around them.

Tom started throwing chunks of firewood onto the ground. "So I stopped at that little market. Back in town." He turned and threw another armload over the side of the truck. "I asked that guy if he knew Elise Brooks, and he looks me in the eye and says, 'Never heard of her.'

Don't you even know anybody around here? I thought you had lived here a long time."

"I have lived here a long time. Most of my life, actually. And I know everybody."

Tom stopped throwing wood. He stood, pushed his glasses up his nose, and waited for her to finish her thought.

"But they don't know you. And I don't know one single, solitary soul who would send a stranger to my door."

"Ah." Tom nodded and resumed his work. "Not even a stranger with firewood?"

Elise shrugged. "If I had ordered firewood, I would have given directions. Did you happen to notice the three trees in the middle of the road? Because you do turn left at the third tree."

Tom glanced at her and plunked down another log. "Huh. Guess I missed that, trying not to hit that raven that kept zigzagging right in front of the truck."

Elise's head shot up, searching for the raven that had just flown over her head a few moments ago. She couldn't see it, and she let out a long exhale.

Tom continued to throw firewood over the side of the truck, finished unloading the cord of wood, and jumped down off the tailgate.

She did not in the least feel like entertaining company, especially this man who made her slightly nervous. She didn't like the idea that he had been peeking in her window. But she felt guilty. He had just driven all this way to bring her wood. His forehead was dripping sweat, and Tom lifted his sleeve to wipe it away.

"I don't have any soda, but I do have nice cold well water," she murmured.

"That'd be great," Tom muttered, knocking his hat against his leg, trying to dislodge some of the sawdust. "I'm parched."

He followed her up to the porch and sat down in one of the wooden rocking chairs. She brought out two glasses of water and an extra bottle and sat down in the other chair. Both of them faced the valley below; they did not look at each other.

"How is it that you are tending to errands for Celestina?"

Tom drained his glass of water and set it on the small table between them. "That's the million-dollar question, isn't it? Sometimes I'm not quite sure myself."

"You weren't guided to go and work for her?"

"Oh, hell, no." He glanced at her quickly. "Sorry—no offense. I just don't go in for that kind of stuff. I'm an engineer. Software engineer. I build programs and panels for running solar equipment. All this psychic babble is *way* outside my comfort zone."

Elise waited for him to continue. "So? How did this happen?"

Tom pressed his lips together and looked away from Elise. "My car broke down. Started sputtering, and the check-engine light came on, and this thin trail of smoke was coming from under the hood. I had just driven into Taos and didn't know my way around at all. So I pulled over, first empty parking space I can find. And I'm looking around, trying to see where I can go find some help. But it was after six on a Thursday evening in January, and most of the shops were already closed. And there, right in front me, is Celestina's place, with all the lights on. I walked in, thinking I could get information on an auto-parts store, or maybe a motel or something, and here's this woman sitting at the counter playing solitaire. At least that's what I thought she was doing, and she looks up and says, 'I've been waiting for you to get here.'" Tom shook his head.

Elise lowered her glass of water.

"Of course, I just kind of shook it off, didn't really think about it at the time. I was more concerned with finding a place to stay, finding a place where I could work on the car myself. You can't really trust most mechanics, you know." He turned to Elise and pushed his glasses up.

"And so I told her what happened, and could she direct me to the nearest motel. And she looks at me for a minute and tips her head"—Tom demonstrated by tipping his own—"and says, 'You can stop running now.'"

"Stop running?"

He swallowed, his body tensed. "I guess you could say I was running away."

Elise studied him for a moment. "You look a little old to be a runaway."

"Huh. You're never too old to run when things get awful." He slapped his hat against his jeans, as if trying to decide whether to go on. His face clouded for a moment, and he stared out at the valley below them.

"I spent my whole life in Tucson. Grew up there, went to school there. Started a business with my best friend. We designed and installed solar equipment. Solar heat, solar cooling, solar hot water. Had a pretty good thing going." Tom stopped and took a deep breath. "Solar air-conditioning is a booming business in the desert."

Tom waited a beat; his voice dropped to a lower register. "And then one day I stopped by the house in the middle of the afternoon. I'd left some programming stuff on the desk, and I needed it for work. Walked in the house, never even thought about the fact that my partner's car was outside. They never heard me. I walked right in on them. My wife and my business partner. Doing the wild thing."

Elise grimaced.

Tom looked over at her. "Yeah. Stinks. Sometimes I think it might be easier for you widows—the ones whose partner has died."

"Excuse me?" Elise bristled at his words; she sat up straighter.

"I don't know, it just seems like it would be less complicated, if it was all over, all at once. At least you don't have to . . . run into them, with someone else. You don't have to see them—in love with someone else. It got to the point where I didn't want to go to the grocery store or out to eat. Afraid I'd run into them—together." Tom looked away for a moment. "Or run into somebody who knew. That was no fun, either. And, of course, everybody knew. Tucson's not that big. People talk."

They were both silent for a long time. Tom let out a heavy sigh. "So. I got divorced. My partner bought out my half of the business, although I have to say, I don't know how he's managing to hold on to it." Tom turned and looked at her. His eyebrows went up. "I was the brains of the operation.

"I let her have the house. Didn't want any part of it, after what I'd seen in there. And I took off. I wasn't sure where I was going or what I was going to do with my life. Just started driving. Did a little hiking around Sedona. Thought I'd come up here and do the same thing. Just check out Taos and the mountains in this area. And then my car broke down. In front of Celestina's shop."

Elise looked at him, his gaze focused on the valley below them. She was astonished that he could relate that whole awful story without one thread of emotion.

Tom cleared his throat. "I never did get a motel room that night. First thing I know, Celestina has it all arranged, and I move into this little guest casita in back of her house. Then she has me getting firewood and fixing faucets for all her widowed friends. And before I even knew what hit me, almost a year has gone by."

"That's quite a story," Elise murmured. "And after all that, you still don't believe in fate? Synchronicity?"

Tom turned and looked at her sharply. "What? You think I was *guided* to Celestina's?"

Elise shrugged. "It is rather interesting."

"Coincidence. Pure and simple coincidence."

"Some people don't believe there is such a thing as coincidence. Carl Jung, for instance. That if coincidence is meaningful and defies statistical probabilities, then there might be something else at work."

"Yeah. And some people think professional wrestling is real." Tom pushed his glasses up once again. "I hate to break this to you, Elise, but psychology and psychiatry are not really science. *Very* fuzzy territory."

"Some people would find that kind of opinion offensive," Elise continued. "Carl Jung had a medical degree. Highly intelligent, by all accounts."

He turned to her; his mouth dropped open slightly, as if intellect and interest in the paranormal were mutually exclusive. "Yeah. Right."

"So how did you end up at Celestina's?" Tom asked.

"Nothing quite as dramatic as your story. I went in for a reading. A little over a week ago."

He nodded, as if that explained everything. "Ah. Did it help? Did you learn anything?"

"I can't say that I actually learned anything new, no. But she sure seemed to know a lot of things about me. About my life."

Tom sat back in the chair and rocked it a time or two. "I have this theory about that. Actually, it's not my theory—lots of people believe the same thing. Scientific people, anyway. That psychics and card readers, palm readers—all those *psychic* types—are actually reading *you*. You know, like they take in your clothing and your hairstyle and the shoes you're wearing. Jewelry. All that. The way retail shops can tell if a shopper can actually afford what they have for sale. Or the way a cop can read whether someone is lying or not. They read all that information, and then say something kind of random, kind of nonspecific, like, 'I see you are feeling lost,' and see how the person responds. Read their facial expressions and body language. Keep going from there." He turned to her and leaned one shoulder forward. "And then these people just start spilling all kinds of information. They keep feeding the fire."

"So you don't think that psychic knowledge, ESP, whatever you want to call it, is possible?"

Tom shook his head. "No. I don't."

Elise leaned back in her chair. "Interesting theory. I wonder how she knew my mother's name was Rose."

Tom's mouth opened, and he hesitated for just a minute. "Did she actually say your mother's name was Rose? Or did she say something vague, like . . . 'I see roses'?"

Elise shot him a look. Now that he asked, she couldn't quite remember. Had Celestina come up with the name Rose? Or had Elise given it to her?

"Well, did she solve all your problems? Tell you the secret to your future?"

Elise shook her head. "No. Her predictions were a little . . . I don't know . . . generic."

"That's my point. I don't think you can prove psychic knowledge if the only information is very general and could apply to almost anyone."

Elise stared at him for a moment, trying to remember what, exactly, Celestina had said.

"So. Did she tell you anything useful about your *future*?"

Elise took a long breath. His words were almost exact echoes of what she had heard from Monica the night of the reading. "She said a man with dark eyes would show up to help me."

Tom burst out laughing. "See? That's exactly what I mean." He slapped his leg with his hat and laughed again. "How useful is that? A man with dark eyes who will help you." He chuckled. "Help you with what?"

"She wasn't really specific about that, either."

"That's great. No wonder she has so many customers. With predictions like that, her success rate is probably very high." He poured down another glass of water. "Well, there's one prediction that we can mark as correct. I have dark eyes, I am a man, and I just brought you a load of firewood." Tom was smiling; his teeth flashed white. "Guess Celestina is a genius, huh? Maybe I need to get my cards read. I wonder if it still counts, since she's the one who sent me up here?"

Elise turned her gaze to the valley below them and sighed. "I didn't actually go in there to find out about my future."

Tom got quiet and pushed his glasses up on his nose. "You didn't?"

Elise looked out at the woods and shook her head. Normally, she would never talk about herself or her life with someone she barely knew. But here it was, spilling out of her mouth. "No. I went in there"—she turned and looked Tom in the eye—"because I think my husband is trying to tell me something."

Tom stared at her.

"My *dead* husband."

"What makes you think that?"

Elise shrugged, wishing now that she hadn't said anything. "I don't know. Just a feeling. Dreams. Sometimes I think I hear him calling my name. Nothing that would qualify as scientific."

"Did Celestina figure it out?"

Elise shook her head. "No. Not really."

Tom was quiet for a moment. He pushed his glasses up on his nose. "Well, you wouldn't go to a dentist if you have a pain in your foot."

Elise scowled at him. She was starting to feel annoyed, ready for him to leave. "What does that mean?"

"Not that I'm a believer in those sorts of things, but if you're looking for a message from the dead, then maybe it's not a tarot-card reader that you need. Maybe you should try someone who specializes in that line of work. Like, say . . . a medium."

Elise went completely still.

Tom leaned back in his chair a minute, as if deep in thought. "I don't know. This is new territory for me. But I've seen the kind of questions Celestina usually gets. Things like, 'Is he cheating on me?' or 'Should I make this investment with my brother-in-law?' or 'Who will I marry?' That kind of thing.

"I mean, I know she sometimes hears . . . *says* she hears messages from spirit, but that's not really her area of expertise. Hard to flip a card that carries a message from the dead."

Elise thought about that for a minute. "What about the other night? With the widows and orphans?" Elise turned to him. "She said, 'He's here.' The man who will help me."

Tom laughed. "And I saw you look straight at me when she said that. Bingo. Here I am. The man who will help you. And then she sends me up here with firewood. Talk about manipulating the situation. Sure looks like a setup to me."

Elise stayed quiet. It wasn't Tom she had been looking at that night. It was the raven.

He pushed his glasses up on his nose again and turned toward Elise. "If communicating with the dead is what you're after, seems like Celestina might not be your best choice." Tom stood and stretched his arms. From the branches of the cottonwood tree, the raven made a soft clucking sound.

# CHAPTER ELEVEN

Early October had always been Elise's favorite time of year. Unlike spring, there was very little wind. Nights were crisp and cool; days were sunny and warm but not hot. The lower light of autumn intensified the colors of the mountains, turning them into jewels. The mountains in the distance were deep-purple amethyst, the sky a blue diamond, the leaves flashing like flickers of carnelian and amber, ruby and garnet and citrine, dancing against the deeper emerald hues of the pines.

The fall perfume of cottonwood leaves wafted through the air—part sweet, part spice, partly the decay of falling leaves. The sumac leaves dotted the hillside with splotches of russet.

Elise was beneath a huge piñon tree, Lorena a few feet away. Both women knelt on a blanket, picking piñon nuts, trying to fill their numerous coffee cans. The Madrid family, like many families in this area, had been harvesting piñon nuts for generations, and Elise had been part of the outing for as long as she could remember. All during the fall and winter, Lorena would take small batches of the nuts, soak them in salt water, then toss them in her heated cast-iron skillet until the water had steamed off and the shells were left with a salty, deep-brown coating.

Piñon was an integral part of winter evenings in the Madrid household—as ubiquitous as the smell of the piñon logs in the fireplace and the taste of green chili and homemade tortillas. Elise remembered sitting in their living room as a child, wind and snow howling outside the house, a fire crackling in the corner, and all of them cracking the shells in their teeth and digging out the nuts inside. They ate them like popcorn, the cracking of the nuts like a musical accompaniment to the stories of Monica's father and mother and uncle Wes.

Monica prided herself on her ability to crack the small shells between her teeth and extract the nut using her tongue. She teased Elise about making a mess, since Elise had to crack the shells with her teeth and then spit them out in her hand, digging out the small white meat with her fingers. Elise's method was untidy, but despite forty years of trying, she'd never been able to master the art of tongue extractions. It was the major reason why her piñon consumption was so much less than the rest of the family.

Uncle Wes, who was actually Lorena's uncle, Monica's great-uncle, sat in a folding lawn chair about fifteen feet away. He had on his black cowboy hat ("If I'm gonna be a cowboy, it sure ain't gonna be one of the good guys," he told them) and long-sleeved cowboy shirt, and he sat with his chin on his chest, dozing. His leather work gloves lay across his lap, one hand resting on top. He'd set himself up in that chair, under the shade of a large cottonwood, about half an hour earlier. "I'm supervising," he told them. "So no slacking." As soon as he had arranged his seat, he pulled the picnic hamper close to his chair and rummaged through the contents. "Maybe I better make sure this fried chicken is still edible. Wouldn't want any of you young folks getting the ptomaine poisoning. Might interfere with productivity."

Monica and her brother Narciso were a little farther up the hill, on a hunt for the best trees—places where the nuts were plentiful and not too small, places that had not already been stripped by the Clark's nutcracker or the piñon jay. The loud squawking of the birds was part of the fall scene, as if they were commenting on every seed the family took away from their own potential haul. The birds hoarded as many nuts as they could get, caching them at strategic locations for the long winter months ahead.

When Monica and Narciso found a good tree, one where the cones were heavy with nuts, they laid a blanket or an old sheet underneath it and then started the shake dance, as Monica called it. They'd whoop and holler and grab branches, shaking them violently, causing nuts to rain down on the blanket like small brown hailstones.

The rest of the family—Narciso's wife and two children, Lorena, and Elise—were left to crawl around under the trees, gathering the nuts that had been shaken loose into coffee cans and plastic ice-cream tubs. It was a sticky business. Sap always managed to drip from the branches and get on their hands and knees, into their clothing and hair. Branches grabbed at their hair, and spiders were lurking in every available crevice, from the branches themselves to the needles below. Picking piñon was not an activity for anyone who wasn't on their toes, ready to slap and flick and escape from the creatures. Elise was already feeling the pain in her knees and back, and she wondered how Lorena managed to gather more than anyone else, despite being seventy-eight years old.

"How about a hand over here, Monica?" Lorena called from her spot under one particularly big tree.

"Me? On my knees?" Monica rolled her eyes and spat. "Have you lost your fricking mind?"

Elise smiled. Despite the beauty of the fall day, she had dreaded this outing. She was certain that Monica had told her mother—probably the entire family—about Elise's descent into insanity and her trip to the psycho witch in Taos. As much as Elise wanted to be immune to what anyone thought of her actions, she knew she couldn't be callous to Lorena's thoughts on the matter. She'd been waiting all morning, trying to find the right moment to talk to her.

She heard Monica shouting farther up the hill, Narciso's answer booming back. She heard them whooping, heard the hard rain of nuts falling onto a plastic tarp. Elise knew this was her chance, and she cleared her throat. "I suppose Monica told you I've gone crazy."

Lorena chuckled and looked up. "I believe her exact words were 'certifiably bat shit.'"

Elise laughed.

"That's the thing about my daughter. You never have to wonder where she stands on any given issue." Lorena smiled and continued plunking nuts in the coffee can.

Elise felt a current of fear rising from her chest, making her face flush. But now that she'd started, she knew she had to continue, had to tell Lorena everything. "Did she tell you about my dream?"

Lorena turned to face Elise. "Why don't you tell me?"

Elise sat down, wrapped her arms around her knees, and spilled the whole story. She didn't look at Lorena as she spoke. Instead, she stared out to the western horizon, at the valley below them and the endless sky. She'd been dreading this telling, had spent months avoiding it, holding in her guilt, her self-doubt, holding on to all the ways she had found to blame herself for Michael's death. Now it came rushing out of her like a mountain spring.

"It's my fault, Lorena. That he died. I should have known not to let him take my car. I should have told him about the dream. I should have stopped him from going."

Lorena turned and looked at her, one of those long, penetrating looks that made Elise feel as if the woman could see straight through to the center of her soul. "There are some dreams, some visions, that are intended to help us make a different decision. To change the outcome." Lorena's voice was quiet and soft. "A warning.

"But there are other situations that we can do nothing to change, no matter how much we may know beforehand. We have stories in my family about medicine men in our tribe who had dreams, visions.

They knew that big changes were in the wind—that the white man was coming, that our way of life would change. But that doesn't mean they could stop it from happening."

Elise focused on the quiet of the words.

Lorena studied her for another moment. "You didn't even know it was Michael in the car, did you? In the dream?"

Elise shook her head.

Lorena exhaled. "So perhaps the dream was meant to show you something else. Something about yourself, maybe. It's been my experience that dreams usually aren't exactly literal like that. The meaning is more subtle—more like a fairy tale or a story rather than an exact translation of events."

Elise exhaled. Now that she had started to unburden herself, she had to continue. She needed Lorena's blessing. Needed the relief of full disclosure. "Did Monica tell you about the card reader?"

Lorena laughed. "Of course. Have you ever known her to hold back on anything?"

Elise did not smile. She waited a beat before asking the most important question on her mind. "Do you think I'm crazy?"

Lorena shook her head and put a hand on Elise's back. "I think you're hurting. I think you're alone. Again. I think you're searching for answers."

"Monica says they're crooks. Just trying to take my money. That it's all a bunch of nonsense."

"The same has been said about herbal healers," Lorena replied. They were both quiet for a moment, thinking of the steady stream of clients, residents of Taos and visitors to the area, who made their way to Lorena's door. Almost every one of them would not want it known to their friends and family that they were taking health alternatives from an Indian woman who talked to the plants. "Monica does not know all the answers, even if she thinks she does. I think if you feel drawn to do this, you should do it."

"Really? But it is so different from the Indian way."

"Maybe. Maybe not. The Indian way is not the only way. There are many paths to knowledge. It is not my job, or Monica's, to try to push our beliefs on someone else. I believe in the idea of finding your own path in this world. If you want help, if you need help, you ask. And you ask the person that feels right to you."

Both women were quiet, their reverie interrupted only by the squawking of the birds and the shouts coming from up the hill as Monica corrected her brother in the right way to perform the shake dance.

"I watched your mother, when she came back here after your father died. She struggled. I know she did."

Elise turned to Lorena. No one ever talked about her mother. Sometimes Elise could almost forget that she'd ever had parents. She had been so young when they died; she remembered so little. Now she found herself hanging on Lorena's every breath.

"I don't know what happened—between Beulah and your mother. But I always sensed that your mother felt very . . . alone. Like she had nowhere to turn with all her grief. I watched her—just fade away." Lorena was quiet for a long moment, as if struggling to find the exact words. She turned and looked Elise in the eye. "I don't want to see you do the same thing. And anyone . . . I mean anyone . . . who can help you move forward? Well, you have my blessing, if that's what you're looking for."

A long sigh escaped from Elise's lips. Always, since that afternoon when she was six years old, Lorena had been her rock, the woman she could turn to for comfort and succor. She almost vibrated with gratitude. And now that they had come this far, she knew she had to tell Lorena everything—had to tell her the rest of what was tearing at her mind and heart.

"Lorena?" Elise searched for the words, searched for a way to convey the desperation she felt over her situation. She swallowed hard. "I feel like Michael is trying to tell me something. Something important."

Lorena tipped her head back.

"I know that the spirits are always around us. Always with us. But this is even bigger than that. Do you believe the spirits of the dead can . . . talk to us? Help us?"

Lorena was quiet for a very long time. "I absolutely believe that they can talk to us. Help us. I've seen them come to help in many situations." She turned and caught Elise's eye. "And it's been my experience that if a spirit is trying to tell you something, it is usually important. I would definitely pay attention to that, if I were you."

Elise sat up straighter. Lorena was rarely one to say what a person should or should not do. She seemed to prefer the path of letting others make their own choices.

"My mother died when I was five," Lorena continued, her voice calm, distant. "I had two brothers and one sister. But after she died, we all got so quiet. No laughing. No loud talking. Even the boys were quiet. The house was so different. Everything was different. But I could feel her there, around us. Watching us.

"And then, just a few months later, they shipped us all off to the Indian school in Santa Fe. The Bureau of Indian Affairs had gone around to all the houses, dug up every child they could find. And they made parents ship their children on the train to Santa Fe."

Lorena turned and caught Elise's eye. "They made all four of us get on that train. I remember standing at the station, watching my father through the window. He stood there, this look on his face like he was completely lost. Broken. Seeing him like that made me feel even worse than being shipped off to strangers. I was petrified that he was going to die, too. It was like the world was crumbling all around me.

"I don't know how he made it, losing his wife and having his children ripped away from him like that. My grandmother stood beside him. And his brother, Wes." She pointed with her lips toward Uncle Wes, asleep in his chair. "I think if it hadn't been for them . . . well, I don't know what would have happened to him. How he would have survived that much loss.

"And then we got to that school, and my whole world went completely dark. They separated us—boys and girls—so that I did not see my older brothers at all. And then they separated us again, by age. My sister, who was eight, had to go to different classes, sleep in a different ward."

Elise watched Lorena swallow, as if she could still choke on the bitterness of those memories. "We slept in dorms, on these hard bunk beds. I didn't see my brothers or sister. I felt . . . alone. And then one night, I heard my mother, calling my name.

"I woke up and there she was, standing at the foot of my bed. She looked healthy, the way she used to look before she got sick. And she smiled at me and made this gesture with her finger—come here." Lorena demonstrated, curling her finger.

"So I got out of bed and followed her. We snuck down the hall to the dorm room next to mine. I was trying so hard to be quiet. I walked slowly, placing every foot very carefully to make sure there wouldn't be any boards creaking. The way my grandmother had taught us to walk in the woods when we were hunting quail. My feet were freezing."

Lorena sighed. "I followed her into that dorm room, and my mother went over to this bed where Delores, my sister, was sleeping. There were kids from every tribe in New Mexico in that school. Laguna, Picuris, San Juan, even some Navajo. I had never been in that dorm room before. I didn't know which bed was Delores's, but my mother led me right to it, the fourth one on the left, under one of the big windows. Delores didn't wake up when we got there. I put my hand on her face, thinking I could wake her up so she could talk to Mom. But Delores was burning up with fever. She opened her eyes, but I don't think she saw me."

Lorena sniffed. "She said, 'Mama? Mama, I'm so hot.' I yanked my hand away. All I could think about was when my mother had died, just a year before. She had seen relatives in the spirit world—had started talking to them, even before she passed. The memory spooked me. I was afraid Delores was going to die. I was afraid that was why my mother was there—coming to get Delores. I started to panic.

"And my mother looked at me and shook her head. Then she moved away, toward the hallway, and gestured for me to follow her again." Lorena looked up the hill, where another shake dance was exploding into the quiet day. "We had already had two girls at the school that had died from fever. I was scared like I've never been scared in my life. And I looked at my mother, standing by the door. She knew all about the plants, the herbs. She made tinctures and teas and poultices. I had watched her concoct some smelly mess to put on my chest one time when I had a horrible cough. She learned from her mother, who learned from her mother. It's been passed down many generations, this knowledge.

"I took Delores's sweater from the foot of the bed and snuck downstairs, in my bare feet. It was October—cold, but not like full-on winter. I followed my mother outside, into this section of bosque, thick trees, not far behind the dorm. And I could see this glow—kind of an orange glow, like firelight—up ahead a little bit. My mother was standing next to a cottonwood, just a young sapling, not more than three feet tall. As soon as I got close to it, the glow faded. I felt as if the plant were speaking to me, saying, 'Pick me, pick me.' So I did. I had to bend the thin branches back and forth, back and forth, dozens of times. All this time, I was so worried I would get caught, worried that I wouldn't know what to do with the sticks, worried that I would be too late to help my sister." Lorena turned to Elise once again. "I'd heard elders in the tribe talking about visions—but this seemed so strange. Nothing like it had ever happened to me before. And the whole time, my mother stood there, watching. Nodding her head, every time I started to falter.

"I kept at it. Gathered up several little twigs, a handful of them, and headed back to the dorm. I almost ran back, despite the gravel and the cold. I headed straight to the kitchen. There was this old woman who helped cook. She was sleeping on a bed in a small room behind the stove. I did not see how I could do anything in there without waking her—without enlisting her help somehow. I kept muttering prayers—in Spanish, in English, in Tiwa.

"I'm not sure what woke her up—if I was making too much noise or what. I've always thought it was because I was speaking Tiwa. I think I must have been crying, tears all down my face, because she came into the kitchen and whispered, 'What is it, child?' She spoke Tiwa. Tiwa! I couldn't believe it! Out of all the mix of languages at that school, she spoke Tiwa. And none of us were allowed to speak our native tongue. We got whipped for it, if the nuns heard us. We were forced to speak English. And here was this woman, this cook, talking to me in Tiwa.

"I spilled out the whole story. I handed her my sticks, told her that I had no idea what to do with them, only that I thought they might help Delores. She never questioned me, never asked how I knew that. She told me that she thought we should make tea—steep those sticks in some hot water. She put some wood on the fire and started a kettle."

Lorena turned to look at Elise again. "That woman made sure my sister got her tea several times over the next few hours. And Delores's fever went away. She recovered.

"When we came home at Christmas, I told my grandmother all about it. She pulled me up on her lap, and told me that she had known ever since I was born that I would be the one. The one who would heal people with plants. The one who would learn all her secrets. The one she would train, every summer for the next several years, in the ways of the plant world. She said I was in love with the plants, just as she was, and that when you are in love with the plants, they talk to you."

Lorena smiled and began to pick up nuts again. "If I had told anyone else, any of the sisters who ran the school, they would have thought I was crazy. I might even have been punished. My sister might have died. But somehow, I managed to find the one adult in that whole place who understood, who spoke Tiwa, who was willing to help.

"And all of it, finding Delores, finding the plant, finding the woman who would help, was because of my mother—my mother's spirit—guiding me. When I woke up that night, after that dream, I had no idea what was around the next bend—no idea how one thing would lead to another. I had no idea that my life would center on healing, on talking to plants. But I kept going, kept doing the next thing that came up, and I kept doing it because that's what felt right."

Both women sat silently, listening to the sounds of Narciso and Monica and the children moving through the trees.

Lorena turned and looked at Elise. "Are you sure this is Michael? Trying to talk to you?"

Elise sat completely still for a moment. "Yes."

"If you think Michael is trying to tell you something, then trust your instincts. Always base your judgment on whether or not it feels right to you. You can't worry about what other people think—not Monica, not anyone." Lorena stopped and looked Elise in the eye. "Not even me." She paused, watching Elise's face. "None of us knows what is right for someone else. None of us can know what's around the next corner.

"From my way of seeing things, these things are all connected. Just like your weaving, one thread laid down on top of another, over and under and in and through. They're part of the warp and weft of your life. You have to just keep going. Keep looking for what feels right. Trust your gut feeling. Trust your heart."

Elise looked away and bit her lip. "That's the really hard part, right there. I'm having a hard time trusting myself. Trusting that I can read the signs and get it right."

Lorena put a hand on Elise's forearm. "If the Great Spirit really wanted you to stop Michael that night, it seems to me the dream would have been more clear. I don't believe you read anything wrong. That dream was given to you for some other reason. It's just a piece of the puzzle."

Elise let that idea sink into her pores. It gave her a small slice of comfort to think of it that way.

"You will figure it out. You will. Watch the signs that are given to you. Listen to the quiet. Trust your own inner compass."

Elise wasn't sure she could do it, wasn't sure what she believed, but Lorena's words had a calming effect. They sat quietly for a few moments, neither of them saying anything.

Uncle Wes woke from his nap and stretched his arms. He looked at the cooler by his feet, then over at Lorena and Elise, and smiled. His voice boomed out into the quiet on the hill. "So what does it take to get a lunch break around here? Do I need to hire an attorney?"

Elise stood and stretched, and when she walked over to the cooler, close to Uncle Wes, he reached up and took her hand. "I smell smoke," he murmured.

Elise started, looking around quickly.

"Not here," Wes said. "In the spirit world."

He continued to hold Elise's hand, and she put her left hand on the old man's white hair. Wes had been part of her life since she'd first met Monica, all those years ago, and she thought of him like a grandfather.

"I will miss you, daughter," he whispered.

Elise caught Lorena's eye, but the older woman said nothing.

# CHAPTER TWELVE

She could see him in the distance, too far away to make out individual features, but there was no mistaking who it was. She knew that walk, that physique, that way he had of holding his shoulders and head. Her body flooded with joy, watching him move toward her.

It was neither day nor night, but somewhere in between. The light was filmy, a gray-green color, like being underwater. The image of Michael, moving toward her, was bent and warped, swaying like a piece of submerged seaweed. He moved as close to her as he could, a few feet away, and Elise realized that there was a fence between them. Only waist high, but she knew that she could not cross that line and that Michael could not leave his side, either. He smiled at her.

For those few moments, Elise remembered how it had felt to be with him. Protected, sheltered, calm. Like going home, even though she had never really understood what *home* meant before him. She had never had that feeling before, growing up with severe, quiet Beulah. She and Michael shared an understanding, a connection that she had never felt with anyone else. They had talked about it, that shared experience of grief, of losing someone you loved at a young age. The feeling of being lost and alone, surrounded by darkness, unable to tell which way was up and which way down. The shared feeling of panic that sometimes flooded the system, as if nothing in the world could be trusted, not even the ground they walked on.

Elise inhaled the calmness that had always surrounded her husband. He was one of the most grounded people she had ever known, and she felt that again, now, as he stood before her. Michael raised his hand, closed in a fist, and held it just over the line of the fence between them. Elise raised her own hand, just beneath his, sensing that he had something he wanted to give her.

His body continued to undulate, to wave back and forth as if it were made of particles of light, nothing that could be grasped or held or touched. And that movement kept his hand rippling and moving. She could not keep her own hand aligned with his. She could not grasp whatever it was he was trying to give her. Her eyes met his, and panic surged up in her system. He was disappearing; wisps of gray-green shimmers, like smoke, moved between them. And then he was gone.

*"Elise?"*

"Ah!" Her eyes shot open, and she stared into the dark, trying to get her bearings after the dense atmosphere of the dream. She had fallen asleep in the chair in the living room, her stocking feet perched on the ottoman, her body covered by a crocheted afghan that Beulah had made many years ago. She breathed heavily, slowly bringing herself back to reality.

Falling asleep in the living room happened so often these days. She would do anything to avoid tossing and turning and fighting the bed that she had shared with Michael for so many years. She would do anything to avoid that feeling of her hand dropping to his side of the bed, finding it cold and empty. Even on the occasions when she managed to doze off, she would jolt awake a short time later, rolling over and wondering why Michael wasn't there. Memory pounded back into her consciousness, always as if for the very first time: *Michael's dead. He is not coming back.*

The soft purr of a car engine invaded her thoughts. Elise stopped, listening with every fiber of her body. Lights flashed across the ceiling of the room, like the headlights of a car turning into the driveway. Her stomach dropped, remembering that middle-of-the-night visit from the state patrol seven months ago. Fear flooded her system in a quick adrenaline rush. She could taste it, like sucking on copper pennies.

Elise stood and moved to one side of the picture window. From this angle, she could see the driveway that led out to the main road coming up the mountain. It was a dark night, with no moon. She could see nothing in the driveway or on the road leading to it—no lights, no gleam of metal other than the soft glow that came from Michael's silent truck. She waited, listening intently. No sound came to her, no click of a resting engine, no crunch of shoes on gravel. Elise shifted her body slightly, trying to decide if she had dreamed it or if it was just the memory, the energetic residue of the night that he died.

The night was black; starlight was the only light outside. This far from town, there were no streetlights, no reflected glow of the lights of town. It was one of those nights when she wouldn't be able to see her hand in front of her face if she were outside. Michael had put in a trail of solar lights along the path that led from the house to the studio, a way to keep both of them oriented on nights like this. They glowed softly. Elise stood at the darkened window, staring out at the night, at the soft curve of the path leading to the studio.

A shiver ran down her spine; the hair on her arms bristled. She watched the darkness, the woods behind Michael's studio, and the slope of the driveway. The dog at the house below her, half a mile away, began to bark, the sound bouncing and echoing up the canyon to Elise. For a moment she wondered if there was a bear or a mountain lion out roaming, but she could see nothing, out there in the dark.

Behind her, inside the house, she heard the soft creak of a door opening. She turned slowly, her breath caught somewhere between inhale and exhale, watching as the door to the coat closet swung open just a few feet away. That closet was the receptacle of all their winter coats and boots; it held a basket of knitted hats and scarves and mittens. She had not opened it since before Michael died, not having a need for any of her winter pieces in the last six months. There was one hook on the inside of that door where Michael hung his denim jacket—the jacket he wore more than any other. The jacket he often wore as he worked in the studio. It was usually covered with sawdust, and he never hung it on the bar with the other coats. Elise had often complained about the sawdust she found in her hats and mittens when winter returned.

Elise moved over to the closet, and raised her hand to touch that denim. She could almost see the way he had come in that afternoon, so many months ago, and hung it on the hook. She lifted a sleeve of that jacket and closed her eyes, inhaling the scent of wood dust. The scent of Michael.

Something fell from the pocket of his jacket and landed on the floor at her feet. Elise bent down and picked it up. It was a piece of obsidian, dark-black volcanic glass, in an oval disk shape. Delicate carving decorated the top of the piece. In the dim light, Elise could see the faint markings of a dog, curled up in sleep.

The dream came back to her. Michael standing in dim, gray-green light, like this. Michael, holding his closed fist over her palm, trying to give her something. Michael.

She wrapped her hand around it and held it to her chest. Obsidian was a common stone in these parts, common in many parts of the world. Obsidian, like the eyes of the raven out in his studio. Obsidian, the stone that so many Native peoples had carved into arrowheads and spear points. Obsidian, the stone that had been christened with the nickname "Apache tears."

Elise held it between her two palms, wrapping her hands around it as if it held the energy of her dead husband, as if it held a connection to him. The stone sent a buzz into her palms and up her arms and through her entire body—just like the buzz of plugging in an electric heater, watching as it fired into life. Something about this stone went to the very core of her being, like tapping into the center of the earth.

She reached inside first one pocket of his jacket and then the other. A small business card, bent in half, was tucked inside the right pocket. "Franklin Cooper. Stone Mountain Carving, Star Route, Olalla, Tennessee." There was no street number on the address, no phone number on the card.

Elise held the card in one hand and the piece of obsidian in the other. She turned and gazed into the dark night.

# CHAPTER THIRTEEN

"Who's the doofus with the pocket protector?" Monica walked into the kitchen and reached for a bite of the chicken salad Elise was mixing. "You went grocery shopping?"

"His name's Tom Dugan. He's a friend of Celestina's." Elise opened a loaf of bread. "And no, no shopping. Celestina sent this basket of food with him."

"A psychic sidekick?" Monica threw her head back and cackled.

Elise smiled. "Engineer, actually. He does all the fix-it for Celestina's group of widows and orphans. He's troubleshooting my solar hot-water heater."

The two women sat down at the kitchen table. They could hear Tom outside, climbing up on the roof, clanging noises trailing down the pipes and into the house. "I think he's trying to get me ready for the winter. He showed up a few days ago with a load of firewood, and now this." Elise pointed to the roof over their heads.

"Why didn't you ask me? Or Narciso? You don't need a strange man coming up here to help you."

"I didn't ask him. He just showed up. Orders from Celestina, apparently. I don't know how she knows what she knows, but she sent him with wood a few days ago, and back up here today. Told him some gadget on my roof wasn't working right."

"What kind of man hangs around doing the bidding of a psychic? Doesn't he have a life?"

"Not at the moment, no." Elise sighed and looked out the window. "We do have that much in common."

Monica shivered. "I don't like this, Elise. Something smells fishy. Almost like you're being sucked into some kind of weird cult. You run into that woman in the park two weeks ago, and now this. A man crawling around on your roof, examining every part of this place. You don't know him from Adam. That could be Charles Manson up there."

"He doesn't have that much charisma." Elise smiled, but her attempt at humor fell flat.

Monica glared at her. "I hardly think you're in great shape for making judgments about people right now. It's not like you're in great shape for making judgments of *any* kind right now."

"Okay, then. You do it. See how dangerous he is with that pocket protector and those glasses that slide down his nose all the time. I don't think he could find his feet without those glasses on."

"That could be a costume, you know. It wouldn't be the first time a white man has practiced the art of deception."

Elise made no protest.

"Elise, what's going on with you? You're as jittery as a drop of water in a hot skillet." Monica gave her a piercing glare. "And don't say noth—"

"Nothing. Everything." Elise jumped up from her chair and paced back and forth by the table. "I'm losing it, Monica. I mean . . ." She stopped. She wasn't sure what she meant, but she couldn't meet Monica's eyes.

Elise turned to the kitchen window and stared out into the woods. "I can't sleep. I can't eat. I see things, out of the corner of my eye. I hear things. I keep waiting for Michael. Waiting for him to come home. I turn my head, and I think I see him out by the woodpile or closing the door to the studio.

"He's everywhere around here. Every corner of the house and the land. Every walk I take. Every book I pull off the shelf. Everything is Michael."

Elise sat down again and put her head in her hands. "I need . . . I'm not even sure what I need. Rest. To be able to sleep." She swallowed hard. "I used to read about people who had a nervous breakdown. I never really understood that. How do your nerves break down? But now it's starting to make more sense. Like all the connecting wires in my body and brain aren't working right. They're all scrambled."

Monica went completely still. This was her greatest fear—that Elise would fall apart. "Why don't you come stay with me? Or with Mom? She'd love to have you."

Elise looked at Monica and shook her head. Her eyes burned red with fatigue. "I don't think that's far enough. I've known Michael since I was seven. I met him at your mom's place. His memory is stitched into every part of this area.

"Sometimes I feel like . . . I just want to get away from here. Away from all these memories." Elise looked out the window and pursed her lips toward the battered old Nissan pickup in the driveway. "And that thing isn't going to take me very far."

Monica stood up and walked to the kitchen window. They both stood, staring out into the afternoon. "Elise? If Michael is trying to tell you something, don't you think you would have a better chance figuring it out if you stayed here? Where his spirit is?"

Elise pursed her lips and blew out a long stream of air. "Maybe. Maybe not. Monica, don't laugh."

"No promises. You are weird as hell lately."

"I need to show you something."

They headed outside, down the path to the studio. From his perch on the roof, Tom stopped working and watched them, sliding his glasses up on his nose. Elise turned the key in the lock and pushed open the door to Michael's studio.

"Oh my God," Monica whispered. She moved to the carving of the raven, walking slowly around the bird, her eyes soaking in the incredibly detailed work. She touched it, barely brushing her fingertips over the tip of one wing, and pulled her hand back quickly. "I think this is the finest piece he's ever done," she breathed.

Elise stood still, nodding her agreement.

Monica stopped and turned toward Elise. "Does Ken Black know about this?"

Elise shook her head. "I told him there wasn't anything that was finished."

"You lied?" Monica's eyebrows rose.

Elise nodded.

"He believe you?"

"I don't know. I think so." Elise stepped closer to the bird, staring at the black glass eyes.

Monica examined Elise for a moment, her head cocked to one side. "I'll bet not. You can't lie for shit, you know."

Elise shrugged and let out a long, slow sigh. "The other night, I had a dream. I could see Michael in the distance. And he walked up to me. We were separated by a fence, and he was trying to give me something. Only I couldn't get it. I couldn't make my hand line up with his. When I woke up, I could have sworn that I heard him, driving up. I thought I saw headlights on the ceiling." She paused and exhaled. "I've done that so many times. Thinking that I hear him, coming home."

Elise stood motionless and blew her breath out slowly, trying to force herself into a calmer state.

Monica turned to gaze at her friend.

Elise pulled the carved obsidian piece from her pocket and handed it to Monica. "I woke up from that dream, and I was standing by the front window, staring outside. And then the closet door swings open, and . . . this fell out of his jacket pocket."

Monica took the stone in her hand. She turned it over, let her hand absorb the etchings and smooth patches. She could see the subtle work that had gone into the carving.

Monica's eyes were open wide, and she was uncharacteristically silent.

"Obsidian"—Elise nodded at the stone that Monica held in her hand—"just like the stones he used for the eyes in that raven."

Monica looked up at the raven again, examining the dark glass eyes.

"And I found this in his pocket." Elise handed the folded business card to her friend.

Monica studied the card. "I don't get it."

"I don't, either. I don't know where he got it. Michael showed me the stones that he was going to use for the raven's eyes. He was really excited about them. I never saw this other piece, though, until the other night." Elise took a breath. "Do you think maybe Michael is trying to tell me to go? To this guy, this place?" Elise pointed to the card in Monica's hand. "Do you think this guy knows something? Because it feels like this might be important. Dreaming that Michael was trying to give me something, and then finding this?"

Monica glanced again at the business card. "I don't know. This really isn't my area of expertise. Maybe you should talk to Mom. Or Uncle Wes."

"Your mom told me to trust myself. To do whatever I think is right."

"Sounds like something Mom would say. But she hasn't seen you when you're like this. On the verge of a nervous breakdown."

Elise shrugged. "She also told me anything that gets me moving is probably good."

Their eyes met for a moment.

"Monica, there's more."

"I'm listening," Monica whispered.

"There's been a raven hanging around here. Ever since I opened Michael's studio a couple of weeks ago. It's shown up a couple of times."

"One raven?" Monica's face clouded. "Are you sure it's the same raven every time?"

"It's missing a feather on the left wing." Elise took a moment to let that sink in. "About one-third of the way down."

Monica looked at the carving. "And you think this raven might be Michael?"

Elise nodded. "And I think he's trying to tell me. To go. To Olalla."

"Last weekend? With Uncle Wes?" Elise watched as Monica's eyes went wide. "He said he's going to miss me."

Monica froze for several seconds. "Miss you? As in he's leaving, or you are?"

Elise shrugged. "I think he meant me."

"Uncle Wes usually knows what he's talking about. If he thinks you're leaving . . ." She turned and looked out the window at Michael's old truck, sitting in the driveway. It was fifteen years old, with more than two hundred thousand miles on it, and had certainly seen better days. It needed work; that was the reason Michael had not taken it to his meeting that night so many months ago. "Please tell me you're not planning on taking that," she said, indicating the truck with her lips.

Elise stared at the truck. She hadn't thought that far ahead, but now, as she considered the idea of driving Michael's truck across country in the wintertime, she shivered.

Monica turned to Elise. "I'd take you myself, but we have a pretty big remodel going on. We're supposed to have it finished by Christmas. I don't think there's any way I can leave right now. Can it wait until the first of the year?"

Elise shrugged. "I don't know. I don't even know if that's what all of this means. I don't really know anything. It's just a . . . feeling."

Tom appeared in the open doorway of the studio, wiping his hands on a rag. He stopped, eyes rooted on Monica. He stared for what seemed an inappropriately long time. Monica stared back, each of them sizing up the other.

Elise moved to break the intense mood. "Tom Dugan, this is Monica Madrid."

"What are you staring at, white boy?"

Tom's mouth hung open a fraction. He closed it with a snap and shook his head. "Nothing." He turned away from Monica's gaze and did a quick back step. "Whoa. What is that?" he asked, taking in the raven on the table in front of them.

Elise and Monica looked at each other. "This is . . . this was my husband's studio," Elise murmured. And just that quickly, she was flooded with discomfort, wanting to get out of this room as fast as she could. She hated the fact that Tom was standing inside this space, this area that she considered sacred with Michael's energy.

She moved toward the door, trying to get the two of them to follow her. They stared at each other, and she knew that Monica was trying to get a read on this strange man who had just shown up in her friend's life. They stepped outside, and Elise locked the door to the studio.

"We're about to have lunch, Tom. Would you like to join us?"

Monica looked at his pocket protector, at the pen and pencil stuck inside. "So, I hear you're an engineer?" she said, as if vetting Tom for a position with her construction firm.

"Electrical, mostly. I write . . . wrote . . . software programs for devices like that switch on your hot-water heater." Tom turned toward Elise. "Which really needs some recoding, if you ask me. There seem to be some holes in the equations."

They trailed into the house, and Tom washed his hands and sat down at the table. Elise brought sandwiches; Monica slipped into a chair and continued her assessment of Tom Dugan.

"Those codes can be really tricky. Sometimes things happen when you're trying to translate one kind of code to another," he continued, munching through a quarter of his sandwich. He caught Monica's eye. She was staring, her face a complete blank. "You're probably not really interested in this, are you?"

Monica pursed her lips. "No, go ahead. I'll just pretend I'm listening."

Tom couldn't take his eyes off her, but if he had heard her words, they didn't register. He continued to spout, staring at Monica as if she were the most interesting thing he'd ever laid eyes on. "Because I know that I tend to get carried away about the intricacies of mapping different types of gadgets. For instance, when the solar heater gets really cold, things slow down, and there needs to be some kind of compensation in the programming if you're going to continue getting hot water. If you've got a hiccup in that part of the program, there will be this *rrrrrr* that really drags everything to a halt."

Monica's eyes glazed over. She sighed and turned to Elise. "Yet another misguided white man who thinks that everything that goes on in his own head is utterly fascinating."

Tom stopped talking and stared at Monica; his mouth hung open slightly.

Elise looked from one to the other and back to her food. Once again, she wasn't really hungry, and she pushed the plate away.

Tom finished his sandwich, took his plate to the sink, and turned toward Elise. "I need to get back. Some friend of Celestina's has something wrong with her woodstove." Tom turned and stared at Monica again, pushing his glasses up. "If that switch doesn't work, let me know. I'll try to design a program, some kind of circuit board, that will keep it from getting bogged down like that."

He reached for his jacket on the back of the chair. "But it will be a couple of weeks before I can look at it again. Celestina is sending me on a cross-country fix-it this time."

Both women turned to look at him.

"A friend of hers just moved back east to live by her daughter. She and her husband found a place in the Smoky Mountains somewhere. Only it's off the grid. Totally off the grid." Tom's eyebrows went up. "Which is great, of course, but right now, they're stuck with a generator. All that noise, all those gas fumes. Not exactly idyllic living conditions. They want me to design some systems that will take care of everything. Electricity. Hot water. Heat. Air-conditioning. I leave on Thursday."

He continued to look at Monica, only at Monica. As if he had forgotten Elise's existence.

"I hope it's not like *Deliverance* or anything. Some backwoods den of iniquity. Podunk, Tennessee."

Elise and Monica looked at each other and then at him, standing by the door. "Did you say the Smoky Mountains? Where, exactly?" Monica asked.

"I don't remember. East of Nashville, I think. Close to the Smoky Mountain national park." Tom reached inside his pocket protector and pulled out a small piece of paper, folded into fourths. "Let's see. Some little place called Olalla." He raised his eyes to Monica's. "Olalla, Tennessee. Got a nice ring to it, doesn't it? Lots of vowels and double consonants. Olalla, Tennesseeeee." Tom drew out the sound and flashed a goofy smile at Monica. He turned and headed out the door.

Elise and Monica stared at each other, but neither of them said anything. They waited, listening to the sound of Tom's vehicle starting up and crunching on the gravel as he backed out and headed down the road.

"Olalla, Tennessee? What are the odds on that?" Monica mumbled.

A shadow fell across the floor of the room, and they heard a thump on the window. Both women jumped. A raven flew up to the glass and tapped on it with its beak.

"What the . . . ?" Monica moved to the glass and watched as the raven flew to the nearest cottonwood tree. It perched on the branch and held its wings spread for just a moment before resting. One feather on the left wing, about one-third of the way down, was missing.

"Huh. So . . . a man with dark eyes who will help you. A journey. To the east." Monica took a breath and turned to her friend. "Looks like the psycho witch is batting a thousand so far."

Elise had forgotten about those predictions, had all but forgotten about that reading only two weeks before. Now it all came back: the hush of that dark room, the flicker of the candle in the middle of the table, the flicking noise as Celestina flipped each card onto the table. She remembered telling Monica about the man who would help her, the journey to the east. But she had never told her friend the rest of the reading. She'd never mentioned the death card.

# CHAPTER FOURTEEN

The predawn sky was thick with clouds, still a deep gray on this cold November morning. Elise had spent the night at Monica's house in Amalia, and now they pulled up to Celestina's shop. Tom was sitting inside his Jeep, shoulders hunched with the early-morning cold. He jumped out now and stood between the two vehicles.

"I understand why you feel the need to do this," Monica murmured. She turned toward her friend. "But keep your eyes open. He may not have the charisma of Charlie Manson, but that doesn't mean he's sane." Monica turned to look at Tom. "Something about him smells funny."

"You say that about everybody who's white." Elise tried to crack a smile.

Monica was watching Tom. "There's more to this than his lack of color. A fifty-year-old man working as a girl Friday for a psychic in Taos?" Monica shook her head. "Everything about that picture is out of focus."

Tom opened the door for Elise, and she stepped out. She grabbed her travel bag from the floor and handed it to Tom.

Monica got out and stood awkwardly in front of Elise. She leaned close, and they hugged. "Watch your topknot," Monica said, stepping back.

Elise nodded. "Watch your'n," she murmured.

Monica moved close to Tom, who was loading the bags in the back of the Jeep. With her back to Elise, she whispered, "If you so much as look at her cross-eyed, I will string you up by your nuts, white boy."

Tom's head jerked up, and he pushed his glasses up on his nose.

Monica walked back to her car, and Tom watched as she pulled away. He moved to the driver's seat and sat for a moment, hunched over the wheel. The chill caused them both to shiver, waiting for the heater and the engine to warm up. Tom pursed his lips toward Monica, turning onto the main street. "So what is she? Your friend, I mean. A lion tamer?"

Elise laughed. "She'd be good at that." She watched her friend disappear from sight. "She and her brother do construction. Monica is quite the tile artist, actually. You don't want to mess with her when she has a tool in her hands."

Tom nodded. "She looks like she could be dangerous even without a tool in her hands." He pulled out onto the quiet main drag of Taos. "Is she partnered up?"

Elise turned to him and snorted. "I can't even picture the kind of man she could put up with for very long. Boyfriends, yes. But the minute they try to tell her what to do, she gives them the boot."

Tom nodded. "Hmm. Yeah. I can see that." He pushed his glasses up on his nose and took a swig from his coffee cup. "So, I've been thinking about your predicament."

"What predicament is that? You mean the *rrrrrr* in my solar hot-water heater?"

Tom scowled. "No, not that. I mean your predicament. Trying to get a message from your husband."

Elise went completely still. "I thought you don't believe in—"

"I don't." Tom laughed. "Absolutely not. But . . . I do like trying to solve problems. I think that's why I went into engineering in the first place. Trying to come up with solutions for life's little predicaments."

Elise turned to him; her mouth dropped open. "Life's little predicaments?"

Tom did not notice her discomfort; he kept his eyes on the road ahead. "So I've been thinking, if I were going to look at this as a scientific experiment." He snorted with laughter. "Sorry. That just sounds ridiculous, coming out of my mouth. Scientific experiment. Talking to the dead." He laughed again and shook his head. "Anyway, the first thing I always do with any problem I'm trying to solve is to find out if anyone else has addressed the issue. Look at the existing information." He checked the left lane and pulled into it.

"You certainly aren't the first person who has tried to communicate with the dead. It's a question that's been fascinating mankind since the beginning of time. Human time, anyway. What happens when we die? Is there anything that survives? A soul or consciousness or whatever. And can we communicate?"

Elise was horrified. "You're turning my life into a research project?"

"So I googled it." Tom pushed his glasses up on his nose, continuing as if she had not spoken. "You would not believe all the craziness that pops up when you type in 'communicating with the dead.' Ouija boards and automatic writing. I found websites where these little ghost graphics are flying across the page, making 'whoooo' sounds. Total craziness."

"You googled 'communicating with the dead'?" She was incredulous, but Tom remained oblivious, as if she were talking to herself.

He raised his right index finger from the steering wheel, as if he were a professor in a college class, trying to make a point. "But then I typed in 'science and communicating with the dead.' A total non sequitur, but there you go. And that brings up a whole different list of sites. A few days ago, I would never have believed this, but apparently there are a few American universities that are sponsoring scientific investigations into life after death. University of Arizona is looking at communication through mediums. University of Virginia is looking at near-death experiences and the aftereffects."

Every fiber of Elise's body was rigid and motionless, irritation spreading to every pore. "I can't believe this."

"The idea of communicating with the dead has been around as long as . . . well, for sure since the beginning of recorded history. Superstitious nonsense, but still. The Greeks, the Romans, the Egyptians, almost all cultures had practices related to communicating with spirits. Abe Lincoln attended séances at the White House after his son died. Arthur Conan Doyle became quite a spiritualist after his son was killed in the First World War. Thomas Edison"—he turned toward Elise for a second, his eyebrows lifted—"looked into inventing some type of machine for it. Several fairly intelligent people have expressed interest in the idea." He turned back to the road, shaking his head.

"You make it sound as if intelligence and interest in what happens after death are mutually exclusive," Elise muttered.

Tom nodded, focused on the road. "Exactly. I was really surprised at some of the names of people who have looked into all this. I mean, Thomas Edison?"

Elise rolled her eyes and looked away.

"But there does seem to be a connection between interest in the afterlife and the loss of someone important in a person's life. The whole spiritualist movement? Séances and all that sort of thing? Swept the country after the Civil War. It's amazing, the kinds of things people will do when someone they love has died. And it does make interesting reading, if you can suspend belief for a while."

"I'm not sure I want to talk to you about this."

Tom completely ignored her sentence. As he became more animated with his topic, his driving became less focused, the Jeep meandering between the lines of the highway. "So I started looking at all the different methods that have been used to try and get messages from spirits. It's been really interesting, being around Celestina all these months, and I've thought several times that I should be writing some of this down. Her predictions and such. You know, trying to keep track of statistics. Her success rate, if you will. Some people do come back, again and again, and I've heard some of them say that she was right. But their assessment is not scientifically valid. Self-assessment is rarely objective. That would skew the results, if I was really trying to do a valid study." He took another long swig of coffee, and the Jeep pulled toward the right side of the road.

Elise put a hand on her door and one on the dashboard. "Do you think you could watch the road?"

"Huh?" Tom held the coffee cup in his right hand, steered the car with his left, and continued. "If you really want to study divination, or talking to the dead, or any of this other woo-woo stuff, you need a well-trained scientist to set parameters and observe results." He turned to Elise again, his eyebrows arched. "That would be me, of course."

"Woo-woo stuff?" Elise let out a gasp of exasperation. What had she been thinking, setting off across country with this man?

Tom put his coffee cup in the holder and reached inside a duffel bag behind her seat. He pulled out his iPad, already running, and opened to a program. "Check this out. I've created a spreadsheet, with columns for all the information you've got so far. One column for your dreams"—Tom raised his eyes to glance at her—"although we'll have to fill in the details.

"And then there's a column for Celestina and her tarot cards, and we can fill in the predictions that she gave you. I already filled in the part about a man with dark eyes that will help you, and taking a journey. So far, so good. So I think I've got us up-to-date with what's happened so far."

"Us?" Elise felt the tension in her brow, and raised a hand to rub her forehead.

"I've done a little research about séances, and Ouija boards, and automatic writing. Some people, ghost hunters and such, use equipment, like recorders for electronic voice phenomena and electromagnetic pulse meters, although from what I've read, those are more apt to be useful if you're talking about a *place* that has paranormal activity. That doesn't seem to be the case with your situation."

Elise wished that Monica were in the car with them. Monica would know exactly what to say. Elise just sat, incredulous, while he continued to spout.

"This is where I come in. I've done some research, since I am the scientist here, and it's up to me to be an impartial observer. It looks like there are two theories about psychics and mediums and all these . . . readings. The first is called a hot reading, and that's where they actually do research on the person first—so that they can nail some facts during the reading. That would be a possibility if we made an appointment with someone. Did you know"—he turned and gave Elise a look over the tops of his glasses—"there are mediums and psychics who are booked for months in advance because of their abilities, so-called? Seems to me you can do a lot of research on someone if you know in advance who you're going to be talking with."

He turned back to the road, but the car continued to meander. "And then there's the cold reading. That's what Celestina does. That's for the medium that just takes whoever walks in off the street. So of course she, or he, has no idea who the person is and hasn't had a chance to do any research in advance." Tom took a swig of coffee and continued: "If a psychic puts a hand on their chest and says, 'I feel pain' . . . that could mean anything. Heart attack. Lung cancer. Broken heart. And people just grab that stuff like it's candy, and buy right into it, and read their own circumstances in that fuzzy murk." Tom sat back and smiled, like he'd just made a basket from center court. "Have you heard of those psychics who do big shows? In theaters and such?"

He turned to look at Elise. "That's the kind of thing they do. They have these predictions, these statements, which could be true for just about anyone. You wouldn't even believe how crazy that can get. Totally ridiculous."

Tom pushed his glasses up and signaled to merge onto the highway. Color was not yet streaking the sky. "So you'll want to be very careful to keep your face and eyes as unreadable as possible. Are you a poker player?"

Elise did not respond. *Fifteen hundred miles of this?* She was already feeling the pinch of a headache. She rubbed her hands on her forehead.

"Because if you'd had some practice with playing it straight, we might get better results in terms of checking statistical probabilities."

"That sounds like something Monica would say," Elise murmured.

"What?"

"Tom, you're weaving. Could you watch the road?" Elise wished she'd never called him, never told him that she believed she needed to go to Olalla. "Have you considered the possibility that some of these people might have *legitimate* psychic ability?"

Tom turned to her and moved his glasses low on his nose. He looked at her over the tops of the rims and pinched his lips together. "Yeah. Right." Then he turned back to the road, pushed his glasses up, and continued.

"There are some people trying to do *legitimate* scientific inquiry into psychic ability, yes. University of Arizona, for example. They have a guy there who has been conducting all kind of experiments with mediums and sitters. I'm not sure I totally agree with his methods, though."

Elise stared at him. No wonder she had hated science when she was in school.

"And then there's this thing called veridical proof. That would be if the medium gets a piece of information that's just . . . I don't know. Too obscure, too difficult, to just be a random guess. Something way outside the statistical probabilities. That could give weight to a reading."

Elise sighed heavily. She closed the iPad and shoved it back into the console between them.

Tom turned to look at her, his eyes large behind the glass lenses. "What? Did you see a design flaw?"

"You mean apart from the fact that you are turning my life into a science experiment?"

Tom swallowed.

"Yes. I do see a design flaw. You've already made up your mind about all of this. You don't believe in communicating with the dead, or in any kind of psychic-intuitive wisdom. Haven't you already violated the first important aspect of research? To approach the subject with an open mind and no preconceived ideas?"

Tom said nothing; he kept his eyes on the road.

"I don't want to go to *any* kind of psychic reader or medium or séance or anything, if you're going to be sitting there with your skepticism, making sarcastic comments and taking notes for your spreadsheet. My life is not your case study into the paranormal."

The silence was uncomfortable, filled with the sharp points of her words.

"All right," Tom murmured. "Fair enough."

Elise sat for a few moments, staring at the window, letting her anger dissipate into the ethers. "Tom, haven't you ever had something happen that you could not explain? Not in any rational, scientific kind of way?"

There was a pause before Tom replied, "No."

"Haven't you ever just had a *feeling* about something? A *feeling* about your ex-wife? Before it all came out?"

Tom pushed his glasses up his nose, but he did not turn to look at Elise. "No."

"No weird synchronicity, coincidence kind of thing? Like the night you showed up at Celestina's?"

"Coincidence has absolutely no scientific value," Tom muttered. "A coincidence is a coincidence. Period."

"Well, coincidence is the reason I'm in this car right now, headed to Olalla, Tennessee. Coincidence. And a dream. And a *feeling*. A gut feeling, that this is something I need to do."

The sun had not yet appeared behind the clouds, but the landscape was starting to lighten. Trees at the side of the road blushed with the gold and peach and apricot colors of dawn. Elise drank in the beauty for a few moments.

"So. You don't want to try any of these . . . methods?"

Elise took a deep breath. "I didn't say that. I'm not sure what I want to do. I guess I just want to see what comes up. If I get a *feeling* I should do something, I will."

"A feeling?"

"Yeah. Got a problem with that?"

"Can I write it down? Track it on the spreadsheet?"

"Can you keep an open mind? Can you bury all that cynicism?"

Tom shrugged. "I can try, I guess."

"All right. You can write it all down." Elise sighed. "But there's one more thing you need to add to your spreadsheet. Something I haven't told anyone yet." She turned and looked at Tom, and he glanced away from the road long enough to meet her eyes. The sky was becoming lighter, but the sun was still hidden in the clouds. "Celestina said a man with dark eyes would help me, that I'd be going on a journey. East." Elise turned back to look out the front windshield. "But there was one other card in that reading."

Tom glanced over again.

Elise turned back to him. "The last card that she pulled in that reading was the death card."

Tom was quiet for a moment. "Death card?"

"Yeah."

"Your death?"

Elise shrugged. "Maybe. That's the thing with these psychic readings, and dreams, and all that woo-woo stuff, isn't it? They're so nebulous. So open to interpretation. Sometimes you don't figure out what it means until after it's already over."

Tom stared straight ahead. "Huh."

# CHAPTER FIFTEEN

"Where are we?" Elise sat up. The sweatshirt she'd been using as a pillow dropped to her lap. The sky was slipping toward sunset; she could see trees and hills passing outside the window.

"Somewhere in northwest Arkansas. I believe we are now in the Ozarks."

"Wow. I slept through Oklahoma?"

Tom turned to her, stretching his shoulders. "Want me to turn around?"

Elise smiled. "No, that's okay. I'll catch it on the way back." She stretched her arms and shoulders. "I think that's the deepest sleep I've had in months." She looked out the window. They were on a two-lane road, winding through heavily wooded hills. "When did we leave the interstate?"

"A while back. I got bored. Semitrucks and four lanes. Nothing very interesting. I like seeing the world from a two-lane. A slower speed. Being part of the surroundings, you know."

"Do these surroundings include a restaurant? I'm starving." Even as the words left her mouth, Elise marveled at what was happening. Sleeping soundly for several hours and feeling hungry were two things she hadn't experienced for a very long time.

"Well, let's see. Sign says, 'Oak Grove, three miles.' How does that sound?"

"We're eating acorns for dinner?"

Tom pulled his glasses down and looked at her over the top of the rim. "You must be feeling better. Sarcasm is a difficult maneuver for the clinically depressed."

The two-lane blacktop twisted and turned the three miles into Oak Grove, Arkansas, population 154, according to the sign. Three blocks long, about the same in width, and other than a service station on their right, there didn't appear to be much more than several houses and a white clapboard church. They pulled into the station, and Elise saw the sign for the Oak Grove Café attached to the north side of the building. The lights were out. She stepped out of the car, grateful to stretch her legs, and turned to look down the streets of town. FOR SALE signs stood in front of several of the homes, announcing what looked like the slow bleeding to death of the community of Oak Grove.

Tom filled the gas tank and started inside. The owner was pulling in his tire sign, preparing to close. "Is that the only place to eat?" Tom asked, indicating the dark café at the end of the building.

"'Fraid so. She's not very predictable in the winter. Unless you predict she'll be closed." He turned to look at Tom and Elise. "Where y'all headed?"

Tom and Elise looked at each other. "The Smokies," Elise answered.

"You need to get there tonight?"

Elise shook her head.

"'Cause if you ain't in no hurry, my great-aunt Venetta runs a little hotel operation out of her house up the road. Mostly summer folks, but she's a good cook, and she'll feed you if you pay to spend the night."

Tom waited for Elise to decide, as if he were the chauffeur in this operation, and her decisions were the ones that mattered.

"That'd be great," Elise answered.

They passed an old white clapboard church, surrounded by dried winter grass and enormous oaks. Three blocks farther, up a little hill that looked down on the town, they pulled up to a two-story white clapboard house. A front porch wrapped around two sides of the structure.

Beside the gate, a sign announced OAK GROVE BED AND BREAKFAST. It hung on two chains, twisting and turning and creaking in the wind. A huge oak tree stood sentinel at the left side of the yard; beyond it they could see the lights from inside spilling across the porch. For one brief flash of time, Elise had one of those déjà vu moments. She opened her car door and walked slowly toward the yard. Tom opened the gate, and they walked up a brick path. Dried brown leaves skittered and skipped across the walk, like children released from school.

They climbed the wood steps and crossed the porch, their footsteps echoing like they were the only living beings in a town full of ghosts. Before Tom could knock, the door swung inward. An older man stood there, holding the handle of the door, and they stepped inside. The man was at least six foot two and had to be somewhere in his seventies. His hair was silvery white, and he had a trim white mustache. His eyes twinkled with the deep blue of the dusky sky, set to glowing by the blue of his shirt. He was wearing a tie, at six o'clock on a Thursday evening.

"Evenin' to y'all. Come in, come in. Make yourselves to home. Ben called and told us you was comin'." Tom and Elise turned to look at the main entrance hall turned reception area for the hotel.

"Name's Henry Jamison," the man said, holding his hand out to Tom. "My wife, Venetta, is in the kitchen."

Tom shook his hand and then looked around a moment, as if he'd forgotten why they were here. He scanned the antiques and mica-shaded lamps, as if this place couldn't possibly offer accommodations. "I guess we need a room."

Elise shot him a look. "I guess we need two."

Henry Jamison's mustache twitched ever so slightly. He looked at Elise and then at Tom. "Well, we have six, so I believe we can handle this situation." He went behind the oak counter and handed each of them registration forms.

"Where y'all from?" he asked amiably, starting to fill out the paperwork the old-fashioned way—with pen and paper.

"New Mexico," Elise said. "The Taos area. I am, anyway. Tom's from Tucson."

Henry nodded and placed paperwork on top of the counter. "You've come a ways, then, haven't you?"

Elise nodded.

"Y'all aren't afraid of ghosts, are ya?"

Tom and Elise looked at each other and then back at Henry.

"I don't believe in ghosts," Tom said, pushing his glasses up.

Henry looked up at Tom, waiting for his credit card to go through, and then handed the card back to him. "I see," he murmured.

"You have a ghost?" Elise asked.

"Yes, ma'am. Nothing really scary," Henry said, taking the credit card Elise held out to him. "She doesn't ever try to hurt anyone. Nothing dreadful like what you see in the movie pictures."

Elise examined this man before them. She could read nothing in his facial expressions or his demeanor, other than perfect southern gentleman.

"But she does like to run up and down the hallway at night. Turn the doorknobs. Just make sure you have your door locked, you'll be fine." Henry put the receipt on the counter for Tom to sign.

"She can't walk through walls?" Tom's mouth lifted in a goofy smile. He pushed his glasses up on his nose, but his attempt at humor fell flat. He bent to sign the receipt and give it back to Henry Jamison.

Henry peered at Tom, and Elise thought she saw the tiniest flash of annoyance, as if Tom's words had ruffled his feathers. He hid it well, though, and murmured, "I suppose she could if she's a mind to."

He turned to Elise and handed her a credit-card slip. "And if you have any pink pretties, best leave 'em in the car. She does like pink." He winked at Elise.

Elise smiled. "No pink. Not my color."

"You should be all right then." Henry smiled at her, a smile that dropped from his face the second he turned to Tom. "And you, sir? Any pink in your belongings?"

Tom looked stunned for a moment, until he caught Elise's smile. He shook his head. "Uh, no. No pink."

"Okay, Mr., uh . . . Dugan," Henry said, looking at the receipt. "Room number four, second door to the right at the top of the stairs. And Miss . . . Brooks, you will be in number one, first door on the left. Doors are open. You can lock 'em up after you settle in for the evening."

Elise took a few steps to the left, studying a dining room surrounded on two sides by walls of windows. Stained-glass panels topped each of the windows, each one a different flower. Roses, lilacs, daffodils, mums adorned the top edge of the glass. A heavy lace tablecloth covered the wooden table. Elise felt as if she'd stepped backward in time, to an age and decor more appropriate one hundred years before, but she was charmed, by both the setting and by Mr. Jamison's barely perceptible smile.

"Supper's at six thirty. It's Thursday, so we'll be having pot roast with potatoes and carrots and turnips from the garden." Henry stopped and turned to look at Tom. "Y'all aren't vegetarians, are you?"

Elise shook her head.

"'Cause we can't really accommodate vegetarians in Arkansas."

"Pot roast sounds wonderful," Elise said. "I'm famished."

They sat at a round oak table in a dining room filled with antiques. A sideboard held the dishes of food that Venetta Jamison had just passed around the table: pot roast with root vegetables, roasted brussels sprouts, homemade rolls. They ate from china plates, edged in an elaborate rose pattern with gold trim. Crystal goblets held water and sweet tea. There were crocheted doilies on almost every surface, and candlelight flickered on the table and the sideboard. The room was bathed in warm, golden light.

Venetta Jamison, like her husband, was somewhere in her seventies, with white hair and blue eyes. Where he was tall and thin, she was short and round, but her smile was warm and friendly as she welcomed the two strangers to her table. "Glad to have you two this evening," she said, slipping into the chair Henry held out for her. "We don't get many visitors this time of year. Haven't had that many visitors period, the last few years, have we, Mr. Jamison?"

He shook his head. "Not so many people interested in these old houses anymore. Everybody seems to want cable television and free whiffy. I've seen it on some of the motel signs over in Fayetteville."

Elise smiled, wondering if he meant Wi-Fi. "This is a beautiful place. Have you lived here long?"

Venetta nodded her head and waited until she finished chewing. "My whole life, actually. My granddaddy built this house back in 1890. Thought he could rent out rooms to some of the folks that came down for the hot springs. I grew up here, with my parents and my grandma. He passed on before I was born."

Elise wasn't entirely comfortable with the question she really wanted to ask. She took a bite of her roast and chewed, trying to work up her courage to ask about the ghost.

"Did Mr. Jamison mention the ghost?" Venetta asked.

Elise breathed a small sigh of relief and nodded her head. "Yes, he did. Is it someone you know?"

"Mmm-hmm. My sister, Viola." Venetta rested her fork against the edge of plate. Her eyes clouded. "When we were eight years old, we got the scarlet fever. She was my twin, you know. We did everything together, absolutely everything. So I guess it was no surprise that we even took sick at the same time. This was before antibiotics, mind you."

Venetta's eyes flickered back to Elise. "We were sharing the same bed, me and Viola, both of us sick to beat the band, and Mama wanting to keep us together and keep the others away. Went to sleep one night, both of us burning up with fever. When I woke up the next morning, my fever was gone. I remember how strange it felt, not to be in that sick fever fog, you know? Almost like I was seeing the real world for the first time. And I sat up and turned to Viola, and she was lying beside me, with her back turned toward me. I put my hand on her arm to tell her I was better, and to see if she was feeling better, too. But as soon as I touched her, I jumped back like a scalded cat."

Venetta stopped for a moment and stared off into a corner of the room. "Her body was . . . cold, kind of stiff. It was the first time I'd ever touched a dead body. I wasn't sure what was wrong with her, but I knew it was very different from anything I'd ever touched before. A body in death is so much different than one that is living."

For a moment, no one moved.

"My mother was sitting in the rocking chair by the bed. She'd fallen asleep sitting up. Been taking care of us for several nights in a row. I don't know how she did it, really. And I said, 'Mama? Something's wrong with Viola.'"

"Of course, soon as she touched Viola, my mama started scream- ing." Venetta looked away a moment, sadness blooming on her face and evaporating into the air. "Blamed herself, you know. For falling asleep. Almost as if she thought she could stop death from coming if she'd just stayed awake."

All four at the table rested their forks and stayed silent a moment. Venetta stared at her plate, and then raised her eyes. "But that was a long time ago now. Been over sixty-five years since she passed."

"I'm sorry," Elise whispered. "That had to be tough. Your twin."

Venetta nodded, her eyes still lost on that distant morning. "You know, I've lost other friends and family since then. But I don't think I ever took any of 'em as hard as I did losing Viola." She lifted her eyes to Elise, as if Elise's own experiences with loss and grief were written all over her, plain enough for Venetta to read. "We were always together.

Always. Same class at school, slept in the same bed. I felt as if I'd lost part of my own body. Like a person who's had their leg cut off. Almost like trying to learn how to walk and talk and move all over again. My whole sense of balance—of reality—was off-kilter."

She gathered food on her fork, and the others did the same. "My mama was a wreck, of course. She was dealing with her own sadness—I don't think she even noticed what I was going through. Everyone was wrapped up in their own shade of sorrow, you know? There was a war on; my brother was somewhere in the Pacific. It was an awful lot for her to handle, too."

Thunder growled, and Venetta's eyes traveled to the window. Wind was blowing; storm clouds filled the horizon. Darkness seeped into the sky and through the windows, creeping up around the four people seated at the table. She sat, motionless, and her next words were whispered. "And then one night, right around dusk. Cloudy and dark and the wind blowing. A storm on the way." She looked toward the window. "Just like tonight. We could hear the thunder, see the flashes of lightning. Mama was getting ready to put dinner on the table, and she told me to run upstairs and check the windows.

"I'd already checked all the other rooms, and was finishing up in our bedroom—my bedroom. The room I used to share with Viola. I had gone to the window and pulled it closed. The room was pretty dark, from the storm, I guess. I felt cold air whoosh against my arm, and it made me shiver. The wind had been gusting in the window right before I closed it, so I didn't think much about that sensation. But as I turned around, I could see the mirror in the wardrobe across the room. The wardrobe door swung open, all slow and creakylike. There was just this tiny flash of movement in that mirror. Looked like Viola, turning away from me. She was wearing this dress with pink flowers on it. Her favorite. She loved pink."

A flash of lightning blazed in the room; thunder pounded right afterward.

"I whispered her name. 'Viola? Is that you?'"

The candle in the middle of the dining table sputtered, the flame dancing a tango in front of their eyes. They all hung on Venetta's words, arrested by the hush that had descended on the room. Outside, wind buffeted the house; tree branches creaked and swayed. Elise shivered, almost as if she could feel the fingers of the departed raking against the clapboard siding.

"There was nothing. No sound. No movement. No more cold air. I could hear my mama, calling out 'Suppertime.' So I walked across that room and came downstairs. I hurried fast past that wardrobe mirror, let me tell you. The hair on my arms was standing up like soldiers on parade."

Venetta shook her head and looked back down at her plate. "I was just a child, you know. Missing her. Hurting so much. There were so many times when I would just stop, in the middle of the room, or outside, or wherever it was. Just stop. And listen. Wait." Venetta glanced up at Elise's face, almost nervous. "I wanted so much to talk to her. To see her again."

Tears pooled in Elise's eyes, and she blinked. She felt connected to Venetta Jamison, a woman she'd only met less than an hour ago. There was an understanding between them, the consolation of knowing that someone else had been through the same pain and loss that she was going through. Someone who understood that need to be quiet and listen, that need to commune with the departed. Elise fought the trembling that crept up her body; she willed her legs not to shake.

Venetta stared at the candle flame; her shoulders slumped. "Well, sometime after that, I started experimenting. I'd find a place in the bedroom where I could sit and see that mirror, from an angle. Get a reflection of some other part of the room, but not able to see myself in it."

Tom cleared his throat. "I read about this." He glanced toward Elise. "Google. It's called scrying. Staring into a mirror, or a crystal ball. Any reflective surface. It's an idea that goes back thousands of years—even shows up in fairy tales. You know that whole 'Mirror, mirror on the wall' thing?"

All eyes had turned to Tom, but no one said anything, and he grew quiet again.

Venetta stared at the candle on the table and continued. "I really wanted her to be there. I wanted to see her. To hear her voice. To hear her laugh. I wanted to know what it was like, to be dead. I wanted to know if she could see us, if she could hear us. I wanted to know if she was . . . okay.

"Sometimes, I'd stare and stare in that mirror. The images would get all blurry, but I never actually saw her again, like that first time. Just these wavy images, warped and kind of smokylike. So one night, I said, 'Viola, if you're there, give me a sign.'"

Upstairs, a door slammed, and Tom and Elise jumped. All four people raised their eyes to the ceiling. Venetta smiled. "She's listening to us."

She waited a beat before continuing. "That night, when I first talked to her, nothing happened. Nothing at all. I stared for probably an hour, waiting. Listening." Venetta shook her head and took a deep breath. "But I heard this . . . I don't even know how to describe it. It wasn't a sound, not really. It was more like a thought, a thought that came from somewhere else. Faint. Faraway. I wasn't sure if I really heard it, or if I just imagined it. It sounded like Viola, giggling.

"And then, the very next day, my mama was looking all over for her pink apron. She'd hung it on the hook in the kitchen after supper the night before, like she always done. And the next morning, it wasn't there. She told me to help her look. We went all over the kitchen and the floor and the back porch. Nothing.

"And then I had this funny feeling come over me. Made me shiver. And I ran upstairs. When I got up there, the door to the wardrobe was open, and Mama's pink apron was inside." Venetta looked up at Elise, and her eyebrows went up.

"'Course, now, my mama thought I did it. She said if I pulled another stunt like that again, she'd go cut a switch." Venetta shook her head. "But that was just the beginning. All kinds of things would turn up missing. It was almost like once Viola got started, she was having too much fun to stop. And I can't even tell you how many times I was accused of taking something pink from my sister or my mama."

Tom sighed heavily, crossed his arms in front of his chest, and shook his head.

Venetta stared at him. "Whenever something pink went missing, we'd almost always find it in the back of my wardrobe. Only I swear by all that's holy, I never did take those things, or hide them there. Myself, I always preferred purple.

"For years, they all thought I was doing it. I think my mama thought it was my way of dealing with the grief. Like it was some kind of subconscious trick that I wasn't even aware I was doing."

Venetta looked up and met Tom's eyes. "She'd look at me, her eyes all sad, and shake her head." Tom had stiffened in his chair. A scowl of disbelief was lodged in his brows and forehead.

"But then I turned eighteen, and left home to go to school in Little Rock. Teacher's college. And one morning, my mama's pink apron went missing again. She'd used it the night before, just like that first time it happened. She looked everywhere, and then finally, she went upstairs to my old bedroom. She said the wardrobe door swung open as soon as she got up there. And the apron was inside."

Henry Jamison leaned forward in his chair. "And now you know why I said to leave your pink things out in the car."

"Which room was that? Where she died?" Elise asked.

Henry's mustache twitched. He rested his fork on his plate. "Number four. Second door to the right."

Tom's head pivoted toward Henry Jamison. "My room?" he asked, his brows pulling together.

Henry looked him in the eye. "You said you don't believe in ghosts."

Tom shook his head. His face flushed with color. "I don't. Absolutely not."

They were all silent a moment, lost in the story. Venetta broke the silence. "I'm afraid I've gone and spoiled our dinner—talking like that. I apologize."

"Please don't," Elise said. "I asked you about it. And dinner was wonderful."

Elise sat for a moment, trying to summon the courage to ask Venetta some of the questions that were pouring through her mind. She didn't even know where to start, and so she sat, staring at her hands, resting in her lap. "Venetta, I . . ."

"You're no stranger to death, are you, dear?" Venetta's question cut through Elise's mumbled words.

Elise shook her head.

"Your husband? Most recently, I mean?" Venetta's words were soft and kind.

"How did you know?" Elise gasped.

Venetta raised her hands to her side and shrugged.

"Yes. In March. A car accident."

"So it was sudden. You did not get to say good-bye?"

Elise looked up at Venetta, and it took all the force of will she possessed to keep from sobbing. She shook her head and dropped her eyes to her lap. "No. No, I didn't."

Venetta leaned back in her chair. "It's been my experience that that kind of loss, that kind of death—sudden, unexpected—is the hardest to deal with. My mama was sick for several months before she passed. It's still hard, but at least, on some level, anyway, you're preparing yourself for it. And if you need to say something, you have the chance to do that."

Venetta leaned forward, her face pulling close to Elise. "Would you like to speak to him, dear?"

All eyes pivoted to Venetta's face. Elise felt her face go slack, as if she were going to melt into the tablecloth. She nodded.

"I can't make any guarantees, of course. But if you like, I could give it a go."

Tom cleared his throat. "What . . . method . . . do you use? Scrying?"

Venetta raised her eyes to him and smiled. She exhaled. "That's how I started, of course. And as I got to be a teenager, I tried a few other things, too. A pendulum, with just yes-and-no questions. Automatic writing."

Elise glanced at Tom. From the look on his face, she could see he was taking mental notes, ready to add everything to the spreadsheet. Ready to dissect and analyze. "And what would you say is the most successful method?" he asked.

Venetta smiled. "Well, I believe anything can work, if a spirit really wants to talk to you. But I also know that anything can be faked, too. The spiritualist movement, the whole history of mediums and séances and talking to the dead, is fraught with fakery and deception. Wouldn't you agree, Mr. Dugan?"

Tom smiled and leaned back in his chair, as if, finally, someone was making sense. "Absolutely." He turned to look at Elise, his shoulders back, a certain swagger to his movements.

"So I don't use any of those methods. Not anymore." Venetta let that sentence sink in a moment. "It's been my experience that it doesn't really matter—the method one uses. What's important is to tune in. To go into this . . . trancelike state. Where I can . . ." Venetta stopped and shook her head, raised her shoulders in a question mark. "I don't know. Where I can tune out this world. And be receptive to the spirits."

Tom glanced at Elise and then turned his powers of inspection back to Venetta. "So . . . do you see them? The spirits? Do you hear them?"

Venetta raised her head and stared off into a corner just over Tom's shoulder. "It's not like that on the other side, Mr. Dugan. I don't believe they are limited to just five senses. Truthfully, I think the living have more than that, too. It's just that most people never use them."

Tom's body was beginning to radiate his skepticism. It filled the air around him, like the smoke from a cigar. Elise coughed. She wanted to kick him.

Venetta brought her gaze back to Tom. "I don't *hear* voices, with my ears. I don't *see* spirits, with my eyes or my mind. But I can sense their presence. Absorb their thoughts. Instantaneously. They communicate on a level that is so far beyond anything we have here, on the physical plane of the living. So much faster. I don't believe they even need words, Mr. Dugan. The feelings . . . the ideas . . . just vibrate through me. Like . . . I don't know. It's almost like tuning in to a certain radio frequency. But instead of sound waves, it's . . . energy. The vibration of energy."

Henry cleared his throat. He glanced at Venetta, and with the surety that comes from almost sixty years of marriage, he said, "Why don't you ladies go on across to the parlor? I'll clean up these dishes and make some coffee and bring dessert. How does that sound?"

Elise nodded. "Sounds wonderful."

Henry stood and started to gather dishes. "Mr. Dugan, would you mind helping me with the transport of these utensils to the kitchen?"

Tom's gaze went from Elise to Venetta to Henry Jamison, as if unsure what was expected of him. As if by sheer force of will, he could have someone invite him to stay and observe. Elise willed him to go. She wanted very much to be alone with Venetta. And at this moment, she could have kissed Henry Jamison for offering that opportunity.

"Uh, sure." Tom stood. He reached for a few dishes and gave Elise a pointed stare.

Venetta smiled, and she and Elise pushed in their chairs and headed across the hall to the parlor. Venetta leaned in close and whispered, "My Henry understands. He will keep Mr. Dugan occupied for a bit. That skepticism is"—her shoulders trembled—"difficult to deal with. For us, and for the spirits."

Elise smiled back. The woman and her husband were incredibly intuitive. A chance to speak to her alone, without Tom and his incessant need to analyze and explain and deconstruct, was exactly what Elise wanted.

They moved across the hall to the formal parlor. It was another beautifully crafted room, with wainscoting and flocked gold wallpaper. Antiques filled almost every space. The parlor, like the dining room, was filled with golden light. Two caramel-colored sofas faced each other, and two wing chairs flanked the fireplace. An elaborate mantel of oak surrounded the fire. Venetta knelt in front of it, adding more wood to the blaze. Across from the fireplace, on the other side of the room, was a bay window. Velvet curtains framed all of the bays, and there was a round table covered in a beautiful damask tablecloth in the center of the space.

Elise turned, taking it all in. She stepped to one wall, to the left of the fireplace, and examined a collection of framed photographs that hung there. "Is this you? You and your sister, I mean?" A black-and-white photograph showed a family, mother and father, older sister, brother in uniform, and the two girls, sitting on low stools in front of the others. They looked young, maybe six or seven years old.

Venetta stepped close to her and peered down the end of her nose. "It's hard to tell the difference, isn't it? People always had us confused. Which could be kind of fun, sometimes." Venetta turned and looked at Elise, a twinkle in her eye. "We enjoyed tricking people, just to see them get flustered. It was one of our favorite activities at school." She turned back to the photograph and sighed heavily. "There at the last, when my mama was passing, she kept calling me Viola, even though by that time I was fifty years older than Viola had been when she died. Even so, my mama was convinced that she was talking to Viola."

They stood companionably together, staring at the photographs on the wall. "'Course, now, I hear tell that folks who are passing see spirits of loved ones on the other side. So maybe she really was seeing Viola."

Venetta cocked her head to one side and stared at the photograph. "It's a sin, you know. To try to talk to the spirits. At least, that's what the church says. That's what my mama would have said."

Elise didn't know that. She had never been much of a churchgoer. A few times with Beulah, when she was young. But she had never found solace there, had never found anything that helped her to cope with all the death and loneliness in her young life. Her church had been the trees; her sanctuary was sitting outside, listening to the sounds of the birds. Her comfort had been Lorena and Lorena's family.

Venetta continued. "My mama would've tanned my hide if she'd ever found out." She turned to Elise and raised her eyebrows. "I suspect she knows all about it by now.

"Still, though, I've always been just a touch afraid, whenever I open myself to the spirits. Afraid my mama is gonna make me go cut a switch.

"One summer, when I was thirteen, I had a cousin staying with us for a few weeks. And the two of us decided we were gonna try and communicate with Viola. This cousin had seen a friend of hers, in Fayetteville, who used a Ouija board. But it scared the living daylights out of her, and tell you the truth, I was a little scared o' that myself. You hear stories, you know? Of all kinds of bad things with those boards. That you can't control what kind of spirits might come through.

"I wanted to be certain that we were talking to Viola—not inviting some stranger into the house." Venetta stood and walked over to the photograph on the wall. She crossed her arms in front of her chest and stood, looking at the family in the photograph. Looking at herself and her sister, sitting on the floor in front of the others.

"We waited till after my mama and daddy had gone to bed. And then we sat up in my bedroom—the room I had shared with Viola. We lit a candle, and I asked Viola if she had anything she wanted to say. I made sure I said her name. Didn't want to take any chances. I stared at the candle until my vision got all blurry. I kind of lost track of time. Maybe I was really sleepy—I don't know. But next thing I know, my cousin has her hands over her mouth, and her eyes all wide, and she's saying, 'Goodness gracious, Venetta.'"

"I honestly don't remember any of it. Probably Mr. Dugan would not believe that, but I didn't. Didn't remember a thing. But Rebecca, she said that I stared at that candle. And that I started swaying, and these words came out of my mouth: 'I'm playing with my brother, Mason.'

"The two of us was scared spitless, let me tell you. We blew out the candle and went to bed, shivering and scared. And we whispered half the night. Who was Mason? I had one brother, John, older than we were, and he was in the war. It didn't make any sense, and I knew if my mama found out what we'd done, she'd tan my hide but good.

"I was in some kind of trance when it happened. So some might say that I did it myself. My subconscious talking. Getting creative."

"That's what Tom would say," Elise muttered.

Venetta nodded. "But the thing is, we neither one of us had any idea who Mason was. We decided to go to the cemetery, down there by the church, and see if we could find anyone by that name. Nothing. We went through every tombstone. No Mason. But several weeks later, after Rebecca had gone back to Fayetteville, I was sitting on the front porch with Mama, shelling peas. And I worked up all my courage, and I asked her, 'Who's Mason?'

"She got this look on her face. Went all white. Hand came up to her mouth, and she stopped breathing. I was worried she was about to keel over. And she said, 'Who told you? Who told you about Mason?'

"Well, I wasn't sure what to say. I knew I was in it, deep, no matter what I came up with. So I just whispered the truth—'Viola. Viola told me she's playing with Mason.'

"My mama started crying. Sat there in her rocking chair, tears just streaming down her face. Had to lift her apron to wipe away all that water. And I just sat there, dumbfounded. Still wondering what the heck was going on.

"Finally, she stops and blows her nose and leans back in her chair. And she tells me that there was a little boy, before us girls was born. He died when he was two. Scarlet fever." Venetta raised her eyes to Elise.

"His name was Mason. And when they buried him, they only had one thing carved on the tombstone: 'Our little angel. Gone too soon.'"

The two women sat quietly, sharing the secrets of the night. Venetta broke the silence. "I don't know how to explain what happened that night. But I know what I believe." She turned, and their eyes locked. "I believe it was Viola, telling me that.

"You know the funny thing? I was so afraid my mama would be fit to be tied. But she wasn't. It was almost like hearing that . . . knowing that Viola and Mason were playing together . . . on the other side. Well, I believe it gave her comfort. She seemed to start doing a little better after that."

Elise exhaled. She felt enormously comfortable in this woman's presence.

"Let's sit, shall we?" Venetta indicated the small round table in the middle of the bay window. They slipped into chairs next to each other. Venetta leaned forward and lit a pillar candle in the middle of the table.

"That's why I do this, you know. Contacting the spirits. Because I saw how much comfort it can bring. My mama got better after I told her about Mason. And I feel like other people have found comfort, too." She turned to Elise. "You're not the first, honey. To show up at my door. Some folks come because they'd heard about what I did with Viola. But through the years, there've been other folks. Like you. That just show up out of the clear blue sky, not even knowing anything about this place.

"I had a feeling about you. Soon as Ben called and said two folks was coming up. I knew." Venetta turned and met Elise's gaze.

They stared at each other. The fire popped. The clock ticked. "I can try, if you want me to," the older woman murmured. "I don't make promises, though. Sometimes I don't get much."

Elise nodded. "I understand." She glanced at the window behind Venetta's shoulders. Dusk had fallen; the sky was the deep turquoise blue of a winter evening. The blue hour. She shivered, remembered standing outside with Beulah. Waiting. Listening. Trying to commune with the woman who'd left them both behind.

"What's your husband's name?"

"Michael. Michael Madrid." Elise looked down at her hands in her lap. They trembled, as if she'd had too much coffee. Her throat was dry.

"We want to make sure to talk to him." Venetta took one long, slow breath. "Michael Madrid?" she whispered. "Do you have something you want to say? A message for your wife?"

Time unfurled slowly, as if everything had turned to a slower speed, the way Elise used to do with her first record albums when she was a child, changing Elvis Presley's "Hound Dog" to something deep and bass and stretched out long and low. And then she felt it, a vibration, a trembling. She could sense it, through the wood of the chair she was sitting on, through the boards of the floor. Venetta's body began to vibrate with energy. The tremor carried through the wood of the table, traveled up Elise's arms, and made the hair on the back of her neck rise.

"He says, 'Stop.' Stop beating on yourself. It was his time to go. You are not to blame."

Tears spilled over edges of her eyes. Her body shook, an earthquake of sorrow rumbling through every fiber of her being. She knew he was close by—so close. And she wanted so much to touch him. To speak to him. To feel him. Elise sniffed, trying to pull her emotions into some kind of control. But she could not. She could not stop the tremors and tears. Her body vibrated.

"You must pick up the pieces. Keep going. Keep going. You will find the way." Venetta's eyes were closed; her body swayed a little. "Across the water. Where the blue notes play. With the dead, she waits."

A gust of air blew across the table; the flame of the candle leaned over sideways. A window behind Venetta blew open, and the flame went out completely. Elise gasped. Cold air blasted in, and Elise jumped up to latch the window. She shivered and ran her hands up and down her arms. She forced herself to breathe. Breathe.

Lightning flashed. The walls of the room lit up with an eerie white glow and then flickered back to darkness. The crash of thunder sounded, and Venetta jumped slightly. "Oh, my! That sounds close, doesn't it?" she asked.

Henry cleared his throat, and they turned to see Tom and Henry standing in the doorway. Henry carried a tray with coconut cream pie arranged on plates, cups and saucers stacked neatly beside. Tom carried a pot of coffee. He scrutinized the two women sitting at the table.

Venetta blinked and looked at Elise. "Well. Shall we have dessert, then, dear?"

Henry passed out the dessert plates, and Venetta took the coffeepot from Tom and started pouring. The two men settled in the chairs by the fire, and Tom took a big bite of pie.

Elise waited, not wanting to return to normal, not wanting to leave that quiet space where Michael had been so close, his words coming through Venetta's vocal cords. She glanced out the window again, searching the darkness.

"You ladies have a nice chat?" Henry asked, a forkful of pie following his question.

"Oh, yes." Venetta smiled. "Just lovely."

*Across the water. Blue notes play. With the dead, she waits.* Elise played the words over and over in her mind.

"Did it make any sense, dear?" Venetta whispered.

Elise lowered her coffee cup and turned to face her hostess. She shook her head. "No. No, it didn't."

# CHAPTER SIXTEEN

"Tom? Are you almost ready?" Elise stood outside Tom's room, knocking softly. He unlocked the door and swung it open, his face a study in irritation. He turned away from her and went down on his knees on the floor, searching under the bed.

"What's wrong? You lose something?"

Tom let out a breath. "Yeah. No. I left my T-shirt and pajamas on the bed while I took a shower, and when I got out . . ."

Elise raised her eyebrows in a question.

"I can't find my T-shirt. It was right there, and now . . ." Tom held up a pair of pajama pants and turned and started sifting through the blankets on the bed, tearing the sheets and blankets out of place.

"Was it pink?"

He turned and met her look, closing his lips in a firm, taut line. "Very funny. No. It was not pink." He got down on his knees again and looked under the bed. "It was kind of a salmon color. I got it in Moab. The color of the canyons."

Elise pressed her lips together, trying hard not to smile. "Maybe a little girl doesn't know the difference between pink and salmon."

Tom sat back on his heels and groaned. "So you're saying the ghost took it?"

Elise shrugged. "Have you checked the wardrobe?"

Tom pushed his glasses up on the bridge of his nose and pressed himself up off the floor. An exasperated sigh rushed into the air. "That is just exactly how these wild paranormal stories proliferate, Elise. Someone makes a suggestion about ghosts and pink things disappearing, and all of a sudden you have people believing . . ." He stopped talking. He stood in front of the wardrobe, holding the door open. A salmon-colored T-shirt lay crumpled in the back corner.

Elise glanced at the pile of color. "Is that it?"

Tom looked at Elise. "And just where have *you* been the past twenty minutes? Because this is most decidedly *not* funny."

"You think I did this?" Elise asked. "Henry, Venetta, and I have been downstairs drinking coffee since approximately seven thirty a.m., until just a few moments ago, when I knocked on your door. Which, I would like to remind you, was locked when I got here."

Tom grabbed his T-shirt from the bottom of the wardrobe and turned to put it in his duffel bag.

Elise leaned against the door frame and watched him. His cheeks were flushed with color; his jaw was clenched and stiff.

"So. How's that spreadsheet coming? Think you have enough columns?"

Tom strode past her into the hall and down the steps. She watched him from the window on the stairs as he banged his way out to the Jeep, barely bothering to say good-bye to the Jamisons.

Elise took her time making her own exit. She stopped at the bottom of the stairs and shook the hand Henry Jamison held out to her. "Mr. Jamison, it's been a pleasure." She smiled.

"Y'all come back anytime," he drawled.

She turned to Venetta, and the two women hugged like old friends. "Thank you, Venetta," she whispered.

She turned and headed down the steps to the Jeep.

"So? Where we headed next? Nashville? New Orleans to visit a voodoo queen? Did your husband leave instructions? A map, maybe?" Tom asked, his voice clipped.

Elise looked out her side window. She took a deep breath and turned back to him. "Can we make a stop in Memphis?"

Tom sighed and rubbed his hand on his temple. "You feel the need to commune with the ghost of Elvis?"

Elise pressed her lips together, trying to control the urge to smile. "Don't be ridiculous. Elvis isn't dead."

Tom snorted. "Fine. Whatever. I'll just be the chauffeur. Any craziness you want to get into? Let me know. I'll drive you. Happy to oblige, Miss Daisy."

Elise turned her smile to the passenger window and let him vent.

"Is there any particular reason we need to stop in Memphis? Is that orders from your husband?"

Elise stared at the Jamisons' house as Tom pulled away. "Not exactly. And Michael was never the type to give orders, by the way. Despite my quiet nature, I can be somewhat disobedient."

"So I've noticed," Tom grumped. "What did she do? That Venetta person. A séance? Scrying? Automatic writing? How does she do it?" He glanced from the road to Elise and back again. "God, I wish I could have watched."

"Did it ever occur to you, Tom, that your skepticism is as thick as smoke around you? And that maybe not everyone can tolerate it as well as I have?"

Tom pushed his glasses up on his nose. "How can we even begin to bring rational explanation to this situation if you won't even let me observe?"

"I'm not looking for rational explanations."

He shook his head and clicked his tongue against his teeth. "I can't believe you let her do that without me there to monitor. Ahh."

He continued to shake his head back and forth, a scowl clouding his features.

"All I want to know is what Michael is trying to tell me. I told you already, I'm not interested in being the bug under your rational microscope."

Tom stared straight ahead. "Elise," he sighed, as if trying to deal with an unruly teenager, "this kind of thing is just too easy to fake. I've watched YouTube videos about this. There are all kinds of so-called mediums out there. Total craziness. You have to let someone make rational observations here—make sure you're not being hoodwinked."

"YouTube? Your research methods are far-ranging, Tom." She paused. "And just how am I being hoodwinked?"

He continued to shake his head, as if he hadn't heard her. "How am I supposed to know? You wouldn't let me stay and listen." He exhaled and breathed through his mouth for a moment. "So what did she say? I mean, he. What did *he* say?"

"'Across the water. Blue notes play. With the dead, she waits.'" Elise unreeled the words slowly, letting them unfurl in the air between them.

"What the hell does that mean?"

Elise shrugged. "I have no idea. But I thought about it all night, and Memphis makes some sense, don't you think?" Elise paused. "Across the water—being, in this case, the Mississippi River. Blue notes could refer to blues music."

"Maybe." Tom turned and looked out the side window. He had reached the two-lane highway they had left the night before and was now turning onto it. "Although 'blue note' is also a jazz reference. There's a Blue Note club in New York, and a Blue Note Records in New Orleans. So if it's 'blue note' you're trying to unravel, we may have to go farther south."

"What are you, a walking fountain of Wikipedia?"

Tom grimaced. "God, no. Some of it is useful, certainly, but you have to be careful. That stuff isn't always referenced, you know. I'll google 'blue notes' later, see what I can find."

"Don't forget to check YouTube."

"And what is that 'She's waiting' thing? Who is waiting?" He glanced over at her again.

Elise shrugged. "I told you, I don't know. This is just a guess. But I figure, we have to go in that direction, anyway. Maybe we could just . . . I don't know . . . stop somewhere. See if anything feels right."

Tom nodded his head. "See if anything *feels* right." He inhaled sharply. "Yeah. Sure. Why not?"

They drove in silence for a few moments. "Well, as long as we're being free and easy with interpretation here, there's something I need to say." He glanced at Elise, head down, so that his eyes met hers over the tops of his glasses. "I don't want to scare you or anything, but there is another way to interpret that 'Across the river' thing."

Elise waited.

"The River Styx. The river of death. From Greek mythology? It's the boundary between this world and the underworld. Hades. Hell. So if you want to consider all the possibilities in that prediction, 'Across the water? With the dead, she waits'? It might not be the Mississippi River that you need to cross."

Like the heavy clouds hanging over the Mississippi River, memories had descended, heavy on her mind. Elise grew more and more despondent the farther east they drove. By the time they reached Memphis, in the early afternoon, she had grown quiet and solemn, as if the storm building on the horizon was building in her psyche, as well. She couldn't help thinking that they were now into November. The holidays would be here in a few weeks—Thanksgiving and Christmas and all the longing for family they always evoked. This would be her first holiday season without Michael in more than twenty-five years. Back in New Mexico, Monica and her family would spend Christmas at the Pueblo, for the Deer Dance. Afterward, they would all go to Uncle Wes's house, where there would be a fire in the fireplace and tons of food: enchiladas and tamales, potatoes and green chili, tortillas, pumpkin empanadas. Elise loved it there, loved the warmth and teasing and laughter, loved the sense of plenty that surrounded that family, despite the fact that the home Uncle Wes lived in, like all the homes in the Taos Pueblo, had no running water or electricity.

When Elise had first started spending Christmas with the Madrids, at the Pueblo, she had found it such a welcome contrast to the years of spending Christmas with Beulah when she was growing up. Laughter and Beulah just never seemed to find themselves in the same location, and Christmas had always been a subdued and quiet affair. Elise could still remember being seven years old, her mother recently buried in the cemetery next to the church on the edge of Amalia. Beulah had cooked a small turkey for the two of them, had managed, somehow, to come up with a dinner. They sat at that wooden table in the kitchen, both of them staring at their plates and trying not to look at the empty chair between them. Neither one of them had eaten more than a few bites. It was the heaviest silence Elise had ever experienced; she felt as if her shoulders bore the weight of a massive animal. All she wanted to do was cry, but when the tears did spill over the edge of her eyes, she swiped at them quickly, afraid of Beulah's reaction. There was no room in Beulah's small house for emotion.

Elise stared out the passenger window of the Jeep. "Do you miss her? Your wife, I mean? It will be Christmas soon, and you were together last year. Weren't you? Do you think about her?"

Tom shifted in his seat. He pushed his glasses up and glanced at Elise nervously. "This is going to sound awful. But no. Not really."

She turned to look at him.

"The truth is . . . I'm not quite sure how we ended up together in the first place. I mean . . . I grew up with two sisters. My mom raised us after my dad died. I was ten when that happened. So I should be comfortable around women, right? But it seems to be an entirely different animal when they are not related."

Elise had experienced that same sense of discomfort, especially when it came to men. And if it hadn't been for Monica and her brothers, her mom and dad taking her in and making her part of the family, she wasn't sure how she could have navigated the intricacies of any relationship. She turned to Tom, and for the first time since meeting him, she felt a tinge of sympathy.

"I spent so much of my time hunched over circuit boards or spreadsheets or trying to imagine my way through the process of whatever I was trying to create. And I just kind of ignored the whole relationship thing. Just didn't seem nearly as interesting as my work.

"My business partner, Wayne, he was the guy who went out and did all the schmoozing—connecting with people and finding financing and buyers and ways to pay our salaries. It was a great setup, really. I stayed in my little cubby, inventing new solar gadgets, or figuring out ways to make things work better. He spent his time at the country club, playing golf and talking to the big guys. He was good at that. I wasn't."

"I felt the same way about my weaving," Elise murmured. "I love the actual creating part. But I hate the whole marketing and sales and trying to find your audience. Michael was a whole lot better at that than I have ever been. I never was comfortable trying to promote my own work. It just feels so . . . I don't know. Pushy?"

Tom nodded. "Exactly. Wayne loved it, though. He got married right about the time we first started—just after college. Nancy. Really nice person." Tom raised his eyebrows and got quiet for a minute, as if lost in his old world. "Anyway, they were always trying to set me up. Wayne kept saying that I needed to get married—that it would be better for business. Nancy said I made it awkward at all the dinner parties.

They always had to find a lone female to pair me up with, so the other people wouldn't feel uncomfortable. Apparently having one single in the crowd makes all the married people jittery. I cannot tell you the number of dinner parties they had. The number of females they picked out for me."

Elise tried to imagine what that would feel like. She was truly comfortable with so few people in her life, and most of them had been around since she was small. She would hate it—the idea of trying to make conversation with strangers, the idea that her friends were trying to "fix" her. "Sounds dreadful."

Tom made a face and shook his head. "It was. And it never worked. I'd start talking about my work, and before I knew what was happening, the woman was looking at her watch or staring across the room. One time, a woman excused herself for the ladies' room and never came back." Tom grimaced.

Elise smiled. "Maybe she was sick."

"Yeah. Right." Tom took a deep breath. "And then one night, there's Alana, sitting at Wayne and Nancy's table. Really beautiful woman. All makeup and hair and glamour. As soon as I saw her, I thought sure she'd be running out the door as soon as dinner was over. But no—she hung on my every word. Stared at me with these big made-up eyes, false eyelashes batting up and down and all over the place. Put her manicured hand with all those lovely fingernails right on my arm. Stood really close to me, perfume so strong I could barely breathe."

He turned to Elise for a moment. "I think that's what happened, actually. My brain went all fuzzy and nonsensical. Probably from all the chemical off-gassing."

Elise pressed her lips together to stifle a smile. Immediately, she thought of Ken Black and his wife, Elaine. So made-up, so false. But no matter how much she disliked the whole idea of makeup and dye jobs, she had always felt slightly "less than" in Elaine's presence. As if

Elise, just plain Elise, would never be good enough. As if all that dress-up and makeup and tanning-booth skin were necessary for acceptance.

"We married four months later. I was so awestruck in her presence. I just couldn't believe I was that lucky—that someone like that could actually be interested in me." Tom tapped his fingers on the steering wheel. "I guess it's true, what they say. If it seems too good to be true, it probably is. My mom didn't like her, although she was much too kind to ever say so. My sisters thought I was making a big mistake—said she was nothing like me—that we had nothing in common."

It struck Elise, all over again, just how lucky she had been in her match with Michael. They were so much alike, so similar in so many ways. The ache of missing him seeped into her bones.

"But I ignored all the warnings. It sure *looked* like she was interested in everything I had to say. I guess I never realized until later that *she* didn't have anything interesting to say. That she wasn't interested in anything but tanning booths and hair color and designer jeans and Gucci bags. I found out later . . . much later . . . that she had been a cocktail waitress at the country club where Wayne hobnobbed with the rich and powerful." Tom kept his eyes straight ahead.

"And here I come, so absorbed in my own little world that I never noticed what she was after. I was the meal ticket. A house and car and the money for all the chemicals and treatments and designers that she craved. Even now, I'm just stupefied by the way I was sucked in. Me, the science whiz. Mr. Observational Analysis extraordinaire. And I never saw it coming."

Elise exhaled. "Wow. I don't know what to say. How long were you married?"

"Four years. Four years of very little in the way of conversation. Four years of sharing a house, and a bed, but pretty much nothing else. Unless, of course, she wanted something. Then she was friendly.

"When everything hit the fan, the person I felt the worst for was my partner's wife, Nancy. She'd been in love with Wayne since high school. They have two children. Married eighteen years. She sure didn't deserve all this."

Tom shook his head and was quiet for a long moment. "I guess what really gets me is that I'm a scientist. I pride myself on my ability to observe and measure and calculate. All the signs were there, as they say. All the red flags. But I chose to ignore them. Chose to believe that there had to be some other reason why she and Wayne were both late to dinner. Why they showed up just a few minutes apart, and why that had happened over and over and over. I ignored all the evidence in favor of what I wanted to believe. Guess I should stick to mathematical equations and circuit boards and let someone else figure out females."

It was raining by the time they reached Memphis. Dark clouds had settled down on the city, and thunder rumbled overhead. They parked near Church Park, and Tom turned off the engine. Rain pounded on the vehicle and windshield. "This isn't exactly sightseeing weather."

"We're not here for sightseeing." Elise got out of the car and zipped her jacket. She pulled her hood up against the rain.

Tom pocketed the keys and pulled his own jacket close. "Yeah. Remind me again, why are we here? Because I'm not sure I really get it."

She looked at him.

Tom raised his eyebrows. "Oh, yeah, I remember. You have a *feeling*."

They ran toward Beale Street, toward the traffic and noise. Music pulsed from every conceivable space, a raucous blend of several different blues bands on the drops of moisture. The noise of car traffic, mixed with the tangle of horns and drums and bass, pounded in Elise's head. The pavement was wet; the bright colors of all the neon signs reflected in the water. After the quiet she had lived in for the past twenty-five years, it was a blast of sensory overload.

"Blues City Café." Tom stopped walking, and started pressing buttons on his phone. "Google and Yelp say it's the best barbecue in the South. Do you have a *feeling* about eating?"

Elise smiled. "If Google approves, I think we should."

They were ushered to a red-vinyl booth in the café. Tom ordered pulled pork, coleslaw, and baked beans. When the waitress turned, Elise looked up blankly. She hadn't really noticed anything written inside that menu, still lost in the strange feeling that had overtaken her on the street a few moments earlier. "The same," she muttered.

"Look at all the famous people who have eaten here." Tom stared at the trivia he was reading. "Bill Clinton, Jesse Jackson, Garrison Keillor." He waited a heartbeat, his eyes still glued on the flyer. "Tom Cruise. Jerry Seinfeld? Wow. We're in prestigious company. Comedians and politicians and actors. Funny, though. I don't see one scientist in the bunch." He lowered the flyer and pushed his glasses up. "Why is it that scientists don't get that kind of attention and fame?"

She shook her head and pressed her lips together. "I can't imagine."

"Don't take this the wrong way, but some people, even nonscientists, say, maybe Jerry Seinfeld or Bill Clinton, would think that what you're doing . . ." Tom met her eyes. "Well, that maybe it's just a little bit crazy. Running across country, listening to these . . . intuitives or psychics or mediums or whatever they are, to guide you."

Elise shook her head. "There are times, Tom Dugan, when you sound just like Monica."

He paused for one fraction of a second. "Rational?"

"*Rational* is not the word I would use to describe Monica," Elise murmured.

Tom raised his eyebrows. "Oh? How would you describe her?"

"She doesn't like this whole psychic reader business. Says they can't be trusted."

Tom nodded. "Sounds rational to me."

"Tom, her mother is a traditional herbal healer. Her uncle is a medicine man. She's very comfortable with the idea of spirits and . . . all that kind of thing."

Tom's eyebrows went up.

"But she doesn't trust all these card readers and mediums and psychics. Thinks they're in it for the money. There are many people that Monica doesn't trust." Elise leveled her gaze at him. "Including you."

Tom looked stunned. He opened his mouth to say something but changed his mind, and shook his head. "She doesn't trust me?"

"She doesn't trust anyone that hasn't proven themselves."

His mouth hung open slightly, as if her words were impossible to absorb.

Elise dropped her eyes to her plate. "I can't explain this. Not really. It isn't so much what Celestina said, or what Venetta said last night. Partly, yes. I am listening to what they said. But it's more than that. And I know you're sick of hearing this, and you think it doesn't have any relevance at all, but . . . I need to do this. Like there's something that I need to know. Something that Michael wants me to know."

Tom sighed heavily and shook his head. "Sometimes I think we speak two different languages."

"Despite what you may think, I am not the first person in history to act on intuition. It happens a lot more often than you might think. There are all kinds of interesting stories out there. Harriet Tubman, for instance."

"The slave who escaped to the North?"

"Exactly. She made . . . I don't know how many trips back into the South to help other slaves escape. To guide them out. She knew where all the Underground Railroad stops were. She knew how to travel to stay off the roads. Traveling at night, all kinds of tricks. But you know what really struck me about her? From her story? Apparently Tubman believed it was her gut feeling that kept her from getting caught. Her intuitive skills were highly developed. She'd get this feeling about something and make everybody hide. And she said it saved them, that feeling. Many times."

Tom shook his head and pushed his glasses up. "It sure looks like you are a hopeless case."

"Soldiers say the same thing. Stories about having a feeling. And if they listened, if they followed it, they survived. Kept them out of danger. Even stories from the World Trade Center. People who were supposed to go downtown and didn't."

Elise sat back in her seat. "Let's just pretend, for a moment, that thought has energy. Hasn't science done some looking into that idea?"

Tom nodded. "I haven't looked into it, but yes, I think there have been some experiments."

"So what if Harriet Tubman was so . . . sensitive . . . that she could pick up on the energy of thoughts. Maybe the thoughts of someone out there who might be out looking for runaway slaves. What if some of those people who didn't die in the Twin Towers had picked up on some vibration . . . some level of energy, maybe as faint as the thoughts of those pilots . . . that kept them from going down there that day? Those people may not have had any idea *what* it was they were picking up on, or why they felt uncomfortable. They just knew that *something* was keeping them from going."

"Quantum mechanics." Tom sat back in his seat. "Not a lot of solid data at this point in time, I think."

"Have you ever walked into a room where two people have just had an argument?"

Tom shoved in a forkful of food and shook his head. "Maybe. Probably. I don't know."

"There's an energy in the room. Even if they stop fighting, even if they're trying to be polite because someone else just showed up. You can *feel* it. The energy of anger."

"I'm not following this, Elise. What does that have to do with your journey right now?"

"I can feel this . . . energy. Pulling me. Something Michael wants me to know. Maybe it has something to do with that stone carver in Olalla. Maybe there's something here, in Memphis. Maybe there's a whole sequence of things. I really don't have any idea what this is about. I just know I need to do it."

Elise leaned back in the booth and ran her hands up and down her arms. "I've been around Michael and Monica and Lorena much too long to ignore this. I've seen what they can do—the kinds of things they just . . . sense. I never could do it myself, not really. Not until the dream, my dream of the car accident." Elise let her eyes roam the café. "I never told anyone else about it. I never asked anyone for help. I thought I knew what it meant." Elise raised her eyes to the doorway across the room. "And I got it wrong."

Tom sat still for a moment, watching her.

"I don't want to make the same mistake twice. This time, I'm open to the idea of help. If I run into someone, someone who can tune in to that sixth sense . . . that psychic wisdom . . . that energy of thought . . . I'm going to ask. Maybe they will be able to see something that I overlooked. Maybe they can add to the picture. Make it more clear. I want to get it right this time."

Tom leaned back against the booth, his plate all but licked clean. "I think Google might be right. This is some damn good barbecue, although technically we would have to try barbecue everywhere in the South before I could say that it was the *best*."

Elise turned her head to look out the window on her right. Outside, the rain continued, a steady dripping on the pavement and buildings. She had no idea why she was here, why she had made Tom leave the freeway and come down to Beale Street. Generally speaking, she had a thick dislike of cities and noise and frenetic energy, and she felt no desire to go listen to blues. Her life had enough blues in it. But she wasn't going to figure anything out by sitting here in this booth. She heaved a sigh. "Are you ready?"

"Aren't you going to eat that?" Tom pointed at the half sandwich still on Elise's plate.

When Elise shook her head, Tom gathered up her sandwich and wrapped it in a napkin. "No sense letting it go to waste."

They headed out into the rain again, and Elise walked slowly, trying to figure out why she was here, trying to make the pieces of the puzzle fit, somehow. She stopped and scanned the buildings on each side of the street and then began a slow amble down Beale Street. Music poured out of the doorways. People jostled past, laughing. Neon lights flashed on the wet pavement, creating a rainbow path at their feet.

"So tell me again, what are we looking for? Because I've already forgotten."

"Can we just walk a little?"

"In this?" Tom scrunched his nose and peered at the rain from under his hood. He huddled inside his jacket, shaking with cold. His glasses were fogged.

"Are you melting?"

"I'm from Tucson. This is more rain than we see in a year."

Elise kept walking, an unhurried stroll down Beale Street, despite the rain and the fact that her shoes and pant legs were getting soaked. Tom walked beside her, his phone tucked inside his sleeve, and he stopped often to read things off the Internet.

"Says here the Orpheum Theater is supposedly haunted. A little girl, killed on the street out in front, who turns up at a lot of the performances. She's been seen wearing a white dress. Want to go see what she has to say? *Feel the energy?*" He raised his eyebrows, and they disappeared under the hood of his jacket.

Elise glared at him.

"I guess that's a no."

He continued to shuffle along beside her, paying far more attention to his phone than he was to the surroundings. "Did you know, Elise, that the first recording of a blues song was in 1902? It's a relatively new genre of music, something that started after the Civil War and Reconstruction. Very southern. Very much a cultural phenomenon."

Elise kept walking, trying to keep her head up in the rain. She had pulled up the hood on her jacket, but water dripped from her hair and eyelashes, flowed down her face, streamed off her coat. Her shoes were wet, her jeans were damp, and she was starting to shiver. And truthfully, she had no idea why she was here, walking the streets of Memphis in a rainstorm, Tom Dugan tagging along behind her, talking almost nonstop.

She stopped at the corner, barely registering the traffic flowing past, an endless sea of headlights and taillights, made double and triple by the reflections in the rain-soaked landscape. This was crazy, leaving home in November, heading across country with a man she barely knew, searching for what? For some message from Michael? For some nameless, shapeless idea formed by the words of an old woman in Oak Grove, Arkansas? *Think, Elise. Pull yourself together.* But the more she tried to gather her thoughts into something that made sense, the more scattered they became. At this point, she wanted to drop to the ground and give up. Tears had started flowing down her cheeks, another river to add to the ocean of rainwater.

She was ready to quit. Ready to go back to the car, ready to leave this noise and commotion. She stopped walking, resigning herself to the idea of coming up empty, and that's when the raven flew directly over her head, going back in the direction they had just left. He sailed down the street another block and turned right. Elise turned and followed.

And then she heard it, even through the noise of the traffic and music, even through the sound of the rain. Across the street, just down from the park where they had left the car, she could hear an occasional note, an eerie *woo* sound, a sound that didn't fit with all the bass and guitar and drums and horns that bounced on the street around them. This sound was unnatural, like a note from another world. Elise followed, stopping now and then to listen.

She spotted the blue bottles, hanging from the front porch of a small clapboard house, set back from the street. The breeze was passing over the mouths of those bottles, creating a symphony of eerie notes, as if the dead were singing. *Across the water. Blue notes play.*

She crossed the street, and her pace slowed as she neared the front gate. The place was a cacophony of color—from the turquoise picket fence to the bright-yellow siding, shutters and porch rails and posts all painted in different colors: bright red, green, orange, purple. Bottles hung from the tree out front, swaying slightly from the wind and the rain. Shadows of blue light bounced across the house. And against the wall of the house, and the posts on the porch, she could see bones, small pieces of skull and jawbone that might have belonged to cats or raccoons or some other small mammal. *With the dead, she waits.* Elise glanced at a small sign attached to one post of the porch. **CONJURE.**

A woman sat in the shadows of the porch, and she stood now and moved to the railing. "That yours?" she asked, and Elise turned in the direction the woman pointed. The raven sat in a tall pine tree.

Elise turned back to the woman and nodded once.

"Best come up, then."

Elise stood outside the gate, staring at the sign, at the bright colors, listening to the sound coming from those bottles. She didn't think; she didn't need to. She was flooded with that eerie sense of déjà vu, that *feeling* that walking up on this porch, the sound of the wind crossing the tops of those bottles, was ordinary. That she'd done the same thing many times before. She opened the gate and walked down the path and onto the porch, on autopilot. As if she were no longer in control of her own feet, her own body, her own forward momentum.

Tom stood at the gate, staring at the riot of color. "Elise? What the . . . ?" He followed her, reluctantly, into the yard.

The woman was dressed in a caftan almost as colorful as the house around her. She stood and looked at Elise, dripping on the wide planks of her porch, and down at Tom, still standing on the sidewalk. She leaned over and spat a long stream of tobacco juice that landed close to Tom's feet. "He can wait outside."

Tom sidestepped the tobacco and followed Elise up to the porch. He sat down in a chair, stretching his shoulders and stealing a look inside. He caught Elise's eye and scowled, his head shaking back and forth. He ran his hand over his face and mouthed the words *poker face*.

"I can hear what you're thinking, mister," the woman said, standing inside the front door. "You just keep that poker face on the porch."

He sighed and shook his head, holding his finger to his temple in one of those *She's crazy* signals. The woman stepped back out on the porch and looked at him.

"You prefer to wait in the street?" She scowled.

Tom looked out at the pouring rain and shook his head. She stepped back inside, and he took out his phone, punching away at the screen even before the door closed behind Elise.

The woman stepped aside, and Elise entered the small living room of the tiny house. She had no idea where she was, no idea what "conjure" really meant, and she searched the surroundings to give her a clue. Shelves lined two of the walls, holding an impressive display of jars full of herbs and sticks, baskets of stones, and what looked like the bones of small creatures. Elise turned in a circle, taking it all in. "What is it that you do, exactly?"

"Some folks calls it voodoo. But it's not. I'm a root doctor. A conjure woman. I can see spirits. Figure out what people need. A charm or a potion. A mojo bag." The woman moved toward her, head tipped as if intent on learning every feature of Elise's face. "Folks around here would call that hoodoo."

A slender finger of a shiver trailed up Elise's spine.

"How long ago did he die?" the woman asked, using her lips to indicate the raven outside the window.

Elise looked out. All she could see were silver threads of rain, the dark branches of a pine tree. But then the raven spread his wings for a moment, shaking them, as if trying to dislodge the moisture, and she saw the missing wing feather on the left side.

Elise turned back to the woman. "Eight months ago."

"Sit," she said, indicating one of two chairs, on opposite sides of a small round table by a window. The table was covered with a brightly colored shawl. The space was remarkably similar to Celestina's back room.

Elise brushed at the water on her jacket and sat down. The woman across from her looked ancient, her face lined with furrows, like mountain gullies. Her hair and eyebrows were gray. Her hands, too, were lined and creased, and they shook slightly as she lit a candle in the center of the table.

"He send you on this journey?" the woman murmured, staring at Elise.

Elise nodded. "Yes. I think so."

"You think so? You don't know?" The woman looked in Elise's eyes.

Elise could swear that this woman could see everything going on inside her body, including the food she was digesting. "Yes. He sent me on this journey."

The woman sat back in her chair. "That's better. Because you need to be certain. A ship ain't got a rudder, it can sure as heck get off course.

"You trust him?" the woman tipped her head toward the outside. "Your husband?"

Elise nodded.

"You're certain about that? Never had no call to doubt him?"

Elise felt her mouth go slack. She shook her head slowly. "No. I never had no call to doubt him. I mean . . . yes. I trust him."

"You best be clear about that. 'Cause you got all kinds of dark around you, girl."

"What do you mean?"

"All kinds of dark. Lies. Swirling all around you. Thick as flies."

Elise stared at her.

"I'm not saying they come from your husband. But they sure as heck come from somewhere."

Several seconds passed, unwinding slowly. Elise wasn't sure where to look. Every time she raised her eyes to those of the old woman, her throat filled, like her lunch was coming back up.

"How well you know that man out front?"

Elise shook her head. "Not very well."

"Hmm." The woman continued to stare at Elise.

She leaned forward, until her face was just inches away from Elise's. "'Cause somebody done worked the hoodoo on you, gal. It's all over you. Dark and deep. Be nice if you could figure out who it is."

Elise took a deep breath, tried to force her features to take a more neutral position. Tried to force herself to keep a poker face, as Tom had instructed.

"You been talking to the dead?"

Elise gasped; her mouth fell open slightly.

"Of course you have. He ain't been dead that long, has he? Natural enough, to want to talk to him." The woman slapped a hand down on the top of the table, and Elise jumped. "But that's a dangerous place to be. With the dead. Don't want to get stuck there."

Elise swallowed. The sound was overly loud in the too-quiet room. She felt certain the woman could hear it.

"You start messing with the dead, you best be prepared. 'Cause ain't no telling what might show up."

The woman raised her hand to her face and rubbed back and forth, back and forth, over her cheek and chin. Her eyes were locked on Elise, as if she were reaching in and trying to pull up all the secrets.

"I smell smoke." The woman closed her eyes and filled her lungs, as if she were actually inhaling something more than the musty smell of the room, the waxy smell of the candle on the table. She tipped her head slightly and sniffed again. "Cheroot. Somebody be burning a cheroot."

Elise went rigid. Wasn't that what Celestina had said, that night at the widows' and orphans' dinner? *Smoke gets in your eyes. Like a cigar, or a cheroot.*

"You been to a conjure woman before?" The woman's eyes sought Elise.

Elise shook her hand. "No."

"You know anybody that smokes cheroots?"

Elise shook her head again.

"'Cause there's a spell on you, coming through the smoke." The corners of the woman's mouth climbed, the faintest touch of a smile. "And they're calling your name. Pulling you in."

Elise felt her mouth go slack. She had heard that, or dreamed it; she wasn't sure which. Someone calling her name. She had thought it was Michael. But that was how she had messed up before, with the dream of the accident. Making assumptions. Elise closed her mouth. She forced her body to stay calm.

The woman continued to stare at Elise. "Where you headed? The Smokies?"

A charge of electricity vibrated in Elise's spine. She nodded.

The woman stared at the candle flame for a moment. Both hands came up to her mouth and nose. She shook her head and met Elise's gaze. "You think you're directing this show. Choosing your way. Looking for answers." The woman shook her head back and forth. "That's not how this works. You coming in here today? That raven, out in the tree? It's all part of the plan. You being pulled right in, like a moth to the flame. No escaping this, girl. Somebody done put something in motion. This some powerful juju going on."

The woman sat back in her chair and crossed her arms in front of her bosom. She stared at Elise, as if reading her face and body for what should happen next. Her eyes closed, she turned away slightly, and sniffed the air again. "I smell . . . blood."

Elise raised her hand to her mouth; she bent forward slightly, feeling as if she might be sick. "Blood?"

"I need to make you a mojo bag," she whispered, putting her hands on the table and pushing herself to her feet. "For protection." She shuffled to the shelves and pulled a red-flannel bag from the top. The bag was small, about the size of a medicine bag, and she opened it with two fingers. The woman wandered the room, pinched herbs from one basket, took a small amber stone from another. She reached into one tray and scooped up what looked like the bones of a mouse. In another, she tore off a piece of something that looked like snakeskin. With each addition, she stopped and tipped her head and waited, as if she were listening for directions from some unseen force. When she had finished, she stood by the table and cinched the bag closed. She tossed it on the table in front of Elise.

"If you going to be messing with the dead, you need protection. You keep that on you, girl. All the time. Keep it right close to you. Around your neck. In your pocket. Just hang on to it."

Elise raised her hand and moved it slowly to the bag. She let her hand rest on top of it, as if she could discern the energy herself, if she just waited long enough.

"You don't trust me?" the woman asked.

Elise met her eyes. "I don't know you."

"That's the smartest thing you've said so far." The woman nodded slowly. "'Cause if I was in your shoes, I wouldn't trust nobody." The woman looked out the window and tipped her head again toward Tom, sitting in a rocking chair. She raised her gaze to the raven in the tree. "And I do mean *nobody*."

Elise could hear the rain on the roof, slowing down now, not quite subsiding. She could hear the woman breathing. She could hear the wind, brushing over the mouths of the bottles outside. But she was disconnected from it all, hanging suspended in the woman's words.

She let her hand close around the bag, pulled it toward her, and put it in the pocket of her jacket. She did not ask what was inside. If she was sitting with Lorena, or was witnessing a ceremony with Uncle Wes, she would never ask such a question. The woman's words came back to her again. *You don't trust me?* Elise rubbed her fingers over the bag in her pocket. Her heart was quieting. And for some weird reason that she couldn't begin to fathom, she did trust her. She did want to take this bag and keep it close.

Elise cleared her throat. "How much do I owe you?"

The woman waited several breaths before she responded. "You pay me what you think it's worth." She crossed her arms in front of her chest and watched Elise.

Elise reached into her pocket, unable to think of anything she could offer the woman that would be worthwhile. Her hand wrapped around the piece of obsidian that had fallen from Michael's jacket, the piece of black glass that had convinced her to start this journey. For one moment, she thought about bringing it out and laying it on the table.

Elise stood, her hand wrapped around the stone, and knew she couldn't part with it. Next to the stone, she felt the change she had been given at the restaurant an hour ago. She had paid with a fifty, so she had more than thirty dollars wadded in the pocket of her jeans. She wrapped her hand around the roll of bills and laid it on the table, next to the old mirror. "Will this be okay?"

The woman nodded, her eyes never leaving Elise's, her gaze never taking in the amount in the wad of bills.

As Elise stepped through the door of the shop, the woman murmured, "Keep your eyes open, girl."

Elise stepped out on the porch, reeling from all that the woman had told her. She walked right past Tom, who had been sitting there looking at his phone. He jumped up and followed her into the rain, softer now, mixing with the drumbeat of blues music, guitar riffs. Neon light blazed from every surface. Elise had had enough of the noise and color, and she made a beeline for their parking spot.

Tom stopped to wait for the walk light, but Elise glanced to the side and shot out into the street. Tom scrambled to catch up with her. "So while you were in there, I googled 'conjure, hoodoo.' This is fascinating. I had no idea. Did you know, Elise, that there are several blues songs that mention hoodoo? I suppose it makes sense, since hoodoo comes from Africa and is tied into the whole slave history in the South. Hoodoo gave them something to believe in, a kind of magic for people to get what they want or need. Like a potion for luck, or protection, or even falling in love. So blues and hoodoo are cultural phenomena that come from southern black roots.

"Remember Bo Diddley? Remember that song, 'Who Do You Love?'" Tom started half singing the lyrics, oblivious to the rain, to the fact that other people were on the street around them. Unaware, apparently, that he could not carry a tune. Oblivious to the fact that Elise was pushing forward and had not said a word.

Tom had stopped on the sidewalk, moving his shoulders in an awkward dance, as he continued to sing, "Who Do You Love?"

Elise stopped and watched him, incredulous.

"It's so clever, don't you think? All this snakeskin and human skulls. Getting his girlfriend to take a walk with him. Who do you love? But it's actually a play on the words 'hoodoo you love.' The whole thing is about a hoodoo love potion. I must have heard that song a million times, and I never realized this before."

"Where do you come up with this stuff?"

Tom held up the phone in his hand. "Google. Not valid for true scientific study, but nevertheless, it does often provide very useful, or at least interesting, information."

"Give me your phone." Elise gritted her teeth and took the phone from Tom's hand. She put it in the pocket of her jacket and turned to head toward their parking place.

Tom jogged to catch up with her again. "What are you doing?"

"Staging a Google coup." She looked at him. Her eyelashes were soaked, her face wet with rain. She turned and continued toward Church Park.

Tom snorted and wiped the rain from his face. "Google coup. Ha! And it's fun to say. Google coup. Google coup."

He turned and hurried to catch up to her. "What happened in there? Why the heck would you go visit a conjure woman? Hoodoo, Elise? Don't you think that's a little weird? Even for you? Doesn't seem like the most likely method for getting messages from your husband."

She stopped and turned toward him. Rain drummed all around them. "Across the water. Blue notes play. Those blue bottles, you know? I could hear the sound they were making. With the dead, she waits. Did you see all those bones on the porch? Tacked up on the walls and the railings? She waits. And there she was, on the front porch. Waiting."

Tom nodded his head. "Of course. Makes perfect sense. You're listening to the . . . I don't know what kind of information, from a woman in Arkansas, and it led you here—to the conjure woman. Perfectly sensible."

Tom looked at her. "I could hear some of what she said. About how you have dark all around you. I've read about this, Elise. Remember when I told you about cold readings? How they read if they're on the right track or not by the person's body language? Apparently there are also these four or five standard lines that the fakes use. And that's one of them. 'There's something dark around you.' It's all just a ruse—a way to get you hooked, so you'll come back for more readings, or for an amulet or a stone or something that they sell for protection. They want you to be scared. The need you to be scared, so they can make more money."

Elise put her hand around the mojo bag in her pocket.

"What? You don't believe me? Take my phone. Look it up. Google 'psychic readings.'" Tom stopped and crossed his arms in front of his chest.

"Stop. Okay, Tom? Just stop." She glanced away, back down the street toward the home of the conjure woman. "I know you don't believe any of this. I know you can't see any rhyme or reason or sense in what I'm doing."

Elise searched for the words, searched for a way to put her own hazy thoughts into some kind of argument that would reach him, and convince herself. Doubt had been her constant companion since her dream and Michael's death. It plagued her now. "Yes, I've been listening to the words of all these . . . psychics. Yes, I am following some nameless *feeling*. But there's more than that."

Tom raised his hands to the sides. "What?"

She was convinced that telling him would only elicit more laughter, more condescension. But she knew she had to do it. "There's this raven." She drew a deep breath and forged ahead. "Ever since I opened Michael's studio a few weeks ago. And it keeps showing up. Every time I'm not quite certain what to do next, that raven appears. Almost as if it's trying to give me confirmation for whatever I'd been thinking. Or feeling.

"It showed up the night I went to the widows' and orphans' dinner. Monica saw it, the day you came up to work on the solar heater. The day you mentioned Olalla. And just when I was ready to give up on Memphis, it flew over my head. To the tree right outside that woman's house."

Tom looked at her. Water dripped from his hair. "Ravens live almost everywhere, Elise."

"This is one particular raven. Didn't you tell me, that day you brought wood to the cabin, that you were lost? And a raven flew up, and you followed it down the road?"

Tom blinked. He raised his eyebrows and shook his head, then shrugged his shoulders and held his hands out as if he could not remember.

"Was it missing a feather on the left wing?"

"I don't know. I don't normally make a mental note about the exact feather count on every raven I see. What are you trying to say?"

She turned to look at him, swallowed all her fear of his reaction, and said it straight out. "I think that raven has something to do with my husband. Maybe even *is* my husband. Or his spirit, anyway. I think he's trying to tell me something. Show me something. Guide me, somehow. Help me stay on track. Maybe just give me confirmation, whenever I'm not quite sure."

Tom burst out laughing. He threw his head back, his mouth hung open, and he laughed until he had to grab his sides. "So, in addition to listening to all these psychics, you're telling me that you're taking this adventure, guided by a raven?"

Elise stood still on the sidewalk and waited. "Yes."

"And that raven led you to the house of the conjure woman?" He turned his face to her and shook his head. Droplets of rain spattered off his hair.

"Yes. He flew past me, on the street, and then he settled in a branch of the tree when we walked up to her porch. The woman had noticed him, too. She pointed him out."

Tom continued to shake his head. "And you think this raven carries the spirit of your late husband?"

Elise nodded at him. "Yeah."

Tom shook his head. "I thought I'd heard everything, working for Celestina. But this beats anything I've ever encountered."

"It's not that far out." Elise felt her voice rising to a higher pitch, and she forced herself to take a breath. "In many Native American tribes, that's a very common belief. That the spirits of the dead can appear in birds. That they can bring messages to the living. Ancient Egyptians believed it, too. Birds and spirits of the dead have been associated with each other for a long time."

Tom looked at her again and pursed his lips. "How does a man of science respond to this?" He rubbed his forehead, as if he were about to try and explain the facts of life to a five-year-old. "Elise, let's put aside all the woo-woo stuff for a minute. From a biological perspective, this is absolute insanity.

"First, it would mean that one particular raven is following you, and that it has flown almost twelve hundred miles in the past two days." He raised his eyebrows and waved his arms in the air. "And if that's not crazy enough, then let's just look at the whole interspecies communication idea."

Elise took a deep breath and braced herself. Why had she bothered to tell him? She sucked in her bottom lip.

"There's a well-known biologist, Bernd Heinrich, who has written all kinds of studies on ravens. He tells this story of a woman, out by her woodpile at their home in the mountains. She's out there stacking wood, completely unaware that a mountain lion is on a rock nearby, watching her. Stalking her. And this raven flies up, and flaps around and squawks, and she turns, because of the raven, and sees the mountain lion and yells for her husband. He comes out, and the mountain lion runs off. And this woman goes around telling everybody that the raven saved her life. That it came up and warned her about the lion."

Elise shrugged. "Sounds like it did."

Tom took a deep breath. "But from a biological perspective, it makes absolutely no sense that the raven was warning *her* about the lion. Think about it, Elise. Ravens eat carrion, so they need dead bodies. They don't kill anything themselves, so they need predators—bears or mountain lions or coyotes or whatever—if they are going to survive. If there was any interspecies communication going on in that situation, it was much more likely that it was the raven communicating with the mountain lion. Probably more like, 'Hey, lion. Look! Dinner. Dibs on the thigh.'"

Tom cackled and slapped his hand on his leg. "God, I'm funny."

Elise waited for him to stop laughing. "So you think my husband is leading me into the jaws of the lion?"

"*NO.* That's not what I'm saying. Seeing a raven six or seven times in the last few weeks does not mean that it is the spirit of your husband. It is just a coincidence. Coincidence is just coincidence. It doesn't mean anything."

"And the missing wing feather? The same raven, apparently?"

Tom stopped. "Coincidence. I doubt very much that *one* raven in New Mexico has followed us to Memphis. There's probably a high statistical probability of a missing wing feather on more than one raven. Come on, Elise. That raven is *not* your husband."

Just as he spoke, a bird flew overhead and dropped a branch, three inches thick and almost eighteen inches long. It cracked on the ground, barely missing Tom's head. "What the . . . ?" He flinched and looked up. A raven flew to the telephone pole, settled on top, and shook its wings. It was missing a feather on the left wing.

They both looked at the bird. It clucked and cocked its head to one side, one eye locked on Tom.

Elise turned and caught Tom's eye. "Yeah. Yeah, I'm sure you're right." She reached for the door on the Jeep.

# CHAPTER SEVENTEEN

They drove into the coming dark. The thick gray clouds of the storm, combined with the shorter days of November, had brought dusk early. Elise stared out the passenger window, watching as Tom tried to maneuver them out of the city. It was rush hour, and they were moving very slowly through the busy streets. Headlights and taillights filled every conceivable space, a constellation of automobiles.

"Tom? Have you ever watched someone die?"

He turned to her as if she'd just spoken Greek. "What? Where did that come from?"

Elise spoke quietly. "I watched Michael's mother, when she died. We were with her, at the end. One minute, she's there in the bed, breathing. She didn't have her eyes open, nothing like that. But she was there. And then . . . not. Gone."

Tom stopped for traffic once again and glanced over at her.

"I know what science says. The body shuts down. No heartbeat. No breathing. No brain activity. Like turning off a computer. Systems down." She shook her head back and forth. "But that's not what it looks like, when you actually see it happen. There was *something* in her body. Something more than just the workings of a machine. Some kind of consciousness, or soul. Or . . . I don't know. What if we used the scientific term? What if we just call it . . . energy?"

The light turned, and Tom focused on finding the way back to the freeway.

"Was it Einstein? Was he the one? Who said that energy is never created or destroyed. That it just changes forms?" She turned to look at him.

He nodded.

"So where did that energy go? Because it sure as hell was not the same as shutting off a computer." Elise stared out the passenger window again. "Monica's family, Michael's family, they all believe that there is spirit . . . energy . . . in everything. Every rock and tree and bird and plant. The stars, the earth. And I've seen them, trying to show respect for that energy, that spirit. When Lorena gathers plants, for her herbal remedies? She takes only what she needs, not the whole plant. She asks permission from the plant. And then she thanks it for helping.

"I know it sounds crazy to you. Primitive, even. Superstitious. But I like that. I like that respect for everything. I like that idea of honoring the spirit in every being. I like the idea that the spirits of my mother and my father, even my grandmother, are still around somewhere. I like the idea that Michael's spirit . . . soul, energy—whatever you want to call it—still exists. Maybe in that raven, maybe somewhere else." Elise was breathing harder. She brushed moisture from her face. Several moments passed before she spoke again.

"And I don't care if science proves it or not. Ever. I don't need that proof."

She sat straighter and inhaled deeply. "But what if science hasn't proved it yet because they don't have equipment sophisticated enough to measure that kind of energy? Just like we didn't know about black holes until telescopes got sophisticated enough to see them?"

Tom concentrated on the traffic, which was beginning to move. They were getting to the outskirts of Memphis, about to head down the highway in the semidark. "Elise, sometimes your arguments are all over the place. What are you trying to say?"

"You act as if you're better, superior to me, more intelligent or something—because you follow *science*. But it seems to me that if you live your whole life constrained by what can be proven with the scientific method, you're going to be just as tossed around as I have been these past few days. Science changes all the time, based on new studies, new evidence, new equipment. Scientific studies used to say don't eat fat; now they say we should. Science used to say Pluto was a planet. Not anymore. When I was a child—you, too, I'm sure—they told us the atom was the smallest unit of existence. Now we have nanoparticles. A hundred years ago doctors prescribed arsenic as a medical treatment. Now we know it's a poison.

"Not that long ago, most people thought the world was flat. Would you have been one of them, Tom? Saying that science hasn't proved the world is round, so it can't be possible?"

Tom pursed his lips and pushed his glasses up. "Nah. I've always been ahead of the curve. Ha-ha."

She turned to him, her eyes bright as she found the words for things that had always felt nebulous and uncertain in her thoughts, as if speaking about it was helping her find the kernel of truth in what she believed. "Seems to me that if you only believe what can be proven by current scientific methods, you're living a life that is pretty narrow and constrained. Shut down to so many possibilities. There is so much more out there than we can ever begin to understand. Or prove. Science isn't ahead of us, Tom. It's behind."

Tom was silent.

"So let me have my raven, okay?"

The drive was tense, and Elise strained forward in her seat, trying to see into the fog and dark, trying to keep track of the lines of the road. The rain was turning to sleet, there were patches of black ice, and Tom slowed almost to a crawl. His shoulders and face were stiff and tense as he focused on staying on the road.

"Have you ever driven in black ice before?" she whispered.

"Not much of that in Tucson."

"Tom?" She turned toward him. "Let's just pull off somewhere. We can sleep in the car if we have to. This is getting pretty awful." She had heard too many warnings, too many ideas about going into the fog and the dark. Her dream, all those months ago, of a curvy mountain road, fingers of fog stretching across. The ace of spades, flipped over on Celestina's table, and her whispered words: "The death card." And now, today, with the hoodoo woman. Someone working hoodoo on Elise. Pulling her forward, to the land of the dead. As if her destiny were already written.

Elise didn't want to travel in this storm. She wanted to stop; she wanted to find someplace safe and just hole up in it for a while.

Tom never turned to look at her, never responded to her words. He continued to lean forward, hands gripping the wheel and eyes locked on the lines of the road. They rounded a sharp curve, and pink light glowed on his face. Elise turned to see the neon sign of a motel, a bright-pink VACANCY sign lighting up the night. Tom signaled and pulled off.

There was no nearby town, and the motel was just a group of log cabins set by the river, used mostly for summer tourists. There was only one left. Two double beds, kitchenette, and all the firewood they needed for the woodstove, since there was no heating system.

"There's been a bad accident up the road a ways. They closed it. You can't get no farther than this," the owner said as he finished the paperwork. "We ain't never been this busy in November, lessen it's a holiday. Must be this weather—people are stopping when otherwise they'd a kept on going." The man stood, waiting for the credit-card receipt. He looked up at Tom. "Uh, sir? Your card didn't go through. Do you have some other way to pay?"

Tom turned bright red and swallowed. Elise looked at his face, and back outside at the ice. "Here. Use mine." She handed over the credit card that she and Michael had used only for emergencies or when they headed out on a trip.

Everyone breathed a little easier when the charge was approved, although the color in Tom's face took a long time to fade.

The manager handed Tom the key to the cabin. "If you can get it warm, which won't take too long, this is a nice little cabin. You can hear the water in the river. Just like a lullaby. On the other hand, you can hear the river 'cause they ain't no insulation. You'll need to feed that fire purt near all night."

Elise came out of the bathroom, wearing her flannel pajamas and Michael's green sweater, towel-drying her hair. The fire was blazing; the room had warmed considerably.

Tom sat at the kitchen table, his iPad in front of him. His brow was creased, his mouth grim. He took his glasses off and rubbed his nose and forehead.

"While you were in the shower, I googled the cultural folklore about ravens."

Elise shook her head. "Oh, here we go. How did we survive before Google?"

He continued as if he hadn't heard her. "And depending on what part of the world you're talking about, ravens have a variety of different meanings. Like in Norse mythology, the god Odin had two ravens: Hugin, who represented the power of thought and the search for information." Tom turned to look at her. "That would be me, of course. And the other was Munin, who represented the power of the mind and the ability to intuit meaning."

"And that would be me?" Elise asked.

Tom shrugged. "Science. Intuition. It does look like we have both bases covered. Some versions of that story say that the ravens went back and told Odin everyone's secrets." He raised his eyebrows at her. "That they were his spies.

"And then the Greeks and Romans have stories that the raven represents the sun, or the light of wisdom, but that he is no good at keeping secrets. In some European myths, he represents a messenger, a shape-shifter. A *keeper* of secrets. And that's not even taking into account the Native American myths about ravens. Some tribes think the raven brought the light of the sun—creation. Some think he swallowed the sun. And some think it represents a trickster figure, like coyote. And still other stories focus on the symbol of change, transformation, clarification. That ravens can help you find the truth." Tom pushed his glasses up on his nose. "So depending on what myth you adhere to, he can be leading you to the truth, or pulling a trick on you."

"Do you do this for everything?" Elise scowled. "Because I can't really see how any of this is useful."

"That's because I haven't finished yet," Tom said. "And the answer is yes. I do this for everything. How can anyone figure things out without doing the research? I mean, really, Elise." He rolled his eyes.

"All right. I'm listening."

"Some tribes believe that evil people can take the shape of a raven. That they can eat your soul. Or that witches can send out ravens to keep track of spells they are working on someone." Tom leaned back in his chair. "And then there's this idea that a raven *foretells* death. That if it flies around the chimney of a house or taps on a window, someone is going to die."

Elise went completely still, remembering the way the raven had tapped on the window in Michael's studio when she had taken Monica out to see the carving.

Tom shrugged. "Just gathering information. I did add a raven column to the spreadsheet. Just to cover all the bases. I put in all the key words, from all the different raven stories."

Elise held the towel in her lap. She stared out the window into the dark, thinking of the carved raven in Michael's studio. She could almost see those obsidian eyes, watching her from the darkness.

Tom slumped in his seat and pinched the bridge of his nose, just underneath his glasses. "As you can see from the literature, that raven could mean any number of different things. Awfully difficult to tell. Or maybe it doesn't mean anything at all."

They sat silently for a moment, and then Tom leaned forward and looked at the iPad. "I think I've got the spreadsheet all up-to-date. What with Venetta's reading, and this . . . whatever it was . . . today. And of course all this raven nonsen—uh, raven information," he stuttered.

Tom put his glasses back on his nose. "You want to look at this?" he asked. "You might find it interesting."

Elise moved to the kitchen table and sat in the chair opposite Tom.

He pressed his lips together, pushed his glasses up, and turned the iPad so she could see it. "So you can see—I have a column for your dream. Icy road. Accident. Death. And then there's a column for Celestina's reading. Man with dark eyes who will help you. Journey. Death."

Elise looked up from the spreadsheet in front of her and met Tom's eyes.

"And that Venetta person in Arkansas, whatever it was she did . . ."

"I think it was kind of a séance," she whispered.

"Yeah, well. I didn't get to watch," Tom muttered, his eyebrows up like Elise had caused all these problems by not allowing him to observe.

"But I plugged in her . . . ideas. Across the water. Blue notes play. With the dead. She waits."

Tom let out a huge sigh. "The conjure woman today. Dark all around you. Messing with the dead. Someone put a spell on you. Pulling you in. Blood. Blah, blah, blah. And now this raven stuff, since you finally told me about that. I put in all the different ideas about ravens—shape-shifter, trickster, a familiar for witches, a spy for the gods. The forerunner of death.

"So if you look at all these columns, with all their weird, disconnected mumbo jumbo, there is one thing that is consistent in every column."

Elise scanned the spreadsheet and looked up and met his eyes. "Death."

Tom pinched his lips together and nodded. "This is not science, Elise. Everything in here . . . everything you've heard from these . . . people? It's all gibberish—like trying to pin down a cloud. If you want to believe all this, then you have to accept the idea that there *is* such a thing as psychic knowledge. And then you have to accept that these *psychics* know what they're doing and really are tapping into that psychic knowledge."

He turned and looked at her straight on. "It is just as likely, probably more likely, that they are just in the business of making money from people who are looking for answers. And then we have to add in the fact that each one of these . . . ideas . . . can have multiple meanings. Everything on this sheet could have several different meanings. Makes no sense at all."

Elise leaned back in her seat. "Then why are you doing it? Recording it all like this?"

He stared at her, as if the question had never crossed his mind. "I guess I thought it would help. Maybe keep everything straight, help you to see any patterns that were developing. I guess it's because this is the way I've always done things. Trying to be . . . objective, you know?"

They were both silent for a few moments. The fire crackled. "Elise, when we started, I really thought this would be kind of interesting Kind of fun . . . seeing how all these psychic types operate. But now I'm not so sure. Are you any closer to knowing what your husband is trying to tell you?"

She shook her head. "No. Not really."

Elise leaned back in her chair. She couldn't just push it all aside. She'd seen too much over the years, with Michael and Monica and their families. Too many things they knew or saw or dreamed—knowledge, information, whatever you want to call it—that was not possible in any rational scientific way. She'd seen this kind of sensitivity too many times to shrug it aside. She knew that there were people with genuine psychic ability. People who meant well. People who really were trying to help.

She looked out the window, and her voice came out soft and ragged, like the sound of paper tearing. "I've been in love with Michael for as long as I can remember. Just about my whole life. Maybe I'm wrong. Maybe this is a wild goose chase. Maybe it's even . . . dangerous." She raised her eyes to Tom's. "But if he *is* trying to tell me something? I have to figure it out." She turned away and looked outside at the dark. "I have to keep going."

Those were the words she spoke. Those were the thoughts she gave voice to. But long after Tom had fallen asleep, snoring in his bed across the room, she sat at the kitchen table, staring out into the darkness. Outside, the mountains and trees were shrouded in thick fog. She could see the thin silver line of the creek that ran past the motel; she could see the branches of one hickory tree, bare of leaves on this November night. She could see the black silhouette of a raven, sitting on a branch.

She ran her hands up and down her arms, fighting off the cold of the night and the cold of her fears. Staring at the raven, she whispered her thoughts to him. *Who are you? Where are you taking me?*

# CHAPTER EIGHTEEN

The one thing Monica had never had a problem with was fear. It was not an emotion that she had experienced very often in her life, and the times when it had popped up had been immediate and short-lived, like the time her truck tires had lost contact with the road on the icy curve by Questa, and she slid sideways for several hundred feet. It had taken a few moments after the truck finally stopped before her heart returned to normal. But those times when she felt that heart-clenching fear were rare and usually very physical in nature.

Monica was not a traditional, in the sense that her uncle Wes and her mother were. They practiced the old ways, revered the old ways. Lorena had grown up on Taos Pueblo lands, had danced the Green Corn Dance every spring as she was growing up. She made the customary white moccasins that she wore for the dance. She fixed her hair in the traditional Pueblo style. And Uncle Wes was a fixture at the Pueblo. He sang old songs to the pounding of drums. Collected eagle feathers. Went to the kiva. Observed all the old knowledge. He knew everyone; he watched everything.

Monica did not. She was never interested in dancing the Green Corn Dance when she was young. "No dresses," she told her mother.

Monica would have much preferred to be part of the foot races at the San Geronimo Feast Day, reserved for men. Running fast was much more enticing than any of the dances. She'd grown up watching it all, loved the songs and the stories and the ceremony. Those things were stitched into the fabric of her skin and bones and blood. But other than attending the normal feast days at the Pueblo, she didn't practice any of the old teachings. She simply lived next to it, watched it, absorbed it on some cellular level.

Over the years, she had seen both her mother and uncle Wes do some startling things. Wes could meet a stranger and just by looking at them know how many husbands they'd had, or if they had adult children who weren't speaking to them. He read people, somehow. Monica had never understood it, but she didn't need to. She'd seen it happen often enough to believe that it was real, and she accepted it. She felt the same way about her mother. How many times had Monica seen her sitting at the kitchen table with a perfect stranger—or not so perfect, as it turned out, since the person was visiting Lorena to find a cure. Lorena always knew that the solution started with the emotional, rather than the physical, and she always managed to find just what was needed.

Monica had seen enough to know that the old ways had power. She'd seen enough to believe that dreams had significance, that medicine men could effect cures, that her mother did indeed talk to the plants, and that they quite likely talked to her in reply. Monica didn't need proof. She didn't need logical sequence. She knew that extrasensory awareness was just as real, and probably more important, than information gathered using the very limited channels of ears, eyes, nose, mouth, and skin.

But none of that had ever affected her, personally. It was just part of the fabric of life around her, part of the surroundings. She wasn't astounded by it; she was never so overcome that she had to stop the routine of her normal day. Until now.

She was over fifty years old, and she had never been interested in learning about the plants and healing. She had never been interested in perfecting her Tiwa. She could speak enough to get by; she understood most of what was said to her in the old language. But she had not felt any desire to learn all she could, to preserve the language and the old ways that could vanish when people like Uncle Wes and her own mother were no longer here.

Growing up with her brothers, Monica had loved the comforts of physicality. She loved running, chasing, or being chased. She loved the feel of the wind in her hair and on her cheeks when they rode horses. She loved climbing trees and hanging upside down. Loved the scrape of bark on her palms and the ooze of mud between her fingers. She'd taken all that and channeled it into a vocation. She still played in the mud, only now she turned it into beautiful tile work. She still climbed and hung upside down, only now it was climbing ladders and hanging in awkward positions so that she could put up tongue-and-groove ceilings for rich white people.

She never expected that anything spiritual, anything intuitive, would come to *her*. She hadn't asked for it, she hadn't studied for it, and she sure as heck didn't want to start now. None of that seemed to matter. Monica could remember every piece of the dream. She lay in her bedroom in the dark and went over it all in her mind, locking in the details.

She was driving up the road, to the cabin where Michael and Elise had lived for so long. Only nothing was the same. The road was crumbling away at the edges, making passage up the hill almost impossible. She pulled into the driveway, too fast, as usual, and caused the tail of her truck to spin out. She slammed the door and started walking up the path, turning to glance at Michael's studio as she did. The glass was missing. The windows were now black holes, empty and lifeless. It stopped her cold. She turned slowly toward the cabin. No glass was in those windows, either. The empty spaces stared at her, like the eyes of an animal hiding in the woods.

Her heart began to pound. She started up the steps to the porch, moving slowly, listening carefully for the sound of another being. She was so intent on listening that she nearly tripped, and when she looked down, she realized that some of the boards on the stairs were missing. Her heartbeat pulsed in her throat, and she watched every footstep she took, placing her feet carefully on the few remaining boards of the porch.

She pushed open the front door, and it fell backward, clattering on the floor. Huge, gaping holes were ripped in the walls and floor; the staircase to the upstairs bedroom was torn to the point of being impassable. Big chunks of the walls and ceiling were missing. Vines had started to grow through the cracks, green taking over the kitchen. The place looked as if it had been abandoned for years.

She turned, taking it all in. As she did, she could see flashes of images, ghosts of the past superimposed on the destruction of the present: a fleeting glimpse of one of many dinners that she and Michael and Elise had shared at the kitchen table, another image of the three of them trying to maneuver that queen-size bed up the stairs when Michael and Elise finally bought a decent bed. There was a strange echo of laughter from the living room, where they would sit until midnight, telling stories and listening to Led Zeppelin and Bob Marley and Carlos Santana.

In the dream, Monica heard a noise coming from the living room, and she placed her feet carefully, trying to avoid falling through any of the missing floorboards. She leaned her head to look in the space. There was the fireplace Michael had built with his own two hands. Monica had helped, the two of them laying the mud and the stones, Elise carting rocks to the pile of supplies. As Monica stared, lost in a heavy gauze of sadness, she heard something just behind her, coming down the stairs. Monica turned to see a flurry of black feathers and beating wings.

She bolted up in bed, fully awake. It had been a raven flying up in her face. A raven, like the one she had seen in Michael's studio just before Elise left on her trip. She sat there a moment, waiting for her eyes to adjust to the dark, waiting for her heart to return to normal. She turned her head toward the window on her left. It was still night, but with the promise of dawn making the sky slightly less black.

The sound came at her again, a sound she'd thought was part of the dream. Now she was fully awake, but she could hear it still, the flapping of wings. Monica flipped the covers off the bed and jumped up. She stood at the darkened window, listening, waiting. The raven flew up once more, using its beak to knock on the glass just above her head. Tap tap tap.

A million thoughts jumped, like popcorn in a popper, trying to grab her attention. Was it Michael, trying to tell her something? And what did the dream mean? She exhaled. So this was how it felt to have dreams that were obviously important but not easily understood. The thought of Elise blew through all the others, a sudden understanding of what her friend must have felt, confronted with her own dream all those months ago. There was a weight to this, a distinct sense that it all had meaning, that there was something she needed to do, something she needed to know, that the future depended on it. But Monica had no idea what that was.

She stood at the window, staring out into the deep gray-blue of dawn. The raven sat on the back of a lawn chair, tipping its head to examine her, one eye at a time.

"Hey, Michael," she whispered. "You hungry?"

# CHAPTER NINETEEN

"Monica?"

"When are you going to get a cell phone?"

"Hello to you, too." Elise chuckled. She had asked to borrow Tom's phone while he was in the shower. "You already know the answer to that. They never have worked up at the cabin, so what's the point?"

"I would like to point out that you are not at the cabin and have not been at the cabin for several days now. We've been worried sick. Mom's been putting out a telepathic APB. Hoping you would call."

Elise felt a pinprick of panic, an almost automatic reaction, as if the only news that could ever be waiting for her was bad. "Has something happened?"

Monica hesitated for one fraction of a second. "How is Mr. Science–slash–Charlie Manson, by the way?"

Elise snickered. "He talks too much. Drives erratically. Has a distinct tendency to bore you with tedious details about concepts in which you are not interested. Clueless, basically."

"That's just to suck you in, make you believe you're safe in his hands."

Elise laughed. For a moment, she considered telling Monica about the conjure woman, about all the things the woman had said, but stopped herself. There wasn't enough time. She could hear the sound of water running in the bathroom. Tom was singing, loud and off-key, belting out the words to "Black Magic Woman" in a way that would have made Carlos Santana cringe. "I don't have long to talk. He'll be out of the shower soon."

"You guys are in the same room?"

"The motel was full. There was an ice storm. We pretty much had to pull off and take this." Elise stopped talking. "Please tell me you're not even thinking what I think you're thinking. Because that's not possible."

Monica was silent for several heartbeats. "I know. It's just . . . weird, you know? You, in a motel room, with a man who isn't Michael."

"It's pretty weird for me, too."

The silence hung heavy between them, like a net, weighted with all the things that neither one of them wanted to say.

"Elise?" Monica said. She waited several seconds. Where Elise held back, Monica plunged forward. "I had this weird dream."

"Oh?"

"About the cabin. It was all torn apart, falling down. Like it had been abandoned for years."

Her heart and stomach and lungs all froze, and Elise could not breathe.

"And then when I woke up, there was a raven out on the patio."

The words, when they left her mouth, were barely audible. "Missing a wing feather?"

"I don't know—it was pretty dark. Hard to tell." Monica waited a minute. "Have you seen Michael? That raven, I mean?"

"Yeah." Elise answered. "Yesterday, in Memphis. And last night, when I couldn't sleep. The raven was out by the creek. Why? When did you see him, Monica?"

"This morning. When I woke up from that dream."

They both went quiet. Monica was the first to speak. "I guess if it's a spirit raven, it can move pretty fast, huh?"

Elise said nothing, but chills went down her arms, thinking of all those stories Tom had told her about ravens. Remembering all the ideas he had typed into that spreadsheet. Spies. Tricksters. A familiar for witches.

"Elise? There's more." Monica took a big breath.

"I went to that shop in Taos. The psycho wannabe. I went in to ask for Tom's phone number so I could call you. It was empty when I first got there, so I just kind of wandered around. And I had just stepped into that back room. You know—the one with all the saints and candles and stuff?"

"Yeah. I know the one."

"I didn't mean to be sneaking around or anything, but these two men came in, and Celestina came out to talk to them, and I just kind of stayed quiet, in the back there. Not on purpose, but I ended up hearing everything. Those men are detectives."

Elise was still.

"They were asking about Cynthia somebody or other. Some woman from Dallas who has a summer home in Taos."

"I've met her," Elise whispered. "At that widows' and orphans' dinner."

"And then they asked about Tom Dugan."

"Tom? Why?"

"Apparently, this Cynthia person's house was burgled. But not your standard drug-addict kind of mess. Whoever went in there took only art. Only Native art. The detectives said that they definitely knew what they were doing."

Elise's thoughts began jumping. "So what does Tom have to do with that?"

"Maybe nothing. But they said they were checking anyone who had been up to the house in the last few weeks. Cynthia told them about Tom—because he had delivered firewood a couple of weeks ago."

"But . . . it couldn't have been Tom. He's been here, with me." Elise could hear Tom; she could hear the sound of water in the bathroom sink.

"He's been there, with you, for two days. The detectives weren't quite certain when the theft took place. Cynthia came back, after a weekend in Dallas, and discovered it. This could have happened before you guys even left."

"No." Elise shook her head. "No, it couldn't be Tom. I don't believe it." She remembered when he had been up at the cabin, working on the solar hot-water heater. He had never even glanced at the artwork in the house, never mentioned the works in Michael's studio as she and Monica stood out there.

"They didn't say it was him. They just want to talk to him. Because he'd been up there. Because he knew his way around.

"Elise?" Monica got quiet, and Elise leaned into the phone, more concerned over the quiet than she would be if Monica were yelling. "The really weird thing? I watched them show Celestina this picture. And they asked if she knew where he was."

"Yeah?"

"She said she had no idea. She lied."

Elise swallowed. "That probably doesn't mean a thing. I mean, if cops were asking me about you, I'd probably lie, too."

Monica snorted. "That would get us both hung." She waited another minute before she spoke again. "Elise? Are you sure about this? Maybe you should come home. There's probably an airport in Tennessee, right?"

There was something in Monica's voice that gave Elise pause—a slender fiber of fear that latched on to Elise's own doubts and fears, grabbing hold and pulling, as if she would unravel. For one moment, she let herself think about going back to New Mexico, getting away from the dread and uncertainty that had gathered around her like a storm system since she'd begun this trip.

But then she remembered the pain and the loneliness, the isolation, the ghosts of the past that waited for her back at the cabin. She reached in the pocket of her jeans and ran her fingers over the piece of obsidian. The stone sent a wave of electricity into her hand, pulling her back to earth. It made her remember that there was a reason for all this, that there were several times along the way when what she was doing felt right. She was so close. Too close to give up now. She couldn't go back. Not yet. She exhaled slowly, trying to push all the doubt away from her, out into the atmosphere. "I have to, Monica. I have to do this."

Elise ignored the tiny knot of misgiving that tightened her stomach. "We should get to Hannah and David's house sometime this afternoon. Provided there aren't any more ice storms."

"Is that supposed to make me feel better? More Celestina groupies? That woman has followers everywhere. Almost like some kind of cult."

There was a long pause, fear and love radiating down both sides of the phone.

"Everybody okay out there?" Elise asked.

Monica took a breath. "Fine. Mom says hey."

Elise looked toward the bathroom. The sound of water had stopped. "Monica, I have to go."

"Elise? Don't drink any Kool-Aid, okay?"

# CHAPTER TWENTY

The day was clear, glistening after last night's rain and ice. Everything around them was washed clean, sparkling in the sunlight. They drove toward the Great Smoky Mountains, and Elise felt her heart stutterstep. Memories pounded over her like waves. There were so many times when she and Michael had left their home, and always, on the trip home, she had this moment, getting into the mountains, where her whole body sighed and relaxed. There was something about mountains, about being surrounded by the hills and valleys and trees, that always made Elise feel safe. And it didn't seem to matter that these mountains were very different from the ones she was used to. The Sangre de Cristo Mountains, back home in New Mexico, had an in-your-face ruggedness, steep and sharp. The Smokies were different. With layer upon layer of soft, rolling blue hills, and patches of mist and cloud, these mountains were softer, like the welcoming embrace of an old grandmother. Her worries, all her questions, just seemed to fade.

They pulled into Olalla around noon. There wasn't much to the place, certainly not enough to warrant the description of "town." One intersection, with four stop signs denoting the road that came in from the main highway and the crossroad that paralleled the lake and river and mountains. The intersection held a handful of buildings: a post office, flag whipping in the cool breeze; a gas station and garage on another corner; a mercantile with a huge wooden porch out front; and one tiny café, set back toward the lake. Half a mile away, they could see a white clapboard church, a steeple pointing into the sky, like a finger raised to signal God. Elise could see no sign of a school or a library. A few homes were scattered about, but there was distance between them, as if everyone here owned at least a few acres.

"Let's get some lunch," Tom said, turning to Elise for the first time.

"Are you always hungry?"

"Pretty much, yeah."

The Olalla Café was the building closest to the lake. It was a small log structure, with a covered wooden porch wrapping the front and sides. Antiques were scattered about the porch—an old wood cook-stove, a rocking chair, various pieces of old irons and cook pots.

Inside, the place was small, with a scattering of tables, all of them covered in red-and-white-checked oilcloth. Windows lined the side of the building that faced the lake, and outside, a large deck held tables and chairs, empty now in the cold weather. Two large pine trees were part of the deck, which had been built around their trunks. White Christmas lights snaked up the trunks, lit even now, in early afternoon.

Elise and Tom sat at a table near the windows, and Elise couldn't take her eyes off the lake. She was fascinated by the water, the way the wind whipped it into froth, moving into swirling patterns of gray and gunmetal and silver. The sky had grown cloudy, as if another storm were on the way.

"Pretty place," Tom murmured. "So wet. So green, even in November."

Elise looked at him, a scowl pulling her brow. Only the pine trees were still green; the deciduous trees had mostly lost their leaves. "Green?"

"Well, more green than Tucson."

A middle-aged woman appeared, a pitcher of water in hand. She poured it into red plastic glasses. "No menu today, sorry. We don't do the full menu in the winter. Not enough folks. But we have meat loaf with scalloped potatoes and green beans. Nine ninety-five, if you're interested. And my mom makes a pretty good pie. Today we have coconut cream."

"Perfect. I'll take it all," Tom said.

"You, miss?"

"The same. Everything." Elise watched the waitress, moving around the room. She was probably close to Elise's own age, her hair black and curly around her face. She moved as if the job of standing and walking and carrying plates had exacted a price from her back and knees. Watching her made Elise remember when she herself had been a waitress at the café in Amalia. She'd been so young then, a teenager. And she'd quit not long after she and Michael had married and built the cabin. It didn't make sense to drive down into town for the sometimes very meager tips, especially in the winter. Elise turned to stare at the lake again. Would she be forced to take a job as a waitress? It was, other than weaving, the only real job she'd ever had. She took a sip of water and wondered if the Amalia Café would even consider a fifty-year-old woman who hadn't waited tables in more than thirty years.

"I called David," Tom said, taking his cell phone from his ear. "He gave me directions. And he says we can both stay there. They have some kind of guest cabin or something, but it sounds like there's enough room for both of us."

Elise nodded, her attention again riveted on the lake.

"David and I have been talking on the phone and e-mailing for a couple of months now. He's already bought all the solar panels and had them put up. So my job, now that we're here, is to connect all the dots, get everything up and running. Design a program to control everything. Which, of course, I've already been working on. I'll just need to iron out the kinks once I see the place." Their plates arrived, and Tom paused to take a huge bite. He raised his eyebrows. "Mmm. Pretty good. Might be the best meat loaf in Tennessee." He shot a glance at the waitress, but she didn't smile.

He shoveled in another bite and continued. "I think it will probably take me a few days to get it all running smoothly. What are you going to do while we're here? Wasn't there some guy you wanted to talk to?"

Elise glanced at him and nodded. "Yeah."

"Another card reader? Hoodoo? Maybe a tea-leaf reader?" Tom smiled and crammed in another bite of food.

"You're not as funny as you think you are." Elise scowled. She reached in her pocket and brought out the business card for Franklin Cooper, the stone carver. "This is the reason I came on this trip. So I could talk to this guy."

Tom picked up the card and read it, flipped it over to look at the back. He handed it back to her. "Does he read stones or something?"

She sat back in the chair. "I don't really know anything about him. I think Michael bought some stones from him. I found this stone and this card in Michael's jacket."

Tom caught her eye. "That's the whole reason you came out here? Because you found this card in your husband's jacket?" He rolled his eyes and shook his head.

Elise stopped and stared at her plate, fork resting in one hand. Memories of that night, less than a week ago, floated back to her. But she did not mention her dream of Michael trying to give her something. Didn't mention the way the closet door opened, the way the stone fell out at her feet. She wasn't about to give Tom another opportunity to laugh at her, to make more woo-woo jokes.

Tom held up his hand, a *stop* gesture. "Okay, okay. I guess this is your decision. But I don't think you should go up there alone. We don't know anything about this place. Or this man." He indicated the card she held in her hand. He began to hum, a barely recognizable version of the theme song to *Deliverance*. "Maybe I should drive you. As soon as I get things settled at Hannah and David's."

The spreadsheet flashed in Elise's mind, columns all lined up, and the one thing they all had in common. Death. Dying. The bones of the dead. Elise swallowed hard. "Okay," she murmured.

They stood and gathered their jackets and moved to the counter to pay. Inside the glass case, tipped so that the lid was open, stood a cigar box. It was faded yellow, flourishes of gold trim along the outside edge. Blue lettering, in a fancy, old-fashioned font, spelled out **OLD VIRGINIA CHEROOTS**. The box held a few of what looked like home-rolled cigars.

Elise raised her eyes to the waitress. "Do you live around here?"

She smiled. "My whole life. Born just up the road. My mother is the one who started this restaurant, long time ago."

"She makes a great coconut cream pie, by the way," Tom interjected.

Elise handed the woman the business card. "Would you happen to know how I could find this man? There isn't much in the way of an address."

The woman read the card, flipped it over, and looked at the back. She looked up at Elise and handed the card back to her. She shook her head. "Can't help you. Sorry."

Elise put the card in her pocket, and they walked out to the Jeep. She stopped for a moment and turned to look back at the café, a scowl crawling across her face. "She's hiding something," Elise said as soon they got in the car.

"What?" Tom shifted the toothpick hanging out of his mouth.

"That woman, the waitress. She's hiding something. I think she does know him."

Tom raised his eyebrows. "Based on what evidence?"

Elise turned and met his gaze but said nothing.

He pursed his lips and nodded and started the engine. "Oh, I see. You have a *feeling*."

Elise shrugged. "Yeah. I do. And look at this place . . . Olalla, Tennessee. It isn't that big. That café is probably the city center around here. How could she not know him?"

Tom pulled away from the café and stopped at the intersection. He exhaled—a long, slow breath that spoke of the trials of dealing with the irrational and unscientific nonsense of the world in general and Elise in particular. "Okay. Whatever. You have a *feeling*. But don't get all worked up, okay? It might be something totally mundane and uninteresting. Maybe they were married and she caught him in bed with someone else. Never wants to speak to him again."

"Maybe you're projecting," Elise murmured.

Tom turned to look at her and pushed his glasses up on his nose. "Really, Elise. You're reading too much into things. All kinds of things. You're almost starting to sound paranoid."

# CHAPTER

# TWENTY-ONE

They followed the twists and turns of the road up the canyon. The pavement ended, and they stayed on the gravel, hugging mountain on one side and creek on the other. Tom stopped and looked at a mailbox, painted robin's-egg blue, comparing the information on the box to the notes he had written down. He stuffed the note in his shirt pocket, and they turned and headed down a lengthy driveway to Hannah and David's house. It had started to snow, and Elise rummaged in her duffel bag for a winter coat. Humidity made the cold more bone-chilling than it was back home, and she hunkered down into the thick fleece.

They pulled into the yard. The bare arms of a weeping willow swayed in the wind, branches sweeping through the grass like long, thin fingers. A huge spruce stood at one side of the rock path, its fragrance sharp. The yard was aromatic, peaceful and quiet in the deepening dusk and the falling snow. The air was sweet with the smell of the fallen leaves and pine. Elise followed Tom up the flagstone walk, feeling comforted by the trees and the snow starting to stick to the grass.

They ran up the steps of the porch, and Tom knocked on the door. Windows on either side of the door spilled soft amber light onto the porch and into the yard. Elise turned and saw the bright-orange berries of the bittersweet, clinging to the dying leaves of the vine, draped over the porch rail. At the far end, Virginia creeper hung like a curtain of red and brown, the leaves swaying in the wind.

The door to the house was old cedar, gray showing through beneath the turquoise paint. It creaked when it opened, and an older woman stood framed in the doorway. She was in her late sixties, not tall, but solid in her bearing and proportions. She wore a black dress, buttoned up to her throat and hanging all the way to her stocking feet. Elise let her eyes take it all in, from head to toe. Bright wool stockings, each toe a different color—orange, yellow, fuchsia, blue, and purple—peeked out from beneath the hem of Hannah's black dress. Elise couldn't help but smile. She raised her eyes from the vivid stockings to the smooth skin and soft gray eyes of the woman's face. Her gray hair was pulled back into a messy bun at the nape of her neck. Strands of silver fell helter-skelter across her forehead and cheeks and neck.

"I'm Hannah." The woman smiled. She took Elise's hand in both of hers. "You must be Elise. We're very happy you could come."

The woman glowed with openheartedness; Elise felt that stiff hard core of her insides begin to relax.

Hannah stuck her hand out to Tom. "Nice to meet you, Tom. Very nice of you to come and help us out like this. Celestina speaks very highly of you."

Tom's shoulders went back and he smiled.

Hospitality poured from the open door, from the eyes of this woman with the pink cheeks. They followed her inside. The hall was long and dark. Halfway back, a staircase rose; the wooden railing and steps glowed dark and smooth with age. A bench stood next to the stairs, and beneath it was a neat row of shoes.

They slipped off their shoes and followed Hannah into the main room.

The house radiated warmth. The outer walls were log, and those on the inside were painted gold and coral and deep brick red. The floor was wood, darkened and smooth with age. They stepped down into the living room, and Elise breathed easier, felt her heart slow. Reflections of flames danced on the walls, from the fire in the fireplace and the candles on the table. The deep blue of the gloaming filled the windows along two walls. A stone fireplace, blazing with light and warmth and the sweet smell of burning pine, filled the space between two windows. The smell of the fire always had the same effect on Elise: like a child's favorite blanket, she felt comforted, quiet, reminded of all her evenings sitting in the Madrids' living room, watching the fire and listening to Monica's dad and uncle Wes tell stories.

Navajo rugs decorated the floor and hung in several places along the wall. Elise examined the patterns: Two Grey Hills, Teec Nos Pos. Even in the dim light, she recognized Hopi kachinas and Laguna Pueblo baskets. She stood in front of a painting, a fascinating study of birds and trees in geometric patterns. "Is that a Tony Abeyta?" Elise muttered.

Beside her, Hannah nodded. "We've been going to Indian market in Santa Fe for, what . . . about thirty years now, I think. Picked this up before Abeyta became such a big name. I'm afraid we are rather hooked on Native art, as you can see."

"It's a beautiful collection," Elise replied. "You spent a lot of time in the Southwest, then?"

Hannah nodded. "Most of my life. I miss it desperately. But . . . I have a grandbaby in Chattanooga, so I'm learning to adjust."

Hannah turned to Tom, standing just behind Elise. "What about you, Tom? Are you a fan of Native art?"

Tom shrugged. "I'm not sure I really *get* art," he said, staring at the Tony Abeyta print on the wall and moving closer to it. "Sometimes it just seems like a bunch of random . . . stuff." He shook his head.

Elise met his eyes, and he pushed his glasses up on his nose.

Hannah held out her arm. "This is my husband, David."

A tall, slender man straightened up from feeding the fire. He was well over six feet tall, and his hair, like that of his wife, was long and gray, held back in a ponytail. Small wire-rimmed glasses could not hide the kindness of his brown eyes. "We're glad you're here, Tom, Elise."

"Don't we look Biblical? Just like we sound—Hannah and David." Hannah laughed.

Elise tipped her head to one side. "Yes, you do. Except for the socks."

Hannah laughed. "It's my first winter in the Smoky Mountains. I'm not used to all this humidity." She shuddered dramatically. "Calls for special measures, I think."

They all turned to look as an older man shuffled into the room, his moccasins making a shush-shush sound on the floor. His face was lined with the deep crags and canyons of age. Dark eyes twinkled with laughter. "And this . . ." Hannah moved to his side, laid a hand on his arm. "This is Jefferson Hayes. Grandfather Hayes. Of the Cherokee."

Elise moved forward and offered her hand to him, keeping her eyes low. "Very nice to meet you," she whispered.

"Not Biblical, I'm afraid." The old man smiled. "But entirely presidential. My mother named me after our third president. I had two older brothers, Washington and Adams. And a sister, Betsy Ross Hayes." He laughed, throwing back his head, showing several missing teeth. "Maybe she thought no one would notice we're Indians."

Elise laughed. He took her hand between both of his and stood there for a moment, holding her hand and looking into her eyes. Elise felt as if he could read right down to her soul.

"Ah," he moaned softly. "You are the woman who brought the birds, then."

Elise leaned into his words, her hand still engulfed by his. "Excuse me?"

"Your friends in the spirit world," he muttered, indicating the air around her with his eyes.

He dropped her hand and stepped back as a tiny woman, hunched with age, shuffled into the room. Her face was just as lined as the old man's, but her hair was still mostly black.

"This," said Hannah, beaming, "is Grandmother Sarah Hayes."

Elise stepped forward to shake Sarah's hand. "I'm very pleased to meet you. They stood for a moment, hands clasped, until Elise stepped back.

"You've got a beautiful place here, Hannah," Elise said. "How long have you been here?"

"About six months now. We wanted to be close to my daughter and her family in Chattanooga, but I knew I could not live in the city. This was our solution. It's nice and quiet; we have all the trees and mountains and nature that we crave. And we can be at my daughter's house in under two hours. Perfect, really. We love it here. Unfortunately, the people we bought it from ran everything on a generator. The noise drives me crazy, and so does the smell of the gasoline. We try to do as much as we can the old-fashioned way—with firewood and candlelight. Doesn't work for the refrigerator, though. I'm hoping that Tom can help us get this place running with solar everything so that we can join the twenty-first century again."

Elise smiled. She had prepared herself to be on her guard, to distrust this friend of Celestina's. Instead, she felt completely at home, surrounded by the art and weavings from the Southwest, by the warmth and openness of the people around her.

"The Hayeses are neighbors; they live just down the road a few miles. We asked Grandfather Hayes to come up tonight and do a blessing ceremony for the new place. And we were hoping to time it so that you could be included. To help Tom with all the solar work he's going to do."

Elise glanced at Tom, willing him not to roll his eyes or make some exaggerated sigh. She caught his gaze and tried to force him to behave himself.

"Are you interested in being part of it?" Hannah spoke directly to Elise, and Elise nodded her head.

"Yes. Yes, of course."

"You, Tom? Would you like to be part of it?" Hannah turned to look at him, and Tom glanced at Elise. She nodded.

"Sure. Why not?"

"Okay, then. Let's get you two settled in, and we'll start."

Grandfather Hayes leaned on David's arm and lowered himself onto a pile of blankets in the corner by the fireplace.

On cue, his wife sat down on a blanket next to her husband. The rest of the group formed a horseshoe shape around the fireplace. Elise ended up between Tom and the stones of the fireplace, directly across from Grandfather Hayes. Everyone sat on the floor. The only light was that of the fire and the candles scattered around the room.

Hayes lit a sage stick, and with his right hand fanned the smoke over his face and head and body. He used a fan made of four hawk feathers tied together with red leather and brilliant red beads wrapping the quills. He passed the bowl of sage and the fan to his wife. She cleansed herself in the smoke and passed it on to David, to make a circle around the room.

Hayes picked up a large hand drum covered in yellowed leather. Painted on the face of the drum were four red-tailed hawks sailing through the sky. The drumstick was hand carved, one end covered in leather. He released one long, slow breath, closed his eyes, and began to beat.

Elise smudged herself with the sage, set the shell bowl in the middle of the circle, and closed her eyes. The drumbeat was like a heartbeat—heavy on the downstroke, more of an echo as it lifted. She had been to many ceremonies with Michael and Monica, but until the pulsing beat filled the room, she had forgotten how familiar and comforting it felt. She sensed her own heart beating in rhythm, felt as if the whole planet were tied to that drumbeat, as if it were the heartbeat of the earth itself.

She relaxed, and almost instantly, the drumbeat carried her straight back to the day they'd buried Michael, straight back to the sound of the Jicarilla men drumming and singing, helping to send Michael to the land of the spirits. The pounding rhythm pulsed in her brain, in her blood, and for a moment, she thought she might swoon, the memories flooding over her in one huge, titanic wave.

Hayes began to sing. His voice was deep and rich, filled with the tremors of age. Elise had heard Monica's mother sing in Tiwa, had heard Michael's mother sing in Apache. But this was the first time she had heard the Cherokee language. Her body rocked back and forth, swaying with the beat of the drum, with the soaring notes of Hayes's voice. She lost all sense of time and place, forgot where she was, forgot everything.

She was pulled under; grief swallowed her like an enormous riptide, powerful and potent. It wasn't just Michael's death; it was the accumulated grief of every loss in her life. They washed over her, huge waves of sadness: the loss of a father she could not remember, the move to New Mexico and the strange quiet of Beulah's house, the loss of her mother not long after. This time, instead of fighting to stay upright, instead of trying to push it all away, she just gave in, let herself be carried away on the tide of loss and loneliness. An ocean of grief, devouring her whole, like Jonah and the whale. She could feel the spirits of each one of them floating around her in the dark: her mother, her father, Beulah. And Michael, larger than life, larger than any of them, with her for so long.

She lost track of everything around her, consumed by the darkness. Somewhere in the far distance she could still hear the pounding of the drum, the sound of Hayes singing. But she was lost in a dream, a vision. She was climbing the steps, up to the porch on the cabin. She could barely lift her legs, could barely force herself to go up the stairs. Something inside her knew, just knew, that when she reached the top of the steps and went inside, the whole world would crumble into pieces. The fear was pounding in her temples; she felt tears on her face.

The aroma wafted to her and went deep into her senses, carried on the notes of the song that Hayes was singing. Lilacs. She could smell lilacs, the fragrance of death. It soaked into her pores, the scent overpowering, almost cloying, as if she were surrounded by the actual flowers. Her mind told her it was impossible; she was inside a house in the Smoky Mountains in November. The perfume could not be real, yet it was so intense that Elise leaned forward, afraid she might be sick.

An eternity passed before she opened her eyes. The sensation was strange, as if she were coming back from a long journey. She looked around. Light from the fireplace danced and flickered on the walls and floor and the faces of the group around her. Grandfather Hayes, directly across from her, held a pipe close to his chest. His eyes were closed. He rocked back and forth, praying in Cherokee, his words barely audible.

Elise sat, numbed now after the intensity of a few moments before. She did not bother to look around her, oblivious to the others. Her body quivered; her hands shook. She raised a hand to swipe at the moisture on her face.

Hayes's voice faded away to stillness. The room went quiet; only the hiss and pop of the fire punctuated the silence. Everyone continued to sit, quiet and still, for several more moments.

Hannah was the first to move. She sighed, pulled her legs out from under her, and stretched them straight in the middle of the circle. She wiggled her multicolored toes.

Elise smiled, a weak twisting of her mouth, but she kept her eyes on the floor, listening to the grunts and groans and creaking of the other stiff bodies as they moved to stand and stretch. Tom stood, stretched his arms over his head, and popped his knuckles. He bent and offered his hand to Elise.

She couldn't bring herself to look at anyone just yet, and she didn't trust her legs to hold her up. She shook her head. He shrugged and wandered off after the others. Elise could hear their voices in another room, could hear the rattle of pots and pans and plates. Every Indian ceremony she had ever attended was followed by a feast, and she knew she should get up and head to the kitchen and offer to help. But she couldn't move. It was as if she had fought some enormous battle; every fiber of her being was spent, the ebb tide of all that emotion leaving her stranded.

"Many from the spirit world were here tonight," Hayes whispered. "For you."

Elise looked up. She had thought she was alone, that they had all left her for the warmth and aroma of the kitchen, but Grandfather Hayes still sat on his pile of blankets across from her. His eyes were pools of darkness in the dim light, but she could see the kindness radiating there.

"Death has followed you, like a dark cloud, my daughter." His voice was low and ragged. "All your life, it seems. Even in your dreams."

It didn't matter that she had spent most of her life around Uncle Wes and Lorena, people who always seemed to know things that they had no way of knowing. It still caught her by surprise, that unearthly knowledge. How did he know? How did he understand so much about her in such a short time?

Elise hung her head, the emotion of all the losses in her life pushing on her shoulders, crushing her. A tear dropped onto her jeans. She melted at the words *my daughter*. She had heard Uncle Wes do something similar, calling people sister or nephew or brother, despite no blood relation. It was a reminder that we are all related, that all are connected in spirit. She could not raise her head to look at him, certain that she would be washed away in another tide of emotion.

"I see you are lost in the darkness. In the fog. You don't know which way to turn." He met her eyes.

Elise couldn't breathe. His words were so close to the same ones that Celestina had used just a few weeks ago.

"It is only natural to want help. Guidance. Answers. You have been looking for answers."

She nodded, despite the fact that he had not phrased it as a question. He already knew the answer.

"Since the dawn of time, it is this way. People look for answers. They go to doctors or churches. Ashrams and gurus. Card readers and witches. Medicine men. Anyone that holds the promise of showing them the right thing to do."

Her mouth hung open slightly, pulled into Hayes and the ragged sound of his voice.

"And sometimes, it helps. Sometimes these others can offer you a part of the answer. There is a time to take counsel from others. To gather information from other points of view. In the old days, when the people were faced with big decisions, we met in council house. Everyone had a chance to speak—a chance to bring their own thoughts to the table. And each voice is important. Each opinion has value."

A jolt ran through her body. She forgot herself and stared at him.

"But each one of us can see only one small piece of the puzzle. One small glimpse of the bigger picture. Even those who know us the best, who love us the most, do not know what is right for us." He rocked back and forth for a moment, his eyes locked on the floor between them.

"Sometimes the words of others can help us. Sometimes, words can deceive. When a warrior goes into battle, he cannot stop and ask for guidance from others. He must find his way through the smoke and the fog on his own. It is the greatest battle that any two-legged ever faces. Learning to trust your own wisdom. Your own knowledge, as Creator gives it to you."

Elise wiped her face with her sleeve. "But . . . what if . . . what if I make a mistake? What if I get it wrong?"

His eyes were kind, flooded with gentleness and compassion for her and her situation. "Do you really think that someone else can protect you? Can keep you from never making another mistake? Can keep you from ever experiencing pain?"

Tears ran down her face in sheets.

"No one can protect you, daughter. Pain is part of living. Pain and joy are two sides of the same coin. If you want to have one, you will also feel the other."

Elise swallowed and wiped her face again.

"Why are you here? Why have you come so far?"

She exhaled and looked him in the eye. "I think my husband is trying to tell me something. I think he wanted me to come out here."

"If he is, he will find a way to let you know. You do not need to keep asking all these . . ." Hayes waved his hand in the air around him. "Others. Even those who study science"—Hayes pursed his lips to indicate the place where Tom had been sitting—"even the experts . . . do not always know." He thumped his hand on his heart. "Listen here. Creator speaks through your heart. The answer is always here." He thumped his chest again. "If you listen."

Hayes stared at the fire for a moment. "We live in a world of so much noise. So much distraction. Cell phones and computers, Wi-Fi, video games. Noise, all the time. Everybody has something to say. Everyone has an opinion about what you should do." He turned to her. "But if you want to know the *right* thing to do, you must shut out all the voices around you. Listen only to your own heart. That is where the answers are."

Elise wrapped her arms around her chest and rocked back and forth. That was exactly what Michael would have said. It was exactly what he used to do whenever he was troubled. Whenever he was working on a carving and it wasn't coming to him easily, off he went. Hiking into the woods or sitting on a rock, sometimes for hours. Listening. Waiting for the spirits to speak to him.

She loved being out in nature, loved sitting by the creek or looking down at the valley. But she'd never been very good at just waiting—waiting for knowledge from a source in which she wasn't sure she believed. Waiting to hear a message she was never quite sure came from *spirit* or from some corner of her own mind that liked to play make-believe. Was it really the voice of *spirit*, or simply her own brain, throwing thoughts around like a Frisbee?

"I've tried. A little. I'm never sure of what I'm hearing."

His eyes took in every angle of her face, studying every part of her visage. "When the answer is right, you will feel it. Here." Again, he tapped his fist on his heart.

She stared at him, at the brown eyes crinkled by age. There was a wisdom there, a calm strength that she wished she possessed.

She waited a beat before speaking. "I'm afraid. Afraid of all this . . ."

He waited for her to go on. "Afraid of what, my daughter?"

She wiped her nose, searching for the answer. "I'm afraid of messing up. Getting it wrong. I'm afraid that someone will . . . die."

Hayes raised his eyebrows and shrugged. "We are all going to die, daughter. Is that so bad? To die? Is that the worst thing you can think of?"

For the first time since her dream of the accident, all those months ago, Elise considered that idea.

"Soldiers always go into battle prepared to die." He rocked back and forth. "Death is not the worst thing that can happen. There are many things worse than death. And one of them is to lose yourself. To lose your confidence. To lose your ability to trust yourself. To give up your own power. Living the life that others say you should live. When that happens, you are a leaf in the wind, blown every which way. You might as well be dead."

Elise swallowed hard. Was it worse than death? To be lost, unable to trust one's own instincts? She tried to sift through the muddle of thoughts.

"There are no mistakes. Only choices. Only different paths. You did not cause your husband's death. He made his own choices that day. He chose his own path. And now you must choose yours. Spirit guides you even now, even tonight.

"Get quiet. Listen with your whole being. Your heart will tell you what you need to know." Hayes thumped his chest once again. "Everything important, everything you need—every answer you seek—is here." His fist rested on his chest. He looked at Elise, a look that reached deep inside her, a look that made her feel as if he knew everything already that she was looking for. As if he had known her forever, knew all her secrets, all her fears.

Elise swallowed and nodded.

They sat in silence, both sets of eyes staring at the space between them, their faces lit golden by the firelight. Sounds of pots sizzling on the stove drifted in from the kitchen, riding with the aromas of red chili and roast chicken. She heard Hannah laugh, a deep, full-bodied laugh that made Elise smile.

"Stop running. Whatever it is you are afraid of, turn and face it. Face it with your head high and your shoulders back. If it is death that comes for you, then so be it. Today is a good day to die." He sat up straight, threw his shoulders back.

Elise swallowed. The tears had stopped. Miraculously, her insides had grown calm. Her breathing had returned to normal. His words were not reassuring, and yet, somehow, she did feel reassured. She felt, for the first time, that she could stop fighting. Stop trying to figure it all out, stop trying to resist. Stop running to one person after another to give her answers, to help her figure out Michael's message. Stop being afraid of *not* being able to figure it out.

Elise stared at him, mesmerized by the low, ragged voice, the kind eyes like dark lake water, reflecting the light of the stars. She exhaled.

The sounds coming from the kitchen reached them; they could hear the rattle of the plates and silverware, the murmurs of conversation and laughter.

Hayes sniffed the air. "Almost time to eat. Shall we join the others?"

Elise nodded and stood up.

"If you don't mind, could you help an old man up?"

She smiled and reached for his arm. He unfolded slowly, as if trying to smooth the creases that had accumulated in his hips and knees and back. They stood, leaning lightly on each other.

"Smells wonderful, doesn't it?" He closed his eyes and raised his face, sniffing the aromas coming from the kitchen. He opened his eyes and found her face again. "I'm starving. I think I could eat a horse." Hayes took a step in the direction of the kitchen, then stopped and put a hand on her arm. "Just kidding! Only the Cheyenne eat horses." He threw his head back and laughed, and Elise caught the warmth in his voice and smiled.

# CHAPTER
# TWENTY-TWO

After breakfast the next morning, Elise and Hannah scrunched through an inch of snow, headed to Hannah's studio. It was behind the house, up the hill, and looked more like an original homestead cabin than a weaving studio. Hannah opened the door, and Elise stepped inside.

"Ah," she gasped. The space was incredible. It might not have looked like much from the outside, but the inside had been completely redone. Windows flooded the space with light and views of the valley below and the Smoky Mountains behind. The roof was high, and the rafters supported knotty pine ceilings. The back wall held spools of thread in every conceivable color. Elise ran her fingers over the shelves, looking at spools of silk and mohair and merino wool and thin cotton.

She turned and took in the looms, sitting at angles around the space. There was a Glimakra, a giant from Sweden. "Wow. This is incredible. You obviously love fiber," she whispered, indicating the

Persian wool rugs on the floor, the weavings that covered every available inch of wall space.

Hannah stood still in the middle of the room. "Yes. Since I was a little girl in New Mexico. We had a neighbor who was a weaver. She dyed her own wool. Used all these natural dyes. Sometimes if she needed some special effect for her tapestries, she spun her own yarn. She made these tapestries that were incredible. They had dimension to them—thick and thin and sometimes with pieces of wood or ribbon hanging off. She was quite a master. I couldn't get enough of her."

"The first weavings that I remember were at Lorena's house, when I was five or six years old," Elise said. "I felt the same way. Like there was magic in those threads. A connection to something deeper . . . something that was missing from my life."

Hannah stood still, her hands resting on the castle of a giant loom. She caught Elise's eye. "It's still there, you know," Hannah said quietly. "That connection. Your weaving will be different now, after everything that has happened. But the magic is still there, waiting for you."

Elise stood next to one of the smaller looms, looking at a colorful striped warp. "It doesn't feel that way," she whispered. She could not meet Hannah's eyes. "I feel like the muse abandoned me the same time Michael did. I haven't been able to weave a thing in all this time. It's like I've forgotten how." She walked slowly around the room. "I sit down at the loom. But all I end up doing is ripping things out."

"Tapestry? Is that what you do?" Hannah asked.

Elise nodded. "It's what I *used* to do."

"Tapestry is pretty difficult. Even under the best of circumstances." Hannah moved to one small strip of wall between two windows. "Let me show you something."

She brought Elise to a narrow section of wall. A tapestry hung there, only eighteen inches wide, about six feet long. It was a blazing trail of color, starting with the deepest purples and moving through burgundy and red and orange, ending with flaming golds and coppers. There were no shapes or corners or difficult threadings. It had none of the intricate patterns and complicated twists and turns of the Navajo patterns that Elise loved so much. This was simply warp and weft, plain weave, in gorgeous sunset colors. "It's beautiful," she whispered.

Hannah moved next to her, staring at the weaving with her. "I just finished that. It's been hard, moving across country. Changing my whole life, at my age. I miss my friends. I miss Celestina. I miss that land. I miss the dry cool air and the sparkling snowfall. Everything out there seems so crisp and clean. Northern New Mexico is enchanting, just as they say."

Elise nodded.

"This is completely different"—she indicated the weaving—"from anything I had ever done when I lived in New Mexico. And yet, it is also a tribute to that place. That land. Those memories. I took all my love for that place, that time of my life, and put it in the weaving."

"It's incredible," Elise said, unable to take her eyes from the long exploration of color.

"But now—" Hannah turned toward a tapestry loom made of copper pipes, sitting in one corner of the studio. "Now I am weaving the Smoky Mountains. I'm starting to weave the land I see around me here. The softness. The curves. The clouds. Also enchanting. Also beautiful."

Hannah ran her hand over the warp threads on a small tapestry loom, and Elise looked at the greens and blues and purples that were climbing the warp strings, creating an abstract study of trees. Of green. Of a land that held moisture and profusion and abundance.

"I don't know how I could survive this change in our lives, moving out here," Hannah whispered, her fingers still rubbing the wool, "if I wasn't weaving. I take all my sadness, but also the excitement of being in this new place—meeting new friends—and pour it into my weavings. I weave my feelings." Hannah smiled.

"They're beautiful. I can see that . . . that emotion."

"That's the secret to all great art, isn't it?" Hannah stood in front of the weaving. "Not that I think this is great art, mind you, but . . . there is something there. Something I don't find in all my creations. Emotion, poured out of my soul."

Elise sat down on one of the weaving benches. "Michael used to say something similar to that. Not emotion, exactly, but connection. Connection to the spirits in the land around him. Connection to his ancestors. To the way of life that they had in those mountains for hundreds of years. Before everything changed. Before reservations."

She remembered that raven, standing in his studio; she remembered the way it had felt to run her fingers over its wings. As if she could feel that connection, that spirit. As if the raven were *alive*, maybe not in any conventional sense. Not in any way that Tom would understand. But still, there was life in that piece. Life that she had never found in her own weaving, in her own work.

"Elise? Why don't you stay awhile? We have that little guesthouse where Tom is staying right now. You could work here, in my studio. I never use more than two or three looms at a time. As you can see"— Hannah turned and held her arm out over the space—"I have a love of beautiful looms. You can use anything here.

"The Penland School of Crafts is just over those mountains, near Asheville." Hannah pointed out the front window. "They do workshops, if you're interested. I'd love to take one sometime. After working alone for a long time, it's good to get out with other people for a bit. Get some new ideas. Feed on the energy of other weavers."

Elise swallowed. "The Penland School. I always thought it could be interesting to take a class there."

Hannah turned and looked at Elise. "Why don't you take all that emotion . . . all that grief and loss. Pick the colors that match your tears.

And pour them into the threads." Hannah stood in front of her New Mexico weaving.

Elise stared at the subtle changes of color that ran up the wall in Hannah's weaving. For one moment, she let her mind explore the idea—the concept of trying to weave all that had happened in her life these past months. Her eyes traveled to the wall filled with cones of different-colored yarns. What colors would she pick? What, exactly, was the color of death?

# CHAPTER TWENTY-THREE

Elise was alone at the house. Hannah had left that morning to spend the day and night with their daughter and granddaughter in Chattanooga. Elise was invited to come along, but she declined. After spending three long days riding across country, without a moment to herself, she had no desire to spend any more time riding in a car, visiting another city. The idea of staying here, in this comfortable home in the mountains, was much more appealing to her. Tom and David had headed out a couple of hours ago, looking for various parts and gadgets they still needed to get the solar system completely up and running.

She sat in Hannah's weaving studio. Hannah had offered her the use of one big floor loom, already warped for dish towels.

"Nothing to it," Hannah had told her. "The only thing you have to do is throw the shuttle." And that's exactly what Elise was doing and had been doing for a couple of hours. She sat at the loom, throwing the shuttle from one hand to the other, grabbing the beater bar and tapping the newly laid weft thread into place. Then back again, the other way.

Nothing complicated, nothing that she had to think about, nothing like the elaborate tapestries she used to do before her life fell apart. This was a rhythm, a musical line, across and tap, across and tap. The rhythm had lulled her, taken her to a place where she was completely unaware of time and space and her own body. It was meditative, and her mind drifted. She was more relaxed than she had been in months.

She was lost to everything except that rhythm. A loud bang made her jump. She caught the shuttle and held still, listening intently. Outside the window, the sky had dimmed. Night was creeping up from the forest, and she realized it now as she raised her head from the weaving. The wind had started to kick up. The same banging noise sounded again somewhere at the back of the house.

Elise stood and moved to the door. There were no lights on anywhere. The generator was not turned on; the solar system was not operational yet. Tom and David had not returned, and for a moment, she thought about trying to find the generator, trying to figure out how to get it going.

The banging noise sounded again, and she started across the ground to the house. A long, covered porch ran the entire length of the back of the house, and she ran the last few steps. She stood at the edge of the porch, looking out at the woods and the mountains beyond. The door slammed, once again, louder this time, right behind her. It was the screen door at the back of the house, pulling out with the breeze and then slamming back against the doorjamb. Elise latched it tight.

*Elise?*

The voice was behind her somewhere, and she turned, slowly, surveying the dark recesses of the property. For a moment, she thought that Tom and David had returned. She scanned the driveway and property. David's truck was parked by the guesthouse, but Tom's Jeep was nowhere she could see. There were so many buildings—a barn, a two-car detached garage, the studio, a tiny guest cottage where Tom had been staying. But she could see no movement anywhere.

It was twilight, the blue hour. Only tonight, with the clouds and the approaching storm, it was more gray than blue. She shivered, thinking about Beulah standing in the dusk all those years ago, waiting to hear the voices of the dead. Her words came back now, whispering in Elise's mind. *The time when the veil between the worlds is the thinnest. The best time to speak to spirits of the departed.* Elise took her hand away from the door. But instead of going inside, she turned back to the edge of the porch. Branches swayed and creaked in the woods behind the house. She stood still, listening. She put her hand in her pocket and rubbed her fingers over the piece of obsidian. That obsidian felt like her lifeline, her one connection to Michael, her whole reason for being here.

*Elise?*

She was staring right into the trees, not entirely sure where the sound was coming from. It had to be out there, somewhere in the woods, somewhere off to the left, heading toward the boundary between Hannah and David's property and the Great Smoky Mountains National Park. Pulling her sweater around her body, she stepped off the porch, headed in the direction of the voice.

She moved slowly, quietly, placing one foot and stopping to listen, just the way she had seen Lorena do when she was out talking to the plants. Step and stop. Step and stop. "Michael?" she whispered. "Is that you?"

She had not walked far when she found a deer trail, worn smooth by years of use, and she started down it, unsure in the falling light. She stopped every few steps, waiting. Listening.

*Elise?*

This time it sounded as if the voice was all around her, louder, more insistent than before. She could not pinpoint the direction from which it came. It could be above her or below her, or ahead or behind. With the way the wind was blowing, there was no way to be sure. She continued her slow step and stop down the deer trail. It opened onto a clearing, just a small slope of grass, surrounded by trees, and she stopped again. Her heart hammered. It took her back to that night, at the cabin in New Mexico, when she woke up convinced that someone was calling her name. Elise waited, listening. Somewhere in the near distance, a dog began to bark.

"Michael?" she whispered once again.

A sound gathered behind her on the path she had just walked. It whooshed through the trees. The raven flew directly over her head, settling into the branches of a bare hickory tree in the middle of the clearing. She was hemmed in by dark woods all around, bare branches of the trees against the darkened sky, the black bird sitting and staring at her, eyes red in the dim light. Branches reached toward her from the forest, like the bony fingers of hands.

Elise moved to the middle of the clearing and lowered herself onto a log. She stared at the bird, remembering the words of Grandfather Hayes a few nights ago. *Listen to your own heart.* She forced herself to breathe, forced herself to stay quiet and still.

The beating of her heart was like the beating of the drum a few nights ago. That pounding, that rhythm, hard on the downstroke, softer on the upbeat, like an echo, pulsed through her veins. The drum, the heartbeat rhythm, pulled her in, like the beating heart of the earth itself.

All the words of Grandfather Hayes floated back to her now, a thick soup of ideas in her mind. She had been looking for someone who could tell her what she needed to know, what she needed to do. And the more she listened to those other voices, the more confused she had become. She wasn't sure about anything anymore.

In her right hand, she held the mojo bag made by the conjure woman in Memphis, her palm and fingers completely enclosing the red flannel and its contents. She could feel the power of those talismans, the herbs and stones and bones that had gone into that bag. They pulsed in her hand, beating with her heart and her blood. In her left hand, she held the chunk of obsidian that had come to her from Michael's pocket.

She thought about all the words she had heard these past few weeks, all the predictions and advice. She thought of Tom, keeping track of it all on his spreadsheet, thought of all the ways the people around her, including those who practiced the art of divination, were trying to help. Trying to protect her. But could they, really? Any more than she had been able to protect Michael from his death?

Maybe it was true, what Lorena and Monica and Celestina had tried to tell her. Maybe her dream of the accident, all those months ago, was never meant to make her stop Michael from going. Maybe there were events, certain situations, that had been put into motion by some force more powerful than she would ever be, some force she had never understood or believed in.

She thought of Michael rushing in from the shop on that March afternoon, grabbing the keys to her car from the table by the door. Taking the hand that fate had dealt, heading off into the night to die. Was she doing the same thing out here in Olalla? Was all this the work of some god with a remarkably dry sense of humor, sending her pinging around the planet like the ball in a pinball machine—racing from one psychic to another, trying to avoid her fate, only to end up here, facing it head-on? The energy of death was all over her, permeating her hair and her clothes, her skin and her blood, like the aroma of a skunk. She had never felt so *immersed* in death before; it was as if she was already covered in her own blood.

Grandfather Hayes had told her that she needed to face her worst fears. That if it was death that awaited her, to turn and face it. That idea, that thought, seeped into her consciousness, and what followed was a sense of absolute calm. She was finished running; she was finished trying to escape whatever it was that had pulled her here. She was finished trying to move faster than the hand of fate, finished with trying to figure out all the signs and dreams and words and warnings. And more important, she was finished looking for answers in everyone else.

His words had stirred up all the mud in her mind, making her sift through all her fears. He was right. Death was *not* the worst thing she could think of. All this time, she'd been afraid of it, that word with the capital *D*. Afraid of what the raven was trying to tell her, afraid of the messages that kept showing up in the cards and in Venetta's words and with that gnarled old woman in Memphis. Not now. The fear was gone. She was finished with careening wildly from one seer to another, trying to make sense of it all and save herself. She cared nothing at all about Tom's spreadsheet and cold readings and hot readings and statistical probabilities. About what was and wasn't possible. Whatever it was that awaited her here in Olalla, she would hold her head up and walk out to meet it, shoulders back, eyes clear. Today was a good day to die.

And now that she had come to this realization, she saw that it wasn't death that scared her. Almost everyone she had ever loved was already gone, passed over to the other side, whatever that meant. She'd have plenty of company there. No, it wasn't flying off the road and into the canyon of death that really frightened her.

Elise understood now why it was that some couples, married for many years, often died within a few months of each other, following their life partner to the grave. She understood now why her mother had grown silent and distant and lost just as soon as they arrived back in New Mexico. She understood why the doctors, and even Lorena, with all the wisdom of the ages to guide her, had not been able to help Rose. Dying was the path of least resistance. Dying was easy.

Her worst fear, the thing she dreaded most, was to go on living—trying to figure out how to negotiate a world that didn't have Michael in it. She did not want to learn how to go on without him. She did not want to figure out how she was going to make a living, or where she was going to live, or how she was going to negotiate the canyons of loneliness that carved through her future. She did not want to absorb yet another loss in her life. All these months, she'd been lost in the icy wasteland of grief, unable to move, unable to think, unable to plan. Frozen, paralyzed, with no interest in trying to figure out her own future.

It wasn't dying she feared—it was living. Living without him. The only thing in this whole world that she wanted was one more moment with Michael. One more chance to get it right. To say all the things she hadn't said on that March afternoon. One more chance to lie next to him at night, wrapped in his arms, his breath in her hair. Just one more time. She hung her head and let her tears drop into the dirt at her feet.

What good was any of it, anyway? Psychic knowledge, intuition, dreams? They had not helped her save the one person she loved most in this world.

She opened both of her palms, looking at the objects she held. In her right was the mojo bag from the woman in Memphis—the bag designed to protect her from the forces acting on her. In her left hand was the obsidian stone Michael had given her. She closed her fingers around it, feeling that same charge of electricity she felt every time she touched it. Elise closed her eyes, the power of that stone vibrating through her, like a direct connection to Michael. Like a direct connection to the world of the spirits.

She wiped the tears from her face and stood. She walked through the darkness, down the path, back to the house, and opened the door into the living room. She moved with purpose, with conviction, her shoulders back, her head high. Straight to the fireplace in Hannah and David's living room. Two logs glowed red, only an occasional lick of flame curling up from underneath. She stood next to the fire. And then she opened her right palm, threw the red flannel bag of hoodoo protection on top. The charm that was supposed to keep her safe. The charm, concocted to protect her from whatever spell she was under. She no longer wanted protection. She did not need protection. She was ready to face her fears, ready to face whatever was coming.

She watched, mesmerized, as the fabric began to smoke. A moment later, flames flashed up, enveloping the bag and its contents, sending sparks of color shooting out into the night. Like smoke signals to the spirits. *Take me. I'm ready. Today is a good day to die.*

# CHAPTER TWENTY-FOUR

They sat at the breakfast table in the kitchen, Elise, Tom, and David. David had made coffee and his breakfast special—huevos rancheros and fried potatoes. Tom had dug in, staring at his computer at the same time; Elise pushed her food around her plate.

Tom closed his iPad and pushed it away. "David, I messed up. We need three of those hose connectors, not two. Do you want me to head back into town and get another one?"

David looked up. "No. That's okay. I'll do it. I need to go back into town, anyway. I forgot to pick up a package for Hannah at the post office."

Tom turned to Elise. "So I guess that means I have a little time this morning. Shall we go look for that stone-carver person?"

David stood up and took his plate to the sink. He turned and looked at Elise. "I asked around yesterday when we were in town. Found somebody who knew the place. Apparently it's on a little windy mountain road, way back of beyond. But we wrote down the directions, so hopefully Mr. Magoo over there won't get you too turned around."

Tom pushed his glasses up and gave Elise a goofy smile. Tom's phone buzzed, and he answered. A moment later, he held it out to her. "It's for you," he murmured. "Monica."

Elise took the phone. Tom's face was flushed with color, like someone coming down with a fever. "Are you sick?" she asked.

He shook his head.

"Good morning, Monica. What is it? Seven a.m. out there?" Elise turned and started walking toward the window.

"Can he hear you?" Monica whispered. "Go outside."

"Hang on, Mo. This isn't a good connection." Elise put the phone at her side and walked out the door and onto the back porch. "Okay. I think this is better. What's going on?" Elise felt a knot in her stomach, pulling tight against her rib cage. She glanced back at the window to the kitchen. Tom had stopped eating and was watching her.

Monica exhaled. "Are you sure he can't hear you?"

Elise turned away from the house and started walking down the path toward the woods. "Yes. Come on, Monica. What is it?"

"Narciso and I went up to the cabin yesterday. After work."

Elise waited, breathless.

"Someone's been up there." Monica's voice went quiet. "You're not going to like this, Elise. That raven? The one Michael was working on?"

The world started to tilt, and Elise sat down on a rock.

"It's gone."

The news hit her hard, almost as if she were losing Michael all over again. The raven. It was only an object, only a thing, and yet it was so connected to Michael. The work he had poured his heart into, the work on which he had spent the last days of his life. She felt dizzy; her stomach clenched. She leaned forward, forcing herself to breathe.

"We looked all over for signs of a car or footprints. Couldn't find anything."

"Hhhh." Elise gasped. "Did you go in the house? Did they take anything else?"

"Not that I noticed. Those other pieces in the studio? That Michael hadn't finished yet? They were still there. We checked the house, too, but if they took something, I sure didn't notice.

"Elise? We called the police. Just the Amalia police, but still. Maybe they know a little bit about what they're doing. We were up there for quite a long time, by the time they took the report and dusted for fingerprints. All that jazz."

Monica sighed. "And maybe they don't know what they're talking about, but they said it looks like an inside job."

"What does that mean?"

"Somebody who knew your place. Who knew exactly where to look and exactly what they were looking for."

Elise forced herself to inhale. Exhale. Absorb the information.

"I keep thinking about this whole Celestina reading thing." Monica waited a beat. "She knew. Knew that Michael was an artist. Knew that he carved wood. Isn't that what you told me?"

Elise nodded, and then forced the answer. "Yeah. Yeah, she knew."

"And then she sends Mr. Science up there, to bring you wood. To work on the solar heater. He walked right into the studio that day. Remember? When you showed me the raven? And then she sends the two of you off on a trip across country."

*Smoke gets in your eyes. Someone has lied to you. Someone is working the hoodoo on you.* Thoughts circled, like ravens, gathering around a carcass.

"Couldn't be a better setup, don't you think? A psychic card reader, probing into the lives of all these grieving widows. All these women, distraught and confused, coming right into her shop, telling her everything."

"But . . . why would Celestina want that raven? What could it possibly mean to her?"

Monica snorted. "What could it mean? Money. That raven is worth some bucks now that Michael is . . ." She stopped midsentence. "There was an article, just a few days ago, in the *Santa Fe New Mexican*. Right after you left. About Michael Madrid, the Indian artist. Another New Mexico treasure, gone too soon. About how prices of his work have skyrocketed. Mom saved you a copy."

Elise forced herself to breathe. She forced herself to try to think. "Well, Tom didn't take it. He's been with me."

"Of course not. Tom was the finger. Think, Elise. Tom is the doofus sidekick, the one who goes to fix something or take a load of firewood. He's the one who goes to the homes of all these grieving widows. He's the one that scopes it all out, learns all about the place. He even had a *key* to that Cynthia's house."

"So you think he knows? You think he knows what Celestina is up to?"

"Maybe. Maybe not. Maybe she was just using him." Monica stopped for a moment.

Elise stared off into the woods.

"Maybe he's entirely innocent, Elise. Maybe Celestina is not involved. But it sure smells fishy. And I don't think you can afford to take any more chances. It's time to get away from that guy."

Elise stood with her back to the house. She held the phone to her ear.

"Elise? Maybe you should hole up somewhere. Let me come and get you." Monica's voice was sober and quiet. "We don't know this guy from Adam. Who knows what he was really doing in Tucson before he came up here. Who knows if he really was in Tucson, even. I don't like this. I don't like the way this feels."

Elise exhaled. She did not tell Monica about her own fears. She did not tell her about the words of the hoodoo woman in Memphis. *Pulling her in, like a moth to the flame. Working the hoodoo on her.* "But . . . all this time, I've never felt like he's *dangerous*. He's just kind of . . . I don't know . . . his head in the clouds, or something."

"Maybe that's because he's trying to pull the wool over your eyes."

Elise turned and saw Tom still standing at the window, watching her. "Monica, I better go. I'll call you soon."

"Elise?" Elise could hear Monica take a big breath on the other end of the line. "Be careful."

Elise hit the "End" button on the phone and held it against her body for a moment. She looked off at the gardens, but her eyes saw none of the plants before her. What she could see were all the many pieces of Native American art inside Hannah and David's house, all the works she had pointed out and admired when they first arrived. Elise turned and started back to the door. She pulled the phone from under her arm. The screen showed recent calls. There was Monica's number at the top. Underneath it was Celestina, three in a row. And a few calls down the list, Elise saw the name Ken Black and a number with area code 505—the area code for northern New Mexico and Santa Fe. Ken Black, the art dealer in Santa Fe, the man who had hounded her for months to see if there was anything Michael had in the studio that might be ready for sale. Ken Black, the man she could barely tolerate, even when Michael was with her to make it more palatable. Ken Black, the man who would stop at nothing, apparently, to make money from Native art.

She clicked the screen away. Her whole body shivered.

The screen door banged, and Tom stepped out on the porch. "Ready?"

# CHAPTER

# TWENTY-FIVE

She stared at him, standing there, holding out her jacket. In slow motion, she reached for it and pulled it on around her. She followed him to the Jeep, folded herself into the passenger seat, moving on instinct.

Like the pieces of a jigsaw puzzle, her thoughts began to snap into place. Celestina, orchestrating this whole show, with her tarot cards and widows and orphans. Elise thought back to the first time she had seen the raven. It was after she had gone in for a reading. The same day that Celestina had called, inviting her to the widows' and orphans' group. The day that Celestina had laughed about asking around and finding Elise's phone number. That raven had been on the porch; she had seen him just after she hung up with Celestina. She bit her nail, trying not to panic.

And then she remembered Grandfather Hayes, just two nights ago, telling her that there would come a time, like a warrior going into battle, when she would not be able to seek advice, would not be able to ask anyone else what she should do. That the only way through the battle, through the storm, was to listen to her own heart, her own gut feelings. *Listen here,* he had told her, thumping his fist on his chest. *And you will know what to do.*

She took a breath, focused all her attention on her own heart, her own inner wisdom. Elise remembered the feeling that had driven her to go to Celestina's shop in the first place, before the raven ever showed up. Michael had something to tell her. She *knew* it, with every fiber of her being. She could not stop now. She could not back down in fear when she was this close to knowing.

She put her hand in the pocket of her sweater and locked her palm around the black glass stone. It calmed her, reassured her, warmed her with that hum of connection that she always felt when she touched it. It beat in time with her own heart. She *had* to go. It didn't matter what Celestina was up to or how Tom was involved or why Ken Black's number was on his phone. She had to do this.

They twisted and turned, climbing up into steep hills. The road was narrow and curvy, a gravel monstrosity that reminded her of her road up to the cabin back home. It was filled with washboard areas that jarred their teeth, and much of it lay in shadow, either from the pitch of the hill beside it or the trees that grew thick and tall on each side.

"Hope he doesn't make moonshine," Tom muttered. "I'm not in the mood to get shot at today." He turned to Elise, a goofy smile on his face, and pushed his glasses up on his nose.

She stared back at him, questions pounding against her temples. *Who are you? And what are you hiding?*

They rounded the bend in the road, and Tom stopped. Next to a long driveway was a bright-yellow mailbox, and Tom reached into his pocket and drew out a piece of paper, folded into fourths. "I think this is it. Yellow mailbox." He turned to the right, and they meandered down a very long, rutted driveway.

Back in the trees, in the shadow of the mountain, was a small cabin, smoke curling out of a blue steel chimney pipe. Two dogs, one a big hound and the other smaller and older and of indeterminate breed, came down off the porch and barked at the truck. Tom killed the engine, and they both sat for a moment, looking at the dogs.

A man came out on the porch. He was long and lean, gray haired, with a beard to match. Elise rolled down her window a few inches. "I'm looking for Franklin Cooper."

The man leaned forward and spat on the ground.

"A stone carver named Franklin Cooper. Would that be you?"

"Maybe. Maybe not." The man stood with one hand leaning on his porch post.

"Do the dogs bite?" Elise asked.

"Not unless I tell 'em to," he muttered.

Elise opened her car door and placed a foot outside. The dogs gathered around her, barking and sniffing, and she took a chance and brought her whole body out of the Jeep. She held a hand in front of the big dog so that he could sniff her and walked slowly up to the porch. "I'm looking for Franklin Cooper. The man who carved this piece of obsidian."

Elise held the stone out to him, and he took it and turned it over a couple of times.

He handed it back to her.

"You from the tax office?"

Elise shook her head. "I think my husband bought that from you, last spring. Somewhere in New Mexico."

The man peered through the windshield of the Jeep, trying to get a good look at Tom. "That ain't him, is it?"

Elise shook her head again. "No. My husband died last March. I found this in his jacket, about a week ago. Along with your card."

Franklin Cooper met her eyes. He did not give away any emotion; his face was every bit as stoic and unmoved as his carvings. "Guess you might as well come in."

He held the screen door open, and Elise followed him into the small cabin. The dogs plopped down on the front porch, heads and paws pointed toward Tom, as if they'd been instructed to keep him in their sights.

Elise looked around the cabin. There were two chairs over by the woodstove. A small kitchen area was on her right side, and behind it she glimpsed a bedroom and a bath. Under the front window sat a long pine desk, filled with tools. A light was trained on a work area, in the center of which stood another piece of obsidian, about the size of an egg.

Cooper stepped forward and turned off the switch. He held out his hand to indicate the chairs by the fire, and Elise sat down. Cooper sat down in the chair opposite.

Elise stared at the floor between them, unsure where to start. "I don't know why I'm here, really. I don't know where Michael found you, or how he got this. But I found it in his jacket pocket, and it just felt . . . I don't know . . . important." She raised her eyes and looked at him.

The man didn't move. He didn't nod. He gave no indication that any of this was remotely connected to him. The fire cracked and popped in the stove. She could hear the hiss of steam from a pot of water.

Cooper leaned forward and looked at the stone in her hand. "I didn't carve that one."

"You didn't?"

"I do carve stones; that's true." He raised his hand and indicated the worktable by the window. "Just not that one."

Elise was totally flummoxed. "I'm sorry. I just assumed . . ." She dropped her gaze to the rug in front of their feet, completely at a loss as to what to do next. She took a deep breath, tried to steady her nerves. "I'm not really sure why I'm here. It's just that . . ." Elise could see now that she really had no good reason to come to this man's house, to interrupt his day. She didn't have a specific question. She could think of nothing she could say to him that would come remotely close to what she had hoped to find when she first left New Mexico. The whole idea seemed ridiculous to her now.

"Your husband was Indian? Long black hair?"

Elise looked up and nodded. "You remember him?"

The man nodded. "I broke down on the highway, just north of Questa. I'd been to that mineral show in Tucson. Had all kinds of stones in my truck. Several thousand dollars' worth. And I'd heard stories about those highways in New Mexico. Not a lot of white people around, you know?"

Elise looked at him, her lips pressed in a tight line.

"I had the hood up, checking out the engine, when I saw your husband pull up behind me. Driving an old, beat-up Nissan truck."

Elise nodded. "Yeah. Yeah, that's his."

"I have to tell you, ma'am, I was a sight uncomfortable when I saw that he was Indian."

Elise went rigid.

"He asked if I needed some help. I was leery. Trying to keep an eye on him and trying to see if he had a partner that I hadn't noticed yet. I was getting a mite itchy."

Cooper leaned over the side of his chair and spit into a copper bucket. "Your husband noticed my license plate. Asked me what part of Tennessee. Said he had always wanted to see these mountains."

Elise nodded.

"Well, we both started poking around under the hood, and he noticed that the plug in my radiator was gone. Completely gone. All the fluid drained out. And he went back to his truck and come back with this piece of wood, and he kind of whittled on it till he got it to fit that hole. Come back again with a jug of water. Said that would probably get me down the hill, back into Questa.

"I told him I was short on cash but long on stones, and I offered to pay him with a couple of pieces I had carved. We jawed about carving for a bit.

"And then I pulled out a few of my obsidian pieces. And I told him to take what he wanted."

Elise wrapped her palm around that stone and stared into a corner of the room.

"He took two pieces that I had carved. And then his eye caught on that piece." Cooper indicated the stone in Elise's hand. "He picked it up and held it for a minute. Looked at the carving. Asked me how much I wanted for it.

"I told him I didn't carve that one. Somebody gave it to me, way back when. I'm not really even sure why I had it with me. I told him if he really wanted it, just take it. I sure as heck didn't remember where it came from. Just thought he ought to know that I didn't carve it."

Elise nodded.

They sat quietly for a few moments. The clock ticked.

"Mr. Cooper, did he say anything else?" She felt desperate, searching for something, anything that would make this whole trip, this whole ordeal, worthwhile.

"Call me Frank. Mr. Cooper is my dad." He smiled. "He said he'd like to come out here sometime. Maybe check out my studio. Said maybe we could work something out with carving. That maybe I could teach him some stone carving. But I had a feeling that wasn't the real reason."

"What gave you that idea?"

The man shrugged. "Can't say, exactly. Just didn't ring true, you know? My God, those carvers at the Zuni Pueblo are the world's best. And a whole lot closer to your home. Maybe he just wanted to see the Smoky Mountains; I don't know. Maybe this was just an excuse."

She wasn't sure what she had expected, exactly, from coming all this way to talk to Franklin Cooper. But this wasn't it. It didn't seem like enough, somehow. Her shock and disappointment must have shown on her face, because Franklin Cooper bent toward her slightly, his voice low.

"Can I get you something, ma'am? A drink of water? A cup of coffee?"

Elise shook her head. "No. No, that's okay. I'm sorry I bothered you." She stood up, still lost in the fog of Cooper's story, and held out her hand. They shook, and he held her hand in his for a moment.

"I wish I had more to tell you. You come all this way." He looked out at the Jeep. He turned his gaze back to Elise. "But I can't come up with anything."

Elise nodded. She swallowed her disappointment. "That's okay. Thanks for your time."

# CHAPTER
# TWENTY-SIX

She could barely put one foot in front of the other, walking back to that Jeep. Tears coursed down her cheeks; she swiped at them with the sleeve of her jacket. She'd misinterpreted everything, once again, just like she had with her dream all those months ago. With her hand in her pocket, she ran her fingers over the stone. She'd been so sure that she needed to come here, to see this man. And all she'd managed to accomplish was leaving home, giving someone a chance to take the raven that Michael had carved. Would she ever get anything right?

She did not want to get back in that car. She wanted to stand here and scream, a heartrending, bloodcurdling scream that would reverberate through the mountains and echo all the way back to New Mexico. Elise took a huge breath, opened the door of the Jeep, and slumped into the seat.

"Buy any moonshine?" Tom's eyebrows arched up.

"Don't you say one word, Tom Dugan." She turned away from him, staring at the passenger window, sheets of tears still blurring her vision, as Tom started the Jeep and began the bouncy return down the driveway.

Suddenly, she was furious. Furious with Celestina and her schemes, with Tom and his glasses that wouldn't stay up, with his incessant chatter. And furious with herself for being so wrong, yet again. Anger surged in her system, and Elise took a big breath and exhaled, like a fire-breathing dragon. "All right, Tom. Tell me the truth. What are you hiding?"

Tom's mouth dropped open slightly; he took his eyes from the road and looked at her. "What are you talking about?"

Elise stared at him. "I know you're not telling me the truth."

Tom turned back to look at the road, and she saw him swallow, his Adam's apple moving up and down. It was then that she knew. He was hiding something; she could see it in the way he turned away, in the way he didn't know how to react. A sliver of fear caught in her throat.

"It's just . . . I didn't really know how to . . . It's embarrassing, you know? Because that's not how I normally behave. You just . . . I got into this situation, and things happened so fast and, well, before you know it . . ." Tom glanced at her again. "I feel terrible, if it's any consolation."

Elise never took her eyes away from his face.

Tom sighed again. "When Wayne walked in on us, and Nancy started crying . . ."

"What? Who is Wayne? Who is Nancy? What are you talking about?"

"It is true, that my partner and my wife were having an affair. Wayne and Alana. Nancy suspected it. I didn't. I'm kind of blind to those things, you know? But that part about me walking in on them? That part isn't true. *He* was the one who walked in and caught *us*. He's the one who would like to put a pistol to my head."

Elise could not hide her confusion. "What?"

"I lied to you. To everyone. Yes, I have a wife named Alana. Just the way I described her. One of the many setups that Nancy and Wayne arranged over the years. We married after four months of dating. And I knew, pretty quickly, that it was all a big mistake."

Tom swallowed again, and Elise slumped against the side of the car door. She shook her head.

"The story is true, just not exactly the way I told it. One morning, I stopped at Wayne and Nancy's house for some papers that we needed. Nancy starts telling me about all these *feelings* she has. About Wayne and Alana.

"She starts crying. Telling me about all the times he's been late. All the times she could smell perfume—Alana's perfume—on his shirts. She's crying, and so I put my arm around her. And . . . ah." He exhaled. "And one thing led to another, and before I knew it, there we were, on the couch, all wrapped up together."

Tom stopped talking for a moment, his eyes on the road. "For the most part, the story is true—the one I told everybody. I just changed a few pronouns. Instead of *my* wife, it was *his* wife. Instead of *I* walked in on *them*, the real story is that *he* walked in on *us*."

Elise stared at him, stunned by this revelation. "Pronouns?"

"I'm not that kind of guy, not really. I don't know what happened. It just . . . there she was, standing next to me, crying." Tom glanced toward Elise.

"If it matters at all, we didn't actually do the wild thing. We were just kind of . . . holding each other, you know. And then here comes Wayne, walking in the door. All wrong, in every way. He'd been the one cheating, and we were the ones who got caught."

Elise shook her head. "That's what you lied about?"

"I've felt terrible, all these months. But I left Tucson in kind of a hurry. And my partner . . . ex-partner and I haven't really reached any agreement on the division of the business."

"And Celestina didn't pick up on all this? What kind of psychic couldn't see a lie like that?"

Tom pushed his glasses up on his nose again. "Actually, Celestina does know. That night, when I broke down outside her place? I told you part of what she said. About how she'd been waiting for me to get there. But she also said, 'I see the lies all around you.'"

"Celestina knows?"

Tom nodded.

A moment passed. Elise was fighting to keep up; this was not at all what she had expected. "What else is there, Tom? What else have you been hiding?"

He looked at her. "Elise, I just spilled my guts with the worst secret I've ever carried. What else are you expecting? Isn't this enough?"

"But . . . you're in some kind of financial trouble, aren't you? The credit card the other night that wouldn't go through? And what happened to Cynthia's artwork? Why is Ken Black's number in your phone? Where is that raven my husband made?" She was sitting up straight, her words punching the air, getting louder with each question.

"What are you talking about?" Tom's brow scrunched up. He had taken his eyes off the road to look at her.

She turned back to look at the road. A raven flew up from the trees ahead, straight toward the windshield. Elise screamed. "Look out!"

Tom turned back to look. He turned the wheel and hit the brakes, trying to avoid the raven, but he was going too fast. The wheels locked; the tires slid on the gravel. The Jeep didn't make the sharp curve of the mountain road. Tom held fast to the steering wheel. "Hold on! We're going over!"

She had seen all this before—that curve to the left, the creek far below her on the right. In one timeless second, she was carried straight back to her dream all those months ago. Her dream of the car going off the side of the mountain. It wasn't exactly the same. The dream had been at night; the road had been paved and icy. But she could feel the essence of that dream closing in around her, could feel the sick realization that absolutely everything was out of her control.

The moment was just as she had always heard. Her life flashed before her, scenes of everything: driving back to New Mexico with her mother, standing at her mother's grave less than two years later. Meeting Michael. Michael's death. And all the warnings, all the words of the psychics, flying up at her. The death card. Being pulled in, like a moth to the flame. The smell of blood. Elise held one hand against the roof of the vehicle, the other braced against the dashboard, trying to keep from hitting her head on the roof of the car as it slammed down the hill, through thick brush and trees.

It worked, for a little bit. And then it didn't. Elise hit her head against the roof of the car. Everything went dark.

The raven flew into a branch of a dogwood tree, cooing softly.

# CHAPTER
# TWENTY-SEVEN

She could smell it in the air. Death has an odor that's distinct, like cedar or the linden trees when they bloom in the late spring. And Hattie should know. She had smelled it often enough in her life. At the moment the scent was still faint, barely discernible in the mix of wood smoke and fall leaves, in the apples rotting on the ground and the smell of the earth, getting ready for sleep. Even through the midst of all that abundance, the smell of death lurked. Not strong, not immediate. But not far off, either.

The first time she'd smelled it, all those years ago, it was faint, just like today. She had been standing out by the wash pot in the yard yonder, stirring the mix of cottons that clothed her little boy. He was playing in the dirt, toddling around on the little leather moccasins she had made for him, chasing the tail of their old dog. Ginger was just wise enough to stay still until the baby got close enough to actually reach the tail, and then she'd get up and move off a ways. Hattie remembered watching the two of them, smiling to herself.

And then that smell, wafting on the breeze, stole her attention. Not like the scent of decay when you find a dead critter in the woods. This was different. More like smoke, tinged with something darker. Burning glass, maybe. Blackness. The aroma of loss, creeping toward her from the dark of the forest.

She'd forgotten all about it, until two months later when they buried that little boy. The spirits had sent her warning. The aroma came back again, not more than a few years after. And this time, she recognized it for what it was. Standing on the front porch, looking off into the mist that shrouded the peaks, that faint whiff of smolder invading her nostrils and sticking on the back of her tongue. It was all she could do not to be sick, knowing now what that smell meant.

That second time, it was her husband. She knew it, long before her neighbor pulled up in the yard, her husband's body in the back of the buckboard, covered with a sheet. Another death. Another loved one, gone to the spirit world. She was not yet eighteen years old. She never married again, never had another baby. But the spirits of those two were always around her, hanging in the trees, her little boy chirping like a chickadee, tiny and innocent. Her husband a crow, cawing now and again just to remind her to take in the wash before the rain hit. She'd grown used to them, keeping her company in the strange way of the spirits. And that's how she lived, staying close to the cabin they had built together, locked in the world between this one and the world of the spirits, a constant connection to the ones who were gone.

She smelled it again, two years into her solitude, riding the wind from up the canyon. This time, though, it wasn't one of her own that was marked. It took Hattie a few days to track that scent to its source. She found it down by the river, and she spent some time sitting quietly. Waiting.

She watched the two children a few days, slowly gathering all the pieces of the puzzle. And she was sitting on the banks of the creek, shotgun resting against one arm, when the children pulled up in her blue boat, tugging it onto the sand, trying to put it back the way they had found it before going out on the water.

"You youngins in the habit of taking what ain't yours?" Hattie asked.

The children were startled and looked at her, eyes wide. They had not seen her sitting on a rock under the pine, had not realized that they were being observed. Hattie had that ability to blend into the landscape until she wanted to be seen. Her skin was the color of tree bark; she knew the art of sitting still as stone.

"We only borrowed it, ma'am," the boy stammered. "See? We didn't hurt it none. And we brung it right back where we found it." The little girl stood still, her belly pushed out in front of her, her chin dropped almost to her chest as she watched Hattie from those big blue eyes. She was wearing a filthy dress and no shoes.

Hattie looked in the boy's face. He didn't seem a bad sort. Had those dark curls that her own boy had had. She swallowed the memory and pursed her lips to indicate the string of fish, held dragging in the sand by the little girl. "Whatcha plan on doing with those?"

"I was planning on frying 'em up. For me and my sister." Ted's eyes were large and serious.

"You got a frying pan?"

The boy shook his head. "No, ma'am."

"Cornmeal, for to coat 'em with?"

Ted shook his head again.

Hattie waited a beat, looking at those dirty children. "Well, I got me a frying pan. And cornmeal. And coleslaw and corn bread. I won't shoot you for taking my boat if you two will share them fish with me. You done the work of catching 'em. I'll do the work of cooking 'em."

Ted was six, Verna four, when she found them on the river that day. Their daddy had been killed in the coal mine; their mama had run off with the first man who could pay for a drink. They had sneaked out of the company house before the mine boss could turn them over to the orphanage, and for the past week or so they'd been camping on Hattie's land, building a fire every night and eating whatever they managed to steal from Hattie's garden and smoke shed. Ted looked at his little sister and then turned back to Hattie. "Sounds like a fair bargain to me."

When the thunder growled later that evening, and the rain started dancing on the roof of the cabin, Hattie told them she had some old blankets and maybe they ought to make a pallet on the floor. Just for this one night, until the storm passed. Hattie realized that night, lying in her own bed, those two children in the next room, whispering softly, that the death smell had been their daddy, and not a warning of an impending death. She'd realized, after she got those children into the cabin, that the smell was in their clothes and their skin and their hair. She rolled over in bed and tried to figure out how she was going to manage getting them all washed up and fresh, how was she going to remove the smell of death that clung to them.

That was the beginning. She raised those two like they were her own children. Loved them like they were her own little boy and the girl she never got a chance at. Cleaned 'em up, taught 'em to weed the garden and chop wood and carry water. The boy, Ted, was useful. Helped her every which way. The girl, Verna, was a sight more difficult. She didn't like chores, and sometimes Hattie would catch Ted doing something she had instructed Verna to do, simply to keep his sister from getting in trouble. Hattie had to smile at that boy. He was a bright, shiny penny, that's for sure.

Something about Ted went straight to Hattie's heart. She'd been broken by her own losses; her heart had ripped and torn, and the jagged pieces often caught on some memory that made them throb and bleed. But now, this little boy with his black hair and blue eyes seemed to be the exact fit for her brokenness. He filled in the spaces of loss and longing and loneliness, smoothed them out, made them less painful. She grew to think of those two as her own children. Sometimes she completely forgot that Ted was not her own flesh-and-blood boy.

There were many things Hattie knew that she couldn't explain. Like the way she knew the minute that Chrysler turned into the driveway, the minute that Ted got out of the driver's side and swung Verna in a huge circle, the very minute that the blonde woman stepped from the passenger door, no one to hold it open for her. Hattie knew. This was trouble.

She didn't have to watch how Verna's face changed when Ted set her on the ground and moved close to the blonde. She didn't have to watch as he wrapped his arm around Rose and introduced her as his wife. She didn't have to see the way Rose and Ted looked in each other's eyes, or the way Verna's body went stiff like a dried-out sponge, this unexpected change in circumstances wrenching her the way Hattie twisted out her dishrag when she was finished washing.

Hattie was no stranger to trouble. She'd seen enough of it to recognize the seed, even before it sprouted, a vine, like kudzu, that would take over their lives. She was so happy to see him. This boy, this man, had been sorely missed around here. Even as she held him and stepped back and looked in his eyes, she could see that the young man before her now was not the same as the one who had joined the navy and been shipped out to Korea just a few years before.

She recognized that look in his eyes. It was the look of someone who had seen too much, had witnessed death and destruction and the total illogical nonpattern of war. How it could leave one person standing and take the friend standing right beside. Ted reeked of it, that day in the yard in 1956. He reeked of all the death and destruction he had seen and experienced. It cast a shadow in the blue of his eyes, and he moved his gaze away quickly, unable to stand there and connect with Hattie, eye to eye.

And his new wife, Rose, was a sparrow, just a reed-thin wisp of a girl. Beautiful, yes, and Hattie could see immediately that Verna felt threatened. Verna had been the belle of the ball around these parts for years, her dark curls and big eyes and petite curves garnering the stares of every man who wasn't already buried. It started when she was only twelve or thirteen, and as her body filled out, Ted had had lots of opportunities to protect her virtue and bloody his own fists in the process. Hattie had observed what Ted had not: Verna walked and talked and moved her eyes in a way that invited that attention. Invited the wolf whistles. She reveled in watching her brother defend her, loved the feeling of power and importance she garnered from those walks into town, and all the attention that followed.

Rose was beautiful in a completely different way. Blonde hair, blue eyes, pale skin—she could double for Grace Kelly if she'd a mind to. Slim and wispy, like a blade of grass. Rose, however, did not swing her hips and bat her eyes and throw out hooks of innuendo. She simply existed, and the world watched, forgetting, for a moment, to breathe.

As a child, Hattie had been taught the value of keeping quiet and watching. The skill had meant everything in her family. Her great-grandparents were among the small group of Cherokee who'd hid in the Smoky Mountains of Tennessee and North Carolina, who had managed to elude the army officers rounding up the Cherokee people for removal to the West on what would come to be known as the Trail of Tears. Hattie's ancestors were lucky: they hid out and eventually were allowed to remain in these mountains, the ancestral home of the Cherokee. They continued to live in these lands when so many of their friends and family had not, when so many of their friends and family had died on the way to the new settlements.

That skill of quiet observation had passed to Hattie. So she watched the way Ted and Rose looked into each other's eyes, the way they leaned against each other. Hattie knew, even before all the introductions had been finished, that trouble had just driven into the yard. Trouble that had the smell of death stitched into the fabric, even years before it actually happened.

Rose was an only child; her daddy had treated her like a princess, and since his death, when she was only thirteen, Rose had been looking for another man to step up to the job. *Ain't it funny how those things work?* Hattie thought. Rose, looking for a man to shelter and protect her, like her daddy done. Ted, trained from an early age to shelter and protect. And here he was, with the sister who would never allow anyone to usurp her role as the most important woman in Ted's life, and the wife who fully expected that the role belonged to her. There would be hell to pay, and Hattie knew it before any of that crew made it up to the porch.

Hattie knew she had work to do here, and she took to the task with all the delicate precision of a surgeon. She could see right off that there was no way for all of them to live in that three-room cabin of hers. Verna and her husband, Ray, shared one room; Hattie had always had another. Despite the shortage of cash, she plotted a way to get Ted and Rose their own house just down the driveway from the main cabin, and she put Ray and Ted to work on building it right away. They felled timber on part of the property and managed to build six hundred square feet of space. Rose and Ted were in there before Christmas.

It helped. First, by relieving the overcrowded main cabin and at least some of the jealous energy between Verna and Rose. And second, it gave Rose a place of her own, where she could spend her days working on improving the place and making curtains and sweeping the floors clean. It gave her a place to dream, a place to be.

Hattie watched as Verna did her best to exclude Rose. Verna had a million stories that started with, "Ted, remember when we . . ." and off she would go, laughing and talking and throwing slitted-eye looks at Rose to see if she was understanding what Verna was saying between the lines of the story. *I'm his sister. I'm his blood. I was here first. You ain't nothing to nobody around here.*

Hattie stepped in. She'd sit on the porch with Rose, and the two of them would shell peas or snap beans. Eventually, Rose got comfortable and started talking. She told Hattie about growing up in New Mexico, about her father who was the foreman at the mine. Many months had passed before Rose shared the fact that her father's position at the mine virtually assured that she would remain an outsider at the small school in Amalia, where many of the students had fathers who worked for her father. Rose had obviously had a great deal of experience of being on the periphery, of feeling like an outsider. She had one good friend, Patricia Jiron, who had accepted Rose despite her father's position. The two of them had become close and were planning to head off to Albuquerque, to college, as soon as high school was over.

Eventually, Rose told her that Patricia had fallen in love with a man named Billy Salazar, who had joined the navy and been stationed with Ted. When Billy and Ted showed up in Amalia, freshly released from the navy, Rose watched as Patricia and Billy sealed the deal and got married. Rose didn't say, but Hattie could see, that with her friend's choice of marriage over college, Rose had faltered, not brave enough to head to Albuquerque by herself.

And Hattie could also see that Rose had fallen for Ted at right about the same time. Just as her own dreams crumbled before her eyes, in walked the man with black hair and blue eyes, the man who had spent his whole life taking care of the women around him. A perfect storm of events, as they so often are. Of course, Rose had fallen for him. She could not stay with the mother who had always been harsh and silent, and she could not push herself to go to school without Patricia. Destiny intervened, offering her rescue in the form of tall, dark, and handsome.

They reached an uneasy truce, but a truce, nonetheless. Rose sheltered on the porch with Hattie, talking softly. And the truce held, sometimes straining at the seams, but still. It held together.

Until the day Hattie smelled death once more.

A day, she realized suddenly, not unlike today. She heard the vehicle leave the road, heard it crashing through the trees. Hattie sat back in her rocking chair, waiting.

Ruby came to the front door and pushed open the screen, a dish towel in her hand. She stood there a moment and turned to Hattie. "Did you hear that?"

Hattie didn't reply. She started to sing, in Cherokee. A song she had sung so many times in this long life of hers. A song she had hoped never to have to sing again. The notes of the death chant rose into the November air, wisping away like smoke.

# CHAPTER

# TWENTY-EIGHT

"Elise? Elise?"

She opened her eyes. Tom was standing next to her, on the passenger side of the Jeep. He'd pried the door open and was shaking her shoulders. "We have to get out of the car. There are fluids leaking everywhere. Do you think you can stand up?"

Elise raised her head from the back of the seat. Blood trickled from a wound on her head; her whole body hurt. But she could move her arms and fingers and feel her feet. "I think so," she whispered.

"You all need some help?" a woman called to them from a few feet away. She had a backpack with her and moved up next to where Tom was standing at Elise's side. "We need to get this seat belt off," she said.

"I know. It's jammed," Tom answered.

Elise laid her head back again and waited while the woman rummaged around in her backpack for a pair of scissors. She cut the belt in two places, and she and Tom helped maneuver Elise out of the Jeep and down to a rock several feet away. Elise leaned back against the rock, her head woozy. The woman balled up a jacket to put under Elise's head, and she leaned over Elise, examining the head wound.

"You look familiar," Elise whispered.

The woman met her eyes for a moment and continued gathering things from her bag. She pressed a rag against Elise's forehead. "Well, I should. I served you lunch a few days ago at the café in Olalla."

"Oh." Elise closed her eyes a moment. She was shaken, down to her core. She fought the urge to cry.

"Name's Ruby," the woman said. "Ruby Cooper."

Elise's eyes popped open, her mind fuzzy and slow. "Cooper? As in Franklin Cooper? The stone carver?" For a moment after the words left her mouth, she wasn't sure if that really was the name of the stone carver. Everything was jumbled.

Elise continued to watch the woman. "Are you related?"

"Not by blood," she said, checking the pupils of Elise's eyes with a tiny flashlight. "He was my husband. Soon to be ex-husband."

Elise took it in. "But . . . but you said you didn't know him. The other day, when we were looking for him."

"I didn't say I didn't know him. I said I couldn't help you." She reached into her bag again and pulled out material to bandage Elise's head wound. "Hold still. This don't look too bad."

"But why would you . . ."

Ruby looked Elise in the eye. "That miserable old son of a bitch went and found himself a redhead. After thirty years of marriage and three children. A redhead!" Ruby flamed. "I'd like to squash his fat head. Flatter than a flitter." She picked up Elise's arm and held her fingers to the wrist, her eyes on her watch. She finished checking Elise's pulse and added, "I'm going to stomp a mud hole in him and walk it dry."

"I thought you were a waitress," Tom said, watching Ruby work.

"I got my RN years ago. But there ain't much call for a nurse in Olalla, and I got tired of driving clear to Gatlinburg to do this work. Started working at the café 'bout a year ago."

Tom reached for the cell phone in his jacket pocket. "You think we ought to call an ambulance?"

The woman looked at him and shook her head. "That won't do you no good. Cell phones don't work up here. There's a landline at my mom's, down the way there. But it takes the ambulance over an hour and a half to get here. If you're dying, you'll be dead by then." She turned to Elise and smiled. "And if you're okay, we won't bother."

Elise grimaced. Every part of her body hurt, and she was completely shaken by the whole ordeal. "I think I'm going to be okay."

"Okay, then." Ruby stood, looking at Elise. "I can go back to the house and get the car and bring it up here, if that would be better."

"How far is it?" Tom asked.

"Right over that rise. Less than a quarter mile. I ran up when I heard the crash."

"Think you can make it?" Tom asked Elise. "If we help?"

Elise nodded and then grabbed her ankle, which was starting to swell. "Yeah. Yeah, I can make it. Maybe."

They managed to balance Elise between the two of them and hobbled slowly down a path that led to a driveway. Elise couldn't put any weight on the swollen ankle; she was swamped with wooziness and had to stop every few feet to put her head down and regain her balance. They topped the rise, and Elise stared down at the homestead. There were two log cabins, a huge red barn. A creek ran at the front of the property, and the road crossed over it. A huge weeping willow brushed its fingers against the ground. Elise looked down at the water in the creek, another wave of dizziness coming over her. When she straightened again, she could see smoke in the chimney of one of the cabins.

She stumbled and whispered, "It's funny. I could almost swear I've seen this place before. That tree. That porch. The barn."

Tom looked at her and pushed his glasses up on his nose. One lens was cracked, spokes radiating from the center of the lens. "I've read about this. Whenever there's a problem in the temporal lobe area of the brain, it can create the so-called déjà vu experience. You knocked your head pretty hard back there. Your temporal lobe is probably scrambled like an egg."

Elise and Ruby turned to look at him, and Ruby scowled. "You got a head injury, mister?" she asked.

Tom raised his eyebrows and shook his head. "I don't think so. I had the steering wheel to hang onto. Kept me pretty stable."

"Then quit yapping like a fool."

They continued their slow, limping progress. When they walked past the barn, Elise stopped once again. She leaned over and put her head between her knees.

"You need to sit down?" Ruby asked.

"No. No, just give me a minute," Elise answered. She stood back up and leaned heavily on Tom. "For a minute there, I thought I smelled lilacs."

"We got a whole big clump of 'em right over there," Ruby said, pointing to a space behind the barn, across the road from the cabin. "But this is November, honey. Ain't no lilacs blooming right now. Maybe you did scramble something. Maybe we oughta call a doctor."

Elise raised her hand to her mouth, afraid she might be sick. The smell of lilacs was overpowering. She turned to look at the cabin on their right. There was a tree, completely devoid of leaves, off to the left. Hanging from almost every branch were pieces of blue glass. Some were disks, like the bottoms of bottles. Some were the bottles themselves, wire circling their necks and holding them to the branches like they'd just been executed. She could hear that same sound she'd heard in Memphis—the whisper of the wind crossing the necks of the bottles.

Ruby raised her right arm and indicated the tree. "Bottle tree. Folks around here think you can catch evil spirits inside the bottles so they won't get in the house. And then when the sun comes up, it burns away any evil spirits that got caught inside the glass."

Elise stopped walking. She swayed slightly between Tom and Ruby. Her mind reeled. *Across the water. Blue notes play.*

From the porch in front of them, she could hear chanting, some kind of singing in a language that sounded a lot like the Cherokee they had heard a few nights ago with Grandfather Hayes. An old woman, brown as a nut, at least ninety years old, sat in the rocking chair. Her gray hair was piled on top of her head. She rocked back and forth, back and forth, singing in Cherokee.

"Grandma," Ruby said sharply, "you can stop with the death chant. Nobody died." She shot a quick glance at Tom. "Not yet, anyway."

The old woman continued to sing for another moment or two, ending the song in what felt like the appropriate place. "I ain't that old, Ruby," she said as they drew closer. "I can still tell the difference between dead and alive."

"Everybody's okay. A little banged up. Car is a mess. But these two are okay," Ruby continued, helping Tom maneuver Elise up the steps of the porch.

The old woman stared at Elise. She stood up, slow and shaky, and made her way toward the group, leaning heavily on a cane. "I wasn't singing someone out of this world," she said quietly. "I was singing someone back in."

Elise raised her eyes and looked at the old woman, at the gray hair piled on top of her head. Hattie moved closer, and Elise could see that her eyes were clouded with cataracts. The woman put her hands on Elise's face.

*With the dead, she waits.*

"I been sending out prayers every day. In the smoke. Burning the cheroots. Praying you'd come back. Praying I would get to see you again before I die. Calling your name, over and over." The woman kept her hands on each side of Elise's face, staring. "That hair color is all your mama, for sure. But the rest of you is your daddy, from top to bottom."

Elise stared into the dark eyes. Her throat threatened to close.

Another woman came to the door and pushed the screen open. Hattie held up one arm to indicate the woman with dark hair. "Do you remember your aunt Verna?"

Elise turned to look at her. She appeared to be in her seventies, though her hair was still black and curly, her eyes still a vibrant blue. It came back in a rush, that dream from a few weeks ago. The dream of being small, running through the meadow. The dream of being scooped up by that man with dark curly hair and blue eyes. This woman standing in the door, staring at Elise, looked just like him. It was like looking into the eyes of her long-dead father.

A gasp escaped from Elise's lips. Her knees buckled.

Tom caught her before she hit the ground.

# CHAPTER

# TWENTY-NINE

Everyone started talking at once. Tom maneuvered Elise into one of the chairs; Ruby knelt down at her feet and watched as Elise opened her eyes.

"Maybe we oughta go ahead and call a doctor," Ruby muttered.

"No. No. I'm not going anywhere," Elise insisted. "Not now. I'm just . . . I can't believe this."

"Oh my Lord!" Verna whispered, both hands coming up to cover her mouth. "You look so much like my brother." She started shaking and crying.

Hattie pulled her chair close to Elise and sat down. "Do you remember us, child?"

Elise shook her head. "Not really."

"Do you remember Ruby? You two used to play together all the time."

"Elise? This is Elise? I don't believe it. After all these years." She studied Elise. "This was not what I expected when I heard that car leave the road." She looked at Hattie and shook her head. "We used to play, right out there, in the yard."

Elise looked out where Ruby pointed.

"We had a pet goat with three legs. Remember Pumpkin?"

Elise shook her head, but then a snippet of memory caught. She did remember curling up against that goat whenever she got tired playing outside. Another memory played at the edge of her mind, tattered remnants of a long-forgotten time. "Sort of. Was there a duck?"

Ruby laughed. "Floyd. Pumpkin had three legs, and Floyd couldn't fly. Floyd used to eat all the rotten apples that fell off that tree." She pointed toward a bare-limbed apple tree in a meadow across the driveway. "He'd get all drunk, lay there in that grass with his feet pointing up and his eyes glazed over. Misfits and miscreants was what Hattie used to call all of us. Remember that? We'd come up on the porch, and she'd say, 'What have you misfits and miscreants been up to now?'"

Ruby kept up her nursing, lifting Elise's foot and placing it on a footstool, somehow finding another bag of ice. Tom plopped into a chair across from Elise and watched the proceedings, bug-eyed behind his cracked lenses.

"What happened to your mama?" Hattie asked, leaning forward in her rocking chair to put a hand on Elise's arm.

"She died when I was seven—pneumonia. She never talked about Tennessee at all. And after she died, I asked Beulah once if I had any relations out here. She said no—that my father's parents had died when he was little."

"Well, that part was true enough," Verna sputtered. "I was four, Ted was six, when it happened. Hattie here"—Verna raised her hand to point at the old woman in the rocker—"she took us in. Raised us up like we were hers." Verna turned toward the door of the cabin and let her hand sweep the length of the porch. "Right here in this very house. Right here is where your daddy grew up."

Elise tried to absorb it all. This was the first connection she had ever felt to that long-lost father. She shook her head back and forth, tears snaking down her cheeks.

"We sent cards and letters out to that place in Amalia. Every one of 'em come back. Marked 'Return to sender.'" Hattie shook her head. "I knew that woman, Rose's mother, wasn't telling the truth. Didn't want nothing to do with us. Wasn't about to let you out of her sight."

Elise thought about Beulah, hanging on to the one person she had left after Rose died. And instantly, she remembered the words of the conjure woman in Memphis: *Somebody lied to you.*

Tom cleared his throat. "Would you mind if I used your phone? I need to call a tow truck, get that Jeep in to a mechanic."

"Oh, Lordy. Forgot all about you," Ruby said, standing up. "I'll call my brother, Teddy. He runs that little garage in Olalla. He'll get you fixed right up."

"This your husband, Elise?" Verna asked, turning to look at Tom for the first time.

Elise shook her head. "No. This is Tom Dugan. He's . . ." She stopped for a moment, trying to decide what Tom was. She still didn't know the answer to all her questions, right before the accident. She didn't know what had happened back in New Mexico with Michael's raven and Cynthia's artwork. But it was Tom who had brought her here to this very road, Tom who had managed to drive them off the road right here, so close to family that she never knew existed. "He's a . . . friend."

Tom looked at her and pushed his broken glasses up on his nose. The lens on the right side looked like a spiderweb, completely obscuring the eye behind it.

She brought her attention back to the two women sitting on each side of her. "My husband died—last spring."

"Ah, honey! I'm so sorry to hear that," Verna crooned. She sat back in her chair, patting Elise's forearm. "I lost my Ray ten years ago now. That's a tough row to hoe, I'll tell you."

Elise nodded. "It was my husband that got me to come out here." She looked up at Hattie, at the cheroot that had been stubbed out in a little ashtray. "Well, my husband and Hattie." She pulled the small oval disk from her pocket and held it in the palm of her hand.

Verna gasped and raised her hands to her face, covering her mouth and nose.

"I found this stone, and this business card, in my husband's jacket, not two weeks ago. Franklin Cooper. Stone Mountain Carving. Olalla, Tennessee." She looked up and met Ruby's eyes. "That's why I came out here. That's why we were on this road." Elise looked up to see Verna's eyes round and filling up once again.

"Can I touch it, honey?" Verna asked.

Elise dropped it in her palm. Verna ran one finger over the fine carving of the small dog. She closed her hand around the stone and sat back. "My brother . . . your daddy . . . carved obsidian. Arrowheads and such."

Hattie nodded. "When those two was little, after they come to live with me, I used to take 'em over the mountain, into Cherokee, North Carolina. I made baskets, out of the cane and honeysuckle around here. Old Cherokee patterns that my mama taught me. And once a year or so, I'd take 'em over to the Qualla Arts and Crafts, in Cherokee. They been selling my baskets for quite some time now." Hattie smiled. "Anyway, your daddy must a been eight or nine. Pretty young. And he seen somebody flint knapping over there. He was fascinated. Sat down with that old guy, and the man showed him a few things. We come home, and before I knew it he was out here, chipping away at them black stones all the time. Got pretty good. We have a whole collection of his pieces, out in that house yonder." Hattie raised a gnarled finger to point at the cabin across the way.

Verna opened her fist and looked at the carving again. "He carved this one, too. This was an old dog we had when you and Ruby were little."

She put the stone back in Elise's palm, and once again Elise felt that buzz of electricity jolting through her hand and arm. She stared at the carving, at the barely detailed head and ears and feet of the sleeping dog. "Festus?"

"You remember?" Verna smiled. "Your daddy was partial to *Gunsmoke.*"

Elise locked her hand on the stone and held it close to her heart for a moment. Her hand grew warm around it.

"Your husband got that from Frank?" Ruby's words were biting with venom.

Elise nodded.

Ruby crossed her arms over her chest. "Well, that no-good, rotten snake. I gave him that years ago. When he was first learning to carve."

Elise sat for a moment, soaking in the whole series of events that had unfolded in their lives and brought them here, to this point. A whole long series of synchronicities, starting with Frank breaking down on the road by Questa, Michael stopping to help him, Michael choosing this very stone and helping her to find it, even after he was gone. And that raven, guiding her every step of the journey, including flying up at the windshield and making Tom swerve, so close to the home of this family. The family she never remembered, the family she did not know existed. Elise turned to look at the cabin across the way. It was tiny compared to this one. White lace curtains hung in one window, and Elise had another flashback—seeing those curtains billowing in over the kitchen table when she was still tiny. "Is that where we lived?"

Hattie nodded. "And that's where you can live right now, if you've a mind to stay for a spell. I had one of the youngins help me get it all cleaned up a couple months back." Hattie sat back and grinned. "I been getting ready for you, girl."

Elise shook her head. "All this time, I thought we had lived in Chattanooga when I was little. That's what my birth certificate says. Isn't that two hours away?"

Verna nodded. "Your mama wasn't the strongest piece of female I ever laid eyes on. She got pregnant once, before you was born, and had quite a struggle. They lost that baby before he ever got borned. So when she was getting close with you, she and your daddy went down and stayed with friends. They were down there about six weeks, I think. Just trying to be on the safe side.

"Ruby, go get that picture box. I'll bet she ain't ever seen her daddy, have you?" Verna turned back to look at Elise. "Your mama forgot that box when she left. I imagine it broke her heart, not having anything to remember him by."

Ruby returned in a few minutes with a pale-gold cigar box with blue trim around the outer edge. On the lid, faded letters spelled out **OLD VIRGINIA CHEROOTS**. Just like the box she had noticed at the café a few days ago. *Cheroots.* Ruby put it in Elise's lap, and she opened the box slowly, lifting out the original of her own birth certificate, the marriage certificate for her parents, Ted and Rose, dated 1956. They had married in Oak Grove, Arkansas.

There were a handful of old photos inside, curled with age. All were black and white; all had the scalloped cut of photos from that period. There were her mother and father, standing together underneath a pine tree, their arms around each other.

Verna leaned over her shoulder. "That was the day they showed up here. Eloped on the way from New Mexico. So we always called that their wedding photo."

There was another photo of her father, sitting on the edge of a blue boat, Hattie sitting on a rock nearby. Elise remembered that boat. She remembered being out on the lake, her father in the front of the boat, her mother in the back. She remembered sitting in the middle, with the dog curled at her feet.

Another showed Ted and Verna standing in front of the café in Olalla, each of them tipping back a bottle of beer. And then Elise raised her hand to her mouth. Here was a photo of her father, dark hair and blue eyes, holding Elise in his arms. She looked to be about three, with long blonde curls and those same blue eyes. He was wearing a denim shirt, sleeves rolled up to reveal his biceps. She could see the outline of a package of cigarettes in one pocket. Just like she had dreamed a few weeks ago.

"Okay, y'all. That's enough for now," Ruby commanded. She was standing with the screen door open again. "I got dinner on the table. Best get yourselves inside 'fore I have to cut me a switch."

# CHAPTER THIRTY

It was evening, the blue hour, and they were all, once again, out on the porch, despite the chill in the air. Hattie and Verna and Ruby sat lined up in their rocking chairs, each of them holding pieces of cane in their hands, working on baskets.

"You ever done any weaving, Elise?" Ruby asked.

Elise smiled. "Not this kind. But I've been weaving for most of my life. With wool. Tapestry weaving."

"Well, scooch on over here," Verna said, indicating the space beside her. "Time you learned to make baskets."

Hattie sat on one side of her, Verna on the other, Ruby on the other side of Verna. They sat in the quiet, picking up pieces of cane, weaving them over and under. Elise took to it immediately—"like a duck to water" was how Verna put it.

"Some of these here patterns were taught to me by my mama," Hattie whispered, her fingers focused on her work. "But some of 'em come from . . . I don't know . . . deep inside." She held her weaving in her left hand, took her right hand and made a fist. She tapped it on her chest. "From here. From the ancestors."

Elise sat still, gazing out at the blue dark. "That's what my husband used to say." She took a breath, remembering those conversations. "He carved birds out of deadwood. Said that something inside him always told him what needed to come out of the wood. As if the ancestors were speaking to him." She looked down at the pieces of cane sticking out from her hands. "I never really understood what he meant. I never had that feeling when I wove. I couldn't tap into any of the ancestors. Any of my relations. My weaving always felt flat. . . like it wasn't enough, somehow. Like there were pieces that were missing."

They didn't speak, and Elise remembered the first day that Ken Black had shown up in their lives, fascinated with Michael's pieces and totally ignoring hers. That same feeling came back every time they ran into Ken, every time they had gone to his gallery in Santa Fe for one of Michael's openings. As if her weavings were never good enough, as if a part of her were missing.

Tom came out on the porch and dropped into a rocking chair. He pushed his glasses up on his nose.

"Can you see out of those things?" Elise asked.

"Better than I can see without them." He held his cell phone in his hand, even though it was worthless up here in the mountains. "Ruby let me borrow their phone, and I made a few calls. David said he'll come and get me pretty soon."

Elise nodded.

"I've been thinking about all those things you were asking me, in the car. Before . . ." Tom glanced at the other women on the porch, who had all gone quiet. "That credit card the other night? The one that wouldn't go through? That one still has Alana's name on it. Apparently, she's been shopping."

Elise said nothing, waiting for him to continue.

"And this Ken Black thing? Celestina called yesterday and said he wants me to do some solar work when I get back to New Mexico. I guess his wife is a customer of Celestina's. Comes in a couple times a year. And you know Celestina. Trying to fix everybody's life. She offers my solar-design services at every opportunity. She made me promise to put his name and number in my phone and call just as soon as I get back."

Elise exhaled.

"I called Celestina while I was inside. And I asked about all that . . . other stuff." Tom swallowed. "I guess there were a couple of detectives in the shop the other day. Trying to figure out who took Cynthia's art. They asked Celestina about me, of course, because I'd been up there. And then they showed her a picture of this other guy. A guy who had come into the shop a couple times. Goes by the name of John White."

All four women stared at Tom. "Not his real name, of course. He's a con man. Apparently he gets friendly with widows and then robs them. He's pulled the same stunt in Sedona. Cynthia had been dating him."

Tom sighed. "Only the worst part of all this? Celestina is the one who set them up. He came into the shop for a reading. Told Celestina how lonely he was. That he wished he could meet somebody. And right away, she does that thing where she tips her head." Tom tipped his head to the side. "Like an old mother hen. Always trying to fix everyone's life. And there you go. A match made in heaven. Or a match made by Celestina. Definitely *not* the same thing."

Tom shook his head. "She may be okay with tarot cards and all that stuff. But her matchmaking skills?" He shook his head again. "I started keeping a spreadsheet months ago, when I first noticed her doing the matchmaker thing. She's tried to set me up with Sonia. And Cynthia. I'm surprised she hasn't tried to hook me up with Pablo."

He shot a quick glance at Elise. "I was a little worried that's what she was up to, sending me up to your place with firewood. Telling you you were going on a journey. Sure had the smell of one of her woo-woo love potions all over it." Tom leaned back in his chair. "You know how she does it? The love-potion thing?"

Elise shook her head.

"In food. She puts it in food. Has to be careful, though, since all hell would break loose if she did it at a potluck or something."

Elise remembered the day that Tom had shown up at her house to fix the solar hot-water heater. He had brought a basket of food, a gift from Celestina. Elise remembered sitting at the table, watching as Tom munched through his sandwich. She remembered that Monica had also eaten a sandwich. Elise had barely touched her food.

"What about my raven? Michael's raven? The one he carved?"

Tom shook his head. "I don't know anything about that. Celestina didn't, either."

They heard the sound of tires on gravel, and everyone looked up to see a car pulling into the yard. "There's David," Tom muttered.

"That's not David, you fool," Ruby muttered. "Are you completely blind?"

Hannah got out of the driver's side, hollering hello to everyone, and started up to the porch. The passenger door opened, and another person got out, hard to see in the dim light of evening. She was short, with black hair.

Elise stood and hobbled to the edge of the porch. "Monica?"

They collapsed into each other for a moment.

"I caught the first plane to Chattanooga. Celestina gave me Hannah's cell-phone number, and she just happened to be in Chattanooga. Came and picked me up at the airport." Monica and Elise stood looking at each other. "Glad you're okay, white woman."

Elise made the introductions. "This is Monica Madrid. She's my . . ." Elise searched for the word that would describe just how much Monica meant to her. "She's my family in New Mexico. She's my . . . best friend."

"I'm your only friend, you mean," Monica interjected.

Elise glanced at Tom. "I might have more than one now." Even in the dim light, she could see he was blushing, right to the roots of his hair.

"Elise? I've got some good news. Your raven is not among the missing."

Elise sank into a chair, and Monica sat down beside her.

"I guess Uncle Wes had a dream the same night I did. Only being Uncle Wes, he figured it out. Got my brother Tomas to drive him up to your cabin. Told Tomas you weren't coming back for a while. They took that raven to Uncle Wes's house, on the Pueblo. He said if it wasn't safe there, then it wasn't safe anywhere." Monica stopped talking and looked at Tom. "Looks like I might have jumped to a few conclusions about white boy over here."

Elise wiped away a tear. "You wouldn't be the only one."

# CHAPTER

# THIRTY-ONE

It was seven in the morning. Elise looked out the window of her cabin and saw Hattie sitting out on the porch. Light was barely brushing the edge of the sky, but Elise grabbed her sweater and jacket and an afghan for her lap and headed over to sit on the porch with Hattie. She was determined to take in every minute she could with the woman. She still had so many questions, so much she wanted to know.

"Aren't you cold?" Elise asked Hattie as she settled into the rocking chair next to her, arranging the blanket around her own legs. She could see that Hattie had done the same. Hattie was smoking a cheroot, pulling the smoke into her mouth, not her lungs, and making small rings of smoke that she puffed out into the morning air.

"Naw. I got to soak in all the sunrises I can. May not have very many of 'em left."

They sat in silence for a moment, smoke rings perfect in the coolness.

"Hattie? What happened? The day my dad died? Why did my mother go back to New Mexico? It never made sense to me. She and Beulah just didn't seem to get along that well."

Hattie sat quietly, staring out at the land. She puffed on the cheroot. Then she leaned forward, ground the end of the cigar out on the bottom of her shoe. She sat back, her face suddenly heavy with age. "Your daddy bought a piece a land, just up the road. That place where Frank lives. Where Frank and Ruby used to live together."

She paused for a moment. "He was pretty excited—working on building a house for you all. Close by, but separate, you know? So your mama could have a little bit a space. A place to call her own.

"Headed up that narrow old road one morning." Hattie pursed her lips toward the road up above their place. "You saw how curvy it is. Old washboard road. Something happened, and he didn't make that curve. Went right over the side, kinda like the two of you did yesterday. Only his truck kept on going. Steeper part of the road. And he went all the way to the bottom."

Inside her blankets, Elise shivered.

Hattie looked out at the mountains, up above them. "I'm starting to think that piece of land has a curse on it. Ain't no good come out of that place. For none of us.

"That day, the day your daddy went over? There's a fellow lives up above. He heard the crash. He was the one went and found . . . Brought your daddy's body back here in the back of his truck." Hattie raised her nose to the wind. "I knew. Even before he said anything. Even before he got out of that truck, holding his hat in his hands, nervous and shaky. I knew. I could smell it in the air. Death. I started singing the death chant."

The memory hit Elise like a two-by-four. She sat up straight. "Was I playing out in the lilac bushes?"

"You and Ruby both. Ruby come out of there when we called her. But you wouldn't. It was like you knew that the whole world had changed. You stayed inside that clump of bushes the rest of the day and into the evening. Wasn't nobody small enough to reach inside and pull you out.

"I was up here, on the porch. Death chant is three days and three nights. And you can't stop singing. So I kept going. I did get some help, later, from old Jefferson Hayes and his wife."

Elise looked at her.

"Known 'em since I was a child. They live not far off." Hattie paused in her talk. Her rocker went back and forth, back and forth, memories stirring the air around her. "He was the one got you to come out of those lilac bushes that night. He was the one that held your hand and brought you up to the house.

"Your daddy's body was inside here," Hattie said, indicating the room behind them, in the big cabin. "Laid out on a door."

Elise could feel the chill of that night walking up her arms, stirring the long-buried memory. The smell of lilacs had surrounded her the entire day: it was getting dark, and she was scared. She needed the bathroom. But she was afraid to leave the safety of the bushes, afraid to walk up those steps on the porch. She knew that something really terrible was wrong, that her whole life had turned upside down.

She could remember the light, spilling out of the windows and doors. She remembered the singing, the chanting. Mixed with that singing was the sound of the breeze, sighing over the tops of all the blue bottles on the tree, moaning like ghosts. She remembered someone calling her name, whispering to her. "Elise? Time to come out of there now." She remembered taking the hand that was offered and walking slowly up those steps to the cabin. Her insides screamed, *No, no, no!* It was almost impossible to lift her legs and go up those steps.

Inside the cabin, she could see her mother, sitting like stone. Not far from her sat Aunt Verna, dark curls hiding her face, but her body shaking and moaning.

Elise remembered moving her eyes away from those two women, to the body that was laid out next to them. She could see the black hair, could smell the blood that still clung to him. She turned toward that body, a scream rising from her stomach. "Daddy?"

Elise leaned forward, her hand on her mouth. It made sense now, the smell of lilacs. The smell of blood. The smell of death. The long-buried memory rose up like a tidal wave, making her feel sick. Moments passed before she could speak.

"I met Jefferson Hayes the other night, at Hannah's. He heard my name. He knew who I was? Who I am? And he didn't say anything?"

"That's not his way. He didn't want to tell you what to do." Hattie reached over and patted Elise on the knee. "You had made it that far. He knew you would find your way home."

Elise leaned against the back of the chair, trying to absorb it all.

"That day it happened, the day your daddy died? Verna fell to pieces. Started wailing and screaming. Your mama just kind of sank to the floor. White as a sheet. She didn't make a whole lot of noise, your mama. Her grief was awful quiet.

"But Verna is a different sort. She went after your mama. Started hitting at her, yelling it was all her fault. That he wouldn't a died if he hadn't been up that road, working on that house. Said nothing was ever good enough for your mama. Said all kinds of things about your mama. All kinds of things that weren't nothing more than Verna's grief, coming out hard.

"Your mama took all that to heart. And as soon as we had him in the ground, she gathered up your clothes and left."

"I always wondered why we went back. It never did seem like my mom and Beulah got along very well."

Hattie pursed her lips and looked off into the distance. "I don't know what happened between your mama and your grandma. But after that mess with Verna, I think she felt like she had to leave here. And she had no place else to go.

"We put him in the ground, up yonder," Hattie said, pursing her lips toward a spot across the clearing. "Underneath the oak tree. You want to walk over there?"

They wrapped their blankets around their shoulders, and Elise and Hattie held on to each other, one old and crippled up, the other still recovering from her sprained ankle. They hobbled across the field, up to the oak tree. One plain stone rested there. Only a name, Ted Brooks, was carved into the granite. No dates, no other information.

The sky was beginning to color. The dark gray of night was turning to the deep blue of dawn. The two women stood, leaning into each other and watching the daybreak. From the silence came the rush of wings just over their heads. Elise heard the caw of a raven.

He landed in the oak tree, close to the top, and cooed softly to the women standing below him.

Elise looked up at the raven. "You know the one thing I still don't understand? All this time, that raven has been helping me, guiding me when I wasn't sure what to do next. How did Michael know? To bring me here?"

"Michael?" Hattie whispered. She turned and looked at Elise. "Honey, that raven is your daddy."

A jolt went through Elise's body, and she stared at the bird. "My dad? Is it missing a . . ." Elise looked up. She could see the left wing, the missing wing feather, about a third of the way down.

Hattie turned and looked at her. "I'd been burning the cheroots, calling your name, trying to sing you back home for quite a long time. And finally, one day in, oh, what was it? September, maybe? October? I asked your daddy if he could give me a hand. Help lead you back out here."

Elise looked from one to the other.

The raven cawed loudly. Elise lowered herself to a nearby boulder. "All this time, I thought it was Michael."

Hattie sat down next to Elise, and patted her leg. "I do believe your husband helped. He got that stone from Frank, after all. Helped you find it. I think you got help in a lot of different places. Psychics. Science. The spirits. But girl, none of this woulda worked if you hadn't been listening."

Elise turned and looked at her.

"You didn't come out here because of that raven. You didn't come out here because of what the psychics told you. You kept going, even when you were getting warnings not to."

Elise nodded, awareness seeping into her brain like the dawn, crawling over the mountaintops. "I had a feeling. All the way along, I had this *feeling*."

"That's exactly what Hayes wanted you to see." Hattie leaned on her cane. "You made a choice. To listen. To trust that feeling."

Hattie looked Elise right in the eye. "Your husband did the same thing the day he died. Whether he knew what was coming or not, *he* made the choice to go. We all gotta follow what feels right to us. No matter where it leads."

# CHAPTER THIRTY-TWO

Tom and Elise and Monica stood on the front porch of Hattie's cabin. They'd just finished dinner, as lunch was called around here. Ruby and Verna had made roast beef with potatoes and carrots, gravy and biscuits, green beans with bacon, and banana cream pie for dessert.

"Banana cream was your daddy's favorite," Verna had informed them.

Now Hattie sat in her rocking chair, dozing in the early afternoon. Verna, too, was out on the porch. Ruby had said her good-byes and left the mess to head off to work at the café in Olalla.

Tom's Jeep sat in the yard, all the dents and dings fixed, the engine running better than it had in years. Apparently, cousin Teddy was quite the mechanic.

"So you're sure about this? You want to stay here?" Tom asked.

Elise swallowed. She had her arm around Monica. She knew she would miss Monica and Lorena and the New Mexico family, as she now called them. But she couldn't go back. Not yet. "For a while," she said. "I'm going to stay in that cabin where we lived when I was a child. I'm going to sleep in the room where my mom and dad slept. I'm going to listen to every story that Hattie and Verna can remember to tell me." She pursed her lips toward the porch and then met Tom's eyes.

"I'm going to learn to weave Cherokee baskets. And spend some time at Hannah's studio weaving tapestries. I have all kinds of ideas, now that I know about all of this." She raised her hand and indicated the land spread around them, the lilac bushes where she had hidden, the place where her father was buried. "Finally, I think I can work again. It was like I was frozen, all those months after Michael died. Frozen and paralyzed in an arctic wasteland."

The raven cawed from a nearby tree, and they turned to look at it. They all watched the bird, preening itself in the branches. Elise looked at Tom. "You still don't believe, do you? Despite all that's happened? Despite the fact that everything on that spreadsheet, every single prediction, turned out to be right?"

Tom smiled and shook his head. "Coincidence. None of this would stand up to the rigors of the scientific method." He looked back up at the raven.

Elise laughed. She and Monica walked to the passenger side of the Jeep. On the seat, Elise saw a stack of books, and the title of the one on top caught her eye. She opened the door and picked it up. *Spook: Science Tackles the Afterlife,* by Mary Roach. Underneath it, she found another. *Proof of Heaven: A Neurosurgeon's Journey into the Afterlife.* "What's this?" she asked, holding up the two books.

Tom blushed. "Thought I'd do a little research. Something besides Google."

Elise smiled. "About time." She put the books back on the seat. "So what are you going to do, Tom?"

Tom opened the door on the driver's side of the Jeep but stood outside, leaning one arm on it. "I'm headed back to Taos."

"Psychic sidekick suits you, does it?"

He smiled. "It's okay, as jobs go." He stopped. "Besides, Monica needs a ride home."

Elise looked at Tom, at the color in his cheeks and the way he kept staring at Monica.

Monica stared back, standing at the passenger-side door. "Don't get any ideas, white boy. We are polar opposites."

He smiled. "Perfectly aligned."

"Diametrically opposed," Monica spat. She rolled her eyes dramatically and turned to Elise. "I knew I should have bought a round-trip ticket."

Elise laughed. "Don't worry, Monica. You have at least one thing in common. You both love Carlos Santana."

Tom grinned. "Relationships have been built on less."

Elise smiled. Monica shook her head and got in the passenger side. "I may have to kill him before we even hit the state line."

Tom raised his eyebrows and smiled. "This could be fun." He leaned on his door for a minute longer. "I'll miss you, Elise. And all that weird psychotic stuff you have going on."

"Psychic. Not psychotic. You need to hone up on your English." Elise pressed her lips together. She walked around to the driver's side and put her arms around Tom's waist. "Thanks for driving me out here, Mr. Magoo. And crashing at exactly the right spot. Just a coincidence, of course."

They stood there for a moment in an awkward embrace. Elise stepped back. "I'll miss you, too. Both of you." She swiped at her cheek.

"Oh, they'll be back." Hattie spoke from the porch, her voice cutting the air and surprising all of them.

All three turned to look at her.

"They are honorary members of the Brooks clan now. They'll be back." She held up a cheroot, burning slowly, smoke wafting through the air. "I have my ways."

# READING GUIDE

1.  Elise Brooks is suffering from intense grief after the loss of her husband, Michael. Discuss the ways in which grief manifests in her life. Does this lessen or improve when she begins her journey with Tom?

2.  At a gathering with the widows and orphans, Sonia talks about the ways our society deals with grief. Discuss the ways in which American culture handles grief, including the duration of leave from work, and so on.

3.  One of Elise's biggest challenges throughout the story is learning to trust her own instincts. She gets lots of advice from friends, from psychics, and from Tom, but ultimately she must discern the path for herself. Discuss the ways in which you see her become stronger at trusting those feelings.

4.  Elise believes she was responsible for Michael's death because she didn't tell him about the dream. Do you believe this to be true?

5.  Tom refuses to acknowledge any information that does not stand up to the rigors of scientific inquiry. At one point, Elise tells him that science isn't ahead of us, it is behind. What does she mean by this? Do you agree or disagree?

6. Elise has spent her life living with the cultures of northern New Mexico, where belief in spirits is part of the fabric of life. Discuss how this cultural exposure has opened her to the idea of communication from spirits.

7. Have you ever experienced a dream or some other form of awareness that turned out to have value?

8. At the end of the novel, Hattie talks about the importance of personal choice, telling Elise that Michael made his own choices on the day he died. Discuss how the idea of choice played into the story.

# ACKNOWLEDGMENTS

Every story has many events and people that help flame the fire. First and foremost, this book is a love song to the land and people of the San Luis Valley and northern New Mexico. It is, as they say, the Land of Enchantment, and will always remain in my heart. I want to thank, in particular, Theresa Vigil, who allowed me to go along with her as she talked to the plants; and Jacob Anaya, who prayed and sang and demonstrated the beauty of his people in so many ways. Tennessee is the land of my father, the first storyteller in my life. His stories are in my blood, and his influence is part of the fiber of my being. My editor, Danielle Marshall, asked the questions that made me go deeper. My agent, Alison Fargis, continues to offer her unerring support. To all of these, and many others too numerous to mention, I am deeply grateful.

# ABOUT THE AUTHOR

Elizabeth Hall, author of *Miramont's Ghost*, has worked as a teacher, communications consultant, and radio host. She spent many years in the mountains of Colorado and now resides in the Pacific Northwest, where she indulges in the fiber arts of knitting, beading, and weaving.